John,
Thanks for
your support!

Diane

Holy Crap ...
We're On Fire!

The Brush Truck Chronicles
Book One

Diane Vetter
And
Paul Miller

Holy Crap ... We're On Fire is a work of fiction. Any resemblance to actual incidents, or persons living or dead is purely by coincidence. References to actual locations and events are written only to give the novel a sense of reality.

Cover design by Paul Miller Studio

Edited by Cynthia Muir

Copyright © 2016 Jackrabbit Productions LLC

All rights reserved

ISBN 978-0-692-78819-6

Available from Amazon.com and other bookstores

Also available on Kindle and other retail outlets

Printed in the United States of America

First Edition

Visit us at:

www.mimbresspringsfire.com

We salute the thousands that have fallen in the line of duty.

We know they would not want us to fall victims to their
unfortunate circumstances, but instead, would want us to
celebrate their lives, bravery, selflessness, and to remember
their laughter.

We will never forget you.

*Laughter gives us distance. It allows us to step back from an
event, deal with it and then move on.*

-Bob Newhart

*Humor prevents one from becoming a tragic figure even though
one is involved in tragic events.*

-E.T. "Cy" Eberhart

*Through humor, you can soften some of the worst blows that life
delivers. And once you find laughter, no matter how painful
your situation might be, you can survive it.*

-Bill Cosby

If we couldn't laugh, we would all go insane.

-Jimmy Buffett

ACKNOWLEDGEMENTS

We would like to thank all those who laughed with us, gave us their honest opinion and cheered us on.

Jackie Ball

Grace Butcher

Phil Comaduran

Nancy Dobbs

Jennifer Fischahs

Regina Ford

Janis Leibold

Tom Louis

Maggie Malaney

John Miller

Sarah Miller

Lily Shulman

Debbie Skeen

Megan Skeen

Mercy Valencia

Reviewed and Edited by:

Cynthia Muir

A bumper sticker reading, WEIRD SHIT 24/7 mysteriously appeared on the back of the truck one week after we came back from the fires in northern Nevada. One clever firefighter placed warning decals on the rear view mirrors of our brush truck, similar to the kind you see on your car. You know the ones that read, "Objects in the mirror are closer that they appear." Only the ones he put on our truck read, "Fires may appear closer than they look!"

I must admit, that particular wildland assignment had its moments and people are still talking about it to this day. I am deciding, once and for all, to set the record straight and tell the stories of what really happens on those wildland assignments.

Believe it or not, wildland firefighting is not all flames and glory. There is a lighter side to all of this, and we hope to shed some light on those humorous moments.

These are The Brush Truck Chronicles

Holy Crap ... We're On Fire! is the first book of *The Brush Truck Chronicles* series. This novel is based on the events that occur between the adrenaline rushes and the mundane daily routines, commonly associated with the wildland firefighter.

Without knowing it, the men and women who enter the ranks of firefighting become part of a larger family unit. They become brothers and sisters in fire, and share a common bond. Firefighters take calculated risks on a daily basis, routinely dealing with the injured, sick and dying and face all manner of natural disasters. Turn on the nightly news and you will see the firefighter pulling people from swollen rivers, taking on residential house fires, and dealing with the aftermath of hurricanes and tornados. They face the chaos of a bloody high-speed car wreck, and endure the smoke and flames of wild fire. These are people who don't hesitate to rush in, while most rational people turn and run away.

In many ways the firefighter shows the same traits found in any average American family. You find pride, resentment, jealousy, respect, sibling rivalry, teasing, practical joking, a lot of laughing, and helping one another through some very tough times. It is because of this tight knit family, that they are able to overcome grief, despair, and sometimes helplessness. Firefighters nurture each other during these times of healing, and that deep love for one another always seems to prevail.

It is a rare profession when a friend is willing to give his life for a colleague. It is more profound that these people are willing to make the ultimate sacrifice for a complete stranger. Courage, compassion, and valor are found in the fire service.

When most people think of firefighting, they think of the big city fire stations, pumper engines, and aerial ladder trucks. In this book you will be introduced to the unique aspect of *wildland firefighting*. You will get to know the men and women who are called in to fight forest fires.

Starting first with the hand crews and the Hotshots, you will see how these men and women are called to work in remote locations carrying 50-pound backpacks loaded with gear. You will learn how they do battle against these fires using only shovels, axes and chainsaws.

Then there are the crews who work on the wildland fire engines. First and foremost, there are the smaller Type 6 brush trucks. The Triple Nickel (B555), the truck featured in this book, is a modified four-wheel drive heavy duty Ford F550 pick-up truck. Type 6 trucks carry a crew of three, are outfitted with a large variety of fire suppression tools, fire hose and around 200 gallons of water. They are nimble enough to take on rough terrain, and can be found working in conjunction with other trucks or individually to assist hand crews during initial attack. Then there are larger engines, the Type 3 Engines. They carry more tools and equipment, have a crew of up to five and carry at least 500 gallons of water.

Sometimes the big-city, Type 1 Engines are called in. These fire engines are becoming more prevalent in the wildland setting, as more and more people are building their homes in wilderness areas.

There is so much more to wildland firefighting than can be mentioned at this time however, once you combine the hand crews with the brush trucks, throw in some bulldozers, air tankers, helicopters, and smoke jumpers, I guarantee, you will experience a compelling tale of courage, humor, and accomplishment!

Holy Crap ... We're on Fire! follows the exploits of Pablo, Diane and Phil, a three-person wildland brush truck crew. You will join them as they travel the American Southwest, and experience some action packed, humorous, and sometimes mildly strange adventures. I'm sure anyone who has experienced life as a wildland firefighter will have his or her own unique and compelling stories. The very nature of the work provides fodder for some exceedingly tall tales.

The wonderful people we have encountered over the years, have inspired us to relay their heroism, passion and yes, even quirkiness onto these pages. If you are a firefighter, and can relate to even one of these adventures, then we all share a common bond. Yes, you can bet this stuff really happens! Some of you may have *even stranger* stories to tell!

This book is written as a fictional novel, loosely based on true events. The events, locations, names and dates have been changed to protect the innocent as well as the guilty. You guilty ones know who you are. Those of you in the wildland firefighting profession will notice some of the characters and events may bear a resemblance to your own firefighters, families or friends and actual wildland fires.

For those not familiar with the world of firefighting, please join us for an educational and behind the scene look at wildland firefighting, and don't hesitate to reference the glossary located at the back of the book.

Enjoy the journey.

Diane and Paul

Table of Contents

1 Fire at First Light

I was jolted awake! The station's overhead tones shat-
tered the silence with a heart-pounding blare! What the ...
where am I? My heart was racing as I tried to get my
bearings.

Through some static on the overhead speakers, I heard
the dispatcher announce, *Mimbres Springs Fire, Engine
550, respond to a brushfire on 7330 W. Glory Road.*

I tried to focus on my watch and blinked at the blurry image, 04:20! In an instant I remembered ... I was in the
bunkroom at the firehouse and could see three firefighters
quickly getting dressed in the predawn darkness.

"Shit, it's a fire!" I yelled to no one in particular.

I threw on clothes, banged my knee on an open locker and
made my way out of the bunkroom.

Captain Smitty was right behind me as we charged down
the hallway and out into the brightly lit engine bay.

Smitty called out, "There's a brushfire at the Glory Road
Hot Springs! Pablo, you and Diane take the brush truck!
Phil and I will man the engine!"

I raced across the parking lot towards the brush truck.
Despite the fact that I was running my ass off, Diane easily
passed me and jumped in the driver's seat. The large doors
of the engine bay rumbled open and Phil drove the fire
engine out. Diane and I pulled out of the parking lot right
behind them.

While en route, dispatch informed us on the radio that the manager of the Glory Road Hot Springs reported a fire on the west side of his property and he was desperately trying to put it out when his phone suddenly went dead.

I told Diane, "I know the manager, it's Victor Caruso. He started the place about 25 years ago and since then it has become quite an attraction.

The Glory Road Hot Springs (clothing optional) was located about seven miles east of town. The accommodations were primitive with RV pull-thrus and electrical hook-ups. The campgrounds had shaded tent sites complete with fire rings and picnic tables. There was also the manager's Airstream along with a smattering of tiny rustic rental cabins on the hillside. The facility had about six or seven mineral hot spring pools that were secluded and surrounded by thick stands of piñon trees.

Since our brush truck was a lot lighter and more nimble, we quickly passed the lumbering fire engine. We could hear their siren fade as we put some distance between us.

Diane was charging hard along the bumpy dirt roads as we quickly made our way into the hills east of town. By this time I was now wide-awake, eager to fight some fire.

As we approached I hollered to Diane, "Keep the siren on; we need to wake everyone up. The place is usually packed with campers this time of year.

"You got it Pablo! Hot Damn! An honest-to-God fire!" Diane shouted with excitement, "It's Showtime!"

"Diane, when we get on scene let's do a quick size-up and see what we've got, especially if any structures are in harm's way. If it looks like a cooker, we need to let the chief know so he can page-out for more manpower and a water tender."

We had less than a mile to go when dispatch announced on the radio, "Brush 555, Engine 550, you've been cancelled.

We re-contacted the calling party, apparently one of the campsites had an unattended campfire and it started the surrounding woods on fire. The manager said it looked like the fire was starting to get out of hand but he was able to put it out with a garden hose. Sorry guys, it looks like everything's under control."

I pounded my fists on the dashboard, "Crap! The fire's out! We could use a little more action around here!" I shouted with disgust.

"Nothing like a fire to get everyone's adrenaline flowing. You don't see us charge out of the firehouse like that on a call for a sick person with diarrhea," Diane said with a snicker.

Smitty radioed us, "You guys continue on in, do a thorough assessment and make sure everything is completely out."

"Copy that!" I replied. I turned to Diane and shrugged my shoulders, "Hey, mop-up is better than nothing."

We arrived at the hot springs and looked for Victor the manager. Victor was a small man, slight in stature, about 5 foot 10, with greying curly black hair. He had a prominent nose with a great *old world* mustache. Although he was about 65 years old, he looked more like 80.

Victor met us in the driveway wearing only work boots, boxer shorts, and a wife-beater t-shirt. He was soaking wet and covered with black soot.

"Ciao! Victor!" I shouted as I exited the brush truck. "It looks like you single handedly put that fire out!"

I shook his hand, gave him a little hug and could feel he was shivering from the early morning cold. He looked like he had been to hell and back.

"Grazie a Dio," he said, "Thanks to God!" Still clutching my hand, he gazed at his blackened property and let out a

long sigh.

As we talked with Victor some of the campers started showing up in bathrobes and flip-flops. With bed hair and bleary eyes, they asked what was going on. Despite the fact that the air was filled with a slight haze and the smell of smoke, we reassured them that everything was under control and they could go about their business.

"We can't assume anything, we better make sure the fire is completely out," I told Diane.

"I'm on it. At least we can return to the station smelling like smoke," she grinned as she put on her fire gear.

As the sky began to brighten, we began to walk the property checking for hotspots. For the next hour we raked and hosed down about a half-acre of charred bushes and trees. We hosed down the last hot spot, put away our tools, took off our gear, and wrapped things up.

Before we left I walked up to Victor, patted him on his back and said, "You really saved the day! Some of this state's largest forest fires have started just like this, by an unattended campfire."

As Diane and I climbed in the brush truck, we looked over to Victor and started the engine. Victor gave us a tired wave as we pulled away.

"Ahhh, I could use a soak right about now. Only one of those pools is marginally warm, all the rest are downright caliente!" I said.

"So are you a regular?" Diane asked with a smile.

"I'm not what you call a frequent flyer, but I've slipped my sweet cheeks in there a time or two. It's very therapeutic, you should try it sometime," I winked.

"In the buff?" she looked surprised.

"Hell yeah, not only is it therapeutic, it's quite liberating. You're a liberated woman aren't you?"

"Well yes, I guess I am. I just might try it someday," she replied with a twinkle in her eye.

"Let me know, maybe I'll join you."

"Not on your life," she grinned.

While driving back on the winding roads, we passed singlewide trailers, weathered sheds, flattened barns, and remnants of adobe ruins. Up around the bend we approached the town's cemetery. In this part of the country, death was celebrated and ancestors were honored and revered. The family plots were well kept, decorated with brightly colored flowers and shiny trinkets, and trimmed of any weeds.

As we passed I commented to Diane. "Look at that, there is nothing scary about a New Mexico cemetery. It always looks like there's a party going on!"

It was about 06:30 when we rolled into Mimbres Springs. As we drove down Main Street we had to stop at the town's only traffic light.

"Damn! Whoever thought this traffic light was a good idea should've had their head examined!" I grumbled, as we idled on the deserted street waiting for the light to change.

When the light turned green, Diane put the truck in gear and said, "We need to stop by Lupe's so we can get some ground coffee. We are almost out. Pablo, we need to ban you from making the morning coffee. When you make a pot, you fill the coffee filter so full we end up going through our stash in no time!"

"Ooh Rah! That's how we made it in the Marines! Nice and thick and strong. It will put hair on your chest!" I said defensively.

Diane glared at me and said, "Ooh Rah this!" and proceeded to push up her sunglasses with her middle finger.

As we drove down the road, the early morning sunlight

flickered through the giant cottonwood trees that shaded the town's Main Street. Quaint little shops lined both sides of the street like strings of colored beads. The old storefronts had large glass windows to show off their treasures, and on nice days their doors were propped open to let the breeze in. I sat back in my seat and had to admit this was all very welcoming.

The Horny Toad Café & Coffee House was at the southern end of Main Street, not far from the station. I knew it was open for business because Lupe Jiménez, who ran the place, got up at the crack of dawn and hand-roasted three kinds of coffee. You could smell the aroma clear down the street.

Lupe moved here about 15 years ago and her café serves up classic New Mexico Cuisine. The dishes she conjured up showcase the red and green chili of the region. Just thinking of her tamale pie made my mouth water. And the grass fed, mesquite broiled rib eye steak, was so delicious; it made me tear up the first time I ate there.

It was now approaching 07:00 as we pulled up to Lupe's café.

Diane said, "Pablo, I got this."

She put the truck in park, hopped out and hustled toward the front door. As I watched her trot over to the café, I had to chuckle. Diane stood about 5 foot 3 inches with a dark Hispanic complexion and a full head of salt and pepper hair. Smiling, I thought to myself, *she must sleep standing up because her uniform was crisp and wrinkle free, her boots were laced and polished, and her hair was neat and trim. She always looked like a true professional.*

I, on the other hand, was not that buttoned down. When I was a Marine, I was all spit and polish, but not anymore. I glanced at myself and grimaced. My shirt was wrinkly and untucked and my boots were scuffed and unlaced. I knew my hair was a mess and I probably could use a shave.

"Man, I really need to clean up my act," I said out loud, knowing I was kidding myself.

Diane has been with the department for 12 years, and was a no-nonsense, by-the-book firefighter. On her days off I would often see her running the trails up in the foothills and knew she could run circles around everyone in the department, and you could always find her in our fire station's workout room, throwing around some serious iron. She was tough as nails, and wouldn't take any guff from anyone.

We returned to the station and idled on the concrete pad. I got out and guided Diane as she backed into the carport.

Our fire station was an adobe ranch-style house, with Saltillo tile floors and white plastered walls. There was a nice big kitchen, a co-ed bunkroom, an administrative office, the firefighter's office, and the dayroom. We also had two bathrooms, one male and one female.

In the large adjoining steel structure there was a small workout room, and two large engine bays that housed a fire truck, an ambulance, and a 3000-gallon water tender. Parked out back under a large carport were our reserve fire engine, an extra water tender and our brush truck, *B555, the Triple Nickel.*

The Mimbres Springs Fire Department employs 22 full-time firefighters plus some part time reserves. There are three rotating shifts, A-shift, B-shift, and C-shift. We work 24 hours on duty, take the next 24 hours off, and shift change always starts at exactly 08:00.

My crew works on B-shift and consists of Phil, who is the new hire this year, starting just six months ago. Diane, who is an EMT, a Technical Rescue Technician (TRT) and a member of our wildland team. And then there is Fire

Captain Howie Smith. A lot of the guys don't even know his first name because everyone just calls him Smitty. Two other firefighters staff the ambulance, and I could see they were out of quarters, probably running a medical call.

My name is Paul, but most everyone calls me Pablo. I am a firefighter/engineer and an engine boss on our wildland team. I got a late start becoming a firefighter because I worked in various occupations before entering the fire service and served in the Marine Corps during the Vietnam War. My military buddies gave me the nickname Pablo. To this day, I don't know why, I am about as gringo as they come. Maybe it was because I hailed from New Mexico, but the name stuck and I've been called Pablo ever since.

As we walked into the station through the back door, I could smell the robust aroma of fresh brewed coffee. I eagerly poured a cup, leaned against the counter, and reflected on this morning's events.

"Hey, old-timer," Diane said curtly and handed me a mop. "These floors aren't going to mop themselves! We need to finish the station duties before A-shift gets here."

She began to put away the pots and pans from last night's supper, wiped down the counter tops, and took the kitchen trash to the dumpster.

I heard Smitty vacuuming the bunkroom and could see Phil walking down the hallway with rolls of toilet paper in one hand and a toilet brush in the other.

I chuckled to myself as I mopped the floor. "Yup, life at the firehouse is not all flames and glory ... someone needs to swab the decks and clean the toilets.

2 Mimbres Springs

The best thing about being a firefighter is, every day is different. There is no telling what will happen once you show up at the firehouse. Just when you think you've seen it all, something unexpected happens.

It was just getting light outside as I drove to the station. I always arrive early, just to settle in, drink some coffee, and get the lowdown on what happened during yesterday's shift.

A-shift was the off-going crew, and as I walked in, I noticed it was dark and everyone was still asleep. The kitchen was a mess, the floors were dirty, and the trash can was overflowing and giving off an unpleasant odor. Worst of all, there was no coffee made!

I shook my head and said, "Those clockwatching slack asses! They aren't going to get up till it's time to go home."

I shoveled ten heaping scoops of ground coffee into the filter and recalled Diane's rebuke about my coffee making skills. I didn't want to piss her off, so I took a scant spoonful out, slid it into the coffee machine, and hit BREW.

A-shift eventually got up and amid a lot of yawning and man-scratching, made a half-ass attempt to finish the morning station duties. The rest of my crew arrived and shift change was over by 08:20. Besides our four-man engine crew, we also had two guys working the ambulance. Tom was the lead paramedic on the box and Javier was a new EMT, who just moved to Mimbres Springs this summer. Every morning we inspect the trucks, do routine maintenance, stock them with supplies and make sure they are ready to go.

As the off-going crew was leaving, they told us they broke the dayroom's light fixture last night, during a rousing game of Nerf football, and they were sorry but didn't have time to fix it. Smitty grumbled and put it on our to-do list.

"Those booger eaters! Why does A-shift break everything? Last week it was the washing machine, today the light. I will write you guys up in a heartbeat if I ever see you playing Nerf football in the dayroom," warned Smitty.

We all jumped in the engine and went to Maxine's Mercantile to pick up some light bulbs. Maxine's was the town's general store, located about halfway down Main Street. It was the largest store in town and had white clapboard siding and a tall false front that said, in faded letters, MAXINE'S MERCANTILE, *Dry Goods, Packaged Goods, Liquor, and Sundries.* I still can't figure out what a sundry is though.

There were hand painted advertisements taped to the two big picture windows that flanked the front double doors.

"Hey look! Today they have beer, pretzels, chips and salsa on sale. I might have to pick some up this weekend for the big game. You guys are coming right?" I asked.

"Does your wife know you're having your firefighter friends over to wreck-havoc on your place this Saturday?" asked Diane.

"Aww, she's out of town visiting her sister in Las Cruces this week-end, and has no idea you guys will be over, except maybe if you destroy something like last time!" I laughed.

"Hey, don't look at me," said Smitty. "I didn't know you put waaaay too much lighter fluid on the charcoal!"

"You needed a new Weber anyway," grinned Diane.

When we opened the front doors, a little bell jingled to announce our arrival. Inside, there were items that were practical, functional, and necessary. The shelves were crammed with canned vegetables, flour, sugar, ketchup, and the like. AA batteries, beauty aids, and medicines, were in the next aisle. Along the far wall, a tall glass fronted refrigerated cooler softly hummed and it was stocked with milk, butter, eggs, sodas, and had a nice selection of beer.

Located directly behind the checkout counter was the *"You must be 18 years or older"* section containing cheap liquor, cigarettes, chewing tobacco, lottery tickets, and assorted girlie magazines. Yup, everything a person needs can be found at Maxine's, except for hardware, of course. For that you go across the street to Ernie Miller's Hardware.

Smitty put the light bulbs on the counter for the cashier to ring up. They always put the charges on the fire department's tab. Smitty signed the receipt, and we ventured across the street to the hardware store to pick up a toilet bowl plunger. The men's toilet was backed up again, and somehow the guys on A-shift forgot to mention it this morning.

"They must have used the women's room all night since their toilet was out of service," said Diane. "I was wondering why the women's room had a funk to it this morning, a kind of man funk. Not to mention the seat on the toilet was still up and there was residual shaving stubble in the sink."

"Don't blame it on men in general," I said. "It must have been an A-shift funk," I laughed.

We walked into Ernie Miller's Hardware to buy the plunger. Now don't get me started with the hardware store,

I could spend hours in there and not buy a single thing. It housed a lot of man stuff. For the ranchers, there were horseshoes and horseshoe nails, hobbles, stock bells, lots of rope, and leather gloves. For the hunters, they had cast iron Dutch ovens, and enamel coffee pots. You could find racks of rifles, shotguns, and caches of ammo. For the do-it-yourselfers, there was a wide assortment of nuts, bolts, plumbing supplies, and a full aisle of hand tools.

When you strolled into Ernie's, you just wanted to walk each aisle and pick up stuff, feel the squeeze of a pair of tin snips or the heft of a hammer. It was like being at Maxine's except the place oozed with a lot more testosterone.

Diane called to me as they were leaving, "Pablo, stop fondling that hammer and get a move on!"

She startled me out of my man-moment. I quickly looked up and knew I had been caught red handed. I put the hammer down and reluctantly made my way back to the truck.

As we were leaving, we got dispatched for a *Rescue; unknown person down,* at the Beaumont Hotel. When we pulled out we could see the ambulance just ahead of us, and were soon following close behind. We pulled into the parking lot, grabbed our EMS gear and entered the lobby. There was a gaggle of lookie-loos circling an elderly woman on the floor. As we approached we realized it was Mrs. Browning, the owner of the Beaumont.

We kneeled down beside her and she said through gritted teeth, "Damn hip, it popped out again when I bent over to pick up a gum wrapper off the carpet!"

Mrs. Browning was third generation Mimbres Springs. Her family bought the hotel when it was still a brothel and saloon back in the day. She was the nicest person you would ever want to meet, and this was the third time her prosthetic hip had dislocated this summer.

"You might have to upgrade on the make and model of your hip. It looks like the warranty has run out," I said with a smile.

"Dang blab, I am going to miss today's bridge club," she sighed with regret.

"You know the routine, we take you to the ER in Deming and they'll pop that pesky hip back in, and you'll be back before you know it," said Tom, the medic from the ambulance.

We loaded her up on the gurney and rolled her out of the lobby. Her daughter was by her side, and all of the bridge players and hotel guests gave her a pat on the shoulder or a squeeze of her hand.

The Beaumont hotel was the town's hub, but it didn't start out that way. Long ago it was barely a back-road watering hole. Back in the town's mining days it started as a squalid dirt floor miner's tent, with rough sawn boards placed on top of two whiskey barrels. It soon became a knuckle busting, dimly lit, tin roofed saloon. As the town grew, so did it. The dingy watering hole evolved into an opulent two-story structure.

She became known as the Pharaoh Saloon, and in her day, was a real showplace. Running the length of the back wall was a large and highly polished oak bar. Behind the bar was an ornate etched mirror, with shelves showing off bottles of hard liquor and watered down booze.

Imported crystal chandeliers graced her ceiling, murals of scantily clad nymphs decorated the walls, and the green felt gaming tables were always crowded with flimflamming card sharks and crusty miners.

In her heyday the Pharaoh was a magnet and many a patron would travel great distances to partake in the three W's: whiskey, wagering, and whoring. The second floor was stocked with the Ladies of Easy Virtue, and the head mistress Gloria 'Goldie' Grayson, ran the upstairs brothel with an iron fist. The Pharaoh fleeced her clientele of their hard earned gold, as most of her customers left in a blissful, satisfied inebriated state.

Eventually the gold ran out, and the Pharaoh fell on hard times. It was stripped of its flourishes and for a brief time, became a common boarding house. She struggled to retain tenants and was almost closed up altogether, until a well-to-do couple from Saint Louis came traveling through and purchased it. They totally renovated it and named it the Beaumont Hotel, and the rest is history.

Today the hotel is a vital and indispensable part of Mimbres Springs. As opposed to the Pharaoh's endless poker games, the Beaumont is proud to host the *59th Street Bridge Club.* Members eagerly anticipate the 8 a.m. start time and there is always a table set up with complimentary coffee, tea, and finger foods. The area's Red Hat Society meets on the third Tuesday of the month, and you can bet there will be Bingo every Saturday night.

The biggest contribution the Beaumont Hotel has made to this town was to create Pioneer Daze. It is a weeklong festival held during the first week in October. The Beaumont single handedly brought it to fruition, helps organize, and vigorously promotes the event. Main Street is closed off and lined with white tents. There are a lot of arts and crafts, a huge flea market, a regional chili cook-off competition and free micro-beer tasting. The air is always filled with the sound of street musicians and the aroma of roasting green chilies.

There are booths crammed with jars of local honey, homemade jellies, jams, pickles, and preserves. You can find roasted corn on the cob, aguas frescas, hot dogs, bratwurst, chili rellenos, churros, and a lot of fresh-steamed tamales. People come from all over to sample the fare.

As we pulled out of the hotel parking lot and headed to the station, I remembered when my family moved here in my youth. I looked down Main Street and noticed the town hasn't changed that much. My parents, as well as their parents, had lived their entire lives in Chicago, and at some point, they felt they needed to get out of the big city.

Coming to Mimbres Springs was a little unsettling at first. There were no tall buildings or skyscrapers, sounds of city traffic or the rumble of elevated trains. Mimbres Springs had only one main street, and the place was deafeningly quiet. I was amazed that you could look toward the horizon and see all the way to the edge of the world. Why my dad chose New Mexico was a mystery to me, but once we settled in, the people of Mimbres Springs immediately embraced us, and we were taken aback by its down-to-earth, Southwestern charm.

On the way to the station we passed Joey Patron's Bar and Grill. Even though it was mid-morning, it didn't surprise me that there were several cars in the parking lot. It was a popular hang out, and my favorite place in town. Joey's was always dark and air-conditioned, with plenty of wide screen TV's playing baseball or football. Joey served up a hefty beefy burger; hand cut fries and ice-cold draft beer.

"Ahhh, there's nothing better on a hot summer's day," I said as we drove by.

We parked the truck and entered the firehouse. After we made the necessary repairs on the light fixture and unstopped the men's room toilet, we worked on the day's assignments, catching up on run reports and some neglected paperwork. After lunch we went outside and did a little yard work. As we scraped out the last remaining weeds of summer, we heard the phone ringing through an open window.

Within minutes, Smitty called us into the administrative office to let us know that our brush truck was being called up to fight some wildfires in northern Nevada.

"They must have been hard pressed for manpower to be calling little ol' Mimbres Springs Fire Department for help," I said. But then again, the fire season this year was intense, and it seemed like the entire West was on fire.

Of course, I always jump at the opportunity to fight some real fire. It was the beginning of September and it seemed like each wildfire season was getting longer with each passing year. We worked a couple of smaller brush fires earlier in the summer, but being called up to any large campaign wildfire like this, was like being called up to the Big Leagues.

One of the best ways we raise money for the fire department is to send out our fire apparatus and firefighters to seasonal wildfires. Most wildfires start up in May and new ones continually pop up until the end of October. The term "wildland" can be defined as an area in which human development is essentially non-existent, except for some roads, railroads, and power lines. Houses, if any, are widely scattered. Normally we let nature take its course and let those fires burn, however, more and more people are moving into the wildland areas, which puts them at a greater risk when those fires pop up.

In the past we have sent our wildland firefighters to Texas, Colorado, California, Arizona, Nevada, Utah, and of

course New Mexico.   Our department, as well as our
firefighters can make good money because the Feds pay for
the use of our equipment and personnel.   They also pay to
backfill our positions back home while we are away.

All the members of Mimbres Springs Fire are certified
wildland firefighters. During the course of the year we take
wildland classes and every February we are required to pass
an annual three-mile hike, carrying a 45-pound pack, in less
than 45 minutes.   This *Pack-Test* proves we can perform
arduous work. As a result, every firefighter receives a *red
card*, an agency-issued document that certifies that we have
the training, experience and physical fitness to perform the
tasks on a wildland fire. You can't work a wildfire without
a red card in your wallet. We take this type of firefighting
very seriously, knowing that fire shows no mercy to those
who are ill prepared, and we do our best to try and keep the
odds in our favor.

I am one of our department's three wildland certified
engine bosses, and I was given the nod to go on the Nevada
assignment. The engine boss is responsible for the operation
and maintenance of the brush truck, along with the safety
of the crew.   I find many similarities between being an
infantryman in the Marines and being a firefighter. I love
the comradery, working in small teams of three or four,
while relying on our wits and using our skills under duress.
The one big difference between the two is, as firefighters we
are lifesavers instead of life takers. It kind of balances it all
out ... good for the soul. Let's just say I have held up well
for an old gray haired guy. I can still dish it out and keep
up with the younger guys both in structure and wildland
firefighting, at least for now, with a little help from my old
friend Ben Gay!

Diane is the most experienced member of the crew and has the most passion for wildland firefighting. Being the *squad boss*, she organizes the truck, documents daily activities, and handles all of the paperwork and payroll for the engine boss. We have worked together for the past 10 years, on both wildland hand crews and brush truck assignments. I think we make an effective team. She has figured out how to put up with my practical jokes and sometimes-ornery disposition, and I have figured out how to stay out of her reach when I piss her off. Actually we get along great and have a lot of fun. There are a lot more guys than gals on a typical wildland assignment, and Diane is never afraid to jump into the fray whenever the crap starts to hit the fan. I am amazed at times watching her in action. She is like a bulldog on a bone.

I recall her saying once … "Wildland firefighters are a breed all their own, not a whiner in the bunch. They come together from all parts of the country, work hard under hellacious conditions, and flat out get the job done!" She then humbly added, "I can't tell you how happy I am to be a part of that."

Phil, was the third member of our crew, and was placed on this assignment to get experience. You could describe him as a young, innocent, clean-cut Mormon boy, standing about 5 feet 10, had dark hair, emerald green eyes and an authentic smile. Being 21 years old, this was his first year as a full-time firefighter. He has a superhero profile and the young girls always look him over, whisper and giggle to each other when we show up on calls. He is modest and easy going, and I never can get him to drink coffee, enjoy a nice glass of Scotch, or even cuss if his pants caught on fire. He is honest as the day is long, and the days on the wildland fire line are always seriously long. He works as hard as a miner's mule and is one tough son-of-a gun, in a polite sort of way. You could say Phil is a *happy to be here* kind of guy.

On this assignment he will be in training, operating as our engineer. Since this was his first time on a big, out-of-state fire, he will be working through his wildland task book. Diane and I will sign him off on different aspects, teach him how to drive the brush truck over rough terrain, operate the water pump, and show him other wildland tricks of the trade.

Once we got our orders, it took us less than an hour to stock the truck, grab some snacks, and get on the road.

Once on the road to Nevada Diane said, "Pablo, do you think it's crazy how we can hardly wait to go on a wildland assignment and willfully endure the next two weeks of suffering?"

"There is nothing wrong with a little sunburn, eating smoke, filthy clothes, monkey butt, wildland boogers, warm baloney sandwiches, and two weeks of crapping in the woods."

"And can you believe it, when we return home we always tell the guys how great it was! And can't wait to go on another assignment," said Diane.

"You've got to love that selective memory," I told her. "A person has a tendency to forget the misery and remember only the glory!"

"What glory?" spouted Diane. "It's just one continuous stream of sleep deprived, bone numbing, nasty, dirty work."

"I'll give you that, but you know you love it," I said with a grin.

"What's Monkey Butt?" shouted Phil over the growl of the engine.

"You tell him Pablo!"

"No no, it's one of those things that can't be explained. You just have to experience it for yourself. He will find out soon enough."

"I don't like the sound of that," shouted Phil.

Diane and I looked at each other and laughed.

The cab of the Triple Nickel filled with riotous monkey noises as we made our way up Interstate 15 to the Nevada fire.

3 The TP Fire

We drove through the night and caught about four hours of sleep near Cedar City, Utah. After almost 18 hours of driving, we pulled into the parking lot at the command center in Elko, Nevada right around noon.

"Did you see all those plumes of smoke off on the horizon as we drove in?" Phil asked.

"Looks like a lot of fire everywhere! Hot Damn!" said Diane.

There was a light blue haze covering the entire state. My eyes were beginning to water and as I cleared my throat I noticed it was getting a little scratchy from the smoke.

The command center was hustling with action. New engines and brush trucks were arriving and lining up for their inspections. Supply convoys were unpacking mountains of boxes, pallets of supplies, and rows of Porta-potties. Helicopters were buzzing overhead, and hand crews were moving out to their new assignments.

"This reminds me of a forward combat base camp back in "*Nam*," I said. "Except there's no big artillery or armored vehicles, just bulldozers and fire trucks."

Today's enemy was wildfire, and lots of it. Lightning-sparked wildfires were ravaging the state's drought stricken grasslands and forests. Rangeland, ranches, small towns, and whole communities, were in harm's way. Nothing was safe! The latest report said there were as many as 14 fires currently in Nevada. Some have been burning for weeks, and some had just started today.

Diane said in an uneasy voice, "God only knows where they will be sending us."

As we got out of our truck to work off our road trip stiffness, we walked across a freshly plowed field currently being used as a parking lot and noticed everything was coated with a fine layer of grey silty powder that reminded me of talc.

I said to Diane, "It's easy to spot the new arrivals from those that have been here for a while. Our clean brush truck stands out like a sore thumb."

"Don't worry Pablo, you know as well as I, after this two-week tour, our truck will be so filthy we won't even recognize the old Triple Nickel," grinned Diane.

We depend on the Triple Nickel, and she is our home away from home. It is a Ford F-550 4-wheel drive, modified pickup truck and has compartments and bins mounted in all available locations, stuffed full of wildland firefighting equipment. There are hundreds of feet of fire hose, hose couplings, fuel cans, road flares, hand-tools, and just about anything that is needed for a wildland fire assignment. With a 200-gallon water tank taking up a lot of space, there is barely enough room for our two-week duffel bags, so we stow our personal gear on the very top of the truck, securing them with bungee cords.

A small compartment located in the cab of the truck is reserved for the most important item of all, *snacks!* Without quality snacks, we don't roll, so we stock plenty of them.

While walking across the parking lot, Phil was overwhelmed with all of the intensity and action. "Man, look at all the trucks!"

"You know Phil, try imagining how a chef makes a big meal and apply that to one of these campaign fires," Diane replied. "The Incident Commander gathers all of his ingredients together. He calls in a little bit of New Mexico brush truck, tosses in a dash of California hand crews, adds a pinch of heavy equipment, a sprinkling of Montana smoke jumpers, and throws in some Arizona hotshots to spice things up. Before you know it, you have yourself an all-you-can-eat buffet."

"A buffet maybe, or a recipe for disaster," said Phil.

"Not necessarily, it all depends on who's running the kitchen. A crackerjack incident command team is the key to success. A crappy IC could mean *Hell's Kitchen*," Diane said with obvious experience.

"Well, butter my butt and call me a biscuit! Let's light the fires and start cookin'!" smiled Phil.

We checked in, and Phil took the truck over for inspection. After our paperwork was processed, we met up with Phil.

"Phil did she pass inspection?" I asked.

"It passed like a kidney stone, slow and painful!" he replied.

Our orders were to support fire units already working the *TP Fire,* located in the far northeast corner of the state, about 20 miles southeast of Jackpot, Nevada. We were given a rough map and some recon about the fire, and they said it would take us several hours to get there. The directions seemed straightforward but the quality of the map was *awful!*

"The copier machine could use a new ink cartridge," I said, looking at the map.

We were soon part of a small convoy heading north. I reviewed the recon and tried to make sense of the lousy map.

"Look at all these roads crisscrossed all over the place; some have names or numbers, but most are just faded lines," I said showing Diane.

"Maybe a recipe for disaster," said Phil.

"Shut your pie hole! Keep your eyes on the road and drive!"

Unfortunately, in the back of my mind, I was thinking the same thing. The map was of little help, so we stuck close to the trucks in front of us and used the smoke plume from the fire to guide us in.

Diane was sitting in the back seat proudly examining her fire boots. "How do you like these puppies?" she smiled and held up her brand new pair of *Whites*.

"Hew Doggie! Those are top of the line fire boots! They don't get any better than that," I crowed.

"Yup, best boots money can buy. It's hard to get boots my size. These were on the year-end clearance sale, and I couldn't pass them up," said Diane. "Since they are brand spanking new and a little stiff, I will need to break them in during these next couple of days."

I was thinking, maybe I should have checked my old reliable boots before we left New Mexico. We were called up in such a hurry I just threw my two-week bag into the truck without going over my stuff.

After leaving the highway south of Jackpot, we traveled for over an hour on some dusty forest service roads before arriving at the TP Fire. When we rolled into camp, there were scattered tents in every color and size imaginable. The area resembled a refugee resettlement camp straight from the plains of the Sudan, and I was happy to see that our truck was now covered in the dry Nevada talc and looked just like everybody else's.

I commented, "There doesn't seem to be any trucks from Nevada. I see license plates from California, Arizona, Idaho, Utah, and Colorado ... nobody from Nevada!"

"The Nevada resources must be thin, too much fire for one state to handle," said Diane.

"Don't worry Nevada, Mimbres Springs is here!" Phil joked, then he began to sing in his best *Mighty Mouse* voice, *"Here we come to save the day!"*

I thought to myself, *where does he come up with this stuff?* Diane and I gave Phil *the stare.*

We parked the truck and got out to take a look around. After we checked in at the command tent, we began to settle in and go through our gear. When I pulled out my old reliable boots I was confronted with my worst nightmare. I held them up to eye level and exclaimed, "Holy crap!"

The boots were deformed; the toes had curled upward, resembling elf shoes.

"Good Lord, Pablo, what the hell happened?" asked Diane staring at the freakish boots.

"On our last fire my boots became water logged. Before we left I thought I could dry them on the warm truck engine ... Well, let's just say I spaced it out and left them on there a little too long."

I managed to squeeze my big feet into them and said, "These babies are *tight!"* and started hopping up and down trying to stretch them out.

"Don't worry, you just need to pace yourself on our assignment tomorrow and don't wander too far from the truck," Diane said with assurance.

Usually on these fires, brush trucks are assigned to work with a hand crew to assist with fire attack or to help with mop up. Very seldom does a truck assignment require a death march across mountainous terrain.

"I can cowboy up for a few days until I replace them. Then again, they just might loosen up enough to be wearable," I said trying to convince myself that the boots were not that bad.

We fired up some military Meals Ready to Eat (MREs) and set our bedrolls out on top of the dry Nevada dirt. Trucks continued to roll in and as we sat there, a light breeze drifted in from the west, and we were soon embraced by the familiar smell of a distant fire.

***

After a fitful night's sleep, I pulled myself up from the bumpy ground, shoved my sleeping bag into one of the compartments, and went to the morning briefing. Phil did a truck check, and Diane stocked us up with some sack lunches for the day ahead.

At the briefing, I was informed that the hotshot hand crews had worked hard throughout the night and the TP Fire was now classified as 100 percent contained. There were no resources assigned to do initial fire attack today, and it looked like this fire had been declared *out!* I was under the impression that we were going to patrol the area in our assigned division, supply water to the hand crews, and assist in mop up and cold trailing. I couldn't have been more pleased. After the briefing I hustled out of the Incident Command tent to inform my crew.

I told Phil and Diane, "We need to head to Division B and meet up with five other brush trucks at the hay bales by 08:00. We are going to assist with the mop up."

During mop up, after the initial attack crews have knocked down the fire, mop up crews proceed to work the edge of the fire line where the charred *black* areas meet the unburned *green* areas. We need to put out any remaining hot spots or smoldering areas so the fire doesn't flare-up and cross over into the unburned areas, making sure the area is cold, thus the term *cold trail.*

We were eager to start, so we wolfed down some morning MRE's and hightailed it over there. When we arrived at our rendezvous, the crewmembers from five brush trucks, gathered around a large stack of hay bales to hear the briefing and receive the assignment for the day.

The division supervisor explained, "You will leave all the trucks parked here and form a hand crew to do mop up. From here you will work the entire length of Division B, cold trailing up and over that small mountain off to the west. There will be sixteen of you guys so take your backpacks, hand tools, plenty of water, and sack lunches, because you will be hiking all day and will not be returning to this location."

Diane and I looked at each other with dismay, and then down at our boots. One pair new, stiff, and shiny, waiting to be broken in. One pair scuffed and deformed, ready to wreak havoc on my feet. Safety depends on mobility, and this death march could prove to be a big mistake for the both of us. Only Phil heeded the advice given to him in his wildland training classes. They instructed him to break in new boots before actually needing them on the fire line.

Before our division supervisor drove off, he assigned a wet-behind-the-ears, young crew boss trainee, to be in charge of today's death march. The *Kid* informed us that we would be picked up at 17:00 on the other side of the mountain and brought back to our trucks.

"Time to cowboy up, Diane!" I said, as we looked at one another with doom in our eyes!

"You got it, Hop-a-Long. It's time to suck it up," shouted Diane.

Diane climbed up on the truck and tossed down some hand tools, a Pulaski, a shovel, and a McCloud.

I grabbed the shovel and commented, "If we are going on a death march, I might as well have the lightest and most practical hand tool on the truck."

Diane climbed down and picked up the Pulaski.

"Hah, a shovel, you wimp! This Pulaski is the best darn tool on the truck," boasted Diane.

A Pulaski is a wildland tool that resembles a double-sided ax. One side has a sharp ax for chopping down light brush and small trees. The other side has a long thick flat blade, for hoeing and digging. It's an ax and hoe in one.

I shouted to Phil, "Hey, buckaroo, you can use this. This is probably the greatest wildland tool ever made." I grinned and handed him the McCloud.

By my estimates, the McCloud tool is probably the most worthless tool on the truck. It looks like a long handled garden hoe on steroids. On one side of the hoe is a heavy flat steel blade about 12 inches wide, the other side is 12 inches wide and has six thick tines, each about eight inches long. It is cumbersome and probably won't do much good in the rocky terrain we're working in today.

The young trainee squad boss hollered for all of us to fall-in and move out to the dozer line. Before I could say anything, Phil hustled to get in line. I wanted to tell him we were kidding about the McCloud, and to switch it out for something more practical. But he fell in line with the rest of them and marched off like a man on a mission. Of the 16 people in line, he was the only one with a McCloud.

As we worked along the edge of the black, our squad boss basically informed us that our crew was going to be the first to finish, like it was some kind of race or something. *The Kid* set a blistering pace along the dozer line and made us go deep into the burned out black area, about 50 feet or so, to put out tiny smoldering embers.

"What a rookie! He is so *smoke happy,*" I said to Phil.

"What's smoke happy?" he asked.

"It's someone who sees wisps of smoke emanating from every nook and cranny and wants to put it out during mop up," I said with a snarl. "We don't need to go so deep into the black, there is nothing left to catch on fire. It's a waste of time and effort!"

"He must have been a track star in high school," Diane scowled. "He reminds me of the Energizer Bunny."

The young crew boss kept up the breakneck pace as we continued to wade ankle deep in the dozer tracks and work the areas deep in the black. Hours passed and we could feel the sun beating down on us.

"Man, I feel blisters forming on the back of my heels," I said to Diane.

"I have a fold in my sock right under the arch of my foot," she replied, "and every time I try to stop and remove my boot, the Energizer Bunny goes faster up the hill. Maybe we could ask Phil to whack the kid upside the head with his McCloud."

"Yeah, that will be the most productive thing that tool will do all day," I chuckled.

Diane and I bit the bullet and pressed on. The sun was scorching, and I could feel sweat pouring down my back and running down my butt crack. The blisters became more painful with each passing mile. We breathed a sigh of relief when the young crew boss called out for lunch. We stopped, dropped our packs and hand tools and proceeded to park ourselves under a scrawny patch of shade. I quickly pried my boots off and peeled away my socks to examine the damage.

"Pretty big! They look like Mount Saint Helen's after the big blow," Phil said.

Diane shook her head and said, "Our foot repair kit is back at the truck, so there is not much we can do until we return."

"Well, if there's any consolation, with the Energizer Bunny setting the pace, we should get back to the trucks in *record time!*" said Phil.

"You got that right!" I grumbled.

I pulled my socks back on and shoved my feet back into my tight boots. I grimaced as I felt raw flesh press into the back of my boot. Just as I finished up my sack lunch, the crew boss rallied the troops. We all shouldered our backpacks and began the afternoon march.

The next three hours were more of the same. As I worked, I couldn't help but notice how Phil handled that McCloud like a pro. I quietly laughed to myself as I watched him scratch and rake the crap out of those hot spots.

"I got to hand it to him," I told Diane, "he is one, hot coal raking, McCloud Muckin' Madman!"

We arrived at our pick-up point *two hours* ahead of schedule and had to wait for our ride back to our trucks. As we waited for our transport, we noticed Phil standing out by the road in the full afternoon sun.

"Hey Huckleberry! Get over here!" Diane shouted to Phil.

Diane waved him over and filled him in on some wildland wisdom.

"Phil, why stand in the sun if you can stand in the *shade?*" she explained.

"And ... why stand in the shade if you can *sit* in the shade?" I added.

"And ... why sit in the shade if you can *lie down* in the shade?" she grinned.

We fluffed up a nice pile of leaves and pine needles, put our backpacks behind our heads and laid down in the lukewarm shade. While we lay there with our hardhats pulled down over our eyes, I apologized to Phil.

"Man, I'm really sorry about the McCloud. I meant it as a joke."

"Not a problem, Boss, I still have time to whack our crew boss with it," he replied.

"Never mind. It would only look bad on our report," I grunted.

Moments later, while sucking on a watermelon Jolly Rancher, I glanced over at Phil resting in the shade and had to smile. It only took a minute or two before I heard soft snoring coming out from under his hard hat.

4 Man Card

Back at camp we decided to immediately take care of our primary concern, the blisters on our feet. I pulled off my boots and blood soaked socks. There, bigger than life, were two blisters the size of fifty-cent pieces, one on back of each heel. Having been split open, the raw weeping innards were now exposed to the dry Nevada air.

"Good Lord!" Diane gasped as she rummaged through her duffle bag in search of the *foot kit.*

I lied down on the bedroll with my heels to the sky. Diane trimmed off the dead skin, and said she had a liquid bandage called *New-Skin* to paint on the raw flesh.

"Pablo, this is going to hurt! ... Real bad!" she warned me.

"Oh, Hell Missy!" I grumbled. "I've endured jungle rot and trench foot back in Nam, this can't be any worse than that!"

"OK, tough guy on the count of *three* I'm going to slap this stuff on. *One, two,*" Bam! She surprised me and slapped the stuff on, at the count of two!

After a few microseconds of silence, I went through the roof like a Roman candle. I was whooping, hollering and cussing up a blue streak because it hurt like hell! When I finally came to my senses, she was finishing up with more layers of the liquid bandage. After letting the layers dry, she applied a layer of moleskin and some athletic tape.

Phil came back with an armful of cold Gatorades and said, "I heard you clear on the other side of camp. You sounded like a school girl that had a lizard dropped down her dress!" Pointing at me he snickered, "Hey Boss, are those tears rolling down those cheeks of yours?"

Not realizing the process produced tears; I quickly brushed them off with the back of my hand, glared at Phil and gave him my best *I hope you die, stink-eye.*

Diane leaned in close and said, "Well, Mr. Jarhead, you were sure acting like a big fat sissy just then! If you don't mind, could you please turn in your *Man Card!*"

I pretended to ignore the chuckling and snorting from the two of them.

I quickly regained my composure, realizing it was now Diane's turn to endure the process. I have to admit, if someone was trying to get secret information from somebody, this would be one hell of a way to do it! Diane had an equally large and painful blister on the bottom of her foot, where her sock had been folded over for most of the day. It was a big nasty, oozing mess, and I was taken aback by the look of it. Having trimmed off the flap of skin I stated, "You know what they say about paybacks?"

"Get on with it, you old coot!" she snapped back.

Yes, it was Diane's turn and I was ready to dish it out.

"Now Missy, this is going to hurt," I said with a little chuckle, "Real bad! Now on the count of three I am going to put this stuff on." I chuckled again and thought to myself, *this otta be good.*

"What are you waiting for, Christmas?" she growled.

I counted one then ... Bam! I slapped it on at the count of one, and stood there smirking, waiting for the Forth of July fireworks to start.

After a few seconds she looked back at me with her eyes narrowed and dryly asked, "Are you done Mr. Giggles?"

"Holy crap!" I couldn't believe it, not a flinch, not a peep!

Phil and I looked at each other with our mouths hanging open like a couple of slack-jawed yokels. I finished up with a few more layers, let them dry, added some moleskin and wrapped her foot with some athletic tape.

Diane got up and gave me a punch in the shoulder and said, "Ooh Rah!"

I turned and started fumbling through my pack and mumbled, "Okaaaay, so where did I put my *Man Card?*"

After tidying up the camp, the next thing on our agenda was to find some grub. We noticed there was a small mess tent set up at the edge of the makeshift camp, with a dozen long tables sitting out in a grassy field. We hobbled over and got in line. The cook staff looked like a rag-tag bunch, with plastic aprons and assorted sweat stained baseball caps, and we were a little reluctant at the sight of them as we approached the chow line. After our morning MRE, and a sack lunch that wouldn't hold over a fifth grader, we realized we were starving! After grabbing some metal trays, we made our way down the line, and the aroma of the food suddenly got my mouth watering.

"Good golly!" exclaimed Phil. "This is some mighty fine eatin'!"

The menu consisted of grilled pork chops, sweet corn on the cob, mashed potatoes, dinner rolls, a garden salad, fruit cocktail, chocolate cake, and cherry pie. We sat down at a table and I couldn't help but stare at Phil's plate. It was piled high to the sky. Next to his plate, standing side by side, were two root beers, a glass of lemonade, and three cartons of milk.

"If this is Hell's Kitchen," grinned Phil, "then let the sinning begin!"

"Wow! That's pretty bold talk for a sweet Mormon boy!" Diane said with surprise.

"I don't know about that, he looks pretty hungry," I said while staring at his plate.

"Hungry enough to sell my soul to the devil," Phil said before tearing into his pork chop.

"Despite the blisters today, I really like getting out there and working these fires. It never gets old," pondered Diane.

"Diane, how long have you been at this firefighting stuff?" Phil asked between mouthfuls.

"Why I chose firefighting is beyond me. I went to college and then worked in food service for six years, and was a restaurant manager for the last three. The pay was pretty good; however, it was tough, you know, long hours, late nights, and there were always staffing issues. People would call in sick at the drop of a hat for no good reason. The hired help was always coming and going. Some of my best people would quit for better paying jobs. It was a constant struggle to find decent help."

Phil chimed in, "During my senior year in high school I worked at the *Pup and Taco* for about a month and a half and I hated it."

"Was it because you had to work with all of those pimply faced teenagers?" I asked.

"No, I think it was because I had to wear that stupid paper hat all day!" Phil laughed.

Diane was holding up a piece of chocolate cake with her fork, staring at it, contemplating its chocolateness or something when she said, "I never even knew women could become firefighters when I was growing up. It was never part of the equation. I would play outside all day with my brothers and sisters, climb trees, ride bikes, play tackle football with the neighbor kids, and get filthy dirty. I just loved the physicalness of it all. I never pulled the *Girl Card* and cried when I got hit by a pitch or got knocked down. The guys didn't cry so why should I?"

"A little Tomboy huh?" I laughed.

"Hey, there's nothing wrong with being a Tomboy! I just loved being outside. OK, it will be a rare day when I wear a dress and put on makeup and heels. Maybe a special occasion, like an anniversary or wedding or something. I have to admit I clean up pretty nice when I have to. There is a time and place for everything, and a girl has to do what a girl has to do to when it comes to being accepted. I don't like to gossip, mess with make-up, shop at the mall, or hang out with many girlfriends. I guess we don't have that much in common, most of my closest friends are men," said Diane with a shrug.

"When I was accepted into the Fire Academy there was a lot of resentment. There were 25 of us, and I was the only woman. The guys hated the fact that there was a girl in their ranks. They felt women had no place in firefighting; after all, they were training to be *firemen*, and goddamn, who let this girl in here? They let me know, in no uncertain terms, that I was not strong enough, brave enough, smart enough or tough enough, and that I had a snowballs chance in hell to make it.

"Then what happened?" asked Phil.

"Their resentment only motivated me. I didn't get mad, I just decided I was on a mission to prove them wrong. Actually, I had to prove to *myself* that firefighting was something I could do, and not just be able to do it, but do it well. I asked the Academy Instructor if I could lead the calisthenics every morning and take point on the runs.

Little did the guys know I was an All-American in track back in my college days and was still in excellent shape. I could still run a mile in under five minutes and 10 miles in just under an hour! I could also pop off 50 push-ups and 15 chin-ups at a crack."

Phil blew out a whistle. "Golleee! Ten miles, those are six minute miles!"

"You bet your sweet tomatoes," Diane said enthusiastically. "I studied my butt off in the classroom too and ended up being the valedictorian of our graduating class."

"You're a real hard ass! Remind me not to mess with you," said Phil.

"Don't worry Phil, I can take a joke. Go ahead and ask Pablo, he has been messing with me for years. I just don't like it when it gets personal. I'm not the one to put up with that crap," Diane cautioned.

"Yo comprendo," said Phil, as he dug into a piece of cherry pie.

Diane went on to say, "It doesn't matter that I eventually settled down in the small fire department in Mimbres Springs. You don't have to work in a big city fire department to do big things. It's been 12 years, and I still find the work very satisfying and rewarding. I feel like I make a difference in people's lives, and I love coming to work every day. I really would like to see more girls become firefighters. They don't have to be Amazons or world-beaters. They just need to have the moxie to work hard, and possess the compassion to serve others."

I looked at Diane and winked. She looked back and gave me a smile.

I polished off my lemonade, crunched up the last of my ice cubes and said, "I found out through the grapevine that we are going to work the TP fire for maybe two more days, mostly mop up, and after that we will be released and reassigned. Thunderstorms have been rolling in throughout the state, with a lot of lightning but no rain. Dry lightning has sparked some new fires and it sounds like there is plenty of fire to go around."

"Not much fire left at the old TP," said Diane.

"Just what do you think the TP stands for?" asked Phil while wiping his mouth with a paper napkin.

"I don't know, maybe Toilet Paper, you know, because we experienced some stupid shit today," I suggested.

"Or maybe Tipi, like the Indian tent, like all the tents in this camp," said Diane.

"How about this one," said Phil with a smile, "Tasty Pie!"

We laughed, picked up our trays, and walked over to the mess tent to drop off our dirty dishes. Phil went over to the camp cooks and let them know how impressed he was with their cooking. We saw him shake the hand of every cook in the chow line. They all laughed and gave him a thumbs-up.

"That Phil, I bet his mother is so proud of him, such a polite young man," said Diane.

"I bet he comes outta here a bit rougher around the edges than when he came in," I replied gruffly.

We returned to the Nickel, settled in, and watched the sun slowly sink behind the distant hills.

"Not a whole lot out there, just grass and sagebrush," commented Phil, as he pointed to the sparse landscape.

"It may not look like much to us, but this is prime rangeland and it is important to these ranchers. They couldn't raise cattle without it. Not to mention, it is habitat for all of the antelope, grouse, coyotes, and other critters who live here," I said.

"You got a point," agreed Phil.

"Well, the critters may love it, but I don't like it much," said Diane, as she rolled out her bedroll, "it's too lumpy."

We tried to get as comfortable as we could, but the hard ground was winning. The air was unexpectedly still and a surreal silence surrounded us. Gazing in awe at the brilliant colors of a slowly changing sunset, it felt as if the earth had exhaled a long deep sigh, and the setting sun, along with the rest of the camp, was beginning to relax after a long hard day.

5 Short Cut

We have been at the TP fire for three days and will be working with a hand-crew from Utah today. We affection-ately refer to hand crews as *Knuckle Draggers* and the hand crews call Type 6 truck crews, a bunch of *Truck Princesses*, but we really have a lot of respect for each other, and I know it is all said in jest. We all work hard and get along just fine.

The TP Fire was considered to be 100 percent contained however, there was still a lot of work to be done. At the morning briefing all remaining crews were told to continue cold trailing. We needed to be sure there were no hot spots creeping into the unburned areas. Cold trailing involves a lot of raking and digging, and it can get real tedious. We get paid the same rate to fight the fire or mop it up, and I figured somebody has to do it. But hopefully, this would be our last day of the monotonous work.

Later in the morning, I was working up a sweat when Diane walked over to me and asked, "Do you have any vitamin-I on you?"

"As a matter of fact I do," I said, and reached into my cargo pants pocket and handed her a couple of ibuprofen.

She downed them with a swallow of warm canteen water, and asked, "How are your blisters holding up?"

"Yesterday was the worst. Who would think something so small could make a person's life so miserable? The good news is, I think my boots have loosened up and I will survive," I said with relief. "How are your feet doing?"

"Not too bad, cowboy, but I think I'm getting a little too much sun today." She felt her cheeks and commented they were getting little warm. "I need to remember to bring my sunscreen with me."

"Yeah it looks like they are getting a little red. Hey, I've got some sun screen in my pocket; it's SPF 50, waterproof and sweat proof!"

"Well, don't Bogart that sunscreen and pass it over to me!" said Diane with a smile.

I laughed when she said that. I didn't think the younger set would even know what that meant.

She applied a thick layer on her face and neck and handed it back to me.

Diane said, "I can't help but think cargo pants are a wildland firefighter's godsend. Whoever invented them should get a medal. When I am working outside all day, there are certain things I always need to have on hand. In my pockets I carry, a small cache of toilet paper, two chap sticks, some cough drops or throat lozenges, assorted Jolly Ranchers, Visine, a Bic lighter, my Leatherman multi-tool, salty snacks, and an extra bandana or two. Man, I can't believe I forgot to pack my sunscreen and ibuprofen."

"Hey, back in Nam I remember stuffing my cargo pockets with battle dressing, ammo, a zippo lighter, bug juice, and other necessities. Oh, and I had a stack of playing cards, not ordinary cards, all of them were ace of spades with a skull printed on them. They were called *Vietnamese Death Cards*. When we encountered the dead enemy, we would place them on their eyes or in their mouths and move on."

"Now that's warped Pablo."

"Hey, it was war and the enemy got really creeped out by it."

"I'm creeped out!" said Diane.

The skies had become overcast and off in the distance I could see veils of rain falling from the clouds, but because the air was so hot and dry, the virga was evaporating halfway down and none of it was coming close to hitting the ground.

It was about 17:00 when we finished up the mundane mop up assignment. The division supervisor arrived and checked on our progress. He inspected our work, walked along the line, and looked at our filthy crew. He grinned and gave us the OK to head back to camp.

At camp, I pried off my leather boots, slid my liberated feet into some flip-flops, took off my smoky brush gear and put on a nice clean T-shirt, and gym shorts.

As we began to wash up, Diane made the comment. "If it weren't for baby wipes, I don't know how I would survive out here." She pulled one out of its pink plastic container and wiped her face and arms. She held the offensive towelette up to inspect the copious amount of dirt she had just removed. "I love them; they are so convenient and handy."

She grabbed another one and scoured her face for a second time. "Ahh, I feel so much better."

Phil walked over to her and gave her a sniff. "And you smell so baby fresh!"

We headed over to the small mess tent and worked our way through the chow line. The cooks recognized Phil and gave him a shout-out. He smiled and gave them a thumbs-up. For today's supper the cooks had produced another tasty meal. It consisted of bratwurst and grilled onions nestled in a large hoagie roll. Along with that they dished out some roasted potatoes and a garden salad. For the ones who were not afraid of passing gas later that night, at the end of the line was a big pan of baked beans and a heaping pan of sauerkraut!

We found a spot at a table where a woman and younger guy were sitting.

The woman stood up and offered us a handshake, and introduced herself. She had impeccable posture, a firm but not overpowering handshake, was about 5 feet 8 inches tall with short blonde hair and looked about 40 years old.

"My name is Virginia, but I really prefer Ginny," she smiled.

As the conversation unfolded, we found out she was a dozer operator and the fella was a water tender operator. They both lived in Middleton, Idaho and worked part time for the Bureau of Land Management (BLM).

"I have been doing this dozer stuff for about six years now. Before that, I served in the Navy, ten years altogether, three of those years on the *USS Nimitz*," she proudly said.

"Wow the Nimitz? No kidding, that's one of those giant aircraft carriers isn't it?" I asked.

"It is the world's largest! The Nimitz is about 23 stories tall from keel to topside, and her flight deck is about the length of three football fields. Believe it or not, she even has her own zip code! She carries about 5,000 sailors, with only a handful being women," she informed us.

"Like the fire service ... only a handful of women," Diane piped up. "You rock!" and they both reached across the table and slapped a hard high five.

The young fella' sitting next to her told us his name was Clint and had fought fire in Idaho, Nevada, and parts of Washington and Oregon. He was manning a Type 2 water tender, which held 3,000 gallons of water.

"I'm a seasonal firefighter and I've been doing this type of work every summer for the past five years," said Clint. "When I'm not on a fire, I work as a mechanic at the gas station in Middleton. The guys at the station don't mind when I get called out, they think firefighters are pretty cool."

"Hey, have you guys figured out what the TP Fire stands for? Phil thinks it stands for *Tasty Pie!*" I asked.

"Good question, I'm beginning to think it stands for the roads around here, *Too many Potholes!*" said Clint.

"I'm guessing it might stand for the crews working on Type 6 trucks, like you guys, the *Truck Princesses!*" laughed Ginny.

I choked on my beans when she said that.

"How do you guys like the chow at these fires?" Phil asked, returning with two lemonades.

"This camp has excellent cooks, and they serve up some pretty good chow. Hey Ginny, remember that fire near Lake Tahoe last year? They had a catering outfit that dished out chow I think my dog wouldn't touch," Clint said shaking his head with a dour look on his face.

Ginny laughed, "Yeah, that chow was awful. I ended up eating a steady diet of MREs and granola bars."

"Well, it looks like tonight's meal could get a little gassy, if you know what I mean," I said looking at my beans and holding up my brat topped with sauerkraut.

I know we would occasionally float an *air biscuit* or two on the Nimitz. Sometimes the air in the sleeping berths would get a little foul," grinned Ginny.

"Ha, air biscuit, I never heard that one before. The guys at the firehouse sometimes refer to it as *barking spiders,*" I laughed.

"When we were growing up we would ask, '*Who let Fred out?*'" snickered Diane.

"Hey, Phil, what corny saying do you have for passing gas?" I asked.

"Well, whenever my dad would rip a good one, he would always ask us, *'Who stepped on a duck?'* "

We laughed, and told more stories while feasting on brats, beans, and sauerkraut.

After savoring the last of my lemonade, I got up and shook hands with Ginny and Clint. "We hope to see you guys on the next fire ... and be safe."

While walking across the grassy field, I noticed more clouds had moved in as the sun was setting low in a blood red sky. When working wildland fires, we experience some of the reddest sunsets on earth, only because there is so much smoke in the air.

"I have to admit this sunset is quite spectacular! I rate it a 10!" sighed Diane as we sat at camp and watched the sun slip below the horizon.

"Get a good night's sleep. It looks like this fire is dead out and, more than likely, we'll be leaving tomorrow morning!" I said with enthusiasm. "Word has it that dry lightning has started a bunch of fires south of Elko, and I want in on that action."

I laid down on my bedroll and couldn't remember anything until sunrise.

***

It was day six. We woke up to a heavily overcast morning, brewed up some coffee, and downed a morning MRE. I made my way to the morning briefing, and noticed the air had become thick with dust from all the activity in camp. Just as I suspected, I was told all units were to report to Elko Fire Command to be reassigned.

While standing in line to have our paperwork processed, I overheard two engine bosses discussing a shortcut through the mountains, west towards the town of Jackpot. It sounded like the shortcut could shorten our travel time to Elko by a couple of hours. The directions sounded pretty straightforward, so I located the roads on my bad copy of a map.

I thought to myself, *Okay we can save some time. Hopefully if we arrive early, we might get assigned to an initial attack team!*

Units were leaving as soon as their paperwork was processed, and I watched as the engine bosses scurried out of the tent, eager to get on the road and back to some real action. The thought of fighting some fire instead of ditzing around with this paperwork made me wish this line moved a little faster.

"Who's holding up the show?" I hollered toward the front of the line. "Move along little doggies, we're burning daylight here!"

Within an hour the Nickel was on its way. With my bad map in hand, I explained the newly devised plan to my crew.

"Are you sure about this short cut?" asked Diane.

"Don't worry, we will head north and take the second left, right here." I pointed to the map and then looked down the road. "After that, we take this winding road for about 10 miles, then pass these ranches and bingo! We are in Jackpot!"

"If you get us lost, Pablo, I get to rip the moleskin right off your blisters," Diane warned.

"I'm not worried; my blisters are safe. I feel real good about this."

It was cloudy and cooler than it had been these past few days. As we made our way down the road, I started to relax and enjoy the beautiful mountain terrain. These were images straight out of a western painting: rustic ranch houses nestled in the pines, windmills spinning in the breeze, and cowboys on horseback herding cattle.

After awhile I put my hands behind my head and let out a long peaceful sigh, "I could do this all day."

"Well, we might just be here *all day!*" Diane glared at me. "It has been way over an hour, and I personally think we're lost. It has taken too dang long for this to be a short cut!"

"Us guys have a natural instinct about directions," I reassured her. "If it will make you happy, I'll stop and ask the next person we see, for confirmation."

Phil was smiling at the wheel. This was his first big campaign fire, and he was soaking all of this in, enjoying every minute.

"Hey, Phil," Diane shouted from the back seat. "Why did you decide to become a firefighter?"

"You know, ever since I was little, I always wanted to be a fireman. I remember on my fifth birthday, I got a little red plastic fire truck and one of those red plastic fire helmets. The fire truck and I would rescue my toy soldiers from landslides in the wash behind our house and save others from puddles after a rain. I even slept with my fire truck at night, and wore that little red helmet everywhere. My mom would make me take it off when we ate supper."

"Awwww, Phil our little fireman," Diane cooed.

"I was in the Explorer program in high school, and hung out at the fire station on weekends and even did ride-a-longs with some of the guys. They taught me a lot. Since you had to be 21 years old to enter a fire academy, I took EMT classes in the meantime and got my certificate and worked on the ambulance for three years. Then I became a certified paramedic before entering the Mimbres Springs Fire

Academy. So there you have it. You are looking at one lean, mean, fire-fighting machine. *I couldn't be happier than a bumble bee on spring clover.*"

"Sounds pretty happy," Diane said with a smile.

"Don't worry," I grunted. "There will be times when you will be hating life out here and wish you were never born."

"I doubt that," he smiled, then looked right at me and said, "I'm ready! I was born to do this!"

Soon we were out of the mountains and heading west into the flatlands. Up ahead I could barely see a town in the distant haze.

"Look at that Missy! There she is, Jackpot!"

As we traveled in the direction of the town, we came upon some cowboys alongside the road. One was driving a pickup truck, the other, an 18-wheeler loaded with Angus.

We pulled off the road and I got out and walked up to them. The cowboy driving the pickup truck was opening a pasture gate for the big rig.

I approached him and said, "Howdy, friend!"

He was a young cowboy with a weathered sunburn look about him. We introduced ourselves, shook hands and he said his name was Jimmy. He slowly took off his cowboy hat, scratched his head, and spit some tobacco juice on the ground. Taking a step to the side, he looked past me toward our fire truck, and looked back at me with a dumbfounded look on his face.

I asked him, "Can you tell me if that town over there, is Jackpot?"

"Say what?" he replied, trying to talk above the rumble of the big rig.

I pointed and asked again if that was Jackpot over there. He stood there, looked down at the ground and silently toed the dust with his boot. He looked up and called over to his buddy in the big rig.

"Hey, Bubba, come on over here for a minute."

Bubba set the air brake and slowly climbed out of the cab and hollered, "Jimmy, what's up?"

Bubba spoke with a slow, real deep *man-voice*, and as he lumbered over to us, I noticed Bubba was older; about 50 pounds bigger than Jimmy and looked even more like a cowboy. He was wearing a sweat stained leather vest, a PRCA baseball cap and was wearing a belt buckle you could pass off as a dinner plate.

"Tell Bubba here what you just asked me."

So I repeated myself for the third time, "Is that Jackpot over there?"

Big Bubba drawled, "Sooo, you think that town is Jackpot, *Nevada?*"

They both looked at each another and burst into hysterical laughter.

After catching his breath, Bubba boomed, with his big man-voice. "That's not Jackpot ... Boy, you're in Idaho! Not just in Idaho, but waaaay up in Idaho!"

Jimmy leaned in close to my face and with Skoal flavored breath said, "I kinda think you boys might be a little bit lost!"

Before I could say anything, they burst out into another round of sidesplitting laughter. After a few minutes, Jimmy calmed down, took a bandana out of his back pocket and wiped his brow and teary eyes, and started to give me directions. He pointed to the horizon and drew the route with his finger, as if the sky was a giant map.

"The name of that town over there is Oakley. If you want to get back to Nevada, you will have to travel another hour northwest, go through Burley, head west over to Twin Falls, then take Route 93 south," He started chuckling again and said, "Or maybe you can just go back the way you came."

I looked at him openmouthed and stupefied. "Th-th-thanks, guys, for all the help." and turned around and marched back to the truck, mad as a wet cat.

As I stomped away, I heard Bubba's booming voice call out, *Jackpot!* ... followed by another round of laughter.

While I huffed my way back to the truck, I could see Phil and Diane leaning out of the windows.

When I passed Diane, she said coolly, "It kind of looks like them boys are having a real rootin'-tootin' time."

I climbed in the front passenger seat and slammed the door as hard as I could. I grabbed the crappy map and *ripped it to smithereens!!*

Phil, still watching the cowboys yuck it up, calmly said, "I take it that's not Jackpot?"

"How could you tell?" I huffed sarcastically.

"Well let's just say," grinned Phil, "*Us guys just have a natural instinct about those kinda things.*"

"Let's get out of here!" I stammered. "We're burning daylight!

6 Welcome To Hell's Kitchen

We decided to head back to Elko in stealth mode and not tell fire command about the nature of our delay. As a matter of fact, we should have already been there and we'll probably arrive three hours late. In my head I started composing a good excuse as to why the trip took so long.

"Maybe we can tell them we got a flat tire," I said in an effort to justify our tardiness.

"They won't let us on the fire without a spare," said Diane.

"We have a spare, I'm just making that part up."

"Oh yeah, but somebody will know your fibbing. Why don't we just tell them the truth about us getting lost?"

"Because Pablo is a macho SOB and doesn't want to admit to it," grinned Phil.

"Diane said, "OK Phil, we know Pablo is an SOB but don't call Pablo an SOB to his face, he's mad enough already. Hey Phil, I've never heard you call anyone an SOB, you're starting to get a little surly young fella."

"You guys must be rubbing off on me," said Phil.

I just sat there and sulked. "We are going to miss all of the action," I frowned. "Stupid map! Stupid short cut! Who's idea was that anyway?"

Phil and Diane gave me a silent stare, and I slouched further down in my seat.

We finally arrived at in Elko at 15:00 and the place was buzzing with activity. Trucks were arriving and others were forming strike teams. All of them were heading out to the newly started fires. As I was checking in, I realized nobody noticed our delay; there was just too much going on. We were immediately assigned to an initial attack team, to assist with one of the three newly started fires.

Our orders were to hook up with a division supervisor and tie in with some fire suppression crews already on scene. The fire was located along the southern aspect of the Humboldt Mountains and thus designated the *Humboldt Fire*. Along with some smoke jumpers, that were dropped in late yesterday, there was a 20-man hand crew from California, a water tender, and a bulldozer.

I returned to the truck and briefed Diane and Phil about our new assignment. Diane took our three Bendix King portable radios to communications to have them cloned to the new fire channels.

As I unfolded the map I gasped, "Holy Crap, I can't believe this! This map is worse than the TP Fire map. This map is horrible! I can barely see the roads. The printer must be running out of toner or something."

"Good Lord! They sure didn't skimp on the red felt tip marker." Phil pointed to a big fat red X drawn where we are supposed to rendezvous with the others.

We fueled up the truck, picked up more MRE's and headed out. My adrenaline started pumping as we traveled south on Bullion Road. Off in the distance we saw a menacing white cloud of smoke. It billowed thousands of feet above the mountains, and drifted motionless to the east. As we traveled down the gravel road, we could see flames in the distant hills. The fires were devouring a combination of desert sagebrush, junipers, pines, and assorted grasses. I checked the map and was relieved to see the road we were on made a big loop out of the fire area and eventually headed back towards Elko.

I showed Diane and she remarked, "At least we have an excellent escape route if we need it. There are not a lot of roads back in here."

"It's nice to know there is a 20-man hand crew already on scene," I said to the others. "And I especially like the news that a bulldozer is already in there cutting line. It won't be that bad."

I could see Diane in my visor mirror; she was putting fresh batteries in our hand-held radios and checking her fire shelter.

"This baby is going to be a good one, so stay frosty and remain calm," she emphasized. "Stay on your toes, there is no telling what's coming up around the bend."

My concern level just went up a notch. In the past, when Diane said those words and had *that look in her eye*, the situation, most likely, would be fast moving and action packed.

The smoke was starting to get thicker. In a few minutes we came upon a wide spot in the road with a large dirt clearing. A jumbled pile of MRE's and cardboard cubees (five gallon boxes of water) were piled in the center of the clearing.

Phil shouted, "Hey, there's a guy sitting on the mound of supplies."

I looked over and waved as we drove by. The guy waved back and gave us a thumbs-up. I couldn't help but wonder who the heck he was and what he was doing out here, all by himself, in the middle of nowhere. We followed the directions on the map, turned off the main road and rumbled down a nameless narrow dirt road.

After a while I said, "This is strange, no flagging or cones to help guide us in! What in the hell?"

Diane chimed in, "This is an awful dumb-ass place for a command post."

The ride was gut wrenching as the Nickel bounced down the deeply rutted road. Phil had a look of determination on his face and was doing his best to avoid the big rocks and potholes. During the drive in, Diane put on her hard hat to keep from smacking her noggin on the sides of the truck. After a while, the road became so narrow, tree branches were scraping both sides of the truck.

The smoke was getting thicker, and after rounding a small hill, we suddenly came to a screeching halt! Dead ahead was a wall of fire coming straight toward us!

"Holy crap!" we shouted in unison.

I realized we didn't have room to turn around, but before I could say anything, Phil was already in the middle of a ten-point turn!

"Whatever you do Phil, don't go off the road!" I yelled.

The sides of the road were made up of deep drop offs and fine loose powder. If we got off the road, we would be in extreme danger of getting stuck.

Phil was pouring with sweat as he ran through the gears, cranking the truck forward and backwards, forward and backwards. He was doing his best to stay on the narrow road, and surprisingly, he got us turned around. Through my rear view mirror, I watched in horror as the wall of fire was closing in behind us!

"Drive it like you stole it!" I yelled.

Phil punched it, and we raced towards the main road like fleeing felons. While speeding down the bumpy road, I saw Diane holding on for dear life. Things in the truck started to fly; hand radios, clipboards, water bottles and Cheetos were airborne. After putting some distance between the fire and us, we found ourselves on the main road. We stopped to catch our breath, and tried to figure out our next move.

"They must have changed their mind about where we were supposed to meet up!" Phil panted.

"I don't know how you did it! That was the best turn around maneuver I've ever seen!" and gave Phil an Ooh Rah and a high five!

Diane punched him in the shoulder and shouted, "Man that was close!"

I let out a big whoop of relief, wiped my forehead with my sleeve, looked Phil straight in the eye and said, "Welcome to Hell's Kitchen!"

We returned to the large clearing with the big pile of supplies. While en route, I tried to reach fire command on the radio, but with no luck, due to the distance and mountainous terrain. Radio relay stations are not established during the early phases of wildland fires, making initial attack assignments even that more dangerous.

As we arrived at the big clearing we saw earlier, the same person was casually sitting on the pile of supplies.

We got out of the truck and I said, "Howdy, friend. Who are you?" and extended a hand.

He hopped down from his perch and said, "My name is Brad, but everybody calls me BJ. I'm one of the smoke jumpers who were dropped in yesterday."

"Where is the command post, and who is in charge?" I asked.

I handed him my sorry excuse of a map. He took my map, looked at it, and paused for a moment. Then he scanned the area with a questionable look, and handed it back to me. "I guess I am the guy and this is the spot."

"Where are we, and where is everybody else?" Diane asked.

He pulled out his equally sorry excuse of a map, and pointed to a dirt road further south of our location.

"My fellow smoke jumpers joined forces with the hotshot crew and a dozer a few hours ago. I came here to start putting together the pieces and form a plan.

He explained there was dry lightning in the area yesterday afternoon and they were dropped in just as the fire was getting started. "The winds shifted on us just as we approached our jump spot. We landed in some trees and ended up way too close to the fire front, and were surrounded by fire, and had to run for it. Our gear got left behind and we lost most of it. I am especially pissed because my jump suit and I have been fighting fire for five years and I am really sad to see it go."

At first I thought BJ was feeding us a line of crap, you know, trying to impress our land-loving brush truck crew with one of those wild smoke jumper stories. I thought about his story for a minute, and noticed my heart was still pumping from *our own* close encounter, so I gave BJ the benefit of the doubt.

He informed me that he was able to get better radio reception higher on the ridge. "I spoke earlier with fire command and they told me more help is on the way, and that a spike camp will soon be set up right here." BJ then asked me, "Where are the other resources that came out with you?"

"Well, I guess we are it for now. As far as I know we're the only truck they sent."

"OK, I suppose we will have to *adapt and overcome*," he said. "You guys can stay and camp here or join up with the crews working the fire down the road."

"Well, we are here to fight some fire, so let's roll," I said.

I shook BJ's hand, and we climbed back into the truck. He walked off to make radio contact with the fire crews down the road. We followed the directions he gave us; headed south and eventually found them. It was around sunset when we met up.

We talked to the guy in charge, found out his name was Troy, and he put us right to work. The dozer was working toward the east and the hand crews were cutting line up the hill toward the west, working to connect our line to a previously burned out area.

"Man, the air has cooled down nicely now that it is nighttime," said Diane, as she wiped her brow and continued helping the sawyers buck wood and branches away from the scratch line.

I looked up the hill and off in the distance I could barely make out something hanging in the burnt trees.

"Diane, I'm going up the hill to check something out."

I hiked in the moonlight to a thick stand of trees, and could see the melted remains of parachutes dangling from the branches. The moonlight shone through them, and in the breeze they slowly swayed like ghosts. On the ground there were jumpsuits lying in the ashes. Even though they were made of Kevlar and Nomex, which is a fire retardant material, they were burned up pretty good. The only thing intact was a charred helmet and wire facemask the smoke jumpers wore to protect them from tree branches as they landed. I picked up the blackened helmet and ripped off the wire facemask and stowed it in my backpack. A short ways away I could see that their cargo boxes, hand tools and gear were burnt to a crisp. I toed the head of a Pulaski that was completely black, and the wooden handle was gone.

"Wow!" I said, suddenly amazed. "The guy was right! BJ wasn't giving us a line of bull after all."

It was approaching 22:00 when the crew boss called it a night. Our small band of firefighters drove back down the road, and BJ helped back up the trucks into the big clearing. This would be tonight's spike camp. Even though the fire was a good ways away, it was still a major concern. I did a 360 and all around us, the distant hills were aglow with fire.

We threw down our bedrolls and fired up some MRE's.

I sat there eating my meal and said, "It looks like we are pretty much surrounded," and swished around the last bit of coffee in my metal canteen cup. "A lot of times ... well, make that most of the time, plans don't go the way you want them to go! Sometimes plans quickly change, depending on the circumstances. You just have to be alert and think on your feet. We have to remember that fire is its own beast and shows no mercy."

Diane added, "I think we experienced a little of the beast today!"

Phil was stabbing at the last bit of meat out of his MRE pouch when he said, "Yeah, kind of like George Armstrong Custer and his plan."

We all got quiet; thinking about Phil's comment and silently began reflecting on today's events.

I slowly raised my aching body to a standing position, and Diane put away our food stash so the night critters couldn't get to it. We tidied up a little and crawled into our icy cold bedrolls, and hoped they would warm up soon.

"Yeah," I said to Phil, while removing some pesky rocks from under me, "but unlike Custer, we live to fight another day.

7 Danger Close!

Morning came quick; crisp, and cold. Additional resources were starting to arrive. Diane fired up the stove while Phil did a truck check. I went to see what the Incident Action Plan (IAP) would be for the day. I came back from the briefing and was greeted with the aroma of steamy, black coffee.

"Yes, there is a God!" I grinned as Diane poured some of the thick, dark goodness into my cup.

"The first thing I put in my two-week bag is some good coffee," she remarked, "and lots of it! And not that cheap stuff either. This coffee is from Lupe Jiménez's Horny Toad Café; it's fresh roasted and fresh ground. Finest coffee on the planet! I figure we deserve the best!"

"Amen to that," I replied, and slurped some more of the piping hot, heavenly goodness.

A dozer operator and tender driver soon appeared at our truck with empty coffee cups in hand. I laughed when I realized it was Ginny and Clint. We poured them a round and brewed up another batch. It was barely light when they finished their coffee, and it appeared that they were in a hurry. We topped off their coffee cups, and gave them a "Good luck and be safe," as they hustled out of camp. I think it is safe to say we became their newest best friends.

Today, we were assigned to support the attack crews along Division C, and assist with line construction and back burn operations. A finger of fire was traversing along a five-mile ridgeline and we were told that the dozer was to clear a swath as wide as a lane of highway, along the crest of the ridgeline. What the dozer could do in 30 minutes, would take a hand crew all day to accomplish.

Our task force was instructed to start at the top of the ridge, anchoring in at the dozer line and cut a perpendicular scratch line using hand tools, down the slope to the wash at the bottom. In theory, the dozer line would keep the fire from cresting the ridge top and our hand line would keep the fire from traversing laterally along the hillside. I was informed that we could call in for air support if things got too hairy. The air tankers, known as *Heavies,* don't necessarily knock the fire out, but the fire retardant they drop, slows the fire down enough so we can work in close and stop it cold.

After a quick MRE for breakfast, we headed out with the same California hotshot crew we worked with the night before. When we met up at Division C, Troy told us his plan.

He kicked the deep loose soil and said, "Our anchor point and safety zone will be this dozer line." Looking along the ridgeline, I could see miles of dozer tracks. He pointed his finger to the line and then down the slope. "We need to start here and cut line down this slope to that dry wash and try to pinch this finger of fire out. This is going to be a textbook maneuver, and should work without a hitch," he said with confidence.

I thought to myself, I wonder if Custer said the same thing to his troops on that fateful morning at the Little Big Horn?

We all acknowledged his instructions, and amidst eager hotshot banter, we gathered our equipment and started the day's work. As we were working, I looked at the miles and miles of rangeland made up of thick waist-high sagebrush, scattered juniper, and scrub pine trees. In the distance we could see heavy grey smoke, and the parched sage was burning fast and hot. Scattered junipers were exploding like dried-up Christmas trees.

The hotshots started cutting their scratch line down the slope, working in a long single file. The first man scratched a line in the dirt and picked the course for the rest to follow. The next guy followed his path using a shovel or a Pulaski and scratched a slightly wider swath of clear area. The next guy expanded the width of the line, chopping out any brush, grass, roots, or small trees. Progressively, with each person working the line, the 20-man crew eventually created a path about 4 feet wide that was free of vegetation.

Once the scratch line was wide enough, a firing crew would start to set the brush on fire using road flares (fusees) and drip torches (metal containers filled with a mix of diesel and gasoline). The fire they created would eventually make its way towards the main fire. That is what we call *creating the black.* Another term for this is *firing out the area.* The more sage we burned off before the main fire got to this point, the better our chances that the fire would be stopped. You could say we were fighting fire with fire. In theory, when the fire gets here, there won't be anything left for the main fire to burn.

Diane, Phil and I put down a progressive hose lay along the newly cut scratch line. This consists of 100-foot sections of one-inch fire hose, known as trunk line. We then placed brass wye fittings to the trunk line and extended smaller branch lines off that. The smaller branches have a nozzle on each end. It looks like a tree lying on the ground with small branches going off to one side.

Diane told Phil, "The water from our hose will help add a wet line to the burned and unburned areas of the scratch line. We'll also be on the lookout for any fire creeping across the line into the unburned side."

"Yeah, I remember in class they referred to that as *slop over*," he said.

"You got that right Phil, slop over is a dirty word around here, and we will have none of that! Also be on the lookout for spot fires. Hot embers from the main fire can be picked up by the wind and deposited into the green side. Depending on the weather, spot fires can pop anywhere, sometimes miles away."

Phil and Diane kept their eyes in the green, looking for slop over and spot fires as they extended the fire hose down the slope.

Diane told Phil, "Every fire operation has a lookout man watching for changes in fire behavior. He will warn us by radio if he sees any questionable fire activity."

Phil scanned the ridgeline, and way off in the distance he could see our lookout man. "There he is," pointed Phil.

"Yup, It's kinda nice to know someone has our back while we concentrate on the work at hand," Diane said as they humped more rolls of hose down the hill.

When I looked up I could see the wind-blown fire front rapidly closing in on us. Due to the curve of the hillside I couldn't see the bottom of the scratch line, as our hose extended about half way down the hill. Just then, I heard from our lookout man that the wind was starting to shift!

Diane called to me, "The wind is picking up and it is getting a little squirrely out here. Keep on your toes, things could get ugly in a hurry!"

An urgent word was spread to hurry up and finish the scratch line. Water from our hose was putting out some slop over and hot spots along the hastily dug line. The hotshots were firing out the sage and were working hard to finish.

Phil and I were about half way down the slope, still not able to see the bottom, when a firefighter from below, quickly marched past us, on his way up the hill.

As he passed us he shouted the letters, "R.A!"

We kept working, and soon two more came marching by us, saying the same thing, "R.A!" I thought to myself, "R.A? Was that some kind of California hotshot slang? Kind of like the Marine Corp expression, *Ooh Rah!*"

I yelled over to Diane, "What does R.A. mean?"

"Beats me," she yelled back.

Just then a group of three came trotting up with a look of concern on their faces.

I gave them a big, "Ooh Rah!"

They gave me a strange look and one of them shouted; "You guys better get the hell up the hill. The fire has jumped the line down below, and is making a run in the green behind us! It's time to *Run Away!*"

Phil and I looked at one another and said in unison, "R.A. Run Away!"

"Shit!" I shouted and started grabbing as much hose as possible, and began racing up the hill. We had bunches of hose draped over our shoulders, with long loops dragging behind us. We couldn't carry all of it, as we made our way back to the trucks. We were thankful the remaining hotshots helped carry as much hose as they could, and they dumped it into a big pile behind the Triple Nickel.

We were all crouching down behind our trucks, anxiously waiting for the approaching fire. Within moments, the fire front roared up the slope and hit us hard, throwing a flaming heat wave of ash and embers against the side of trucks.

Embers cascaded over the tops of trucks and after a few intense minutes, we got an *all clear,* and walked around the buggies, watching as the fire made its way down the ridge-line.

"Man, that was close!" said Phil.

"Wow, that happened fast!" gasped Diane.

"R.A., we'll have to remember that," I shouted and let out a sigh of relief.

We regrouped and spread our manpower along the dozer line. Some embers had crossed the ridge top, and were now starting small spot fires in the green. The crew boss immediately sent some people out to take care of them.

All in all, the dozer line did its job, keeping the fire from cresting the ridge. It was a close call and the fire could have caught us in the middle of the sagebrush. Fortunately, we all made it back to the safety zone, and no one was injured. We only lost a few hundred feet of hose and a couple of fittings and nozzles. We weren't worried knowing we had extra hose on the truck.

It seemed like everyone working the Humboldt Fire today was having problems with the wind, and the heavies were being called upon to help in all divisions. After several requests, Troy was able to divert two air tankers to our location.

The crew boss quickly rounded up the troops and discussed the new plan. It sounded pretty much like the first plan, but this time we'll have air support. It was business as usual for the hotshots and they loaded up their gear and got in their buggies.

We loaded the spaghetti pile of hose onto the back of the Nickel and I thought to myself, *I wonder if Custer really had a plan?*

Our new plan was to drive about a mile down the dozer line and regroup. We took off for about a mile and Phil parked up on a small knoll under some spindly trees. We took advantage of the sparse shade, agreeing that we would have a perfect view of the airshow. I radioed the hotshots and told them our location. Troy came up and said they were delayed and would remain in place until after the drop. He radioed the air tankers and advised them to look for a brush truck on a small hill, and told them they needed to make their drop a little downslope and to the west of our location.

We commenced to off-load the big pile of spaghetti that was once orderly and clean rolls of white fire hose, and began to unravel the mess. I told my crew that the two aircraft would be approaching from behind us, and start dumping their load, and to continue down slope to the streambed at the bottom of the hill. The two connecting drops should put down a nice wet line of slurry, pretty much the whole length of the slope.

I got a queasy feeling knowing the air tankers were on their way, and told Diane and Phil, "This brings me back to a day in Vietnam when we were in a platoon defensive position. Things got desperate as we were about to get overrun by enemy troops. A call went out for a *Danger Close Airstrike!*"

"What's Danger Close?" asked Phil in earnest.

"Whenever a Danger Close was called in, it meant we needed an air strike PRONTO! Our company commander let forward air control know it was only a matter of minutes before the enemy would overrun our position and we needed close air support *now!* Danger Close maneuvers were extremely risky and we knew they would be dropping their ordnance real close to our perimeter. If they were off by just a fraction, they would be dropping their bombs right on us!

I remember we were way outnumbered, and since we were low on ammo, a call went out to prepare for hand-to-hand combat. I was fumbling with my bayonet, trying to attach it to the end of my M16. My hands were shaking so badly, I dropped it twice before I could secure it! I dug a shallow foxhole and stayed motionless, desperately scanning back and forth at the jungle, waiting for the enemy to break through. The sting of sweat was burning my eyes, but I didn't dare move a muscle to wipe it away. My heart was pounding like a bass drum, and my fingers were cramping because I was holding my rifle so tightly.

"How awful, I can't imagine how that must have felt!" Diane said.

"God, I was messed up in my head and feeling panicky! I was scared, soaked in sweat, getting the dry heaves and was about to throw up! We were running out of time and I was thinking to myself. *Christ, I'm just a young kid! I don't want to die!*

"God Pablo!"

"You know, I find it kind of strange now … that when I was facing my last moments on earth, my thoughts turned to the people I loved, and to the memories I had with my family and friends. Suddenly, I was calm, and the terror I felt vanished."

"Amazing!" Diane said with wide eyes.

"Did the enemy overrun you guys?" Phil asked with excitement.

Man! From out of nowhere, a flight of F4s roared in and started dropping Snakes (bombs) and Nape (Napalm) directly over our heads. It was chaos! I could feel the earth violently shake, as the bombs hit close to us! Hunks of rocks and dirt were dropping on us like rain. Shrapnel from the bombs sheared off whole trees. We desperately took cover in our shallow foxholes. I wanted to see what was happening, so I started to peek up over the lip, but my friend Luther pulled me down and yelled at me to cover up. If I had stuck my head out, it would have been torn clean off. I pressed myself as flat as I could into the bottom of that hole, and immediately felt the heat on my back from the Napalm. The noise was deafening and in an instant, it was over. It got real quiet and slowly we emerged and saw that the air strike had decimated the area. The jungle was smoldering black and splintered to hell. There was absolutely nothing left standing. Those F4s took out the enemy troops and saved the day. Without their help we surely would have been goners!"

"Holy crap!" gasped Diane.

"You got that right!" I said with gusto.

Diane tugged at the pile of hose and said with excitement, "I remember the first time I saw a slurry drop. We were so close and it was so loud! It was awesome!"

Suddenly we could hear the distant rumble of aircraft engines.

Diane sprung to life and yelled, *"Baby, it's Showtime!"*

Just then a small plane appeared out of nowhere, flew in low and buzzed us! It continued down the slope and headed north over the next ridge.

"What was that?" yelled Phil.

"It's a spotter plane. It guides the air tankers in. The heavies follow the *Bird Dog,* and the small plane tells them where to drop their load."

The air began to vibrate with the low rumble of the big radial propeller engines. Because of how the truck was parked, we couldn't see the aircraft, but knew from the sound they were getting close.

I looked around and said, "Where the hell are they?"

We all stood up looking back over our truck in the direction of the deafening noise. Suddenly, we were eye to eye with the pilots!

The huge aircraft was flying low and Phil hollered something, but it was too loud to understand him.

"Holy crap, get down!" I yelled and franticly motioned my crew to get on the ground!

Just then, a cloud of red exploded from the belly of the plane, turning the whole sky crimson! We flopped face down on the ground, holding our helmets and covering our faces. Branches were being torn off the trees, and rocks were tossed aloft as clods of undissolved retardant came crashing to the earth. Everything immediately turned monotone, as the red mist slowly settled down on the hillside.

"God dang!" I yelled, lifting my head looking at the carnage.

Phil was staring up at the sky with a look of excitement and awe on his face.

"Another heavy!" Diane yelled, as she covered up again.

The rumble was even louder this time and the ground shook even more. We were face down, hugging the earth, WHOOOOOOOMMMM! The plane came in low and loud. The belly of the beast exploded open. Its contents fell further down the slope, picking up where the other heavy left off. It slathered the remainder of the slope and part of the streambed with slurry, before it gracefully gained altitude and drifted over the next ridge.

"Yee, doggie!" hollered Phil, as he got up, dusting himself off.

I shouted, "Mamma Mia! Marinara!" and pointed to our pile of hose, it looked like someone ladled spaghetti sauce all over it.

"Look at us!" Diane said, *"We got slimed!"* We laughed even harder.

The front side of us looked normal, yellow shirts and green pants. But when we turned around, our backsides were covered with slurry and were completely red. We turned back and forth, back and forth. Yellow, red, yellow, red.

The hotshots soon met up with us, and of course they gave us crap about our two-tone brush gear.

Troy snickered, "I see you Truck Princesses have been lying down on the job!" He pointed down, and to our amazement, we could see the slurry outline of three figures lying on the ground.

We all had a good belly laugh and proceeded to work the hillside the same way we worked the last one. With the help of the retardant, we managed to stop the fire cold. While walking back to the Nickel, we became aware of the surrealistic sight; the hillside was painted three distinct colors, black, red and sage green.

Diane gave the sight a well-deserved, "Far out!"

"It's kind of nice how a plan comes together," grinned Phil.

We just stood there and marveled at it all.

We washed the retardant off the windshield the best we could with the remainder of our onboard tank water.

While driving back to spike camp, we found a 3,000-gallon water tender parked at the intersection where our dozer line and the main road met. We recognized it was Clint. He took one look at us and couldn't stop laughing.

"Stop your braying, you jackass, and top off our tank," I grinned.

Diane helped with the hose from the tender and asked Clint, "By the way, where is Ginny?"

"After lunch she was reassigned, loaded her dozer onto the lowboy and headed off to Division E."

After parking the truck at spike camp, we proceeded to get out of our red splattered fire clothes. I dug around in my duffle bag and pulled out a clean T-shirt, some sweat pants and tennis shoes. Diane fired up the coffee pot and we tried

to find a comfortable spot to sit down and rest our weary
bones.

"What's for supper?" asked Phil.

Diane pulled out a large cardboard box and rummaged
through the MREs.

How about some *red* beans and rice?" she offered.

"Or maybe some *spaghetti with marinara sauce,*" grinned
Phil.

"Looky here," I said, pulling out another MRE. "It's R.A.!
... *Rigatoni Alfredo!*"

We polished off the MREs and slurped down some good
Joe.

As we watched another spectacular sunset, I said to
Diane, "All in all, not a bad day."

Turning to me she said, "It doesn't get any better than
this!"

"You got that right, Missy, but then again, these old bones
could use a nice soak in the Glory Road Hot Springs right
about now. We could light up some nice cigars and toss back
a generous two fingers of Scotch on ice."

"OK, it doesn't get any better than that!" she winked.

We watched in silence as the evening sky turned as bright
as burning fusees, and then go dark.

"Yup," I said, as I spread out my bedroll in the darkness.
"We burned all the daylight outta this one."

8 Go'she' Li'gai

We awoke to the sound of more trucks arriving. As we ripped open our morning meals, Phil remarked, "We must be getting low on MREs. I've never had Cajun jambalaya for breakfast before," and sprinkled some Tabasco on it. "I think everything tastes a little better with some hot sauce on it, but then again, I've never put hot sauce on ice cream."

Diane elbowed him in the ribs and said, "Let me know how that one turns out."

Diane ripped open a small generic looking pouch labeled, *Wheat Snack Bread.* She pulled the bread out of its envelope and sniffed it, trying to figure out if it was edible. The bread, if you want to call it that, was about a quarter inch thick, and five inches square. It was dense and heavy, resembling a thick piece of cardboard. It came with a small pouch of grape jelly and a pouch of peanut butter.

She hesitantly nibbled on it and said in a surprised tone, "Not too bad. It tastes like a molasses cookie, soft, chewy, and a little sweet. I must admit the grape jelly sends it right over the top. I can't wait until I put peanut butter on the other one."

"Hey, don't complain! These are pretty good *for heat and eats*," I said and wiped the gravy off my mustache. "It's a far cry better than the *C-rations* we had back in Vietnam.

We used those small P-38 can openers to open tiny cans of potted meat product."

"Wow, potted meat product, sounds appetizing!" said Diane.

"Yeah, they were real *yummy!*" I said with sarcasm. "We had a variety of them and our squad leader mixed up all the rations and tipped an open box of 12 on the ground, upside-down so we couldn't read the printing on the top of them. We'd randomly choose one and prayed to God it wasn't the one that read, *pork steak cooked in juices.* When you first opened the can, it looked all greasy and jiggly. God knows what kind of juices they used."

"My mom's pot roast kind of looks like that," laughed Phil.

"Well her pot roast couldn't be as bad as the dreaded C-Rat labeled *ham and lima beans.* That one was the most detested. It was universally known as *ham and mother-F***ers.* The most palatable one was *spaghetti with meatballs.* My favorite ration was *beans and frankfurters.* The guys called them *beans and baby dicks.*"

"You cannibals, those poor babies," snickered Diane.

"Those poor babies! Heck I can't even eat franks and beans after coming back from Nam. Just the thought of *those poor babies* makes me want to gag!"

"Did you eat them cold right out of the can?" asked Phil.

"Naw, sometimes we heated them with the stinky heating tablets that came with the C-rats. The best way however, was to take a pinch of C-4 explosive, about the size of a large marble. We'd dig a small hole and place the C-4 in it, light it and place the C-ration on top. That way, the enemy couldn't see the white hot fire in the hole. Most of the time, we weren't allowed to make a fire. The rations were OK when they were heated up, but God they were awful when we had to eat them cold." I cringed just thinking about it. "No wonder we didn't win that war."

"I guess that's why they say war is hell," smiled Diane.

"You know, the only thing good about C-rations was, they came with a small pack of cigarettes. I didn't smoke, so I saved them and when my buddies were Jonesing for a cigarette, I bartered with them. Heck, I would take canned peaches or pound cake over cigarettes any day!"

Diane put our coffee away and went over to restock our food supply. There was a big pile of MREs at the edge of camp, and we made an effort not to get the nasty vegetarian ones.

Phil made a comment about the layout of the cramped spike camp. I explained to him about the difference between this camp and the one we experienced at the TP fire.

"Small spike camps like this are set up in the field away from the main base camp. The reason is, in a larger fire such as this Humboldt Fire, it would take too much time to shuffle manpower and equipment, back and forth from the main base camp to here. These camps are closer to the action and a bit more primitive. They tend to be somewhat scruffy and untidy. It is a real *Man-Camp*, no porta-potties, mess tent, supply tent, or hot showers. Some of the larger base camps even have a laundry service."

Diane chimed in, "Yeah, no fluff and fold here. Luckily we packed several sets of clean shirts and pants. Our slurry splattered, two-tone brush gear will have to wait until we get back to the base camp before they get washed."

I returned from the morning meeting and began to brief my crew. "Today we are going to work in Division E, so set your radios to channel 2. The good news is, due to a manpower shortage, I will be our acting task force leader! I'm glad because I could use the experience and finally get it checked off in my wildland task book. I expect things to go smoothly, no R.A.s for us today!" I pointed to the map and explained, "We need to expand this containment line along this hilltop and prevent the fire from entering that nearby basin."

Our convoy headed out and soon arrived at Division E. It was a mixed group, consisting of two Type 6 brush trucks, a Type 3 engine, a 20-man hand crew, and a 3,000-gallon water tender. We all met at the hilltop and looked down to the basin below, discussing the locations of our safety zones and escape routes. Everyone seemed to be on the same page, and the team promptly got to work. I designated Diane to be Division E's weather gal.

Phil went over to Diane and asked, "How does this weather stuff work?"

"We call this *Slinging Weather.*" She took the small weather kit out of its case. "The weather kit consists of a compass, a little wind gauge, and two 6-inch thermometers mounted on this little board. One is an ordinary thermometer. We call this the dry bulb. The other thermometer has a little cloth cover over the bulb. I will wet the cloth-covered bulb with room temperature water. We call this the wet bulb."

"Why is there a long piece of string attached to the board?" Phil asked.

"This is where the *slinging* comes in." She poured a little water from her canteen on the wet bulb and said, "Stand back!"

She began to twirl the thermometers overhead like a lasso.

"I twirl these for about 100 revolutions, then record the temperatures. Because of evaporation, the wet cover cools one of the thermometers. The difference between the wet bulb temp and the dry bulb temp helps determine the relative humidity. Every hour I radio the results to Incident Command ... let's see what we got. Time, 09:00, dry bulb 85 degrees, wet bulb 65 degrees, relative humidity, 17 percent, wind is from the west at about 5 MPH."

"Cool beans! *That's slicker than snot on a brass doorknob.* How do you get the relative humidity?" he asked.

"See this little chart on the back of the board?" pointed Diane. "There's a formula here that takes the difference between the two temperatures and converts it to RH."

"Golleee! You learn something new every day," said Phil.

"I predict the RH today will eventually go below 10 percent. You know the saying, *it's a dry heat.*"

"Here Phil, give it a try," said Diane and handed him the tiny weather kit.

Phil proceeded to sling a round of weather and called it in to Incident Command.

As an Apache hand crew was emerging from their transport trucks, I noticed it was a mixed crew, with women outnumbering the men 2:1.

"I'm glad they are working in our task force today!" I remarked to Phil. "Those guys have a reputation as being hard charging, hard-working, a get-the-job-done hand crew. That will make my job as task force leader a whole lot easier. I'm not here to be a baby sitter, and know I won't need to get on them. Those guys can out work any crew on this fire."

In our division, there were a lot of dead and dying trees close to the fire line that needed to be cut down with chain saws, and I knew these Apaches were excellent sawyers. They were the first to suit up, fire up their chainsaws, and head out to cut timber. They were a serious and quiet group, keeping to themselves, preferring not to socialize with the other crews. This intrigued me and I wanted to get to know them better. Being today's task force leader should give me that opportunity.

We worked hard along the division, felling trees and clearing out a lot of brush. It was 13:00 and I called out for lunch. Making my way to the truck, to grab a sack lunch, I saw the Apache crew heading to shade-up in some nearby piñon pines. Each one was carrying a chainsaw, fire shelter, water, extra fuel, chain oil and a backpack filled with more essentials, and I knew their gear weighed close to 40 pounds. Before they sat down, they dropped their heavy packs, took off their protective chaps, gloves, hardhats and yellow fire shirts. Every one of them was drenched in sweat.

The tallest man in the group was wearing a T-shirt that caught my eye. It had a silkscreened image of six arrows sticking out of his back. From a distance it looked as if he was the target in an archery contest. I thought to myself, *This is my opportunity to start up a conversation with the elusive group.*

"I'm going over to talk to them," I told Diane.

"Don't be starting any trouble you old buzzard!" she growled.

"Who me? Don't worry!"

As I worked my way up the hill, I started singing an old nursery rhyme, "One little, two little, three little Indians, four little." *Whhhhiiizzz!!!* I ignored the stick that went flying past my head.

As I reached the shade, I walked up to the sawyer with the unique T-shirt.

"Howdy, friend, I'm Pablo. My crew and I are from New Mexico."

He stood up and said, "My name is Élan, and we are based in Arizona."

"I couldn't help but notice the design on your T-shirt."

"Oh that. Have you heard of Custer's Last Stand?"

"You know I was just thinking of that a couple of days ago, when we were surrounded by fire," I chuckled.

"Well ... this is Custer's Last Shirt! I can arrange for *you* to have one as well," he said dryly as he pulled out a huge Buck knife from its sheath and slowly thumbed the blade. He grinned and looked back at his crew.

Things went quiet in a hurry. All eyes were on me, waiting for a reply.

I swallowed hard, and after a brief pause I asked sheepishly, "Can I get three?"

"I'll see what I can do," he smiled and then laughed out loud.

He shook my hand, and everyone in the shade started to laugh. That was the icebreaker I needed. I sat down with them and motioned to my crew to come join us. While we ate our sack lunches together, they explained that this was their sixth major fire of the year.

Élan said, "I've been doing wildland for three years now, and it helps pay for my college education."

"Where are you going to school?" I asked.

I just finished with community college and now I'm attending the University of Arizona. I want to get a degree in wildlife, watershed, and rangeland management."

"Good for you," said Diane as she got up to brush off some cookie crumbs.

During our lunch I noticed a beautiful young Apache woman quietly sitting at the far end of the group, keeping mostly to herself. I soon became mesmerized as she fueled up the saw and topped off the chain oil. With her long black hair loosely braided and tied back, I noticed her shoulders and arms were nicely toned from working the heavy tool. Through the entire break she meticulously sharpened the chain with a small file. Her strong authentic features were riveting, and I was captivated.

With my head cradled in my hands and my elbows propped up on my knees, I let out a slow long sigh and thought, *Yes, truly a Cover Girl for the Apache Nation.*

I sat there transfixed, as she put on her yellow Nomex shirt and protective chaps. She stood up, packed out, and headed over to the line to cut more timber.

Suddenly, Diane gave me a hard elbow to the ribs. "Shows over Romeo, back to work!" Diane looked over at the sawyer and then back at me and grinned, "If I didn't know better, Pablo, I would think you were in love."

"Yes, what's not to love? ... You know, I have always had a thing for beautiful women in chaps."

I sighed and walked my weary bones back to the truck. Diane grabbed her weather kit and headed off to sling this hour's weather. After calling in the weather, she informed me that she needed to *drop the kids off at school* and would be back shortly. I chuckled at the remark. It was an inside joke and it meant she needed to go to the bathroom.

On these fires the crews are outside, usually from sun up to sun down. It is backbreaking work, done in smoky conditions, and stifling heat. After days in this smoke, I know my eyes really begin to sting and my throat becomes raw and scratchy. Despite all that, I never hear anyone complaining or grumbling. They all possess a *can-do attitude*, which makes my job as the strike team leader a lot easier.

It was about 15:00, the sawyers were working on the last stand of timber when our lookout radioed in, warning that the main fire front was rapidly approaching from the west.

"Let's go give them a hand and be their swampers!" I called out to anyone within earshot.

"What's a swamper?" Phil asked, as Diane and I grabbed some protective chaps and goggles from the truck.

"A swamper is a sawyer's helper; they pull away the cut branches and slash from the area where the sawyers are working. That way the sawyers don't trip and fall while working those big chainsaws," I informed him.

I, of course, took this opportunity to make my way over to the Cover Girl. I pantomimed to her, over the roar of the chainsaw, "Me ... Your ... Swamper."

She gave me a quick glance and resumed with her cutting. I gathered up a load of branches, quickly disposed of them and returned for more. Standing a couple of steps behind her and a little off to the side, I got her attention to make sure she saw me.

"Man it sure is hot this afternoon." ... *No response.*

I gathered another load, dumped it, and hurried back. I stood near her again and made yet another opening comment.

"Missy, that's a mighty big saw for such a small gal like yourself." ... *No response.*

As she worked on a large overhead branch, I moved in closer, and held up the limb with both hands. Before I could say another word, she slammed on the brake, swung it around, and placed the smoking hot blade *close to my crotch!*

"*You too close!*" She looked me in the eye, gritted her teeth and said something in Apache.

Crap! There I was with both my arms up in the air, feeling the heat of the blade through my Nomex fire pants.

"Whoa! I can take a hint!" With my arms up in surrender, I slowly stepped back.

Diane motioned me over to her as the gal started cutting timber again.

"Quit bugging her, you're being a damn pest!"

"I was just trying to help," I said with a shrug.

Diane snorted, "Yeah, I bet you were!"

Diane had worked with the Apache gals in the past so I asked her what she thought she said.

"It sounded kind of like *Go'she' Li'gai.*"

"Do you know what it means?"

"I haven't a clue! But I don't think she was paying you a compliment!"

"Well she was not being very friendly," I said in a huff. "I was just trying to make some friendly conversation. She acted like she didn't hear a word I said."

"I wouldn't want to be making idle conversation with someone working a freshly sharpened chainsaw," Phil exhorted. "It could be dangerous! That thing could lop off a leg or something!"

"Yeah, *or something,*" I repeated as I looked down at my crotch.

"Pablo, I can tell you why she acted like she didn't hear a word you said!" Diane turned and glared at me, "She wasn't being rude. *She's wearing earplugs you moron!*"

I gave her my best defensive response, *"I knew that!"*

Hiding my embarrassment, I walked away and muttered to myself, "I knew that, I knew that."

Our work in Division E progressed smoothly. We cut extensive fire lines and managed to create a lot of black before the main fire came into our area. The division supervisor drove up and told us to wrap things up and head back to the spike camp. We settled in for the night, and enjoyed another round of those tasty MREs,

***

The next morning our assignment was to mop up and cold trail the black we created yesterday in Division E.

When we arrived, our task force spread out and worked the black. Everyone could see how our work done yesterday prevented the fire from progressing down into the basin below. After a long day of digging, and scraping, we finished the mop up assignment around 16:00, and headed back to the spike camp.

It was another long hot day and after we settled down for the evening, we received word by radio that the entire spike camp was to pack up and head to the main base camp! Just the thought of going to the base camp lifted our spirits and the camp was filled with energized chatter and laughter!

Between being at the TP Fire and now the Humboldt Fire, we had been at it for nine days. I was really looking forward to a real home cooked meal, some ice cold drinks, and a level cot to sleep on.

"I can't wait to get out of here!" yelled Phil. I could use a nice hot shower!"

"Hey Phil, I don't want to bust your sweaty balls but, we all could benefit from you taking a shower, you reek!" laughed Diane, pushing Phil aside while holding her nose.

For the rest of the day, every time I passed Phil or Diane, they would bump into me on purpose and say " *You too close!*" followed by a good laugh. I really did a number on myself, and it looked like I wasn't going to live this one down.

"We sure carry a lot of stuff on this truck," said Phil, as he tossed his gear bag up to Diane, who was standing on top of the truck.

I explained, "When working on these fires, we have to be pretty much self-sufficient. That's why we carry so much crap on the truck. If our truck breaks down for any mechanical reason, we have to try to fix it ourselves."

Phil fumbled through the engineer's compartment and said, "There's radiator coolant, brake fluid, motor oil, air filters, light bulbs, fuses, wrenches, screwdrivers, pliers, liquid wrench, and radiator stop leak. Not to mention a roll of duct tape. Hey! What's this coat hanger doing in here?" he laughed.

"That is our universal fixer-upper. It has 101 uses! I wouldn't leave home without one!"

Phil nodded and tossed the coat hanger back into the crowded compartment and slammed the door.

"Yup, if we can't fix it ourselves, our truck gets towed off the fire line. That's why it is important that *you* do a truck check every morning. We all need to try and prevent any mishaps before they happen. For every day we are out of service, it means a day without pay."

"It would suck to come all this way and not get paid," said Phil

"Yeah, tell me about it. I have been on fires where our truck broke down, like the time up in Taos last year, when we blew our transmission on the very first day!"

"Bummer Pablo."

"Bummer doesn't even begin to describe it. We were out of service for 5 days on that one!"

We felt revived and were joking and laughing as we finished packing. All the trucks convoyed back on the same road we came in on that first day, and it soon became a solemn ride as we passed miles and miles of scorched earth.

"Look at all the destruction!" gasped Phil.

Diane pointed to the barren moonscape and said, "Despite all of our training and physical conditioning, we still have to realize that the forces of Mother Nature are a heck of a lot greater than we are, and this is just a reminder that wildfire shows absolutely no mercy."

I said, "You know, we never talk about the danger but ... Phil, several years ago a few friends of mine, veteran guys, who were excellent firefighters, got in a situation while fighting fire in California. The wind shifted on them, and they got burned over pretty bad, and almost died. They never expected it ... never saw it coming."

As we drove down the road, I looked out into the black and felt a pang of remorse.

"I knew them as friends, just like I know you guys. In an instant their lives were changed forever, and I saw how they suffered physically and mentally during their long recovery. After that, reality set in for me, and the dark side of firefighting really hit home. You just never know ... it could happen to us."

"I got'cha Boss," said Phil in a hushed tone.

The words *no mercy* echoed in my head and the truck was dead quiet as we made our way to the base camp.

9 Base Camp

It was slow going on the road leading to base camp, traffic was backed up and people were walking past us faster than we were driving. As we waited, we struck up a conversation with a passing firefighter. He told us that the fire was three times larger than it was yesterday, and more units were being called up, and the Humboldt Fire was declared the largest fire in the state.

Diane grinned when she heard the news, "This is significant! The bigger the fire, the longer we stay!"

"The longer we stay, the bigger the pay!" I chimed in. I looked at Phil and Diane, and we all gave each other a round of high fives.

Just as we pulled into base camp our division supervisor flagged us down. *"Good job Mimbres Springs!* The firing operation in Division E was a huge success. Nice work!"

We drove slowly down the makeshift streets, looking for a potential campsite.

"Ye doggie!" shouted Phil as we continued in. "Wow! Look at all those rigs! This all popped up while we were away at the spike camp? This set up is bigger than our home town!"

There was a large grassy field about the size of four football fields, and a big white mess tent was erected near the far end. Semi-trucks loaded with food, ice and supplies sat idling nearby, and a large supply tent was located a little further to the west.

At large campaign fires, a supply tent is usually established so firefighters can replace any damaged or destroyed gear, and it is where firefighters can check out cots, sleeping bags, and tents. Supply also issues fresh AA batteries and seems to do so by the handful. Good communication is key in ensuring our safety; a dead radio can easily result in dead firefighters.

"We definitely need fresh batteries for the radios, I will stock up first thing," Diane said.

As we drove past the mess tent, Phil raised his nose and started sniffing the air, "Good golly! Warm peach cobbler! *I'm happier than a tick on a coon dog!*"

We continued to drive in, looking for a halfway level piece of ground to camp on.

The local elementary school was located just up a small hill next to the field. The Fire Operations, Logistics, and Finance Divisions were all headquartered inside. Being it was the beginning of September, school would normally be in session, but with the recent fire activity, it looked like the kids' summer vacation was going to be extended.

"Stop, stop! Don't park too close to the porta-potties. They can get really rank," I yelled. "We also need to create some defensible space between us and the crapper flappers."

"What's a crapper flapper?" asked Phil.

"It's any moron who lets the porta-pottie door slam loudly, usually around 04:00, when we are all trying to get some sleep."

"But not too far away! I don't want to run a half marathon just to take a leak," pleaded Diane.

Phil found a nice compromise and pulled into a perfect spot. It was equal distance from the mess tent, supply tent, and the johns.

Our base camp was established several miles away from the main fire and the wind was in our favor, blowing toward the fire. The sky was blue, and the air was crystal clear, free of any smoke. We parked the Nickel, piled out and took in a lungful of fresh air.

"Damn that feels good! After those long days of eating smoke, my lungs were beginning to feel it," and coughed up a big black goober and hawked it into the dust.

"I know what you mean, especially what you said about those wildland boogers," Phil added.

Diane agreed, "And how! Sometimes it feels like I have boulders growing way up in there."

Phil whipped out his hankie and forcefully blew his nose into an already blackened bandana.

He tucked it back into his back pocket and added, "And I kind of know what that Monkey Butt is all about," digging a little at his butt crack.

"Well, Phil, I've got some good news for you," Diane commented. "See those semis parked over there? Those are the camp showers. They stay open pretty late, usually till eleven o'clock. So it looks like your Monkey Butt will soon meet its match."

"The sooner we set up, the sooner we soap up, so let's start unpacking," I said in earnest.

Phil and Diane looked at each other and said at the same time, "We're burning daylight!"

I walked to the school, to find out the latest news about the fire. While crossing the field, I saw two white transport trucks rolling into camp with NDF printed on their sides in large green letters. They parked far away from us, on the opposite end of the field, and about two-dozen guys emerged wearing bright orange clothing. They were stretching out a little and started to gather around their supervisor.

Who are those guys? I thought, as I continued walking.

The check-in went without a hitch and I returned to our camp. Phil had gone to supply and brought back three cots. Diane had acquired some fresh batteries, and had already swapped out the old ones.

Struggling to set up her cot, Diane said, "That ground at spike camp was miserable. It was so lumpy, it felt like I was trying to sleep on watermelons. These cots are going to be soooo nice!" She pulled it to a spot that was remotely level and threw her Thermo-rest inflatable mattress and sleeping bag on top, fluffed up her favorite Hello Kitty pillow and sighed, "That looks like heaven!" and plopped down, to give it a test spin.

The sun was low, just barely peeking through the trees when we finally wrapped things up. The three of us moseyed over to the mess tent and noticed the chow line had formed half way around it. As we approached, there was a long table with a dozen hand sinks. They were supplied with warm water, soap dispensers, and paper towels. I rolled up my sleeves and ran my hands and arms under the warm water.

"Ahhhh!" I said and splashed some warm water on my face and into my hair and scrubbed a little behind my neck. It had been nine days since I shaved, and I remarked, "I'm beginning to look a little rough, don't ya think?"

Phil chimed in, "Yeah, like something the cat dragged in!"

I gave Phil a quick disapproving glance, paused, and looked into the mirror.

"Do I look that bad?" and wiped off some of the dirt with a paper towel.

"Naw, not that bad. I've seen you looking worse," said Diane. "Much worse!"

"What about me?" asked Phil. With his hands on his hips he gave us a quick profile.

I pinched his baby face cheeks pretty hard. "Nothing but peach fuzz Phil. Has anybody ever issued *you* a Man Card?"

Parking ourselves at the end of the chow line, we worked our way into the large tent. Plastic trays, plastic utensils and Styrofoam plates sat on a large table by the door. Further down the line were steam tables overflowing with copious amounts of food. I could smell the aroma of roast pork and black coffee. Mixed in was the faint odor of diesel exhaust, dust, and burnt sage, not to mention a whiff or two of B.O. The tent was packed to capacity with hundreds of firefighters, and there was a lot of raucous chatter and hearty laughter.

Soon it was our turn, and we slid our trays down the line. The kitchen staff heaped generous helpings of roast pork loin, potatoes au gratin, green beans, and applesauce on our plates. There was a buffet table off to the side, showcasing a garden fresh salad bar, slices of coconut cream pie, and peach cobbler.

"Man, this sure beats MREs!" said Phil with a smile. "Not that I'm complaining or anything, but, gosh darn, look at all this! Warm peach cobbler, and a scoop of vanilla ice cream! *You can't beat that with a baseball bat!*"

As we walked among the long cafeteria tables to look for a place to sit, I noticed the Apache hand crew waving us over. We squeezed in between them and another crew from Colorado. Phil started eating his dessert first.

Remembering the remark Phil made the other morning about hot sauce, Diane asked, "Would you like to try some Tabasco on your ice cream today?"

"Not today, maybe next time," he mumbled while shoveling in a mouthful of the frozen vanilla indulgence.

I went to grab a cup of coffee, and when I returned, I noticed Phil had finished with his plate and was getting in line for seconds.

I grinned and shook my head, "That boy must have a hollow leg, but then again, I would give anything to be a 20 -year-old again."

It made me chuckle when I saw three guys from Wyoming across the table from us, with napkins tucked in their shirts just under their chins. They were as filthy as Kentucky coal miners; the only clean part on them was their hands. Their once bright yellow brush shirts were now a dingy olive drab color, and I could just make out where their backpack straps came over their shoulders, as this was the only place where their shirts were remotely yellow.

I elbowed Diane and whispered, "Like that tucked in napkin is going to make a difference." I chuckled and looked down at my own shirt and realized if I dribbled any gravy down the front, I would be hard pressed to see where it landed.

10 The Wild Bunch

We were yucking it up pretty good when a hand crew dressed in bright orange, came marching in, single file.

"Who are those guys?" I asked, knowing they were the guys I saw earlier.

"I think you need glasses because them ain't guys," chuckled one of the firefighters from Wyoming.

"Hokey smokes, they're a bunch of girls!" gasped Phil.

"If I'm not mistaken," said the engine boss from Colorado, clearing his throat, "them gals are known as *The Wild Bunch.*"

"The Wild Bunch?" asked Phil. With a look of curiosity, he watched them as they made their way through the chow line.

"From what I hear, they're an inmate crew from the federal prison. They are under constant surveillance and their supervisors always keep handguns holstered and loaded shotguns at the ready. They are hard core prisoners, felons and the like."

His buddy chimed in, "They're meaner than mongrels and won't hesitate to rip your heart out if you look at them the wrong way."

"You mean like armed robbers and murderers?" asked Phil.

"Yup," said one of the Wyoming guys while he adjusted his napkin. "They are the worst of the worst. I heard they even have lifers on their crew."

"No kidding!" gasped Phil in disbelief.

"That's not the worst of it," said the other guy with the napkin. He slowly leaned over the table to Phil and in a hushed tone explained, "From what I hear, if they see a young fella like yourself, one they *really* fancy, they manage to snatch you from your camp under the cover of darkness, and sneak you into their camp."

"What happens then?" asked Phil, all wide eyed and flustered.

"I don't exactly know. Let's just say, you go in as a boy and come out as a *Man!*"

We all stopped eating and stared at Phil.

The Colorado engine boss sitting next to Phil, stated with a serious tone, "If I was you, I wouldn't wander too far from your camp, and be on your toes when you hit the showers."

The Wyoming guys quickly finished their meals, stood up, and made their way to the exit.

"Well, there you go Phil, here's your chance to get your first real Man Card." I could barely keep a straight face when I said, "Someone needs to take one for the team!"

I could hardly believe it. Phil was buying into the story, hook, line, and sinker.

I glanced around to see that Ginny had joined Diane and they had both moved over to sit with the Apache women. They were all silent, slouched in their chairs, staring at us with perturbed looks on their faces. I could almost see the daggers emitting from Diane's eyes. I could tell the women were truly annoyed with our shenanigans. I shrugged my shoulders as if to say ... *What?* They looked at each other and said in unison. "*Go'she' Li'gai!*"

We all got up to leave, and I thought, *I can't argue with that, whatever it means.*

We tossed our trash on the way out, and Phil said, "I can't believe it, hard core criminals right here in our camp! I've never seen a real criminal up close before."

"You could be seeing them up close for real if you aren't careful," I replied with caution.

We got back to our camp, and Phil let us know he better go shower now while the Wild Bunch was still eating. He quickly grabbed his shaving kit, towel, and clean skivvies, and hustled over to the showers.

As I watched Phil disappear in the darkness, I started to chuckle to myself.

Suddenly Diane got in my face, "You guys may be getting your jollies feeding Phil this line of crap. I, on the other hand, know better and have a lot of respect for those young women!"

She went on to enlighten me about inmate hand crews.

"The inmate crews are usually made up of low level, non-violent offenders. Yes, they are constantly supervised, and follow strict policies and rules! For every day they work, their sentence is reduced by one day. They work just as hard as the rest of us but only make one dollar an hour, starting from the day they leave the prison until the day they return."

"Wow, I didn't know that."

"Here is another tid-bit of information, you old coot. They may not see a lot of initial attack action on the fire line. They usually separate them from the rest of us, but the inmate crews, male and female, get out there and do a ton of conservation and fire rehab. They do soil stabilization, reseeding, fence repair, and they eradicate miles and miles of dozer lines."

"Wow Diane! I'm really impressed. You won't find me doing this kinda work for a dollar an hour."

Diane started digging in her bag for some shampoo when she finally said, "I know you like stirring the pot, and you guys can mess with Phil all you want. I'll be a good sport and play along, only because things could get interesting. But let me tell you one thing. Those gals are serious hard workers, and I don't think for a minute they would jeopardize all of that hard work for a little *Boy Toy* action."

With that said, she grabbed her bathroom kit and towel and hustled off to the showers.

"Hey, Diane!" I hollered, as she headed across the camp. "Back in the mess tent you and the Apache gals called me something. What does *go'she' li'gai* mean?"

She yelled back, "It means *white dog.*"

I laughed, and in the darkness, gave her a barrage of yipping coyote calls.

While walking away, she raised her arm and gave me the finger.

Laughing even harder, I fumbled with some gear and muttered, "Damn women!"

11 Jungle Time

The practical joker in me reared its ugly head, and I couldn't resist taking this a bit further. Tearing a piece of paper out of my note pad, I wrote down a few words and sketched a drawing of a heart and dagger. I imagined the look on Phil's face when he read the note, "*We really like you, see you tonight!*" and ominously signed it, "*The Wild Bunch!*" I laughed, folded the note in half and made my way to the showers.

Each mobile shower stall had two compartments, an inner shower area for washing up, and a small outer room that had a bench for getting dressed and a shelf to place your bathroom kit. It was easy to find the one Phil was in and knew he couldn't see me as I reached through the outside curtain and took his clean underwear from the bench and replaced it with the note.

Hurrying back to camp I couldn't help but think, "This will stir things up." I was so pleased with myself I could hardly stand it.

Diane was the first one back. "Pablo, we need to talk! *Now!*" she barked as she stomped over to me in a huff.

She threw her stuff on her cot and glared at me. "What the hell are you up to? Phil just told me that his underwear was stolen from his shower and a note was left in its place. A note from the *Wild Bunch*."

"No, really?" I said dryly.

"Damn it, son of a bitch! Are you really that dense?"

"I haven't heard you cuss like that in a long time," I snickered, and in my best John Wayne voice said, "Aww Missy, you look mighty purdy when you're angry."

That remark made her even madder! She got in my face and said, "Phil is coming back here *Commando!* I'm not naming any names but whoever took his undies probably doesn't realize that those are his *Temple Garments.*"

"What the heck are temple garments? They looked like run of the mill, white boxer shorts and a T-shirt to me."

"Ohhhh, Pablo, or should I call you, shit-for-brains! The Mormons, male and female, wear the garments 24/7. To them it's some kind of expression and commitment to their faith."

"Really?" I said raising an eyebrow, "24/7?"

"They consider them sacred. What you just did was like knocking the pointy hat off the Pope."

"Whooooops! My bad," I said dumbfounded.

"If I were you, I would start thinking about how you are going to save face and get those chonies back to him. If you don't, I am going to spill the beans about the whole situation. When he finds out you guys made all of this up, he won't like it. He especially won't like you. He might even start *hating* you."

"Oh, Diane, come on now, *hate* is such a strong word."

Just then, Phil came into our camp and showed me the note. He didn't go into any details about the garments, except to say that they were swiped. I could see he was shaken up about the whole thing. He now felt that the Wild Bunch had singled him out, and it was only a matter of time before they came after him.

"I don't know about you," Phil said seriously, "but I'm taking my virtue and virginity into the truck where it's safe!"

He grabbed his bedding off of his cot, climbed into the cab of the Triple Nickel and locked the doors.

"See what you have done!" Diane whispered with venom.

After taking a nice hot shower, I came back, sat on my cot, and tried to devise a plan. I needed to undo the damage without Phil knowing it was I who swiped his skivvies. After all, the Wild Bunch never existed in the first place. We just made them up, so getting them out of the picture shouldn't be a problem.

I was exhausted and sore after working at the spike camp, but after tonight's supper, and that long hot steamy shower, I knew I would be asleep in no time.

***

Our patrol was scurrying through the jungle in single file. Somehow, our patrol lost its bearings earlier in the day and now the Viet Cong were in hot pursuit. We were following a well-traveled enemy trail, and the air hung heavy with the humid smell of perspiration and wet vegetation. Our point man was up ahead, scouting for booby traps and trip wires, when the sound of gunfire sent us scattering in every direction.

There was more gunfire and the air was thick with lead! Three of us had gotten separated from the rest of the patrol and were now sprinting through the jungle, heading in the general direction of the river. We could hear the voices of the enemy, and their shouting was getting closer!

Christ! They're almost on us!

Another smattering of rapid gunfire, and my two buddies face planted just in front of me! Their backs were riddled with bullet holes! I was sprinting as fast as I could, ducking and dodging tree limbs and branches. I was crashing through the jungle, and sweat was pouring off me. I couldn't afford to slow down, and my legs were getting as heavy as concrete. My lungs were on fire and I was franticly gasping for air! Up ahead I could hear the sound of the river!

The river, I've got to make it to the river!

Pushing my way through a clump of bushes, I quickly stopped on a dime!

Holy crap!

I was standing at the edge of a steep cliff. The jungle dropped away, and the river was 200 feet below me.

I'm so screwed!

I turned around and was now confronted by a dozen Viet Cong. My back was to the river, and I was trapped! Making a semi-circle around me, they had their AK-47s trained on me and were slowly closing ranks.

There's no escape!

I dropped my weapon and raised my hands slowly over my head in surrender. Strangely enough, I realized all of the Viet Cong facing me, were *women!* And they were all wearing *orange Nomex!*

One of them said in a cold, calm voice. *"You too close! Go'she' Li' gai!"*

With a click of a trigger, they began to blow me to smithereens!!!

AAAAAHHHHH!!!!! AAAAAHHHHH!!!!

I was screaming bloody terror and Diane was shaking me.

"Wake up, Pablo! Wake up!"

I sat up in my cot, confused, disoriented, and breathing like a freight train.

"God, they're after me!" I gasped.

"Who?" Diane asked.

I paused for a moment and could feel my heart racing. I shook my head, trying to clear the fog from my brain and blurted out, "The Wild Bunch! It was the Wild Bunch!"

Diane cautiously remarked, "OK ... now you're freaking me out!"

I got up from my cot, walked around in the cool night air, grabbed some water and splashed it on my face. After gulping a couple of big swallows and taking a few deep breaths, things began to settle down and look normal.

How could something so innocent as messing with Phil turn into a night terror?

Still shaken by the nightmare, I crawled back into my sleeping bag and pulled it up over my sweat-chilled body. I rolled to my side, stared into the darkness and vowed,

I definitely need to fix this mess tomorrow!

12 Burying The Hatchet

I headed over to the morning briefing half awake, still trying to devise a plan. Phil and Diane did a truck check, cleaned up our camp, and restocked the truck with drinking water, Gatorades, and sack lunches. We met up at the mess tent.

The chow line was short. We were greeted with mountains of scrambled eggs, tons of bacon, toast, jelly, assorted Danish, and a big table covered with those tiny cardboard boxes of cereal. The kind you had when you were a kid: Sugar Pops, Frosted Flakes, Cocoa Crispies, and Fruit Loops. At the end of the tent sat large Igloo coolers of orange juice, cranberry juice, and milk. At the very end of it all was steaming hot coffee!

Diane said to Phil, "I know you aren't supposed to drink the stuff, but personally, I feel if there ever is a *Food Hall of Fame*, coffee will be at the top of the list. I like it hot with a spoonful of sugar and a little splash of half and half. I love the smell of it, its bitterness, the creaminess, and its sweetness."

Diane slurped some down as we made our way to our table. "Man, pure heaven," she sighed and took another sip. "Not as good as Lupe's Horny Toad Café Coffee, but I'm not complaining."

During breakfast I let my crew know the details from the morning briefing.

"The fire is reported to be 65 percent contained. Our strike team will be comprised of five, Type 6 engines like ours, and we will be working in Division C."

While eating, I noticed that Phil was not his normal self; he was quiet, introverted, and had a concerned look on his face. He was not the usual *happy to be here* kinda guy, that we have come to know and love. I was sure it was my evil doing that had provoked his glum mood, and I felt bad because of it.

Before leaving base camp our supervisor pulled me aside and informed me I would be in charge of today's air-to-ground helicopter operations in Division C.

"You need to protect the communications complex located at the very top of the Humboldt Mountains," he explained. "Stage at the complex and direct helicopter bucket drops. The helicopters will be dipping out of a nearby reservoir and you'll have plenty of water, so don't hold back, those towers are expensive and we can't afford to lose them."

The area surrounding the complex was partially overrun with fire yesterday and was mostly in the black today.

Our job is to put out any remaining smoldering fires and have personnel identify hot spots, flag them with pink flagging (pink plastic ribbon) and call the helicopters to drop water on them.

He also advised me, "Since your strike team will be working at the southern tip of the fire, you will be spiking out again after today's activities."

I told my crew, "We need to pack up again. We are going to the spike camp at the end of the day."

Phil started whining, "Ahhh Pablo, we just got here!"

Diane turned to him and said, "Cowboy up, mister! We're on a mission. This ain't the Waldorf Astoria, bub! We're here to fight fire!"

Phil apologized, and admitted he was being a wimp, and started to pack up.

"If it's any consolation Phil, at least the spike camp will be a good ways away from base camp and the Wild Bunch!" said Diane with a wink.

Phil suddenly perked up and looked happy, "What are we waiting for? *It's time to put the fatback in the wagon, load up the children and the chickens! Let's move 'em out!*"

Our division supervisor assembled our strike team and advised us about our plan for the day. "We are entering an area that is considered to be a *dirty burn*. We have a lot of scattered, patchy, unburned areas mixed in with the burnt stuff. These unburned fuels have been preheated, dried out, and are ripe for fire. The temperature is going to be in the high 80s today, and the humidity will be around 10 percent. The winds will be squirrelly again. These conditions are a recipe for disaster!" he said with caution. "Remember, bad things can happen during mop up if you aren't careful. So stay on your toes and pay attention out there!"

As we entered Division C, the strike team leader began to spread our trucks along the Tower Road. Some crews were sent out into the slurry lines to check for hot spots. The Triple Nickel progressed up the winding mountain road until we were at the communication towers. From the complex we had a 360-degree view of the fire area. In the distance I could see the large smoke plume of the main fire that had passed through the area yesterday. I surveyed the surrounding terrain for signs of active fire. I noticed the NDF buggies and the Wild Bunch setting out soil erosion barriers in a wash not far from our location. The images of what took place last night, flashed through my mind. I needed to do something to fix my evil doings or I would surely rot in hell. A plan started to materialize.

"Diane, I'm going over to talk with the Wild Bunch." I made sure Phil heard me. "I will be back in a few. Diane, you're in charge and keep the drops coming. I'm going over there to see if I can bury the hatchet."

I picked up the Pulaski out of the tool cache, gave Diane a wink, and Phil a thumbs- up. I hopped into the truck and started down the road.

"Good luck," yelled Diane. "We will keep an eye on you with our binoculars. Radio if you need to be rescued. Just give us the code word *Wild Bunch*, and we'll come a running."

I rumbled down the road and pulled up to the Wild Bunch to meet with their supervisor.

"Nice looking crew. It looks like they do nice work," I remarked.

She greeted me with a handshake and said, "Thank you, I really like working with this group. They work real hard."

We made idle chitchat and I began telling her of the harrowing tale about our initial attack during our first day here. I was *very* animated about it, and began waving my arms all over the place. I told her about how we were driving like a bat out of hell, trying to out run the fire. She was now staring at me like I was a nut case. I pointed to her uniform and asked her if that was a special kind of Nomex that was used to make their orange pants and shirts.

She responded, "Beats the heck outta' me."

"What does that stand for?" pointing my finger to the NDF stenciled on her shirt.

She stepped back with a puzzled look and told me, "*Nevada Department of Forestry.*"

I asked her if she had seen the model of Pulaski that I had in my hand, and offered it to her.

With a questionable look, she reached out for it, felt the heft of it in her hands and replied, "It's not the kind we use, but it looks like it can do the job."

"Go ahead and give it a swing," I said.

She looked at me again with a puzzled look, and gave the Pulaski a good plunge into the ground. When she pulled it back out and handed it back to me she said, "Not much different than ours."

I gave the tool a good swing and left it sticking in the ground. "You know, that is probably the *best ... tool ... on ... the ... truck!*" Emphatically pointing at it with each word spoken.

I wrestled it free and shook the supervisor's hand nice and hard.

"It was very nice meeting you," I said with a smile and walked towards the gals working in the streambed. I pointed to them repeatedly, and yelled out, *"We ... love ... you ... gals! ... Great ... work!"* I turned around and marched to my truck.

At this point, their supervisor must have really thought I was off my rocker. I knew my crew was watching the whole ordeal with binoculars, so I turned and waved to them.

As I sat in my truck, I said out loud, "The United Nations couldn't have patched things up any better."

I returned to the communication towers, parked the truck, and Phil ran over, asking in earnest, "Well, what happened?"

Hitching up my pants a little I said, "I wanted to keep my cool, but I kind of got in a heated argument with their supervisor. *But don't worry!* I laid down the law and said if they didn't stop the harassment, I was going to report them and get them kicked off the fire!"

"We saw that, it looked as if you were really letting them have it. Your arms were flying all over the place!" said Diane.

Phil added, "And we saw a lot of finger pointing and chest thumping!"

"You betcha, there was! I told her I wouldn't report the shower incident if they agree to return your skivvies and leave us alone. She promised me she would personally return them. I insisted we need to bury the hatchet on the whole thing, and made them show us a sign of good faith by burying the Pulaski into the ground. We both plunged the Pulaski into the ground, and shook hands on it. Then, I went over and laid into the Wild Bunch a little, before I left!"

"Wow! I saw that! Is it for real?" asked Phil.

"I guarantee you, they won't be messing with us anymore. You have my word on it."

"Gosh, Pablo, I don't know how to repay you," gushed Phil.

"Don't worry about it kid ... It was nothing, it was *really nothing.*"

Phil smiled and hustled down the hillside to flag another hot spot.

"From here it looked so believable," grinned Diane.

"Boy, I really pulled that one outta my ass, I will tell you later what really happened down there. I hope their supervisor doesn't report me for being a nut case! Tomorrow I will return Phil's skivvies and all will be back to normal. Well ... kind of!" I gave a long sigh of relief and said, "It's amazing how a little good clean fun can get so out of hand."

After an hour, I called out to Phil, and signaled him to come up for lunch.

After lunch I paced on the walkway of the communication complex directing bucket drops. There were still a lot of burning and smoldering hot spots down below.

The helicopters working the fire were very similar to the ones we used in Vietnam. Back then we used them for everything. They brought us ammo, tons of supplies, transported personnel, flew out the wounded, and of course brought us our precious mail, but most important, they provided a lot of effective air-to-ground fire support.

This process was the same except today the enemy was wildfire. Even though the fire wasn't shooting at us, it could still hurt us or maybe even kill us if we weren't careful. We continued to work the tower site for the rest of the day. As the hours passed, Phil had become his happy-go-lucky self again and Diane was glad because she didn't have to wring my neck.

Yup, I thought as I scouted the area with binoculars, *we are an effective team again.*

I heard a call on the radio from one of the Type 6 crews. They advised command that while they were traveling off-road, they got *two* flat tires. Their brush truck was about one mile from our location and their engine boss said the burnt sage had pierced through the sidewalls of their front tires, and they needed to be towed off the fire grounds.

The division supervisor arranged for a tow and alerted all other crews not to drive into the burned up sage. If a truck needed to go off-road, they would have to leave the truck and hike in to work a hot spot.

The burned up sagebrush had created large swaths of stumps and stubble that resembled thousands of Punji sticks. Back in Nam, Punji sticks were used as booby traps. They were groups of short sticks stuck in the ground by the enemy, and were as thick as your thumb and about 12 inches tall. Their ends were sharpened and dipped in feces. Sometimes they were set in holes to be stepped in, or camouflaged and set out over a section of the trail. If an unsuspecting soldier tripped and fell on them, he would become impaled. It was always a long and painful process to extract them, and the wounds would almost always become infected.

It had been another long hot day, and at 19:00 the call came in, telling us to wrap things up. We packed up and gathered the group for our trip to the spike camp. Our stay at the main base camp was short lived, but rejuvenating for the body and soul. I knew it would make the next few days a lot more bearable.

I told Diane and Phil, "As you guys know, our two-week assignment is winding down, and we are all dog-tired. I need to make sure we come out of this assignment in one piece. Phil, take your time driving to camp. You did the lion's share of the work, running up and down the hillside ... you must be exhausted. I have to admit ... you are one tough son-of-a-gun. I can make you do any crappy task, and you muster up the gumption to get it done!"

"You got it Boss. Just point me in the right direction and *I'm all over it, like ants on a honey bun!*" laughed Phil.

"He's all over it like grease on bacon," Diane chimed in.

"All over it like a cop on a donut," I replied.

"Oh yeah, like a duck on a June bug," Phil exclaimed.

"Oh yeah, like ugly on an ape," I said grinning.

"Oh yeah, like ... Phil on a pork chop!" Diane added.

"Oh yeah, like ... like ... Monkey Butt on my Patooty!" laughed Phil.

"OK, OK, that one takes the cake, I can't beat that," I laughed, and we soon found ourselves at the spike camp before we knew it.

13 The Butter Bean Gang

I was still in my sleeping bag when I heard Phil shout, "Ha! Look what I found! My Garments, they brought them back last night!"

In the brisk morning sunlight, I could see him holding up the underwear.

"Well look at that!" said Diane as she gave me a wink.

Phil added, "Those girls aren't that bad after all!"

During the morning briefing we were assigned to a task force of newly arriving brush trucks. We could tell them apart from the others because they weren't covered in the grey Nevada talc. Today the plan was for our task force to pinch off one of the last remaining fingers of fire, which was making a run to the east. The area we would be working in had smooth rounded foothills covered with tall grass and light brush. We had adequate resources for the job, two water tenders, six brush trucks and a team leader with a spotter truck. We even had two pumpkins (4,000-gallon, orange portable water tanks) sitting on the side of the road for the tenders to top off their tanks when they ran low. Our division supervisor split our task force into two groups, one taking the north flank of the fire, the other the south. We would extinguish the slow moving fire along the edges and eventually work our way to the tip of the fire. There we would make a frontal assault and hopefully stop it in its tracks.

After coffee and an MRE, we were ready for the day's action. We drove half way around the blackened edge of the main fire and finally came upon a mile-long finger of fire moving steadily to the east. The plan was to stop its progress before it reached a stand of large dry trees that meandered through the valley below. The Triple Nickel, two other brush trucks, and a water tender would take the north flank. The remaining trucks would work the south flank. We did a radio check before we began.

"This is Team Leader 620, Radio check, north team, how do you copy?"

"Tender 633 copies."

"Brush 555 copies."

"Brush 616 copies."

"Butter Bean copies."

The team leader paused and asked again. "Last unit please repeat!"

"Butter Bean copies."

Phil asked, "Who in the heck is Butter Bean?"

"What is your designator Butter Bean?" asked the team leader.

"We have a problem with duplicate designators. Sir, there is another truck on this fire with the same number as our engine so we are using our truck name," they replied.

I said to Diane, "I need to talk to them later. There's got to be a good story to go with that name."

The team leader informed us that we would work at 100-yard intervals. "If you catch up to the truck in front, leap frog past them. Everyone keep in mind that we have an excellent safety zone in the black. The tenders will bring up the rear. Drop back to top off your water tanks, and then jump back into your rotation. Does everybody copy?"

"Tender 633 copies."

"Brush 555 copies."

"Brush 616 copies."

"Butter Bean copies. That's a 10-4 good buddy."

"Awww man, those guys are going to be a handful," I moaned to my crew.

These were perfect conditions for a *pump and roll* operation. During a pump and roll, a brush truck drives slowly alongside the fire. A firefighter walks, carrying the fire hose, while gently spraying water along the fire's edge. We're talking real *slow* here. No more than 1 mile per hour. The conditions today are mild, with a light, downslope breeze. What we will be doing today is almost boring. You won't find any film footage of this type of firefighting on the evening news.

As I drove the Nickel along the fires' edge, Diane walked behind the truck, operating the pump panel as Phil walked the fires' edge, extinguishing it with the hose. It was a pretty straightforward procedure, providing the wind remained light and the fire front maintained its course. Occasionally we stopped and used hand tools to work some heavy brush.

"That *Butter Bean* truck likes to hog the radio," Phil commented. "They let us know their every move. For crying out loud, we can see them! They are just over there!" Phil pointed 200 yards ahead. "They even talk about stuff that doesn't have anything to do with the fire."

"Some people just like hearing themselves on the radio," I replied.

We slowly extinguished the fire along our assigned flank and were now in a position to see the other units on the opposite side. Things were coming together nicely. I let Phil and Diane know I was going to contact the team leader by radio, to make sure we were all topped off with water before we started the final frontal assault. But first, I had to wait for the Butter Bean truck to finish blabbing on the radio.

"How hard is it to pump and roll?" Phil angrily blurted out! *"Shut your Butter Bean butt holes. They are as full of wind as corn-eating asses!"*

Diane cautioned him, "Hold on Phil! Calm down! Are those guys really starting to bug you? And did I hear you say *ass*?"

Diane and I gave Phil a double take.

I finally managed to get through on the radio. The strike team leader and all of the engine bosses met up on a small hill for a quick bull session. The team leader allowed the strike team to rest up for a few, before the final assault.

"I am going to walk over to that Butter Bean truck and talk to those guys!" Phil snorted.

Diane quickly warned him, "Be nice, we already have one trouble maker on board, we don't need another!"

"He is in rare form today and is really feeling his oats! Our Phil is turning into a real firefighter. He's getting a little feisty and even said *ass* today!" I beamed with pride.

"It's probably a good thing. This is more than likely, our last day on this fire," said Diane.

"Yup, I hear you! But there is still a chance we can take the required two days off and get reassigned to work another two-week tour somewhere else."

"I noticed for the last few days, the humidity has been steadily rising. It looks like some rain will be here any day, instead of just the dry lighting. I think Mother Nature wants us to go home," she said. "I'm up for another two-week tour, but whatever the outcome, this has been one heck of a fire assignment!"

"Yes it has!"

Diane looked up and watched as Phil marched over to the Butter Bean truck. "Pablo, go and chaperone Phil, I don't want him coming back here with a shiner and a split lip on his last day."

"OK Mom!" I said sarcastically. "I'll play the big brother, but just this once!"

I jogged up to Phil and patted him on the back, "I thought you might need some help. I tamed the Wild Bunch for you, but this is your shootin' match, I'm just here for moral support."

We approached the Butter Bean guys. There were three of them and I let Phil do *all* the talking.

"Howdy, boys! Mighty fine weather today!"

He shook hands and played nice. Their engine boss looked like he had emerged right out of the High Sierra. He had a rough-hewn mountain man look about him, was barrel chested, and had a full shaggy beard that probably hasn't seen a razor since he was 12 years old. There was some chest hair sticking out from under his T-shirt, and he sprouted some knuckle hair to boot.

The squad boss was a Hispanic guy, about five feet, four inches tall, and was as thin as a rail. He had a head of black curly hair shaved close at the sides, and had an impressive mustache, that was thick and long, with pointy ends that curled up.

The third guy was their engineer. He was a blond hair, blue-eyed Beach Boy lookin' dude, about six feet tall, with a great tan and a muscular build. There were no tattoos, earrings, or body piercings, but I noticed a small quartz crystal on a leather string, hanging around his neck. It must have been there for good Butter Bean karma.

Phil asked the big guy with the shaggy beard, "Where are you guys from?"

"Our home base is in Basin, Montana," Shaggy replied.

"We are from southern New Mexico," said Phil.

"Wow! You are a long way from home."

"What's with the Butter Bean handle?" asked Phil.

"Oh, that! That's my dogs' name! Come over here," and motioned us toward their truck.

We walked over and right there on the door was a picture of *Butter Bean*. The dog was a scruffy, black and white Chihuahua-terrier mix, and looked like he could have won the *Ugliest Dog in America* contest.

"We are strictly a wildland outfit, and have eight, Type 6 brush trucks that we deploy all across the country."

"Do all of your trucks have a picture of the dog on them?" asked Phil.

"Hell yeah! *That dog is famous!*"

"That's not all!" said the Blondie. He climbed in the driver's seat and pulled a lever on the dashboard. The truck sounded off with a specialty air horn that sounded like a bugle call.

"Holy cow! Can I give it a toot?" asked Phil.

He climbed in, pulled the lever, and the air filled with the sound of the bugle.

"That's *First Call*," Shaggy stated. "Kinda sounds like we are ready to run the Kentucky Derby don't it?"

"Wow!" said Phil. "Do all of your trucks have those horns?"

Shaggy laughed, "Yup, each truck has its own unique horn. One plays reveille, another plays uhh ... "

Blondie spouted off the calls. "Truck 1, that's us, we have First Call. That one is my favorite! Truck 2, Reveille. Truck

3, Fire Call. Truck 4, Mess Call. Truck 5, Mail Call. Truck 6, Fatigue Call. Truck 7, Assembly. And lastly, Truck 8 has Calvary Charge!"

"Yee doggie," crowed Phil. "By the way, what's your name?"

"The name's Dylan pleased to meet you." They shook hands again.

"This little guy is Luis," Dylan patted him on the top of his curly head. "But he likes to be called *Chico*."

"And that there is the big boss Mike, but most people call him *Chopper*."

"Sounds like you guys have a lot of fun," Phil said with a grin.

"We sure do."

"Well, the main reason I came over here is … I want to talk to you guys about radio communications. It seems you guys are kinda' hoggin' the air waves, and we can't get on the radio to call the other units," said Phil. "We need to keep the frequencies open at all times. You know, just in case something important comes up."

"I get your drift," said Chopper. "I know, we have a tendency to chat it up some."

"So, are you guys going to limit the chatter?" asked Phil.

"Not a problem," said Chopper.

"No hard feelings?" asked Phil.

"None at all," said Chopper.

"By the way," asked Phil, "can I blow the horn one more time?"

"Be my guest!"

Phil climbed in and let her rip. *Saddle up Sea Biscuit! It's off to the races!*

When we returned to our truck, Diane was tidying up the back seat, and Phil started to tell her about the Butter Bean Gang.

"Guess what? He named the truck after his dog Butter Bean! Can you believe that? They have a big picture of the dog on the side of their truck!"

I told Phil, "Heck, I named our truck the *Triple Nickel* eight years ago. Obviously, because of the 555 designator, but also after the 555th Tactical Fighter Squadron that had the most Soviet MiG shoot downs during the Vietnam War. I think they shot down close to 40 MiGs. They were known as the Triple Nickel and their motto was, *'World's Largest Distributor of MiG Parts.'* So what do you think of that?"

"That's pretty cool," said Phil. "I didn't know that."

"Neither did I," said Diane sounding impressed. "I must admit, the Triple Nickel has a much better ring to it than Butter Bean. Hey, you know how pilots stencil an icon of some sort, on the side of their plane for every enemy plane they shot down? We could do that with the Triple Nickel. You know, a little flame stenciled right here on the front quarter panel. One for each big fire this truck has knocked down."

"That's a great idea! I like that," I said. "When we get back home we need to do a little research to see how many large fires this truck has been called out for."

A few hours later, our two attack crews met up at the tip of the fire and after a brief frontal attack, we managed to knock down the fire. We backtracked along our assigned flanks, making sure we had a secure edge leading back to where we started. It was 17:00 when we finished up. Our team leader corralled all of us and asked for a volunteer truck to make one final drive around the fire. Since it was our last day, we gladly *cowboyed up.*

As the rest of the group drove back to the spike camp, we headed out to do a 360 around the fire line. We finished the sweep and attempted to radio in, to let the team leader know we found nothing of any concern, and were heading back to the spike camp. For some reason we couldn't make contact. I was in a hurry to get to camp and decided to head back along an old dozer line to save some time.

Diane said in a questioning voice, "Pablo this isn't a *short cut* is it?"

"Nah, don't worry, I know this area like the back of my hand."

I told Phil to bypass a steep gully section up ahead, where a brush truck got stuck yesterday. We soon found ourselves pointed down the steep slope of the ravine I was trying to avoid! It was super steep, but with the help of gravity, and some cool headed driving by Phil, we made it to the bottom. Unfortunately, it was the exact place I didn't want to be.

"We need to get out of this ravine and back on to the top of that ridge," I told Phil.

We stopped, got out of the truck, locked the hubs, got in and put the truck into 4-low, four-wheel drive mode. Phil turned the truck around and pointed her up the ravine.

"Since you are in training, this will be your required test in driving a four-wheel drive truck. I will sign you off on your wildland task book when we make it to the top of the hill. Now Phil, keep a firm grip on the wheel, take it nice and easy, and keep a steady speed. Not too fast, not too slow. Keep your wheels out of the deep ruts and make sure you don't spin out the tires in the loose stuff. It's as simple as that."

"Maybe you should drive Pablo," Phil said hesitantly.

"Cowboy up mister! Everyone has to learn eventually. Just do it!"

Phil took a deep breath and started up the hill. It felt like we were on a bucking bronco! I could see Diane holding on for dear life in the back seat. The next thing I knew we were sliding backwards, almost sideways. Our truck was losing grip and all four wheels dropped down into the deepest ruts. We bounced backwards and I heard a loud scraping sound, as we stopped with a jolt!

"It's OK!" I said. "Crap happens!" We all bailed out to analyze our predicament. I realized we were high centered on a big rock, and three of the wheels were off the ground.

Diane stated with concern, "We are kind of screwed here, we need to call in and get some help. There is no way we are going to get this baby off of that big rock by ourselves."

"We don't need no stinkin' help," I said. "We've got this covered."

First, we emptied the remaining water in the tank to lighten the load. That didn't help. We then tried placing rocks under the tires but that made it worse. We even tried rocking the truck back and forth, but nothing seemed to work.

After all of our attempts failed, I finally conceded, "OK, it's getting really dark out. We need to call for one of the other brush trucks to winch us out."

When I tried to make radio contact with the strike team leader, I couldn't get through.

"Guys, I'm really sorry for getting us stuck like this," Phil said sadly.

I told Phil that he would probably have to pay for the towing charge, and before I could say another word, Diane smacked my hard hat off of my head.

"Knock it off, this is serious!" she said, gritting her teeth. "If we can't get in touch with somebody, we might have to spend the night in the truck. I don't want to be hiking out of here in the dark."

"OK, just messing with Phil," I replied meekly.

Phil was mortified and walked over to sit on a rock.

Diane walked over and tried to console him. "Hey, don't worry we will get out of here. You did a pretty good job, you made it to within twenty feet of the top. If we had a bomb-proof anchor point up on top of the hill we could have winched ourselves out of this mess."

I thought for a moment, "OK, here is my plan. I will hike up to the top of that large hill over there and try to make radio contact with the guys at spike camp. We should have better reception on higher ground, instead of down in this ravine."

"Sounds good," said Diane. "Take this flashlight and don't sprain an ankle or get bit by a snake."

I grabbed my radio and flashlight and trudged up the hill. Phil was like a puppy and tagged along with flashlight in hand.

We followed the dozer line along the crest of the hill for about a quarter mile. Just then, off in the distance we saw headlights bouncing down the rutted road.

"Start waving your flashlight!" I yelled to Phil.

We were jumping up and down, hollering, and praying they could see us. Next thing we know, we heard it ...

A bugle call ... like you hear at the Kentucky Derby!

"The Butter Bean Gang!"

Pulling up to us, Chopper rolled down his window, and said in a sweet little southern voice, "Need a ride sailor?"

We squeezed in the back seat, and made our way back to the Triple Nickel.

"Man, am I glad to see you guys! Did you hear us calling?" I asked.

"Nope, can't say that I did," said Chopper.

He turned to Phil, slapped him on the shoulder, and said with a laugh and a loud voice, "I was probably too busy talking on the radio!"

Dylan added, "We were worried about you guys when it started getting dark and you didn't show up in camp."

After arriving back to our truck, Chico attached their winch cable to the Triple Nickel, and the Butter Bean Gang slowly pulled the Nickel off of the boulder. Once it was out of the ruts and up on flat ground, Phil and Chico crawled under the truck with flashlights, to see if there was any damage. They reported that the drive shaft was a little scraped, but fortunately it wasn't bent.

Diane was happy she didn't have to spend the night in the truck. I was glad I wasn't the one driving up that slope. It looked like a challenge, and I probably would have gotten us stuck too. The Butter Bean guys became Phil's new heroes; he couldn't stop talking about how great they were for the rest of the drive back.

After arriving at camp, we parked next to their truck, brewed some Joe, laughed, and swapped stories until the wee hours of the morning.

It was 02:00 when we called it a night, and set out our bedrolls on top of the cots we acquired from base camp.

"Man, I thought we had some tall tales. Our stories pale in comparison to the ones the Butter Bean guys told us! They had some real knee slapping, sidesplitting whoppers!" I commented, as I got comfy on my cot.

"Yeah, I especially like the story about the fire they fought near Mt. Hood. The one that involved Chico and the lovesick moose, the hornet's nest and the nudist camp! You can't make that stuff up!" laughed Phil.

It was a short night and we got maybe three hours of sleep before the sun started to brighten up the horizon.

The camp was beginning to stir when Chopper came over to us and said, "I heard through the grapevine that IC wants everyone to pack up and head back to base camp.

"Base camp! All right, let's pack up!" I hollered with enthusiasm.

After we finished packing, I walked over to the Butter Bean Gang and said, "Chopper, thanks for the rescue last night, you guys really saved my bacon."

"Aw heck, it was nothing, come up and see us some time," he said with a grin. "We don't get down New Mexico Way very often."

We all shook hands and got in our trucks.

As we were driving back to base camp, I commented, "It just goes to show you, you can't judge a book by its cover."

"Or a brush truck by its name," Diane chimed in.

Soon, a convoy of trucks filled the road and off in the distance, further back in line, we heard it ... the unmistakable call of a bugle.

Phil laughed, "I have to admit, they're not half bad, for a bunch of gas-passing corn eating asses."

14 Holy Crap!

After nearly two weeks of working the fires, our time had come to demob.

"God I'm dead tired," groaned Diane.

Her comment took me by surprise, Diane is usually revved up and raring to go, but today she looked like the rest of us ... like death warmed over.

"Hey guys, we should never have an empty water tank, so top the tank with water. I will try to get us placed on another two-week assignment. We traveled this far, might as well try and fight some more fire," I said.

"Hey Diane, we need to turn our paperwork in to finance for this Humboldt Fire, is it good to go?"

As she handed me the clipboard I said, "Let's grab some grub, I will slog through the demob process after breakfast. There are a lot of units checking out today, so it may take a while. We may get put on a new assignment, but I really doubt it. If we can get out of here at a reasonable time, we will be well into Utah by sunset, and I am looking forward to our first night under fresh clean sheets!"

After breakfast, Diane and Phil reorganized the compartments, and I gathered up all the empty water bottles, Gatorade bottles and snack wrappers off the cab floor. I was afraid to even look at what had accumulated behind the back seat. Diane rummaged through the snack bag, trying to salvage anything that had not melted or rolled in the dirt.

"My favorite snack of all times is Cheetos," Diane said while holding up a rumpled bag she found. "They're salty, have a nice crunch, and hold up relatively well while being tossed around while we drive on those crappy forest service roads. You can work me all day until I drop, but dangle Cheetos in front of me with a Gatorade chaser, and I'm good for another round."

I smiled at the remark and began to walk up the hill to the elementary school. As I figured, it took me two and a half hours to muddle through the demob process. Even though our paperwork was in order, other crews with poor organizational skills slowed down the process considerably. Unfortunately, we weren't placed on another assignment and I slowly walked back to the truck. I turned the corner and saw that Diane and Phil had all of our clothes sitting on a cot, washed, dried, and neatly folded.

"Wow, clean clothes!" I held them up to my nose and inhaled deeply. "Aaah! You guys are awesome!"

"Let's wait to change, no sense putting clean clothes on these filthy bodies. A hotel somewhere near Salt Lake City should do the trick. We can take a long hot shower, and then change into something clean and comfortable. It will be like a fresh start," I said with a smile. "Let's saddle up, we're burning daylight."

We packed the clean clothes in our gear bags, and I tossed them up to Phil, who was standing on the top of the truck. He crammed them in where there was room and cinched them down with a bungee cord. Diane returned the cots to the supply tent, and we were finally ready to clear out.

I stood there for a moment, staring at the vastness of the base camp as it emptied out. There was a lot of excitement.

In the distance I could hear a lot of laughter and shouting. As the fire trucks rumbled past us, I could smell the distinct aroma of bacon mingled with the smell of dust and diesel. I was happy that we were homeward bound, but as always, I felt kinda sad to see it all end. Despite the bone numbing fatigue, I was a little reluctant to be heading home. This was one hell of a fire assignment, and we probably wouldn't fight this much fire for the rest of this year.

"Guys, we all want to get home, but let's not drive like a bunch of maniacs. Let's take frequent turns driving and make this an uneventful trip," I cautioned them.

"I'm all for that," said Phil.

"Copy that," said Diane.

Just then, Élan, our new friend from the Apache hand crew, ran up to our truck and handed me a package wrapped with newspaper and duct tape. He didn't say a word. We just shook hands, and he turned and ran back to his truck.

"A man of few words," I said.

"What's in the package?" asked Phil.

"I don't know, I think we should open it when we settle in at our hotel tonight."

Rather than climbing back on top of the truck to put it in my gear bag, I stuffed it under the front passenger seat instead.

"Let's move out!" I yelled with a smile.

We climbed aboard the Triple Nickel and Phil started her up. We rumbled along the bumpiness of base camp, and turned onto the welcome hum of paved roads.

I decided to wait until we were further down the road to empty our tank water. We could use it to wash the exterior of the Nickel. We found a gravel storage area a few miles out of town. It was the perfect spot to wash the layers of dust, vegetation, and dried fire retardant off of our brown, nasty looking gypsy wagon. Diane climbed on top and pushed our two-week duffle bags aside to get to the topside hose reel. She handed the nozzle down to me, and Phil fired up the water pump. Dumping the 200-gallons of tank water would lighten the load considerably. I can't imagine what kind of gas mileage the Triple Nickel gets when fully loaded, but I figure she will feel a whole lot better after we dump the burden of 1,600 unnecessary pounds.

Just before I turned the nozzle on her, I rubbed a circle of dust away with my finger. "Check this out, she's actually a red fire truck under all of this grime."

After 30 minutes of scrubbing Phil called out. "We're out of tank water!"

We toweled her off and stood back to admire our handiwork.

Phil said, *"She looks prettier than a suckling sow laying in sunshine!"*

Diane and I looked at each other and I said, "Where does he come up with that corny stuff?"

Since it was Sunday, I noticed traffic was pretty light as we headed east on I-80.

Phil was at the wheel, and Diane was in the back seat relaxing and humming a little tune. I was focused on trying to finish up the paperwork and log book. It would take a few days to get back, and I needed to finish everything while it was still fresh on my mind.

I turned off the squabble emitting from the fire dispatch radio and found a local Country-Western station. After driving awhile, we took turns calling out items on our wish list.

"A nice long hot soapy shower," Phil pondered.

"Maybe a hotel room with air conditioning," grinned Diane.

"Give me a single malt Scotch whisky and a good cigar," I added.

"And clean clothes," said Phil.

Closing my eyes, I sat back and said, "Good God I can't wait to get home and enjoy some of the wife's home cooking."

After a while, I noticed a car in the fast lane pulling alongside of us. They honked their horn, and everyone inside was waving. The car stayed next to us for a moment. There were kids in the backseat, and their faces were pressed against the windows, staring wide-eyed at our truck.

"Aww, isn't it nice how people just love firefighters and fire trucks," Diane said, looking out the window at the family driving by.

"Yeah, this is the third time a car has passed us with people waving like that, it's like they have never seen a fire truck before," added Phil.

Then the car took off, passing us as if trying to outrun a tornado.

"That was strange!" I said as I watched them speed away.

A little later I noticed Phil looking off and on in his driver side rear view mirror. He gave me a puzzled look and said, "Hey, I think we might be burning some oil!"

I looked over to my side mirror and couldn't see crap. The mirror was all messed up. It took a hit from a tree branch a couple of days ago and was loose and angled down. In order for me to see what he was talking about, I had to roll down my window. I leaned out and looked back.

"Holy crap! ... We're on fire! Pull over!"

Diane said stoically, "Not funny, Pablo! Stop kidding around!"

Phil couldn't see the flames wrapping around the entire right rear of the truck! On his side he could only see an occasional hint of black smoke. The fire must have been raging for some time! The folks following behind us must have been getting quite a show! No wonder they were all honking and waving when they passed us!

Phil pulled the truck to the shoulder and screeched to a halt! Cars were honking as they whizzed by. None of them were stopping! I figured they wanted no part of this unforgivable event ... *a fire truck on fire!*

The three of us bailed out, all asses and elbows. We immediately ran to the rear of the truck. Larry, Mo, and Curly couldn't have scurried out any faster. The flames were boiling up at least 20 feet high, and a plume of thick black smoke drifted down the highway. The water pump was on fire, its plastic fuel tank had melted and its five gallons of gasoline poured all over everything! The empty 200-gallon plastic water tank was melting and gobs of plastic were pooling onto the pavement. The truck's wood decking, hand tools, a case of motor oil, and all of our personal gear bags on top of the truck were engulfed in flames! A case of road flares was blazing bright red, and the two extra five-gallon fuel cans were jetting flames like rockets. Through the smoke I could see flames surrounding our two mounted fire extinguishers.

"I can't believe this is happening!" I screamed.

The three of us stood there in horror, as we watched the Triple Nickel self-destruct before our eyes! There was nothing we could do without water, or fire extinguishers. We were helpless! Diane grabbed her fire gloves from the cab and climbed on top of the burning truck and frantically threw down two smoldering shovels. Without saying a word, Diane and Phil started shoveling dirt from the side of the road, and focused their efforts to subdue the flames near the mounted fire extinguishers. While shielding my face, I reached in using my hat as a glove and yanked them from their mounting brackets and quickly tossed them on the ground.

The extinguishers were really hot, so I folded my hat double thick, picked one up, aimed the nozzle and pressed the lever. To my disbelief it malfunctioned! The heat caused the air pressure in the extinguisher to vent, leaving me with just two short blasts of retardant. The second fire extinguisher was no better. Diane and Phil frantically continued to cover the truck in a cloud of dirt.

At some point during the chaos, a large water tender roared past, and ground to a halt just in front of us. It was one of the water tenders we had worked with on our last fire.

I ran up to the driver and yelled, "Give me your fire extinguisher!" I grabbed it, ran to our truck and sprayed it with every last drop.

The tender operator told Phil, "I dumped my water back in Elko to lighten my load, but I always keep a hundred or so gallons left in the tank just in case something like this happens."

Phil and the tender operator quickly deployed the hose and knocked down the fire. The air was filled with the rubbery, steamy, smoldering smell of a car fire. We stood there staring in shock at our once shiny fire truck.

After a few minutes of recovery, we learned the tender driver's name was James and he worked with the BLM out of Bakersfield, California. He corralled a couple of cold Gatorades, and we all sat down on the side of the road, staring in disbelief at the Nickel. After we regrouped and caught our breath, we dusted ourselves off and started to survey the damage. Everything from the crew cab on back was a black, muddy, ash-covered, melted mess. There was a piece of hose sticking out of the rubble, or maybe it was part of a leather boot, I couldn't tell because everything was charred beyond recognition.

Walking over to the shade of the tender, I leaned my forehead against the cool empty hull. "Damn! This is going to look bad on my report. Why meeeee?" I yelled to no one in particular.

Phil climbed on top of our truck and used his shovel to throw down the remnants of our still smoldering two-week duffel bags. They contained all of our clothes and personal items. The tender operator used the remainder of his tank water to cool down our personal gear, or what was left of it.

I don't know what came over me, maybe the stress got to me, but I turned to Phil and said in my best professional engine boss voice, "I hope you know, since you were driving the truck when the fire started, you are responsible for all the damages."

"No way! You're kidding me!" he gasped.

"When we get back, you will fill out the required paperwork and the department will start taking installments out of your paycheck. It won't be all at once. It could take few years to pay it off," I said with a straight face.

"No freaking way!" cried Phil with a look of disbelief on his face.

"The department did it to me when I hit a bull in Texas a few years back. I had to pay for the damages to the truck *and the bull!* Hey, you're the one who wants to be a driver and engineer, now it's time to own up to that responsibility and pay the piper."

Diane whispered in my ear, "You jackass, you never quit do you?" She punched me in the shoulder and with her head down; she walked around to the other side of the truck and tried to hold back her laughter.

15 Back to Reality

I made a mental note to get back with Phil to let him know I was just kidding about paying for the damages. Fortunately, we all came through it OK, only suffering singed eyebrows. The only lasting injury will be the pain and embarrassment of burning up our fire truck. Now, I needed to take care of the realities at hand, and started to make a mental checklist of things that needed to be done.

I called the Elko Fire Dispatch to let them know what happened. To my surprise, they already knew of our predicament, and asked us if everyone was OK. Apparently, there was a surge of 911 calls from every trucker and passing car on I-80. Dispatch informed me the local fire engine that was chasing us was being cancelled and a fire investigator was en route to our location.

As we helped our new friend rack his fire hose, I said, "James, thanks for stopping. You probably saved my job. I am already in hot water with our chief and losing our truck would have been curtains for my firefighting career. I'd like to repay you for your act of kindness; nobody else stopped to help us. What's your favorite bottle of spirits? Or are you a Mormon like our Phil here, and can't imbibe in the sinful fire water?"

"Oh heck no, I enjoy a stiff drink or two to help me unwind. I am partial to Hennessy if you're buying."

"Consider it done! When I get back home I will send you a bottle. It's the least I can do," I said with a grin.

We exchanged addresses and phone numbers. As he climbed up into his tender, he turned and said, "This is the most fire I have seen all week!"

The tender pulled into traffic, and gave us a long loud blast from his air horn. We climbed into the cab, and waited for the inspector to arrive. I decided to call our chief back in Mimbres Springs, to inform him about the Triple Nickel.

"Hello Chief! The first thing I want you to know is that everyone is OK, and no one was injured."

There was a brief pause on the other end, and then he asked, "OK, Pablo, what happened to the truck?"

"Well, just a little fire damage to the back, nothing a little paint and wax can't fix."

Diane did a double take when she heard that. "A little paint and wax!" she hoarsely whispered. "Are you nuts?"

I shrugged my shoulders and went on, "The fire inspector is on his way and everything is under control. I will document everything and give you a full report when we return." We talked briefly, and Chief said he was happy everyone was OK and was glad that the truck wasn't badly damaged.

The two-day drive back home would give me time to figure out how to better explain our little fiasco. Last year, while working on an assignment, the transmission blew up. Then one night, a couple of years ago, I took out a Brahma bull on a deserted stretch of highway in Texas. As an engine boss I have acquired a reputation as being hard on the equipment. Today's incident, however, takes the cake! I know I painted a prettier picture than what was in front of us, and all hell will break loose when our chief lays eyes on the truck.

We waited in the warm shade of the cab for the inspector. I turned on the fire dispatch radio and caught the tail end of some fire radio traffic. The dispatcher was reporting multiple spot fires along some highway.

"Oh my God!" Diane blurted out. "Multiple spot fires! I can't believe it! We have just lit northern Nevada on fire! ... Again!"

She cussed, grabbed a water bottle, hopped out of the truck and huffed off into the surrounding desert.

Phil said, "Wow, I think she's kind of pissed!"

I watched as she made her way to a large boulder about six hundred feet up the side of the mountain, where she sat on the rock and started sulking. Phil got out of the truck, walked to the side of the road and tried to talk her down.

Phil shouted, "Diane, come back, it's not that bad."

When Phil climbed back in, I asked him, "What did she say?"

"I don't know exactly, I could barely hear her. She said something like *No way!*' And then something about working in a circus and needing some *me-time!*"

The investigator showed up, and we got out to examine the truck. He poked around, scribbled a few things on his fire report, and took a few photos of the carnage. He discussed what needed to be done to make our truck roadworthy again. Phil and I took the inspector's list and MacGyvered the necessary repairs. We salvaged various truck parts and duct taped the melted taillights and brake lights by removing the emergency light lenses from the front of the truck. The license plate was warped from the heat, so we flattened it out the best we could, and replaced the right rear fire damaged-tire with the spare. How the spare survived the inferno was a mystery to me. The investigator surveyed the repairs and made sure all the turn signals and brake lights were in working order. We drove forward a little to test the brakes, and he finished his report. He handed us our copy and put his copy in his satchel.

With the investigation over, we were given permission to continue homeward. In the report he stated the cause of the fire might have been due to an electrical short under our gear bags. Electrical wires have a tendency to rub and fray while driving over the rough roads. Or maybe it started when the bags shifted and came in contact with the fire pump's exhaust pipe, which extended up through the gear bag storage area. The exhaust pipe doesn't have a protective shroud, so I thought the second scenario seemed to be more realistic.

The investigator climbed in his truck, rolled down his window and said, "You better put a tarp over that! There is a hefty fine for littering in Nevada, and I don't want you to get a ticket. You guys have suffered enough."

We gathered the burnt scraps from the side of the road and placed them into a five-gallon bucket we found in the weeds.

I stood back and said sarcastically, "The only thing left is a nice paint job."

"And don't forget the wax!" Phil added.

I dug through the remains of my bag to see what was salvageable and recovered my burnt wallet from the back pocket of my burnt jeans. To my surprise it still had about eighty-three soggy dollars, along with seventy-five cents. Phil was not so lucky; most of his money was charred, and he had only twenty-two useable dollars. Unfortunately, the fire department's fuel card, my driver's license, and all my personal credit cards were melted and warped out of shape, so were Phil's. We found a slightly blackened blue plastic tarp in a forward compartment. We could barely pry the melted thing apart and covered the back of the truck with it, to prevent any loose debris from flying off while we were rolling down the highway. But more importantly, it was there to hide our embarrassment.

"Well that takes care of that," I said as I cinched down the tarp. "We sure as hell don't want to add a ticket to our little mishap here. It's going to be a no frills trip from here on out. We'll be eating all of our left over snacks, MRE's and the last of the Gatorade."

"Man, I was looking forward to a nice tasty meal," frowned Phil.

"Damn, I had my first meal all picked out too," I said. "It was a big juicy T-bone steak and a baked potato with lots of sour cream."

"We might have to panhandle for gas money. I can see us now at the intersections," said Phil. "You, all unshaven and frumpy, holding up a cardboard sign saying, *down on my luck, need cash!*"

I elbowed him, "Yeah, and your sign will say, *anything will help, I don't drink!!! God Bless.*"

Phil and I sat in the truck and waited for Diane to *find herself* and come down off the mountain. While we were waiting, we heard on the fire dispatch radio that the fires reported earlier were located along a highway, way north of here, somewhere near Jackpot, Nevada. It had been determined that they were started by a cattle truck dragging a chain, causing sparks. Those sparks in turn set the roadside grass on fire. The dispatcher stated the fires were in the process of being extinguished.

"Hmm, I could get some mileage on this one," I said while rubbing my grizzled chin. "I need to come up with a funny spoof to play on Diane about those fires, which she thinks *we caused.*"

I was getting excited about the possibilities to prank Diane.

"Boy, I could get real twisted with this one ... Phil, help me out!"

"Ohhhh, no way José! Back home at the fire station I saw what happened to a guy who messed with her. I'll tell you what, it wasn't pretty! Diane doesn't get mad she gets even! Pablo, you are on your own on this one. I don't want any part of your shenanigans."

Just then the truck door swung open, and Diane jumped into the back seat.

"Ahhh, I feel so much better!" she sighed. "I take back the stuff I said about working with clowns. You guys are all right." She smiled, reached in her back pocket and triumphantly held up her shiny, unburned credit card! "Who wants ice cream?"

16 Czechoslovakian Playboys

With the sun behind us, we started to head for home. We found a little ice cream stand in the last town before we entered Utah. With soft serve in our bellies, and a full tank of gas, we were on the road again.

"Whoa!" I shouted, as I stared straight into Phil's eyes, "Utah is a dry state on Sundays! If we don't find a good bottle of Scotch before Utah, I might have to hurt somebody!"

Phil felt a Vietnam flashback brewing and said, "Don't worry Boss, I'm on it *Like Barbeque On Chicken!*"

It didn't take us long to round up some booze. Finding liquor in Nevada is never a problem. I also picked up a few quality cigars and we hit the road again. Our next stop would be in Utah, where we needed to buy some cheap clothes and find a place to spend the night.

I turned to Diane and asked, "How much do you think you have left on your card?"

"It's kind of hard to say, I might be right at my limit," she replied with a frown. "Maybe you should have asked that before you bought that big $45 bottle of Scotch with your surviving cash."

I knew that hefty bottle of 12-year-old, single malt Scotch was money well spent, and I couldn't wait to taste it.

It was around 16:00 when we pulled into Mona, a small town south of Salt Lake. We still had time to buy some clothes, bathroom essentials and get a room for the night. As wildland firefighters, we are required to take 12 hours off at the end of our assignment, and I was looking forward to the down time. It would be our first decent night's rest in two weeks. Unfortunately, we had absolutely nothing to wear except the clothes on our backs. They were pretty dirty when we left base camp, but after attacking the flames that consumed the Triple Nickel, they stunk even worse.

It was Sunday, getting late, and the only stores open in Mona were a drug store, and a mom and pop second hand clothing store, called *Bee Boos-Better Than New*. Phil and I were counting our remaining money when Diane asked if she could contribute.

I immediately replied, "No way Missy, us guys got it under control. By the way, you may need to bail us out for gas money on the ride home."

We all walked into the second hand shop and immediately experienced a trip back into the '60s. I detected a slight smell of incense and patchouli oil, to go along with that familiar thrift store funk. There were dated concert posters on the walls, the Monterey Pop Festival, Newport Folk Fest, and some from the Fillmore Auditorium. Other posters featured rock bands from that era, like Frank Zappa and the Mothers of Invention and the Velvet Underground. On the back wall were posters of The Grateful Dead and Jimi Hendrix. Colorful ones of Bob Marley and the Wailers along with Big Brother and the Holding Company hung behind the cash register. All classic '60s and '70s stuff. You name it; Be Boo had it up on the walls.

As we wandered farther in, we found tables loaded with garage sale cast-offs, assorted junk, and tons of costume jewelry.

We rummaged through the accumulated chaos when Diane came across some old metal lunch boxes. She held up a box with a picture of Quick Draw McGraw and Baba Looey. In the other hand she held up one with a picture of Johnny Quest.

She sorted through the collection a little more. "Look at this, an old Mickey Mouse School Bus, complete with thermos!"

Phil let loose a loud whoop! He found a lunch box from the old TV show *Emergency!* It was a little rusty and had a dent on one side, but it had a picture of Johnny and Roy and Rescue 51.

Phil was excited, "Can I have it, please, please, pleeeeease!" he begged.

I wagged my finger at him and in my best *mom-voice*, said, "Phillip, you know we came in here to buy clothes. If you can't behave yourself, you will have to wait out in the car!"

He frowned, put the lunch box down and reluctantly headed to the clothes section.

"Wow! Far out!" gushed Diane. "Hey, Pablo, it's like back in the day!" She held up an Easy Rider leather fringed motorcycle jacket while sporting some cheesy rhinestone sunglasses.

I laughed and started rummaging around for some shirts and pants. Since we were low on cash, we decided to buy the cheapest clothes we could get our hands on, and soon found some inexpensive retro duds.

I picked out a blue and green paisley polyester shirt with a big pointed collar. It reminded me of stuff I wore back in my younger days. Back then we thought we were way cool, and I had to laugh, seeing how ridiculous they looked today. A pair of plaid bell bottomed pants and a wide, lime-green leatherette belt completed my ensemble.

Phil picked up a Dashiki tribal shirt but decided turquoise was not his color. He sized up a tie-dyed T-shirt with a peace symbol and held it up against his chest.

"Too small, too bad," he frowned and tossed it back in the pile.

Finally, spotting a purple long sleeve polyester shirt with white daisies, he sniffed it, gave it a reassuring nod and put it in his basket. He then started to look for some pants.

In no time, he proudly held up a pair of red corduroy hip huggers and picked out a wide white belt.

"Perfect! Not a bad get-up for $12, if I do say so myself."

"We may look like freaks but who is going to know us in Utah? No one will ever see us again," I remarked.

"I don't know about that," announced Phil. "I might run into a distant third cousin up here, and *boom,* pictures of me and my hippie firefighter friends will be splattered all over Facebook."

We walked up to the counter to pay for our duds. Bee Boo cheerfully rung us, up and I couldn't help but think the guy had seen it all. He was an aging hippie, slight in stature, about 5 feet 6 inches tall with a short greying ponytail and a goatee. He was wearing a plain white cotton tunic, and around his neck were some Hindu Rudraksha beads.

"Nice place you have here," I said.

"It's a living. I came here about 12 years ago. Not much demand for retro stuff in Utah, though. Internet sales are my saving grace. I might head back to the Bay Area ... lived there all my life. The weather here is so nice though, it will be hard to leave. The Bay area is always cold and wet. My arthritis just kills me back there."

"The Bay Area huh?" I asked. "I bet you have a few good stories."

"Man, the '60s ... now those were the days. The vibe was cosmic back then. I had a small head shop on Haight Street. There were eight of us living in one small apartment. We were penniless and impoverished, but we didn't give a shit about material things. Just being there was wealth beyond compare."

"You were living the life huh?" I smiled.

"Man was I, I remember one day Janis Joplin came into my shop to buy some rolling papers. She was so unassuming and down to earth and had such a great smile. I just stared at her the entire time. I was so smitten with her presence, and loved her music. When it came time to pay, I told her the papers were on the house."

"Wow, Janis Joplin, I'm jealous!" gasped Diane.

"And dig this, before she left, she slid one of her bangles from her wrist and gave it to me! I was floored!"

He held up his wrist and proudly showed off the bangle.

"No kidding? Far Out! Can I see it?" asked Diane.

He slid it off of his wrist and handed it to her. Diane put it on, picked up a wooden spoon, pretending it was a microphone and immediately started to sing *Piece of My Heart!*

"That was the last time I saw her. She died in 1970," frowned Bee Boo.

"Did you see any concerts at the Fillmore?" I asked pointing at the posters.

"God, the music scene was so epic. If the concerts weren't free, they were really cheap, maybe $3 to get in. Backing up the music on stage were the light shows! They were so trippy and fantastic! That whole era was mind blowing! I can't believe I was a part of it. I toked in it, danced in it; I was neck deep in it. Man it was a great time to be alive!"

"I'm even more jealous," said Diane.

"Unfortunately that whole music scene was over way too soon. Now, the Haight has been bought up by a bunch of affluent SOBs, and all the shops are high-end boutiques, snobby restaurants, and coffee houses. It's a bummer."

We ended up telling him about our recent escapades as wildland firefighters, and surprisingly, despite the paltry price on the tags, Bee Boo gave us 50 percent off! Diane handed the bangle back to him and we escaped without spending too much of our precious dough.

Because we couldn't stand our own stink, we altered our plan, walked outside and changed our clothes right there in the parking lot, not noticing the onlookers gawking at us from afar. Phil and I looked up at each other and burst into laughter. Diane rounded the rear of the truck and almost peed her pants.

"You guys look like the Czechoslovakian playboys from the old *Saturday Night Live* sketch!" she laughed while pointing at us.

"Yes we do. *A couple of Wild and Crazy Guys!*" I laughed.

I looked at Diane and said, "You're lookin' pretty dapper yourself Missy."

She was wearing old camouflage cargo pants, a red bandana do-rag, and a T-shirt that said, "*Game over man!*"

"You look like you just stepped out of the movie *Aliens*, looking all Vasquez and shit," I said.

Phil waltzed over to her and quoted a line from the movie, "Have you ever been mistaken for a man?"

She came back with, "No! Have you?"

We all cracked up!

Donning our brightly colored mix-matched paisleys and plaids, we ventured into the adjoining drug store to buy toiletries and snacks. Some of the curious locals followed us.

When it came time to pay, the lady at the counter dryly asked Phil, "You boys aren't from around here, are you?"

Phil smiled his *happy to be here grin* and while handing over his last few dollars and proudly stated, "No ma'am, we're *firefighters* from *New-Mex-i-co!*"

She looked us up and down again and deadpanned, "Well if you boys believe that, I've got some real nice ocean front property to sell you this side of Salt Lake."

We all had a good laugh, decline her offer, and paraded out of the drug store in search of a cheap motel.

17 The Safari Room

We drove down the main drag searching for a motel that looked affordable. Up the road we saw it, the Safari Motel and Motor Lodge. It looked like it came straight out of the '50s. We pulled up to the lobby and the three of us walked into the office with the rank smell of burnt truck and a hint of patchouli oil following us. I was pretty sure we resembled immigrants fresh off the boat. With credit card in hand, Diane approached the front desk.

A well-dressed elderly lady was standing anxiously behind the front desk, and with some hesitation at the sight and smell of us asked, "Do you need *help*?" She quickly corrected herself and said, "How can I help you?"

"We would like a room, please," said Diane.

"Two or three rooms?" she replied.

Being short of cash I blurted out, "Just one!"

The lady told us, "We only have a few rooms remaining ad each room has only one queen sized bed."

Prior to arriving in Mona, we discussed the motel arrangements. Since we all work at a fire station that has one coed bunkroom, we felt comfortable sharing one room. Not to mention, we were short on cash.

The woman at the front desk paused, looked at the strange trio in front of her, and reluctantly allowed us to sign in. She stated in no uncertain terms, "I want you people to know, *this is not that kind of Motel.*"

Phil took her hand as she handed him our keys, "I reassure you ma'am," he said politely as he leaned in a little closer, "*We are not those kind of people.*"

As we sashayed out of the lobby I couldn't resist the opportunity to say loud enough for the lady to hear, "Phil, do we need to go get more scented massage oil?"

Diane turned to me and hoarsely whispered, "Don't make me cram my fist down your smart-ass throat!"

We climbed in the truck and looked for our room. We found it around the back, near the dumpsters. I think the desk clerk put us there so no one could see us.

"Massage oil!" Phil laughed. "You never quit do you, Pablo?"

"I can't help myself," I proudly replied.

"I have to admit that was pretty funny," smiled Diane.

We opened the door at the end of the building and were faced with a long hallway decked out in an African motif. Cheesy African shields and spears lined the walls.

Phil said as we passed by, "If the natives get restless, we can defend ourselves with this stuff hanging on the walls."

Phil keyed the doorknob, threw open the door, and we immediately fell silent. There was a fake zebra skin hanging on the wall, a tacky leopard skin bedspread covering the bed, several homemade sock monkeys lying on the pillows, and the mini bar was stocked with bamboo-drinking glasses.

I turned to Diane and grunted, "Me Tarzan, ooh ooh ahh!"

"Me Jane, ooh ahh!" Diane grunted back.

"Me Cheetah!" cried Phil.

With our arms over our heads, we all started to make screeching monkey noises and danced around the room. Phil started to jump up and down on the bed, and I nailed him with a flying stuffed monkey. After laughing ourselves to tears, we gathered our meager possessions and settled down for the evening.

I was the first one to jump in the shower and cranked the faucets on full blast. The bathroom filled with steam and I didn't hold back on the soap or shampoo. While lathering up, I sang the Deep Purple song, *Smoke on the Water.*

After a few minutes I could hear Phil pounding on the door. "Don't take so long in there! You're using up all the hot water and the natives are getting restless."

I exited with a towel wrapped around my waist, and grabbed another towel and began to dry off my head. Phil squeezed past me and eagerly shut the door and turned on the shower.

Diane gave me a wolf whistle and said, "Hey G.I. Joe, you go for boom-boom? Five dollar, you holler! Love you long time!"

I responded with my best John Wayne voice, "Well Missy, I'm a little short on cash right now. Can you spot me a freebie?"

Suddenly, a stuffed sock monkey hit me right between the eyes.

After we all took turns experiencing hot shower bliss, we put on our retro clothes, and decided to order out for a pizza. Diane looked in the phone book and to our surprise; there were three pizza places in Mona!

She ran her finger down the page, cleared her throat and announced, "These are our choices, listed in alphabetical order ... *THE ARCADE, Pizza & Games.* It says here that they are famous for two pies, one is called *The Addiction,* and another is called *The Home Slice.* Sounds like pizza for the younger crowd. Then we have, *MONA-CHELLI'S, Mona's First and Finest Home Made Pizza Pie!* Boy, that sounds homemade delicious! Unfortunately, they are closed on Sundays. Last but not least, we have *ZZZAPPA'S!!! Greazzzy and Cheezzzy ... Freee Deeelivery!!!"*

"I'm all for Zzzappa's, and extra cheezzze pleazzze," I voted. "Any preference Phil?"

"Zzzappa's is fine with me. If it's edible I'm all over it."

"And you can't beat *freee deeelivery!* I'll call the number and place our order," said Diane

I filled the ice bucket from the noisy ice machine down the hallway and got a couple of root beers for Phil. I made my way though the sliding glass door, out to our front patio and poured a round of drinks. The patio had two mismatched motel chairs, a small metal table, and was landscaped with a border of gravel, white washed rocks, and wilting vegetation. I borrowed a chair from our next-door neighbor and as I sat down on the warm metal chair, I could feel the heat emanating from the desert and a cool stream of air conditioning flowing through the crack in the sliding glass door.

After much anticipation, we heard the rattle of a mufflerless car. The pizza guy had arrived! We waved him over to our patio, and he rumbled right up to the sidewalk. The delivery guy's old beater car was rusted down past the primer and looked like it was in worse shape than the Triple Nickel.

With dark moppish hair hanging down over his eyes, the pizza guy had an unshaven patchy beard, and a half burnt cigarette dangling from his lips. With a rebellious attitude and a teenage slouch, he shuffled over to us and handed Phil the precious cargo.

Despite the fact that the words *Freee Deeelivery!!!* were printed across his rumpled red T-shirt, Diane decided to tip the guy anyway; in hopes he could afford a better set of wheels.

We placed the pizzas on the small patio table, flipped the top open and dug in like this was our first meal after a month-long hunger strike!

"Isn't it way cool that in *Any-Town USA*, you can order out for pizza?" said Phil as he wolfed down a slice. "Pizza, it's so wholesome, so All-American!"

"I don't know what it is about pizza, the way it smells, the crispy crust, the cardiac clogging greasy pepperoni, and all that gooey drippy cheese," I said. "I could eat pizza every-day of the week."

Diane held up a slice to examine its excellence and said, "Not to mention it has the potential to scald the skin right off the roof of your mouth! It's just so dangerous and magical. I'm glad I ordered two!"

"I don't know about you, but I think we should have ordered three," mumbled Phil, gorging on his third slice.

With full bellies, Diane and I poured another three fingers of Scotch over ice, fired up a couple of good cigars, sat back and gazed into the glow of the surrounding desert.

After two dry weeks, the Scotch tasted great and went down easy.

Phil took a long pull on his root beer and said hoarsely, "Smoooooth."

I looked over to him, raised my glass, and laughed.

Diane took a long drag on her stogie, sent aloft a few smoke rings and said, "All we need now is a Jacuzzi!"

We polished off our drinks and cigars and went inside. Diane offered to sleep on the floor, but Phil and I quickly rebuked her. Since our sleeping bags somehow managed to survive the fire, we elected to sleep on the floor instead.

The soft carpet, extra blankets, pillows, stuffed sock monkeys, and *air conditioning*, will be a luxury compared to what we have been experiencing during the past two weeks. I figured we should show some chivalry ... after all it was Diane who paid for the room and bought the pizzas!

"If you guys want to be macho, be my guest," she said eyeing the clean bed.

Surprisingly enough, the three of us sat up until the wee hours, talking and laughing, reminiscing about the events that had taken place on our two-week fire assignment.

"Remember two weeks ago, when all of this all started?" I said.

"Yeah, it took us almost 24 hours to get to the fire command post from Mimbres Springs," recalled Diane.

"It doesn't seem like it has been two weeks. Time sure does fly," said Phil.

"Remember the first fire we were assigned to when we got there? It was the TP Fire," Diane said.

"We never did find out what the TP stood for," said Phil.

"How about this one ... *Trashed Pablo*," I said with bloodshot eyes and slurred speech.

I laid down on the floor and the last thing I remember was, the blankets and pillows were so soft, the air conditioning was nice and cool, the room was a getting blurry, and started to spin counterclockwise.

18 The Middle Sister Café

While lying on a chaise lounge in the shade of some coconut palms, I woke to the sound of waves gently breaking on the shore. The sun sparkled on a shimmering sea, and the air was pleasantly humid, and smelled like the salty ocean.

A native gal approached and handed me an ice cold Mai Tai, garnished with a maraschino cherry and a little pink umbrella. There were two other women surrounding me. One was rubbing sun tan oil on my shoulders, and another was giving me a foot massage. The one rubbing my shoulders had a flower in her hair and a lei around her neck. Her skin was the color of mahogany, and was as smooth as silk. As she got closer, I detected the fragrance of tropical flowers.

Strangely, instead of a grass skirt, the girl was wearing chaps. I suddenly noticed they were all wearing sawyer chaps!

How strange, I thought to myself.

"Am I in heaven?" I asked the one massaging my feet.

She looked at me and giggled, "No Howlie Pablo, you are in Utah!"

Just then I felt a nudge on my back, and I opened my eyes. The two beady black eyes of the stuffed sock monkey were staring back at me.

Slowly awakening, I sat up and grunted, "Damn, another one of my dreams."

The curtains were closed, and the room was just barely lit. Looking around I tried to get my bearings. With much disappointment, I realized we were still at the Safari Motel.

"It must have been better than the Wild Bunch nightmare," Diane laughed, as she packed away her meager belongings. "You were talking in your sleep. You said something about someone putting more sun tan oil on your shoulders, and it sounded like you were *really enjoying it!*"

"Yes I was. I was dreaming I was in Hawaii. No! On second thought, it was ... heaven, Yeah, I was in heaven," I said with a smile.

"How was it? Is heaven all that it's cracked up to be?"

"Missy! If that was a snippet of what heaven will be like, you can off me right now."

"That good huh? Well mister, welcome back to the real world. We have to pack up and move out, it's getting late."

Just then we heard a purring sound coming up from under a sleeping bag in the corner of the room.

"This boy can sleep anywhere," I said, as I shook Phil with a vengeance. "Rise and shine pussy cat, we need to vamoose, we're burning daylight."

He got up, shook his head and wandered to the bathroom.

After washing up, and brushing his teeth, Phil quickly emerged from the bathroom and waltzed over to the front window. He forcefully threw open the curtains, and struck a Superman pose, while being silhouetted by the blinding sunlight.

"Heww doggie, I feel good! That was some mighty fine sleeping. I feel so refreshed, so invigorated, I feel super!" he shouted while stretching his arms upward.

He walked over to the dresser and held up a half empty bottle of Scotch.

"It looks like you party animals were doing a little dancing with the devil last night."

I squinted at him and said, "Not so loud Mister Happy Pants!"

"I'm kinda pissed at you!" snorted Diane. "You downed the lion's share of Scotch last night!"

"Don't I know it," I moaned, as I tried to drive the ashtray taste of stale Scotch from my parched mouth. "My head is killing me. You know how much I love that stuff."

I grabbed the bottle, stuffed it in my plastic shopping bag, and said defensively, "Hey, I may have drank a little more than my share but I didn't see you holding back Missy!"

"OK, you got me on that one, thank God for Phil, at least we have a designated driver," said Diane holding her head.

Within minutes Phil gathered up his personal belongings and made his way out to the truck.

While gathering my stuff, I looked at the clock on the nightstand. "10:04! Geez! I can't remember ever sleeping in this late."

"Too much time in heaven," Diane smiled sarcastically.

We checked the room one last time, looking for anything that might get left behind.

As we exited, I stopped in my tracks when I laid eyes on the Triple Nickel.

"I can't believe the way she looks. She looks so sad."

Diane chimed in, "At least we have a functional truck to get us home. It could be worse, we could be on a Greyhound bus right now."

As I scanned the truck, I remembered we needed to get a new spare tire. "We can't drive all the way back to New Mexico without a spare."

"I agree," said Diane. "That would be stupid. Without a spare we would be asking for trouble. The one thing we don't need is more trouble."

Phil gushed, "I did a quick truck check, cinched down the tarp, washed the windshield, and checked all the fluids and tire pressure. We're good to go. This is going to be a great day! I feel like a rooster in a hen house!" He tucked his hands into his armpits and started flapping his elbows.

With his head tilted back, he gave us a rousing *"Cock-a-doodle-do!"*

Diane and I turned and looked at each other, and with bloodshot eyes I said, "He must be from another planet! Well, pull up to the lobby, Mr. Cock-a-doodle-do, so we can turn in the room key."

"Wait!" shouted Diane. She hopped out of the truck and dashed into the room. She emerged with a stuffed monkey in hand. "I left a ten-dollar bill and a little note saying I took the monkey for good luck. I told them they could bill my card if that wasn't enough."

She hopped in the back seat and held up the little guy, wiggled him and said, "Booga, booga, booga! What should we name him?"

We pulled around to the front lobby and Phil grabbed the motel key and said, "I got this."

Phil hopped out of the truck and waltzed over to the lobby. I had to laugh as he strutted like James Brown, in his red bellbottom hip huggers and purple daisy shirt.

"Hey, Happy Pants! Make sure you bring back the receipt," shouted Diane. "I need the fire district to pay me back for all the expenses."

Phil came back and I asked, "Did everything check out?"

"Everything is groovy baby! We're cool! It's far out man!"

"Hey that's my line," yelled Diane.

Giggling, he hopped in the truck and I put the receipt in an envelope and stowed it in the glove compartment.

Phil said, "I told the lady that we had a wonderful stay and she wished us a safe journey home, I asked where we could get a tire replaced and she said the Four Star Truck Stop is about 40 miles down the highway, right next door to the Middle Sister Café and bakery."

"Perfect! Let's roll!" I said. "We can gas up, tire up and grub up, all at the same time."

In little less than an hour, we pulled up to the truck stop. There were big rigs everywhere, not to mention, a parking lot full of cars, and I couldn't help but think this was unusual for just a wide spot in the road.

I walked into the main office and explained our dilemma to the truck stop manager. He looked me up and down, glanced at our truck, and shook his head.

"No problem, I will get one of my guys on it, toot sweet," he grinned.

Phil unbolted the spare and wheeled the lumpy thing over to the shop.

We pulled around and parked in front of the Middle Sister Café. As we moseyed to the front door, people were staring out the windows at the sight in front of them.

"Are those folks staring at us or the truck?" Diane asked.

"Probably both! It's not every day you see Czechoslovakian Playboys emerging from a burnt up fire truck."

"True Dat!" she replied.

Just before we opened the front door, Phil smiled and flashed the onlookers a righteous peace sign.

The Middle Sister Café was a sight to behold! There were objects and artifacts nailed and attached to every inch of wall space, with even more stuff hanging from the rafters!

Framed autographed photos of the famous and not so famous, as well as postcards from all over the world, were mounted to the wall near the cash register. A trombone, two wooden tennis racquets and several deep sea fishing poles were mounted above us.

"Look at this!" said Diane, "It's so tacky, yet wonderful," and she lightly stroked a velvet painting of Elvis.

We were flabbergasted with the spectacle. On several small shelves were signed World Series baseballs, old *Texaco* oil cans, and a smattering of bowling trophies.

Phil giggled and pointed to a shelf, "It's the *Book of Mormon* next to the *Joy of Sex!* How funny!"

Looking down the back hallway, there was a mounted elk head over the kitchen door. Christmas ornaments, old keys, and large fishing lures, hung from his antlers, and he proudly wore aviator sunglasses and had a corncob pipe sticking out of his mouth.

"He kinda looks like an elk version of General MacArthur!" I laughed.

The café was much bigger on the inside than what it looked like from the front. The booths had old church pews cut to size, and the tabletops were a testament of time, as patrons carved decades of names and dates with their pocketknives.

"Hokey smokes!" stammered Phil, "I've never seen anything like this!"

"Far out!" said Diane. "This is awesome!"

I asked the hostess, "Do you let your customers add to the collection or is it up to the management?"

She proudly told us, "Our customers donated 100 percent of those items. We do, however, have the right to refuse anything that we feel is off color, in bad taste or just plain stupid. This place has been around since the '40s and from what I hear, way back when ... someone ran a little short of cash when it came time to pay the bill, so he went to his car and gave the owner five cans of Texaco motor oil and a new Chicago Cardinals football pendant ... and the rest is history."

"Can we put something on the wall?" I asked.

"Knock yourself out," she smiled.

I ran out to the truck and came back with three things. I thumbtacked the crappy map with the big red *X*, a half-burnt $20 bill and the blackened wire cage left behind by the smoke jumpers.

With my hand on my hips, I admired my handiwork and said, "That outta do it."

The hostess said, "I bet there is a great story that goes along with that stuff."

"I can't even begin to tell you," groaned Diane shaking her head.

"Maybe you should write a book," the girl replied.

"Maybe *YOU* should write a book about *this* place!" laughed Diane. "There must be a million stories hanging off of these walls! Maybe we both should write a book."

Just then, we got the OK to sit at one of the booths. We slid into the butt polished church pews and the waitress handed us some menus.

"Can I start you all with something to whet your whistle?" she asked.

She was a tiny thing, about 5-foot nothing, had a head of curly red hair, with most of it tied in a ponytail. She was about 25 years old, had a splash of freckles across her nose and was as perky as a chipmunk. Her attire consisted of faded blue jeans and a light blue, long-sleeved checkered shirt, with the sleeves rolled up. Around her waist was a white apron that had three pockets, one for a menu pad, one for extra napkin wrapped silverware, and the third one was bulging with tips. Written on a little pin-on nametag was, *This is your lucky day! You are being waited on by, JULIE!*

"Diane and I will have coffee, Phil what would you like?"

"Some lemonade would hit the spot," he flirted, giving Julie his best cheesy smile.

"Coming right up!" quipped Julie with a blush. She giggled, spun around, and disappeared into the crowded café.

Breakfast Served All Day was printed in bold letters across the top of the menu. It was almost noon, so we could choose between the best of both worlds.

"The price is right, I hope the quality is good," said Diane.

"You're right! The prices are downright cheap, no wonder the place is packed!"

Julie came back with the coffee and lemonade and asked, "So what are you-all hankering for?" She pulled out her menu pad and pointed her pen at me.

"I'll take your *Breakfast Special*, three fried eggs, over easy, hash browns, a slice of country ham and some of your homemade sourdough toast."

Diane went next, "I'll have your country-fried chicken and waffle dinner, mashed potatoes, and some of your red-eye gravy."

"Good enough," she said. "And how about you, Mister Purple Daisy Shirt?"

Phil smiled and said, "Well, little Miss Ponytail, I'll have the breakfast steak, medium rare, but mostly rare, home fries and a short stack of sourdough pancakes with huckleberry syrup."

She looked right at Phil, smiled, and said with a wink, "*I'm on it like wool on a sheep.*"

We all laughed, and I said, "Is she related to you Phil? That sounds like something you would say."

They must have had maniacs working in the kitchen because the wait was very short. I looked at the table with all of that food, and eagerly tucked my napkin under my chin.

Phil and I looked at each other and said at the same time. "Let the sinning begin!"

My country ham slice was as big as the plate it came on, and was homemade delicious.

Diane said, "I can't describe how crispy and juicy this chicken is, and whatever they used in the spices for the crispy coating is sending me to the moon!"

"How's your steak?" I asked Phil.

He held up a piece and showed us. "Charred on the outside and bloody in the middle. Good golly, it don't get much better than this!"

While savoring the entire Middle Sister Café experience, Diane said. "I might have to come back on vacation just to eat here again."

"That little stuffed monkey of yours must be bringing us good luck," I said and wiped my mustache with a napkin.

Diane paid the bill and stuffed the receipt in her cargo pants pocket. We headed for the garage, and the mechanic brought the spare tire to the truck. Phil crawled under the charred beast, and I helped him mount the tire.

Diane joined us carrying a white bakery bag containing a dozen fresh peach empanadas. "That bakery is something else. God I love the smell of a bakery! There were shelves full of fresh baked bread and stacks of tortillas, and they had a large glass display case filled with pastries, donuts, cakes, and pies. Absolutely incredible!"

"I think the sunshine is extra sunny, and the air is extra pure at this wide spot in the road," I marveled. "It's like we are in a *Vortex of Goodness!*"

"Maybe we are experiencing another slice of heaven," said Diane.

"I think so! When we get back in the truck, I am going to circle this spot on the map and write *Vortex of Goodness!*"

Diane went into the truck stop office to pay for the spare tire. She came out and put the receipt in the envelope, and stowed it in the glove box.

"Man! That tire wasn't cheap! It cost 275 bucks. After paying for fuel, my clothes, the drug store, the hotel, pizza, breakfast, peach empanadas, and the new tire, it looks like I'm maxed out on my card. You guys might actually need to panhandle for gas money come Phoenix."

"Crap, you just burst my bubble," I frowned.

"Well, it looks like life in heaven can get a little pricey," said Diane.

We all climbed in the Nickel and headed south.

19 Bryce Canyon

It was approaching 14:00 as we pulled away from the truck stop and headed down Interstate 15. We decided to camp overnight somewhere, because camping would cost a lot less than a hotel. Thankfully, our camp stove and all of our sleeping bags were still intact, and the weather was holding up nicely.

"How about Bryce Canyon?" said Diane. "I hear it is a spectacular sight. A bucket list destination."

"I've never heard of it, have you, Phil?"

"Oh heck yeah! My uncle and cousin, who used to live in Panguitch, would get an elk permit every year. I would come up to hunt with them when I was in high school. Bryce is in a really remote part of the state, not close to much except Panguitch, but well worth the drive. Some say it is equally as beautiful as the Grand Canyon."

"Naw, the Grand Canyon?"

"Yeah, some say it is the place where God tried his hand at sculpture. It has miles and miles of spires, pinnacles, and rock formations called Hoodoos, a natural wonder of the world. Quite spectacular if you ask me."

We took a vote, "All in favor of Bryce Canyon raise your hand." Three hands and a monkey paw shot up, "It looks like Bryce Canyon gets unanimous approval."

I found Bryce Canyon on the map and said, "Yup! Pretty straight forward, it looks like it'll be easy going, and not too far out of the way."

"I've heard that one before," said Diane.

"Pipe down in the peanut gallery, Missy! I have this one under control. Besides, this map is a heck of a lot better than the crappy map we had before."

The little monkey appeared between Phil and me.

"Booga, booga, booga!" he said.

"Pipe down too, ya little fur ball. By the way, what is the little guy's name, anyway?"

"*Mortie*," said Diane, "*Mortie the monkey*. He looks kind of like a Mortie, doesn't he?"

"OK, Mortie, tell the lady in the back seat we are *not* going to get lost."

Mortie shook his head yes and clamored "Booga, booga, booga," to Diane.

"Take Route 20 East, to Highway 89 South."

Phil said, "You got it Boss, I know the way."

Eventually we drove through Panguitch and followed Route 12 East.

The directions were spot on, and before we knew it, we were pulling up to the front entrance. After we chitchatted with the ranger at the main gate, he handed us an overnight camping permit, a map and some literature of the area. I think he felt sorry for us and waved us through, free of charge.

We scouted around for the Visitor's Center and I began to feel a sense of urgency overcome me.

"We need to find a restroom pronto; my bladder is ready to burst."

"Must be from trying to re-hydrate after your dance with the devil last night," admonished Phil.

"No, it's because I'm old!" I told him, "I can't wait till you get old Phil."

Phil pulled over at the first restroom he spotted. I made it just in time. When I emerged, I heard some raucous laughter from around the corner. Diane and Phil were having an animated conversation with three guys next to our truck, and behind them was a nice shiny Type 6 USFS (Utah State Forest Service) wildland truck.

The older guy said, "I'm Johnny, a Forest Service Ranger and wildland firefighter. We work on severity patrols in and around Bryce Canyon during the summer season. This is Ranger Vincent and Ranger Jennifer."

"Pleased to meet you, Vincent."

"*Vince,* please, nobody calls me Vincent except my mother."

Vincent ... Vince was about 5 foot ten, in his early 30s, and looked like he was born to be a Forest Service Ranger. He had a good build, was as fit as a Navy Seal, and looked like he could carry an 80-pound pack to the back of beyond and then some. Jennifer was taller, about 6 feet, with straight, shoulder length, sandy blond hair. She was about the same age as Vince, had fair skin, and had a great smile. She was wearing a Smokey Bear, wide brimmed hat that had some wildflowers and native grasses tucked in the hatband. They both had a way about them that exuded a love for the great outdoors.

"Jennifer?" I asked.

"Jen," she said, and gave me a handshake that could've crushed walnuts.

Johnny, on the other hand, was shorter than the two, about 5 feet 6. He was older and when he removed his hat I could see he was balding slightly and had deep widow peaks, with greying temples and side burns. He was their leader and did most of the talking.

"We've been assigned to keep an eye out for wild fires in the park. We caught a few this season, some started by careless smokers, another one started by an unattended campfire. We had one fire last week that was started by someone who parked his car in some tall grass. I'm sure you guys know how quickly things can get out of hand during the dry season."

We all nodded in agreement. I noticed how Johnny kept glancing past me looking at our truck.

Johnny went on to say, "When we are not working wildland, we are members of the Technical Rescue Team (TRT) and are called in to assist with any rescues that involve rappelling, to get to hikers that have gotten themselves in a jam. We sometimes carry out an injured hiker using the Stokes Basket. We even had to extricate people from cars that went over the edge. Those were pretty much body recoveries."

"Did they go over the edge by accident?" asked Diane.

"No, not really, a person would really have to work to get their car off of the roadway. They were mostly suicidal maniacs."

"Diane here, is a member of our fire department's technical rescue team," Phil said.

"I can relate," replied Diane. "Technical rescues can get a little complicated, and most of the time the rescues are at night, or take place in real crappy weather."

"Tell me about it," nodded Jen. "Rarely does somebody get lost or hurt on a nice sunny day."

Vince added, "When we aren't putting out fires or saving lives, we empty trash cans, clean restrooms, stock toilet paper and talk with the tourists. We give them directions and answer their questions. It's a very transient population that comes and goes through Bryce Canyon. We rarely see a person who spends more than a couple days here. You guys are the first wildland guys we've seen here."

Johnny was getting a little antsy, put his hands in his pockets and started to rock back and forth, and finally asked, "Ok, guys, tell us about your truck!"

"Johnny, I knew it was only a matter of time before you brought it up, I have to admit our truck looks a little under the weather. She experienced a little fire herself!" I laughed.

We went over and sat in the shade of a ramada and told them the tale of the Triple Nickel. Phil really got into the drama of it all. He began spewing about how we were driving home and our truck caught fire on the interstate! Phil went on to tell them about the second hand clothes store and the Safari Motel.

The Rangers were laughing so hard I thought they were going to piss their pants.

"You guys have been on quite the adventure!" laughed Johnny.

"Yes we have," grinned Diane.

"I don't want to be a party pooper," I said, "but we need to find a campsite. The sun is getting low."

"I can tell you where you can find the *perfect* campsite," Vince said. "It is not on the tourist map; only we know where it is. We camp there sometimes when we feel the need to get out of the bunkhouse." He pointed to our map and said, "Take the main road past Rainbow Point. Look for flagging on a newly cut forest service road. Look for a makeshift gate that has a sign on it saying KEEP OUT. It has a lock on it. It looks locked, but it's not. Go through the gate and re-set the lock and chain. Drive a little-ways to a large boulder on the left hand side of the road. Park behind the boulder, kind of close to the edge of the cliff."

"Set your brake and chock your wheels with a big rock so your rig doesn't go over the edge," warned Jen. "Then walk around the boulder to a nice, flat, soft sandy area where you can bed down for the night. This is the absolute best spot in the park. It has a Multi-Million Dollar View!"

"We will check in on you guys after we make our rounds," Johnny said. He honked his horn as they drove away, and we headed off in the opposite direction.

After parking the truck on a slight incline, about 15 feet from the edge, we set the parking brake, chocked the wheels with a big rock, and hauled our meager possessions to the other side of the boulder. The secret spot was all they said it would be and then some. The area was flat as a Marine's crew cut, with a six-inch layer of red sand. The campsite was surrounded by a stand of Douglas and White firs, and the view to the north was to *die for.*

"This must be the highest point in the park," Phil gasped.

As the sun was getting low in the sky, the entire amphitheater of hoodoos, pinnacles, and spires started to glow, as if set on fire. "Wow, this is another slice of heaven, you were right about Bryce Canyon," I said to Phil. "Despite burning up the truck, this is the best wildland campaign I have *ever* been on."

Diane fired up the camp stove and made some coffee. While sitting on our sleeping bags and poking at our MRE pouches, we couldn't help but marvel at the mind-boggling glory of the natural world.

Just then, the Rangers walked around the big boulder and grinned, "Well, what did we tell you guys?"

"I didn't even hear you pull in," I said with a start.

"That's because that big boulder back there blocks a lot of noise at this camp," explained Johnny. "That's just one of the reasons why this place is so peaceful."

"It sure meets all of our expectations and then some," Diane smiled.

The Rangers rounded up some coffee cups and joined us as we watched the sun set below the lowest Hoodoo.

"Wouldn't you know it, I have to answer nature's call *again*," I said as I stood up. "I think it's the coffee."

"Don't blame the coffee," shouted Diane. "Blame your aging gut."

Wandering off into the woods, I began to feel like life was about as good as it gets. Contemplating my thoughts, I began to feel totally relaxed and at ease, at peace with *everything!* This all-knowing, almost intuitive grasp of reality must have been brought on by the perfect events of this day. You could say I was experiencing an epiphany.

I snapped out of it and realized my stay in the woods was quite a bit longer than expected. It was now dark as I made my way back to camp. Despite the fact that there was no moon and as dark as hell, it was amazing how the multitude of stars cast the most delicate shadows on the ground.

The group wasn't hard to find, as there was a lot of laughter just in front of me. I could see they were swapping stories by headlamps and enjoying the homemade peach empanadas from the Middle Sister Café.

"Hey, Pablo," Jen called out. "I thought we might have lost you in the woods. We were about ready to send in a search party!"

"Let's just say I had a quality BM out there."

"It must have been a good one," said Phil, looking at his watch. "It took you almost 30 minutes."

Just then the Ranger's radio fired up and startled us all! Johnny radioed in with their location and informed the guys at headquarters that they were heading back.

"We have to go. Have a good night and make sure to see us before you leave," Johnny said, as they walked to their truck.

The group quietly pulled away, and we sat on our sleeping bags and watched the *Milky Way* magically work its way across the night sky. I eagerly broke out the last half of our Scotch, and passed the bottle.

"Here's mud in your eye," I said, and took a generous swallow.

"Here's slurry up your nose," hailed Diane, and took a snort.

I offered the bottle to Phil, but he politely declined.

Phil ambled over to the truck and retrieved a couple pair of binoculars.

"Have you ever seen the stars with binoculars?" he asked.

"Never have," I replied.

"On a dark night like tonight, you can see thousands of stars with the naked eye, but wait until you see them with binoculars!"

I raised the binoculars to my eyes and gazed into the abyss.

"Look at all the stars! There are billions of them. Look at the *Milky Way!"*

"And the *Milky Way* is just our galaxy; can you imagine how many galaxies are out there?" said Phil.

"It boggles my mind! This is *Incredible!"* I said with amazement.

We stayed up until Diane and I sucked the bottle completely dry. After punching down my pillow, I made myself comfortable, and felt myself slowly starting to nod off.

"Maybe I'll dream of heaven again. But what could top this?" I mumbled through half closed eyes, "We were just looking at it through binoculars."

20 I'll Be Damned!

The sun came up in dramatic fashion. The valley was awash in bright morning sunlight. My head was a little foggy, but not as bad as the night before.

"I must have slept hard last night, I don't recall anything except my head hitting the pillow and then opening my eyes to daybreak."

Diane and Phil were still asleep in their bags when I got up to take a leak. I headed over to the truck to get my toothbrush and some water. While wearing just my boxers, I noticed it was pretty darn cold this morning. I rounded the big boulder and stopped in my tracks. *Where is the truck? The truck! It's gone! It's freaking gone!*

I ran over to Phil and Diane and yelled, "*The truck is gone!*"

"What do you mean gone?" mumbled Diane, sitting up and squinting in the early morning sunlight.

"I mean, not there, missing ... vanished ... vanished into freaking-thin-air! Gone!"

"Are you saying it was maybe-stolen gone?" asked Phil.

"Who would want to steal a burnt up old truck?"

"Beats me," said Phil as he got up and shuffled over to where the truck was, wearing only his skivvies.

"Pablo were you up messing with the truck last night?" asked Diane.

"No ... no way! I never got up ... or at least I can't remember getting up!"

"You know how you get after hitting the bottle, you old coot."

Diane crawled out of her sleeping bag, dressed in gym shorts and a black sports bra.

"Man, it's cold this morning." She peered down into the valley, and asked Phil, "Can you grab the binoculars for me please?"

Phil retrieved the binoculars from our campsite and handed them to her. Diane focused them and scanned the valley floor.

"*Holy shit!*" she shouted. "Look over there, just to the right, in that thick stand of juniper trees."

I grabbed the binoculars, and with my hands shaking, tried to focus on the valley floor. Looking 800 feet straight down, I saw half hanging in some treetops, a blue shredded and slightly charred plastic tarp. Scattered on the hillside were burnt bits of fire hose and debris. I looked at the ground, and next to my feet were gouges and scrapes, about 4 feet long, that lead over the edge of the limestone cliff.

"Holy Crap! She rolled over the edge!" Diane shouted. "She must have rolled over the edge last night!"

At first I was in shock, but when reality set in, I began to lose it! "Damn it! Damn it! Damn! Damn! DAMN!" I yelled and stomped all over the place.

"It sure looks that way," said Phil. "What are we going to do now?"

"There is nothing we can do," Diane frowned. "She's gone!"

After a moment of reflection, Diane sprang into action. "OK, guys, we have to stay frosty and remain calm," she exhorted. "The park rangers will be making their rounds, and we need to report this. Let's get dressed. Just be glad we kept our clothes by our sleeping bags; otherwise we would be walking to the main road in just our underwear."

We quickly got dressed. Phil and Diane rolled up the sleeping bags, and I grabbed the empty Scotch bottle and angrily hurled it over the cliff, hearing it smash on the rocks on the way down.

Diane yelled and shook me hard. "Get a grip cowboy! Let's be glad nobody got hurt. One of us could have been sleeping in the truck when it rolled over the edge! Now grab your stuff and let's move out!"

My heart was pounding, and my mind was racing. "How could this happen? Did we not set the parking brake? Did we forget to put the chock stone under the tire? What the hell happened?"

We gathered our stuff and started walking toward the main road. As we got to the paved section, I was overcome with rage, threw my sleeping bag down on the asphalt, and started kicking it repeatedly. I began cursing up a storm, and was losing it all over again!

Just then the park rangers pulled up next to us, and Vince yelled, "What's up?"

"The truck is gone!" I yelled. "I think it rolled over the edge!"

"What? No way!" shouted Vince.

"Over the edge? Are you sure?" asked Jen. "It looked pretty secure when we saw it yesterday!"

"Let's go back and take a look around," said Johnny.

We piled into their truck, and the questioning began. We returned to the scene of the crime and they glassed the valley below, seeing the same tarp and debris we saw earlier this morning.

"Doesn't look good," Johnny said. He bent down and rubbed his hand along the scuffs leading to the edge of the cliff. "Not good at all."

We drove back to the ranger station in complete silence. I stared blankly out the windows, wondering what would happen next.

As we pulled into the Visitor Center, I looked with envy at the kids racing around, laughing, buying things from the gift shop, and eating ice cream cones from the snack bar.

"They don't have a care in the world," I mumbled to myself.

Once in the ranger's office, Jen walked directly over to the file cabinet and started thumbing through some manila folders. She pulled out a few official looking forms and with a click of her government issued black pen, filled out the necessary names and dates. She held up the first one and told us it was for search and rescue.

"What! Search and rescue?" I cried.

"Search and rescue needs to hike down there and look for the truck. We are pretty sure it's down there. It is in the most remote part of the park. We just have to get the exact location and GPS coordinates so a sky crane can haul it out of there. We probably won't be able to get a group assembled for a couple of days, since this is not a true emergency," she stated with authority. "The sky crane will have to wait until spring. That is the earliest we can haul it out. Then we will have to arrange for a flatbed truck to come, so we can raise it to the top of the rim and cart it out of here. The flatbed truck will take it to a salvage yard where it'll be scrapped."

"Sky Crane! Scrapped! What the ... First the Nickel is in a crumpled heap at the bottom of a cliff and now she will be hauled out and scrapped! I can't stand it! This is killing me!" I cried out loud.

"Then there is site cleanup," added Vince. "We will have to remove all of the burnt debris, scattered truck parts, and every tiny piece of broken glass."

Vince asked us if there was anything of value that the search and rescue team could bring back, after they located the truck. I was in a daze and couldn't remember anything. My brain was turning into marshmallows.

Diane replied, "We need to recover three Bendix King portable radios from the cab of the truck. It doesn't matter if they are working or not; they just have to be accounted for. Also all of our travel receipts are in an envelope in the glove box. If I don't have the receipts, I am out all the money I paid with my personal credit card."

"Don't you guys have a company credit card?" asked Vince.

"Got melted in the fire," Diane frowned.

"Ouch!" said Vince.

"One more thing; there is a stuffed sock monkey in the cab. If he is still there, can you mail him to me? His name is Mortie, and he is our lucky charm," Diane added.

I did a double take on that one. "Our *lucky* charm? Good Lord, help us all," I mumbled.

Jen said reluctantly, "So, search and rescue, the sky crane, towing, and site cleanup, will add up to a lot of money. To whom do we send the bill?"

"Holy crap, I am so screwed," I said walking over to the counter and began signing the forms.

I was so bummed I couldn't see straight. At this point I couldn't care less and didn't even read the forms. I just signed where Jen pointed, scribbling my name on one page after another. There must have been a dozen in all.

"Well, it looks like we are stuck here," said Phil sadly.

"Don't worry, we can get you on a Greyhound bus by this afternoon," replied Johnny. "I'll even buy you guys some lunch."

"Thanks but don't bother. I'm not hungry," I frowned, looking down at the floor, "I'm feeling kinda sick to my stomach."

"Hey Pablo, I've got something that might cheer you up," Johnny said with a smile.

I shook my head and said, "Sorry Johnny, I don't think anything can cheer me up right now."

Johnny walked all of us down a hallway toward the back of the Visitor Center. We exited through the back door, and Jen lead us across a dry grassy field, over toward an old maintenance shop. I could hear a chain rumble as she rolled up the garage door.

There in the shadows I saw it. There she was! The Triple Nickel in all of her charred glory! I stared and looked! Rubbed my bloodshot eyes, and looked again!

Everyone was busting a gut, shouting, and laughing!

It took me a moment to realize that the joke was on me! It was all an awful, horrible, rotten prank!

"What the hell? What's going on here?" I said looking at them laughing at me.

Phil said, "We've put up with your practical jokes long enough, and I have learned a thing or two from Diane." He elbowed me in the ribs. "We don't get mad, we get even!"

I sputtered, "All of you guys were in on this? How? When?"

Diane began to tell the story, "When you went into the woods last night, we discussed a plot for revenge. Phil stood as our lookout man, and we took the tarp off of the truck and tied a rock to it. Vince threw it over the cliff, along with some burnt equipment. While we were doing that, Jen grabbed a Pulaski off her truck and scraped some gouges in the rock by the edge of the cliff. It only took us a few minutes, and the dirty deed was done."

Vince added, "Diane said you had a half bottle of Scotch to polish off, so we returned to your camp late last night. We figured you would be in a Scotch induced coma and Diane left the keys in the ignition for us. We quietly backed up the truck, and brought it back here!"

"All we had to do was imply what had happened, and you fell for it, hook, line, and sinker," laughed Diane.

"Vince and I will have to hike down there on our next day off to retrieve the stuff we tossed over the edge. It'll be a long hike, but man, it was worth it!" laughed Jen.

"Well I'll be damned!" I grinned, running my hand through my hair, "I'll be dang blasted damned!"

I started to laugh, and couldn't stop. Tears were rolling down my cheeks, maybe from relief, or maybe because I loved that truck so much and was so glad to see her again. I grabbed Phil's bandana out from his back pocket and wiped my eyes and blew my nose.

"Johnny," I hollered, "I heard you say, you wanted to buy us some lunch!"

"Guess you got your appetite back."

We all laughed and headed to the snack bar for a hot dog and milkshake.

As we headed back into the building, I made a proclamation. "No more pranks! No more Scotch! I have learned my lesson, and I'm a reformed man!"

"Yeah, when hell freezes over!" shouted Diane.

"I swear I will do my best."

"For now I believe you. After today and what you went through, I think you may have learned your lesson the hard way," she said with conviction.

I crossed my heart and raised my right hand and said, "Never again!"

"Cross your heart and hope to die?" asked Phil.

"Stick a needle in your eye?" they all chimed in at once!

"Come on, guys, *let's be reasonable!*" I said.

As we were walking back to the office, I glanced back to the garage one more time, just to make sure. I sighed when I saw her. There she was, the Triple Nickel, with Mortie sitting on the dashboard, looking back at me. I looked closely and did a double take. If I didn't know any better, I could have sworn that little monkey winked at me!

21   Mystery of the Desert

After polishing off the best chocolate shake I ever tasted, we walked over to the maintenance shop. Diane and Phil couldn't stop grinning, and the rangers were happy because I didn't do anything desperate or stupid after I thought the truck was a goner.

Phil pulled the Nickel out, and Jen found some old dusty drop cloths to toss over the back of the truck. We all helped tie them down, and the truck was now draped with greying canvas, stained with forest service brown paint. It couldn't have gotten any uglier, but the truck looked beautiful to me.

I elbowed my way past Phil and planted myself behind the steering wheel and fired her up. I really wanted to drive this truck back to New Mexico. We all got in and slowly pulled away.

Johnny yelled, "Come back and see us some time, we loved having you around."

"I bet you did," I shouted above the sound of the engine.

We waved good-bye and headed toward Arizona under a clear blue sky. It was midday, and we had a lot of miles ahead of us. Phil stretched out in the back seat, and Diane was in the navigator seat, checking the map and looking down the road.

"Man, I can't tell you how much I love this truck," I beamed. "You really don't know how attached a person gets to something until it is taken away."

"To tell you the truth," recalled Phil, "I was feeling real bad when you started to lose it on the road to the Visitor Center. You were kicking your sleeping bag over and over again, stomping and cussing up a storm. I was going to confess right then and there that it was all a prank."

"Yeah, I saw that look in your eye, Phil," recalled Diane. "I remember grabbing you by the arm and saying something like, 'Don't even think about telling him!'"

"Yeah, and I was thinking you were pretty cold-blooded and heartless."

"Phil, believe me, I was enjoying every minute of Pablo's misery. The more he agonized about it, the better I felt! Pablo has been dishing it out all these years. And Phil, you being the new guy, can't even begin to imagine how long I have suffered with this practical joker. I've been putting up with his crap for 10 years now, *10 long years!* God knows he's probably been a pain in the ass all of his life. I'm surprised the Marines didn't take him out with some friendly fire back in Nam."

"Now that you mention it, I pulled off some pretty good ones back in the day," I reminisced with a grin.

"So there you have it, *payback and then some!* It was a long time coming, but definitely worth it," said Diane.

As we continued down the road, I began to wonder if my crazy antics have caused others that much grief over the years?

"Hey Pablo," smirked Diane as she held up a manila folder, "Jen handed this to me as we were leaving. Get a load of the paperwork you signed back at the ranger station."

Diane began to read the forms I signed while in my delirious, tormented state.

"Here is a requisition for toilet paper, 17 cases of toilet paper! And here is another one you signed for 16 cases of mousetraps."

"This one is for more *Woodsy Owl, give a hoot! Don't pollute,* coloring books, plus nine boxes of *Smokey Bear* iron-on patches. Here is one for more *Good and Plenty* and *Snow Caps* for the snack bar."

"Did Pablo order some *Jujubes?*" asked Phil.

"Nope, no Jujubes," Diane said with sadness.

"Crap, I really love those things," frowned Phil.

After reading the forms aloud, she handed them to Phil in the back seat. He read them and laughed all over again.

"Oh! And look at this one!" Diane laughed, wiping the tears from her eyes. "This one is an *Employee Performance Review.* It looks like Jen gets the *highest marks* in *every* category and you approved her for a hefty raise in pay!"

Phil chimed in, "Aww, you only knew her for one day, and you gave her a raise. How sweet!"

"They all have your signature on them. I can't wait to show the guys back at the station," she laughed.

"That Jen, she looked so serious at the time," Phil recalled, laughing as he read the forms. "She was having as much fun out of this as you were Diane!"

"You women were ganging up on me," I grunted.

"Can you blame us?" said Diane. "That was a once-in-a-lifetime opportunity."

As we headed south toward Arizona, we tuned the radio to an NPR news broadcast, trying to catch up on what had happened in the world while we were away. It was the same old, same old. Conflict in the Middle East, politicians bashing each other, the cost of living going up. Nothing had

really changed. Despite the world in chaos, it still felt good
to be heading home. We switched to a Country-Western
station and settled in to some twangy, cry in your beer
music. We decided to drive through the night, as opposed to
stopping at a hotel or campground.

Pushing past Flagstaff and muscling our way around
Phoenix, I remarked, "Man, I'm glad I live in rural New
Mexico, Phoenix smells like concrete and car exhaust! By
the way, we are getting low on fuel, and it will be awfully
hard to panhandle for gas money at this hour."

"Don't worry Pablo, I was just messing with you back
there. I have plenty left on my card," Diane smirked.

"You rotten little sneak you," I grinned.

It was way past midnight when we dove through Tucson,
and we all agreed we could use a brief rest. I pulled over at
the Triple T Truck Stop so we could grab some shut-eye.

We woke up in a huff, the sun was high in the sky, and the
traffic was flying by us on I-10. Despite the rumble of the
big rigs, we managed to sleep way harder that we thought.
We got out and went in to the truck stop to snag some strong
coffee.

Diane took a sip and started coughing, "This swill is so
strong it could erode the enamel off of your teeth!"

Diane elected to drive, and we pulled back out onto the
interstate. As we were driving, from out of nowhere, in the
yucca filled desert, we started seeing big yellow billboards.
They occurred in orderly intervals and in tall blue letters, on
a bold yellow background, they read,

THE THING?

Below the big blue letters was a subtitle.

Some said, *THE THING? Have You Seen It?*

Others said, *THE THING? Worth the Stop!*

Another one said, *THE THING? Mystery of the Desert!*

"Wow!" said Phil, "Mystery of the Desert! We can't pass that up.

Our curiosity started to get the best of us and we took Exit 322, drove the exit loop and pulled into a big asphalt parking lot. We saw a Dairy Queen to the right; a gift shop to the left and in the very center was *THE THING?* Museum. It stood proud in all of its tacky, touristy glory.

"I've heard about this place but never took the time to visit," I said.

"Me too," nodded Diane. "We might even experience the seventh wonder of the world behind those doors."

We ponied up the required one-dollar admission and followed the yellow footprints painted on the floor. We marched past the gift shop and on toward the *Mystery of the Desert!*

"I wonder how many people have walked on these footprints?" asked Phil.

"Beats me, probably millions. Somebody has to pay for all of those billboards."

Inside, we found a menagerie of artifacts on display. Paintings, books, old rifles, covered wagons, antique cars, even a Rolls Royce they claim to be Hitler's Car. It looked like a *Ripley's Believe it or Not Museum,* except everything was kind of shabby and covered with dust.

We slowly worked our way past the exhibits and followed the footprints to the main event ... *THE THING?*

"I'm all a-twitter!" I said sarcastically as we got closer.

We approached a coffin-like container and peered down inside. We all gasped! What we saw was indescribable! Hideous beyond words! Worthy of our worst nightmares and will haunt us for the rest of our days! ... *NOT!!!*

We laughed at the exhibit inside the coffin, only because it was so incredibly hokey.

"At least we didn't pay a lot for that one," laughed Phil. "I think we got our one-dollar's-worth."

"I can't really explain what we saw, you really have to experience it for yourself," I said.

As we were leaving, Diane bought a little infant's t-shirt at the gift shop to put on Mortie. It was of course, bright yellow with *THE THING?* logo printed across the chest. Under the logo was written, *My mommy saw the Thing? And all I got was this lousy T-shirt.*

I told Diane, "Mortie shouldn't be too upset; the monkey probably got the better deal."

We walked into the bright sunlight, grinning and shaking our heads.

"After this is all over," Diane smiled, "we can donate the Triple Nickel to the museum. They can park the burnt up old truck next to Hitler's Car."

People had started to gather around our truck to gawk while we were inside, and began to disperse when they saw us walking toward them.

"Yes, we are indeed *a Mystery in the Desert*," I said. "Since we are dressed in these paisley Jimmy Hendrix styled shirts and bell bottomed pants, we should put ourselves on exhibit and charge people a buck just to see *us!*"

Phil decided to drive, and we were back on the road. We started to get antsy during the last few hours of travel, happy to be almost home, yet sad in a strange way that the trip was coming to a close.

"I wonder if the department will ever send us on another wildland assignment?" asked Phil.

"Why not?" I replied. "Firefighting is always about taking calculated risks, and sometimes it can become downright dangerous. Sometimes bad things happen out there. We just happened to burn up our fire truck, that's all. Since I am the engine boss, I take full responsibility for you guys and the truck. I know Chief is going to put the screws to me ... I might even get fired! You guys, on the other hand, are off the hook and good to go."

"Just be glad the truck didn't roll off a cliff," said Diane with a wink.

"Well, since you put it that way, I can't wait till next season," grinned Phil.

Diane rummaged through her stuff and pulled out a rumpled plastic shopping bag.

"Hey Phil, before I forget, I got you a little memento to remember this trip by."

On the bag was the logo from *Bee-Boos, Better Than New* thrift shop. Diane opened the bag and showed its contents to Phil. A giant grin crossed his face.

"The *Emergency!* Lunch box!" he hollered.

"It wouldn't be right if we left something like that behind," Diane said with a smile.

"If I weren't driving, I would kiss you right now!" he gushed.

"Hold off on the kissing; I can tell you really like it," said Diane.

I cupped my hands over my mouth to simulate fire tones going off.

"Station 51... Engine 51 ... Rescue 51... respond to a motor vehicle accident on I-10, at exit 322. The calling party stated, the driver of the vehicle lost control, due to an overwhelming moment of giddiness. KMG365."

At that moment, because it was Phil being Phil, he began to sing the theme song to *Emergency!* We couldn't help ourselves, and joined right in.

The sun was getting low when we finally arrived in Mimbres Springs. We decided not to return the truck to the

fire station right away. Our cars were still at the station
and I decided to drop them off at their houses and pick them
up tomorrow morning, to face the chief together. As sure as
the sun comes up, there will be a lot of explaining to do, and
right now we were not up for it. I know Chief is not going to
be a happy camper. As far as he knows, all this truck needs
is a little paint and wax.

I dropped Diane off first. She gathered her meager
possessions and plucked Mortie off the dashboard. She gave
me a shabby salute, and Phil a high five. She walked toward
her small adobe house, and shouted out a weak *Adios*.
Marigolds bordered the walkway, and a flock of plastic pink
flamingos stood in the vegetable garden, knee deep in green
chilies, tomatillos, and tomatoes.

I thought, *What a cute little place for such a crusty old
hard ass. It just goes to show ya, she must be a real softie
at heart.* I changed my mind real quick on that one ...
thinking back to the Bryce Canyon payback.

Phil lived in a modest doublewide at the edge of town. It
had a carport with a small tool shed off to the side. It was a
sparse piece of property, tidy, clean, and free of tall weeds
and rusty junk cars.

He gave me a, "It's been unreal," and pulled his gear off
the truck.

When I backed out of the driveway, Phil gave me a
thumbs-up and a snappier salute.

"Yes, unreal about sums it up."

I managed to call my wife before my arrival, giving her a
heads up that I was almost home.

After what seemed like an eternity, I pulled the Triple
Nickel into my driveway. Our golden retriever, Scout, ran
up to me with his feathery tail a-wagging. He gave me a
chorus of happy barks and began to inspect my plaid

bellbottoms with a lot of curious sniffing. He then raised a leg and pissed on the Triple Nickel.

No respect, I thought to myself as I gathered up my stuff.

I looked in the cab to see if I forgot anything important, and out of the corner of my eye, I saw the newspaper package Élan gave me, peeking up from under the front seat. I reached in, grabbed it, and ripped off the newspaper and duct tape. There were three silkscreened T-shirts with the *Custer's Last Shirt* design. With a Sharpie marker, Élan wrote on each of them, "*To My Brothers and Sisters in Fire. Be Strong and Stay Safe.*"

"Wow!" I said as I held them close. 'That Élan he is truly a man of few words, but very powerful words. I'm glad I didn't put them in my duffel bag. They would have burned up with the rest of my clothes."

Walking to the house, I noticed the western sky was just barely lit and the porch light was giving off a warm welcoming glow. Hearing the sound of mourning doves roosting in the mesquite trees, I stepped onto the front porch and caught the smell of supper cooking on the stove.

God, it was good to be back home!

My wife greeted me on the porch and laughed at the sight.

"It looks like you hippies are back from your *Summer of Love!*"

She hugged me, and I gave her a squeeze and a big kiss.

"How was your trip?" she asked.

"Boy! Have I got a story to tell you!"

"You always do," she smiled, looking back at the Triple Nickel, "You always do."

22 One Year Later

I couldn't have been more disgusted as we walked out of Chief's office. "A-shift! God, A-shift! Smitty, can you believe it, we've been put on A-shift!"

Smitty said, "God, we will become one of those booger eaters."

Over this past year, the department has hired five new guys, and the chief has decided to move some people around to even up the crews. He wanted to mix some of the old dogs in with the young pups. New probationary firefighters are known as *probies*, or as we like to call them, the *boots,* and Smitty and I have been moved over to A-shift to work with two new guys, Jeff and Lenny.

I said to Smitty, "Now don't get me wrong, the boots Lenny and Jeff are good guys. However, the A-shift reputation sucks, and I don't want the probies turning into some clock watching slack asses."

"Yeah, the A-shift image needs to be revamped, and I think we are just the guys to do it."

Chief told us the news just as we were coming off of B-shift, and instead of going on our four-day break; we now have to work back-to-back shifts.

"I really hate working 48 hours straight," I grumbled.

Just then, the overhead tones went off, stopping us in our tracks, the dispatcher said, "Engine 550, Paramedic 553, respond to childbirth at 3230 Black River Road. Patient states she's pregnant, isn't due for three more weeks, and her water broke! Her contractions are now about eight minutes apart. She is home alone and can't reach her husband, and she sounded really panicky and desperate!"

"Oh hells bells!" Smitty said as we hustled out to the fire truck.

I eagerly jumped into the driver's seat. Smitty was up front with Jeff and Lenny in the back. As we raced down the road, I said in a singsong voice, "A baby! A baby! We're gonna have a baby!"

"Since this is calving season, her husband Gilbert, must be out with the cattle," Smitty said. "Mrs. Albertson is home alone, can't reach her husband and the baby is ready to pop out! I bet she is on the verge of hysteria. I hope she doesn't have it before we get there! Pablo, can't this thing go any faster?"

"Captain, I'm giving you all she's got!" I yelled. I glanced at the new guys in the back seat and said, "I bet you two haven't delivered a baby yet have you? Is this your first time?"

Jeff and Lenny looked at each other and nodded in agreement. I could see fear in their eyes.

"Ohhhh, this will be good, we have delivery virgins," I grinned.

As the engine raced down the highway, Smitty turned to the new guys and said, "OK, this is the plan. Lenny you bring in the EMS jump bag and oxygen cylinder. Jeff, you grab the OB kit. When we get on scene, don't open the OB kit right away. Look for crowning first. If you start to see crowning, open the kit and gown up for the delivery. Do you guys copy?"

Jeff and Lenny nodded in agreement again. I glanced back and could see more fear in their eyes.

We knew the ambulance had left the hospital, returning from their previous call and wouldn't arrive on our scene for at least 15 more minutes.

The road to the Anderson ranch was bumpy as all get out. Smitty grinned at me and said, "Jeff, looks like he's getting a little pale back there and is about ready to throw up."

We made great time and were there before we knew it!

After entering the house, we found Mrs. Albertson lying on the couch. She was soaked in sweat and looked really anxious.

I knelt next to her and said, "Don't worry, we are here, things will be just fine. Try to relax and take some deep breaths."

She said with pursed lips, "Thank God you're here! I've tried three times to call my husband on that damn cell phone of his, but he's not answering."

I wrapped the blood pressure cuff on her bicep and grabbed a stethoscope to listen for her pulse and blood pressure. Her heart was racing, and she was crying out with each contraction.

Jeff walked to the kitchen counter and said, "Is this your husband's cell?" He found the phone half buried under a towel next to the microwave.

Mrs. Albertson looked over and rolled her eyes, "Yes damn it! That man would lose his head if it wasn't attached."

Smitty placed a run report on his clipboard and started to write down all of Mrs. Albertsons pertinent information, name, age, date of birth, any medical history or medications and how many children she has had. He also wrote down her vitals as I called them out.

I told Jeff to come over and look for crowning. He gave me a double take and looked behind him, pointed to himself and said with wide eyes, "Who me?"

I pulled Lenny aside and whispered in his ear, "Yes you, numb nuts! Get over there and take a peek."

"Why can't Lenny take a peek?" he whispered back.

"Lenny is outside in the driveway helping guide the ambulance in, now cowboy up and take a look."

"He cautiously lifted up Mrs. Albertson's robe, took a look and said, "God there's crowning!" His eyes rolled back, and he passed out cold.

"Good Lord!" said Smitty. He ran to the door and yelled for Lenny. "Get in here, we have a man down!"

Lenny ran in, and they dragged Jeff out of the way.

"OK Lenny, open up the OB kit and gown up, we can see crowning and it looks like we're going to have a baby!" I grinned.

We placed some blankets and sheets on the kitchen floor, and gingerly carried her over to them. We placed a couple of pillows behind her head, and tried to make her as comfortable as possible.

"You guys are great! No sense messing up the couch or the carpet," she said.

"Now let's try to remain calm, remember to pant like crazy and push with the contractions, and let nature take its course. This is going to be great, we can do this!" I said.

"This is my fourth and I know the routine," she said with a weak smile.

As I held her hand, she squeezed it like a vice. Every time she had a contraction, I felt the pain too! I could sense she was both happy and terrified ... but then again, so was I!

During the next few minutes there was a lot of panting, increased moaning and then one long agonizing scream! Whoosh, before we knew it, the baby came sliding out into Lenny's hands!

Lenny shouted, "It's a girl!"

Prompting Lenny, I said with excitement, "Use the bulb syringe to clear mucus from the baby's nose and mouth, and lightly pat the baby's feet to get her to cry."

I helped towel off the slippery crying newborn, wrapped her in a blanket and placed a little yellow knitted cap on her head.

Lenny grinned, "She has pinked up nicely," and handed her off to momma with the umbilical cord still attached.

The room was now filled with the sound of crying. The baby was wailing, Mrs. Albertson was crying, Lenny was bawling, and I was getting misty myself. I even saw a weepy eye on Smitty! The whole event was a fantastic newborn miracle! And wouldn't you know it, Jeff missed it all! He came to just as the ambulance was pulling away.

During the childbirth, Smitty took some pictures of the blessed event on Gilbert's cell phone. After cleaning up the kitchen, we left a note next to the phone, to let him know what had happened, and where to call.

As we were ready to leave I joked, "Let's make like a baby and head out!"

I got a collective groan from my crew, and we climbed into the fire truck.

Making our way back to the firehouse, I took a deep sigh and marveled at the nearby mountains and flowing grasslands. Spring was in the air, and it was appropriate that we welcomed a new baby girl into the world. I pondered what it was like back when the West was young and when Mimbres Springs was in its infancy.

From what I heard, back in the 1870s, the Barrow brothers hit pay dirt up in the foothills. Word got out that there was *gold in them thar hills!* Miners showed up in droves to pick and peck at the hillsides. A makeshift town was established but was soon overrun by raiding Apaches who were hell bent on protecting their land from the foreigners who were ripping up the mountains. The town was quickly re-established by the miners. Nobody was going to keep a bunch of ornery miners away from their gold! There were more skirmishes between the indigenous and the white man. The mining camp took several hits and was eventually burned to the ground. Many lives were lost before the US Army was sent in to secure the area. The town was rebuilt and quickly flourished. When the gold diminished, the town began to slowly die out. Once the saloons went belly up, the raucous ways of the miners gave way to the high hopes of the homesteaders and ranchers like the Albertsons.

The diversity of the land was the town's saving grace. A town site plat was registered, and plots of land were awarded to anyone who ponied up some bucks to buy land.

Womenfolk were scarce in this part of the country, so the town's founding fathers advertised that during the first two years, plots of land were to be given away for *free*, to any woman who wanted to settle in the town. Mrs. Albertson's great-great-grandmother was one of the founders of Mimbres Springs.

The new homesteaders tapped into the richness of the valley. There was plenty of game in the nearby mountains and trout in the streams. The diversity of the land is prevalent even to this day. There are stretches of grasslands and forage for cattle, abundant water, and good soil for farming.

Zinc, gold, silver, and copper, can still be found in the area. A large copper mine lies about 40 miles west of the town, and a lot of the locals make the commute to work the high paying 12-hour shifts.

Farming is the main vocation, and the area's cash crops consist of pinto beans, chilies, squash, apples, pecans and pistachios, with some vineyards sprouting up.

Ranching is still strong in these parts. Some ranchers raise beef cattle and believed, the bigger the steer the better the selling price. Other ranchers, like the Albertsons, raise cattle for calving and their stock is made up of mostly cows and heifers. It's nice to see the multitude of baby calves running amok in the springtime pastures kicking up their heels and suckling up to momma. It's reassuring to know there is a new baby Albertson kicking up her heels today as well.

As we pulled into the station, several firefighters from the other shifts were going through their wildland gear, and stuff was spread all over the floor in the adjoining engine bay. After parking the fire truck, I walked over to the guys and asked what's up?

"We heard on the news this morning that some wildfires are starting up in southern Arizona, and we think it's just a matter of time before our department gets called out for an assignment," said one of them.

It was the end of May, and rainfall in the southwest had been scarce. The Rain Gods had been good to New Mexico and we weren't in such a severe drought as Arizona. I don't think it has rained here since early April, but I know in southern Arizona it hasn't rained since February. The region had a real hard freeze this winter, and some believe it was the *Hundred Year Freeze*. By combining those conditions, there must be tons of dead wood in the forest.

Yup, the stage is set for a big fire, I thought to myself, as I watched the guys sort through their gear.

With their gear spread out everywhere, I was like Pavlov's dog and could smell the faint odor of ash, smoke and dust, and began to get excited. If I had a tail it would be wagging right now. All that euphoria vanished in an instant, when I remembered that our chief had grounded me from fighting wildfires forever.

Being the engine boss, I was held responsible for burning up the brush truck last year. Then there was the little matter of blowing up the transmission in Taos the year before, and to add to the list, I had a run-in with a prize Brahma bull in Texas a few years back. Hey, it was dark and he came out of nowhere! The impact took out the windshield and the right front quarter panel of the Triple Nickel. Those mishaps have a way of staying with me, and I have acquired a reputation for being hard on the equipment, and even harder on the fire department's budget. Worse still, nobody wants to voluntarily be on the butt end of my practical jokes. The chief really ripped me a new one after last year's Nevada fire and banished me from any future wildland assignments.

Feeling remorse, I walked outside to the Triple Nickel that was parked in the carport just behind the station. She just came back from the shop and had a lot of work done to her this winter. She looked fantastic! The entire back end had been replaced, including a new 200-gallon water tank. There was a new water pump mounted at the rear, and just below it was a bumper sticker that read *Weird Shit 24/7*. The exhaust pipe had a protective cage around it, and I grinned as I opened and closed the new overhead storage bins. It looks like our personal gear can now be stowed in covered compartments away from the elements.

Walking to the passenger side, I ran my hand along the new paint and wax. There were new lenses on the front emergency lights, and when I walked around to the driver's side, I laughed out loud, seeing 18 stencils of 2-inch-high flames painted on the front quarter panel, representing all the big fires the Nickel had knocked down over the years. And of course it knocked down a bull, so mixed in with the flames was a 2-inch stencil of a Brahma bull. She was in fine form and ready to fight some fire. Rumor has it, the repairs cost about 25-grand, but heck, I know she's worth it.

Walking back into the station, I could feel there was a lot of excitement in the air. I poured a cup of coffee, then all at once, everyone's cell phone started to beep, chime or chirp. It was like watching *The Gunfight at the OK Corral,* as everyone whipped out cell phones from their belt holsters. A manpower page was being issued for a fire in Arizona, and I felt depressed watching them frantically speed dial the battalion chief (BC), to get their names on the list.

The message read, Need *one engine boss, one squad boss and one wildland firefighter for a two-week brush truck assignment in Arizona.*

Also need a Driver and one wildland firefighter for a two-week water tender assignment in Arizona. Call the battalion chief ASAP!!

Wildland firefighting was what I enjoyed most, and I thought, *It sure would have been nice to get one more wildland season under my belt before I retire.*

While slumping in a Lazy Boy and looking forlorn, the guys scurried around, all excited about the page out.

"Hey Pablo," said one of them. "I think you have a black cloud following you to these fires. You know, bad karma, bad juju, or something."

"Well you guys don't have to worry about my juju. The chief has banned me from all future wildland fires. From here on out, it looks like I am an old washed up, ex-wildland guy." The guys at the station patted me on the shoulder and said, "Sucks to be you *Mister Mishap.*"

"Hey! It could happen to anyone. It was just bad luck! It was all just an unfortunate series of bad luck!" I said in a defensive tone.

A second page came across, it read, *Tender assignment filled and ready to go. The squad boss and firefighter position are filled for the brush truck. Only need one engine boss for the brush truck assignment. I NEED ONE OF OUR ENGINE BOSSES TO CALL ME ASAP! BC.*

I wanted to answer the page, but knew better.

A third page came across. *Tender assignment is manned and leaving for Arizona in 30 minutes, wish them a safe journey. Still need one engine boss for brush truck assignment. Call the BC ASAP.*

Some time passed before a fourth page came across. *Pablo, call me I need to talk to you ... BC.*

There was no way they wanted me to go on this assignment. They probably wanted me to cover some shifts for the ones that were going to be away. I was too depressed to respond.

Fifth page. I looked down at my phone. *Pablo, call me PLEASE. YOUR FRIENDLY BATTALION CHIEF!!*

Possibilities ran through my mind as to why the BC wanted to talk to me. Back filling the wildland shifts would be OK. Working out of an air-conditioned fire station while those guys were suffering out there in the heat and smoke would be nice. I could work the overtime, and the extra money would come in handy.

Just then, Smitty came over and told me he found out that the other two engine bosses were unavailable for the assignment. Three days ago, Kenny threw his back out while riding his ATV. Kenny said it was a *"watch this"* maneuver. He ended up getting thrown over the handlebars, and face planted into some prickly pear cactus. The other engine boss, Bruno, has procrastinated to the point of no return and needs to take a paramedic recertification class next week. He has to pass the class, or he could lose his hard earned paramedic certification, and will be tied up for five days.

Wow! Could Kenny's unfortunate mishap, and Bruno's procrastination be my ticket to Arizona? The thought of that gave me goose bumps.

I couldn't call the battalion chief fast enough. After 15 minutes of harsh lecture, idle threats, and stern warnings, he put me on the assignment

The BC put out another page, *"Pablo has the engine boss spot. All brush truck personnel,* please *report to the Wildland Shack for assignment and briefing."*

After grabbing some extra skivvies and my shaving kit from my locker, I headed for the Wildland Shack, where all of the department's wildland gear was stored. With a newfound pep in my step and a song in my heart, I met up with the battalion chief. He informed me that all of the firefighters who called to be put on the brush truck assignment are now asking to be taken off the list.

"They're all calling off? I thought there was a waiting list? They were all chomping at the bit to get put on this fire," I said with shock.

"Seems like your reputation as an engine boss, shit magnet, and practical joker has reared its ugly head. Some of the guys are reluctant to spend two weeks with you."

"Wow, that's harsh!"

"Can you blame them? I'll send out one more page. If I don't get any takers, we will have to scrub this brush truck assignment. If we cancel on this fire assignment, we may not be placed on the list for the rest of season. The people at the top don't like it when someone gives them the *brush-off.* It will be a shame too, we really could use the money."

As the BC put out the page, I wondered, *Am I really that much of a jerk that people don't want to work with me?*

The battalion chief's cell phone buzzed with a text message, and then his phone rang. After a brief moment I heard him say, "That's great, get here as soon as you can."

He turned to me and showed me the text. *"Here we come to save the day! The Wild Bunch is on the way!"*

It took me a few seconds to respond. "Diane and Phil?"

"Who did you expect? It seems they are the only ones that can put up with you, ya old dog!"

23 Westward Bound

As I was anxiously waiting at the Wildland Shack, Diane pulled up in her beat up '89 Ford Ranger. It had a faded custom license plate on the front that read, EMMYLOU, and her car must have had a hundred bumper stickers plastered on it. Diane has driven that truck as long as I have known her, and she probably has put a million miles on that baby!

Diane got out and pulled her two-week bag out of the bed. She walked up to me, plopped the bag down into the dust and gave me a soft punch to the shoulder.

"I thought you were blackballed from all wildland assignments you old hoot-goat?" she grinned.

"It looks like this old goat has one more fire in him."

"The department must be scrapping the bottom of the barrel," she said laughing.

"The other engine bosses aren't available, so it looks like it's the bottom of the barrel or nothing," I boasted while admiring the Nickel.

"Well those other guys are missing out, the season is just starting, and I am *ready to rumble*." She opened the back door of the Triple Nickel and tossed her bag in.

"The old truck looks great!" She looked over my shoulder and walked around the Triple Nickel, "I almost don't recognize her," and ran her hand over the reconstructed truck. "Look! 18 little flames painted on the front and a stencil of a bull. Very impressive! I wasn't there when you hit that Brahma over in Texas. Did they let you keep the meat?"

"Nope, the only thing I came home with after hitting that bull was a broken windshield and a brown spot in my shorts," I said, hiking up my pants. "Oh Missy, why weren't you on the list when the first page went out?" I asked her.

"I had a rock climbing trip planned for this week-end. My climbing buddies are heading out to Hueco Tanks Friday night. This might be our last chance to climb there before it gets too hot."

"Man I'm really sorry about that," I said, shaking my head.

"Don't worry Pablo, the summer is just starting, and there are plenty of other places to climb," she said with a smile.

Diane and I were talking with the battalion chief when Phil pulled around the corner and parked next to Diane's truck. After the dust settled, he walked over and we all slapped high fives.

"Pablo you owe me big time for this one," said Phil, slapping me on the shoulder. "I was about to go on a 7-day backpacking trip into the Gila Wilderness. I was virtually out the door when the last page-out was sent. When I saw that you were the engine boss, and nobody was signing up, I figured it was my civic duty to call the BC. So I'm warning you now, if you so much as think of pulling a prank, I have every right to aggressively retaliate. And you know what happened the last time you messed with us."

"Don't I know it!" I said shaking my head.

"What happened last time?" asked the battalion chief.

"Don't go there!" we all said in unison.

The BC gave us a quick briefing about the assignment. "You will be heading to southern Arizona, to a town called Sierra Vista. High winds are predicted, and temperatures will reach close to 100 degrees. To go along with that, there will be lip chapping, single-digit humidity. The fire was started by some traveling illegals in the mountains west of town, and the forest is mostly oak, half diseased, and tinder dry. Sierra Vista is nestled butt up to the mountains, and the chance of a massive wildland/urban interface fire is imminent. A lot of homes could be lost on this one!"

"The conditions are ripe for a perfect storm," scowled Diane.

"You can say that again! The Arizona Governor has declared a state of emergency and has called up a lot of Type 1 fire engines (house-fire type trucks), as well as a buttload of hand crews and brush trucks. The National Guard is being sent in to help with civilian evacuations.

The battalion chief paused for a moment, looked us square in the eye and cautioned, "This fire has the potential of being a real man-eater. People could get killed and a lot of property could, and most likely will be lost. So keep on your toes and don't do anything heroic or stupid!"

"Yes sir!" we replied in unison.

We took his warning to heart and finished stocking up the truck with fresh supplies. "If we leave now, we should arrive by late afternoon. Once there, we can go through the check-in process, grab some grub and get some sleep," I said.

"Good Lord!" said Phil, as we climbed into the Triple Nickel, "This sounds serious!"

"Hey! Every fire is serious and has the potential for disaster," cautioned Diane.

"Don't worry Phil, we have our lucky sock monkey mascot."

I pointed to Mortie who was sitting on the dashboard all decked out in his little yellow *The Thing?* T-shirt. "That little stuffed monkey pulls a lot of rank around here. He is our lucky charm. We should be all right. Oh, Diane did you pack some of that gooood coffee?"

"Pablo, I went over to Lupe Jiménez's Horny Toad Café as soon as I called in for the assignment. I have a whole bunch of it. It is good and strong, fresh roasted, and fresh ground. Mrs. Jiménez said a *Vaya con Dios* to me, made the sign of the cross, and gave me a hug, so I think we are good to go."

"Wow! We got a *Vaya con Dios*, the sign of the cross, and a hug? Well I think all of our bases are covered. What are we waiting for? We're burning daylight!"

While on the road, we noticed the wind was starting to pick up, and big tumbleweeds were becoming airborne. As we crossed over into Arizona, we could see a massive pyrocumulus cloud forming over the Huachuca Mountains.

"Holy crap, look at that!" said Phil.

"It looks like the fire is starting to blow up," I replied.

"Good Lord, it's a monster," gasped Diane.

I turned on the truck radio to see if we could catch any news about the fire. The radio selection was sparse. One station had a preacher delivering up a sermon about Armageddon, damnation, and an eternity of fire and brimstone. Switching channels, I found another station playing some happy Oom-pah Norteño music. I turned the dial and found a talk show dishing up some long-winded GOP propaganda and vitriol rhetoric, so I turned it off.

"No news here, we will get the low-down soon enough."

I was happy that Diane and Phil were on this assignment. We all seemed to get along pretty good; they were both level headed and Phil was now a seasoned veteran sort of speaking. He saw more fire last year than most of the guys have seen back at the station. We are all EMT's, paramedics, and career structure firefighters, so we have a lot of know-how in a lot of different areas. We will react to what the fire brings to the table and rely on our training and experience to get us through.

I felt hopeful that this assignment would be a good one. But then again, I couldn't shake an ominous feeling deep in my gut. As we approached base camp, I noticed the area just north of the camp was really burned over. We pulled up to a firefighter walking over to the command post, rolled down our window and started talking to him.

He said, "The fire came roaring out of one of the side canyons yesterday. Even though this camp is several miles away, the wind shifted and the fire crossed the highway and headed south in a hurry. Luckily, two bulldozers were in camp and cut a line to the north. Some heavies were diverted and flew in low hitting the leading edge of the fire pretty hard. If it weren't for the dozers and heavies, the base camp would have been toast!"

"Things are looking pretty extreme," I said, as I observed the area. "Phil, after we check in, take the truck through the inspection and find a place to park over with the other Type 6 engines. We will meet you later."

"You got it Boss, *I'm on it like Bag Balm on a chapped udder,*" said Phil.

Diane and I hopped out of the truck, and I grabbed the clipboard, looked up, and grinned at Phil. I slammed the door and we started walking over to command.

Diane asked, "Does he sit at home and make up those corny hayseed sayings?"

"He sure comes up with some good ones," I laughed shaking my head.

The fire was only three days old, and the base camp was already bulging with all kinds of fire apparatus. There must have been several dozen, Type 1 fire engines alone. These Type 1s are big city fire engines, the ones that go on residential house fire calls.

"Look! There are engines from Tucson Fire, Phoenix Fire and Mesa Fire," I said, and started to read the names of the trucks as we passed them. "Sierra Vista, Benson, Green Valley, Casa Grande, Glendale, Scottsdale, Rural Metro, and Northwest Fire! It looks like all of Arizona's big city fire departments are here!"

"I have never been on a wildland fire assignment where there were so many Type 1 engines," marveled Diane.

After finishing the check in, we scouted the parking lot trying to find where Phil parked the Nickel. While walking back, we passed Type 6 trucks from Montana, Illinois, Utah, and Washington. There were trucks from California, Colorado, and even a Bombero truck, from Mexico.

Further south, I could see a lot of hotshot buggies and inmate hand crews parked in the field. Thankfully, there was no evidence of the Wild Bunch. Phil flagged us down, and we settled in at the truck.

We went to the mess tent and grabbed some grub, and as we ate, I opened the IAP and started going over the info about the fire.

"Look, there are houses and subdivisions scattered in the foothills, and the main town is located just across the highway, within a stone's throw from the Huachuca Mountains," I remarked. "If the fire crosses the highway, the whole town could go up in flames."

"It says here, Ramsey Canyon is about four canyons to the north, and many endangered species call Ramsey Canyon home," Diane said. "If it is overrun with fire, it would be devastating to them!"

"Phil pointed to the map and said, "And, further north is an Army base named Fort Huachuca. It says here, the base is dedicated to military intelligence and their expertise extends into covert cyberspace operations."

It was already dark when we walked back to the truck, and Diane said, "We will probably be rode hard these next few days, so we'd better get some quality shut-eye now."

"It looks like we have our work cut out for us!" Phil said, as he pulled his sleeping bag from one of the compartments.

I rolled out my bedroll, crawled in and said, "Yeah, Phil, there is a lot at stake here, the fire is gaining ground, and time is running short, so pay attention and stay on your toes."

"You got it Boss, don't worry about me, I'm gonna be on my toes like Baryshnikov."

I chuckled, punched down my pillow and tried to get comfortable. Rolling to my side, I glanced to the north and off in the distance was the ominous silhouette of the mountains rimmed with a huge glowing necklace of fire.

24 Miracle In The Woods

Because of the thick layer of smoke that settled in over the base camp, and the droning of the generators, it turned out to be a long miserable night. We were up before sunrise and I headed for the morning briefing while Diane and Phil made their way toward the mess tent to grab some breakfast.

The base camp had doubled in size since yesterday, and the mess tent was abuzz with excitement. The aroma of sausage and bacon filled the tent, and there must have been over 600 firefighters eating breakfast. I grabbed a tray, dished up some scrambled eggs, a bagel and few strips of bacon, and poured myself a cup of hot coffee.

"Ahh, don't ya just love bacon?" I said as I sat down next to Phil.

I ran my finger down the IAP (Incident Action Plan) and began to tell them about the morning briefing and assignments.

"We will be working in Division D, joining forces with a Type 1 engine from Green Valley, Arizona, a 20-man hotshot crew from Illinois, two Type 6 brush trucks, and a local water tender." I pointed to a series of steep canyons, lined up one after another. "The fire has charged down two canyons already, and there are four more canyons waiting for their turn to make a downhill run into Sierra Vista. Our job is to create some defensible space between the approaching fire and around the houses at the base of these canyons."

We finished our breakfast and met up with the other members of our task force. The team leader gathered the engine bosses to discuss the day's assignments. We agreed on an action plan and headed down the highway. As we approached our division, we could see the destruction from the days before. Ranch houses and sheds were now piles of blackened rubble, and all of the oak trees were gone. Telephone poles were charred; their bases burnt away. Some were hanging by their wires like puppets, while others were lying on the ground.

As our convoy approached our division, the task force leader began to assign one or two trucks to dirt roads that emerged from the woods. Trucks started to peel off from the convoy, venturing into the forest. We turned left on the third dirt road and behind us was the hotshot crew from Illinois. After several miles, the road dead-ended at the National Forest Boundary. We turned around and slowly began to work our way toward the highway.

The area had been evacuated and looked like a ghost town. We pulled into the driveway of the first house we came across. It was a nice rustic, red ranch style house, about 1,500 square feet, surrounded by oak trees, and it had a large front porch with a suspended swinging bench and two white rocking chairs. Located on the other side of the driveway were a tool shed and a small guesthouse. As we approached the house, we saw a white envelope thumbtacked to the front door.

Diane read the handwritten note out loud, "Dear firemen, my name is Louise Manning and this is my home. Please do what you can to save it. The door is unlocked, so help yourself to some cold sodas in the fridge. I had to leave in such a hurry, the only thing I took with me was a suitcase with some clothes and my cat Kibbles. Everything I own is still here. I am afraid for you and all my friends who live here. This is all so horrible! God Bless You Firefighters."

Diane took out her pencil and wrote, "Dear Louise, we will do our best. I hope when you return, your house will still be here and this note will be waiting for you. God Bless You Too! Signed, Mimbres Springs Fire Department, New Mexico, and the Midewin Interagency Hotshot Crew, Illinois." Diane opened the front door and placed the letter on a small table.

We walked around the property to appraise the situation. The back of the house had a once grassy yard, which was now straw brown and mowed short. There was a large back porch with several dead and dying trees growing next to it. Our crews huddled up and discussed our escape routes and safety zone. We found a ladder, and some of us climbed onto the roof to shovel off years of accumulated oak leaves and dead branches. The others cleaned out the acorn-chocked gutters. Meanwhile, sawyers cut down the dead trees close to the house. The rest of the hotshots eradicated some tall grass, and removed a thick layer of leaves that had piled up around a large propane tank located at the edge of the property. When that was finished, we started on the guesthouse and shed. There was a flurry of activity and as Phil would say, "We looked like ants on a honey bun."

After securing Louise's house, Phil, Diane, and I wiped our feet on the doormat and went inside to take a peek. The house was furnished with lace curtains, oriental rugs, and antique furniture. While standing in the living room, I detected the slightest hint of mothballs and could hear the slow mechanical, tick, tick, tick of a grandfather clock. Aside from the soft drone of a housefly, the place was eerily quiet and looked like it was frozen in time.

I picked up a silver framed photograph that was sitting on the fireplace mantel.

"This must be Louise."

She had snow-white hair, rouge on her cheeks, and wore red lipstick. She was wearing a light blue floral print dress, a pearl necklace with matching earrings, and had a white apron around her waist. Two children were sitting with her on the front porch swing, and I figured they must have been her grandkids. But most importantly, she had that wonderful maternal smile!

I placed the picture back on the mantel, and Diane said, "I bet there are some fresh baked chocolate chip cookies waiting for those kids in the kitchen. She kind of reminds me of my grandma when I was growing up."

"What's in the fridge?" asked Phil.

Even though the electricity was off, the fridge was still cold and stocked with an assortment of those tall, full sized glass bottles of soda. There were Coca-Colas, Sprites, Fanta Grapes and Oranges.

I grabbed one and ran it across my forehead. "Ahhh," I sighed.

The bottle had tiny white letters *Hecho en Mexico* printed next to the Coca-Cola logo, and I knew these were the good ones, made with real cane sugar, as opposed to the ones made with high fructose corn syrup.

While Diane and I each enjoyed a Coca-Cola, Phil popped open a Fanta Grape Soda. Savoring their coolness and thirst cutting carbonation, I tipped mine completely upside-down to extract every last drop, and let loose a resounding burp.

"Nice burp!" said Phil.

"Oh yeah ... How about this," said Diane. She chugged her last swallows of Coke and let loose a loud, long, unladylike belch!

"Wow! That was impressive, I didn't know you were so talented Diane!" I said with surprise.

"It's a gift," she said sarcastically, and placed her empty on the kitchen counter. "We use to have burping contests when I was a kid and would drink Bubble-Up because it had great carbonation. I was a pretty good burper, but my younger sister Janis was the champion belcher. She could recite the alphabet all the way down to the letter L in one long loud burp!"

"No kidding?" asked Phil. "Let me try." He polished off the last of his soda and let loose a loud grapey burp.

"A-B-C ... that's all I got!"

We laughed and placed our empties on the counter next to Diane's.

"Well that was a nice break," Phil said.

"Yup, a pause that refreshes!" said Diane.

"Well, let's get our refreshed butts outta' here and get some work done!" I quipped.

As we exited the house, Diane took the note and wrote ... *P.S. Thanks for the sodas!* She put it back on the table and we left.

About a quarter mile down the road, we approached a beautiful two-story house. The first floor was built with native fieldstone. The second story was made of wood, covered with white vinyl siding, and had a sturdy green metal roof. The yard was professionally landscaped, and a dozen tall pine trees were mixed in with the oaks. There was a large storage building located off to the left. Surprisingly, the owner of the property was still there and was getting ready to evacuate when we met up with him.

"Howdy, friend," I said and extended my hand to the homeowner.

The man shook my hand pretty hard and said, "Boy, am I glad to see you guys!"

He was an older gentleman, 75ish, about 6 feet tall, wearing a white, long sleeve shirt, and denim jeans. A big 10-gallon cowboy hat complimented his white handlebar mustache, and he was wearing some pretty expensive ostrich skin cowboy boots.

There was a desperate tone to his voice when he said, "If all else fails, let the house burn, but please save the storage shed!"

The house was gorgeous, so I was taken aback when he said that.

"Sir, we will do our best to save all of it, however, if you don't mind me asking, what's in the shed?"

He walked us over to the shed, which was more like a small warehouse.

He unlocked the garage door and raised it up. Walking into the shady coolness of the building, we were astounded at the sight. Parked in the darkness were about 12 vintage automobiles in various stages of restoration. We gasped at the sight! We were easily looking at millions of dollars worth of cars!

"These are my babies and my life's work. I don't have enough time to flatbed them out of here. I pray to God they will survive the fire. I've seen the ruins down the way and am sick at the thought of losing it all!" he frowned.

"Wow!" said Phil with excitement, as he walked over to a bright red racecar, "What kind is this?"

"That's a 1938 Alpha Romero 8C 2900 Mille Miglia. The black one next to it is a 1938 Bugatti 57 S Atlantic. I bought them from Ralph Lauren. He drove a hard bargain, but I think I made out OK and landed me a couple of real beauties," he said with a glint in his eye, and looked at them like a father admiring his children.

As we were leaving, I kept looking back at the cars and said, "Well sir, we will have to work quickly. We need to remove some of the trees that are next to the house and shed."

"Do whatever you feel is necessary," he replied.

"You, on the other hand, will have to get outta here, the fire is heading this way!"

With that, he handed me a slip of paper with his cell phone number on it. "Let me know what happens, good or bad. I can take the news, but call me regardless. Not knowing is the worst part."

The old guy quickly climbed into his powder blue, 1950s pick-up truck and headed to town.

Diane and two Illinois hotshots fired up their chainsaws and cut down trees next to the house, and proceeded to cut the low hanging limbs off of some others. The other hotshots removed pine needles from the roof and gutters, and worked at clearing away the dead and dying vegetation from around the buildings. We finished up knowing we could have done more, but time was of the essence, and there were more houses to deal with down the way.

Down the road we found a small yellow house. We all sat on the front porch to eat a quick lunch. The crew we were working with, were hardworking son-of-a-guns called the Midewin Interagency Hotshot Crew. Their crew boss was tall and lanky, had a full red beard, and long red hair. They were all wearing white hard hats with the Forest Service Emblem on the front as opposed to our generic yellow ones.

Phil said, "You guys are a long way from home."

"Yup, a long ways away. Oh, by the way, my name is Jerry."

"My name is Phil, it's a pleasure, and where the heck is Midewin?"

"Well Midewin is the name of a region. The Midewin National Tallgrass Prairie is located in northeastern Illinois. Midewin is a Native American name meaning *Healers*. The Potawatomi Indians of that area had very powerful leaders and they used their medicine to help heal their nation and keep the peace among the many tribes."

"We could use some of those Midewins up on Capitol Hill," said Phil. "To keep the peace between the Democratic and GOP tribes!"

Jerry said, "I have never worked on a fire in Arizona before. We've worked some fires in the West but mostly up north, Montana, Idaho and the likes. Our season starts pretty early, sometimes as early as March. We work a lot of prescribed burns in New York, Illinois, Minnesota, Indiana, and Ohio."

Diane informed them, "The fire season here starts pretty much in late May and early June. We are fairly close to the Mexican border, and we get a lot of foot traffic coming up from there. Sometimes unattended campfires are responsible for some of our early-season fires."

Phil added, "And when the seasonal thunderstorms start to move in, about the middle of June, we get a lot of dry lightning starts."

"The supervisors went over some of the hazards at the morning briefing, you know, high temperatures, low humidity, high winds, and such. Possible heat exhaustion and dehydration were also mentioned. What else do we have to look out for?" Jerry asked.

"They are right about the heat exhaustion and dehydration, so don't take that lightly," I cautioned. "With the humidity being so low and the temperatures being close to 100 degrees, a person doesn't realize how much they are sweating. In reality, when we are working this hard, we sweat like crazy. We just don't see it or feel it because it evaporates off of our skin so fast, due to the low humidity. So drink a lot of water and Gatorade. You can never have too much."

Diane started to clue them in on more desert wisdom. "In the desert southwest we have other stuff to worry about. For starters, there are the killer bees."

"The Africanized bees, right?" asked Jerry.

"Yup, those are the ones. When a dozer knocks down some old timber or stirs up a woodpile with a hive in there, they come streaming out, mad as hell. There can be as many as 50,000 bees in a hive, and all they want to do is eliminate the threat."

"What should we do?" asked Jerry.

"Turn tail and run, but most importantly, cover your mouth and nose. Those bees are attracted to CO2 and go straight for your airway. Once they get in your nose or mouth, the bee stings will cause your airway to swell up and you won't be able to breathe. You will be a goner in no time. They can fly as fast as you can run, so get a move on, cover up, and keep going for a long ways."

"What else do we have to worry about?" asked another hotshot.

"We have rattlesnakes everywhere." I said. They are mostly nocturnal, but watch where you place your hands when removing brush and timber, and watch where you sit your fanny down."

Phil chimed in, "There is a scorpion named the Bark Scorpion. They are small, about one-inch long, reddish brown in color and have skinny, long pincers. You will find them in woodpiles and rock outcroppings. But check your sleeping bag before you turn in, and tip out your boots in the morning, before you put them on. Their sting is pretty painful, and some people have severe allergic reactions to them."

"Anything else?" asked another.

"And who are you beautiful?" I asked, trying not to sound like a chauvinistic pig.

"I'm Katherine, but most people call me Kate."

She was tall and fit, with brown hair, and dark green eyes. Even without makeup and covered in Arizona dust, she was easy on the eyes.

"Well, Kate, aside from heat exhaustion, dehydration, and creepy crawlies, we have to look out for the wily, Jumping Cholla Cactus. It stands about five feet tall, has branching arms studded with these gnarly spiked balls. I swear, you can be standing clear of the darned things and find yourself howling in pain, as one of the spiked cholla balls mysteriously jumps from where it was and becomes attached to your forearm."

"What do you do if that happens?" she asked.

"Whatever you do, don't try and pick it off with your fingers. If you try and pry them off, you will just have spines in your other hand as well. It takes a pair of pliers to pull the ball off of your skin. Some guys carry a sturdy long toothed comb in their cargo pants pocket just for that reason. You kinda slide the comb under the cactus barb and then flick it off."

"Killer bees, rattlesnakes, bark scorpions, jumping cholla! Good Lord!" said Kate.

"Ha! And all you thought you had to worry about was fire," I laughed.

"Silly me!" she said as we all got up to begin working on the yellow house.

We worked pretty hard for the rest of the afternoon. Despite the homeowner's attempts to beatify their property, if the landscaping looked like it could be a threat to their house, we ripped it out, chopped it down and cleared it away. This was what hand crews call creating defensible space. I liked to refer to it as extreme landscaping. It was always a lot of grunt work and after several hours of chopping and digging, I sensed our crew was starting to become exhausted from the heat. Despite the fatigue, we sucked it up, drank some more water, and pressed on.

It was about 16:00 and we had been at it since 07:00. The air was filled with the constant buzz of aircraft. Sky crane helicopters and air tankers were flying in and out of the canyon at a fevered pace, and the radio was crackling with non-stop traffic. I could feel some tension brewing.

Diane came over to me and said, "The air is getting hotter and drier, and there is a lot more smoke. This is usually the hottest part of the day, so we have to stay frosty and be on our toes. If these conditions continue to worsen, we may have to bug outta here."

I agreed and rounded up the troops to inform them of this *Watch Out Situation.* After finishing our seventh house, we heard an urgent call on the radio!

"All units move to the safety zones! I repeat, *All Units Move To Your Safety Zones!*"

"Let's get our butts outta' here!" I yelled.

We jumped in the Nickel and I radioed Jerry. He did a head count to make sure all of his hotshots were on the buses and accounted for. All systems were go, and we quickly left

the woods and headed for the highway. We parked the
Triple Nickel on the far shoulder with the Midewin guys
right behind us. It looked like someone had stirred up an
ant's nest, as other units were coming out of the woods in
droves. Dozens of trucks were parking along the highway,
and we could barely see their red and blue flashing code
lights due to the heavy smoke boiling out of the canyon.

The afternoon sky was becoming as dark as night, and the
air tankers were flying low, barely above the trees. The wind
was howling and suddenly, a wall of fire as tall as the
telephone poles, erupted from the forest! Our brush truck
started shaking as the enormous wall of flames rolled over
us.

"Holy Shit!" yelled Diane.

Phil was staring open mouthed at the wall of fire, and did
a duck and cover when it roared over our truck.

"Christ Almighty!" I yelled, and watched as the fire
jumped the highway and headed for the town!

Just then, we heard a frantic call on the radio from our
division supervisor!

"All units get back in there and save any structures you
can!"

Immediately, all the trucks staged on the highway, drove
right back into the fires returning to their assigned areas
they had worked earlier.

I yelled at the others, "God, I wish we had more on than
these flimsy yellow shirts and green pants!"

"Me too!" yelled Diane.

With the main fire front past us, we went back and started
attacking the fires impinging on the houses.

Jumping into firefighting mode, we pulled our goggles
down over our eyes and covered our faces with a bandana.
We parked the trucks and started to put out a porch that

caught some hot embers. The air was ferociously hot, and my bandana, shirt, and pants were a flimsy barrier against the heat. My adrenaline was pumping, and I was sweating up a storm!

After saving the house, we jumped back in the truck and I could hardly sit in the seat, my clothes were so hot.

We worked the length of the road, put out more hotspots, and realized we didn't lose a single house! We circled back and double-checked our area and marveled at it all.

"I can't believe all these houses are still standing!" shouted Jerry.

"It's like a guardian angel has placed her hands over each house and steered the flames away!" yelled Diane.

We regrouped and returned to the two-story house with the antique cars. Everything had miraculously survived! The metal shed was scorched but still standing, and it looked like the cars had survived. The house had lost all of its beautiful landscaping, and the vinyl siding had melted and was hanging off the house like pulled taffy.

"Isn't that amazing!" gasped Kate.

After determining our area was secure, we headed out to the main road to regroup. We could hear the big Type 1 fire engines racing into the neighborhoods, and looking across the highway, Diane said with astonishment, "Look at all the houses on fire!"

We could see black columns of smoke rising into the sky, and they resembled the fires in the oil fields of Kuwait, during the Iraqi War.

We raced into the neighborhoods and worked for several hours dousing hot spots. It was almost dark when Incident Command told our task force to wrap it up and return to base camp. I looked at my watch and couldn't believe we had been at it for 16 hours. As we put away our gear, the fatigue set in, and I noticed we were all filthy and dang-dog-tired. As we headed back to base camp, I said ... "Holy cow, I need to call the man who owns the cars!"

I pulled the slip of paper he gave me out of my wallet. It said, *God Speed Firefighters*, his name, and his phone number. I dialed the number, hoping the cell phone towers were still intact.

"Hello, is this Benjamin? This is Pablo, the firefighter you met at your house."

There was a moment of silence at the other end. He cleared his throat and said quietly ... "OK let me have it."

"Benjamin, the house and the cars survived! Everything is a little scorched, your landscaping took a big hit and you will need to replace the vinyl siding on the house, but all in all, everything is in good shape!" I beamed.

"Whump!" The phone must have dropped and hit the floor, and there was some scuffling and fumbling, and then he said with a loud and teary voice. "Thank you God! Thank you all!"

"Yeah, thank God and then some," I said. "We needed all the help we could muster. The angels were with us today. The entire area was over-run with fire. And I'm not talking a little bit of fire. There was a lot of it! It was nothing short of a miracle. A true miracle!"

We chatted a bit more and then said our good lucks and goodbyes.

Later, back in the mess tent, I relayed the news to the rest of our task force over a well-earned dinner of fried chicken and mashed potatoes. We finished our meal, high fived each other and parted ways. Returning to our camp in complete darkness, we checked for rattlesnakes and bark scorpions, and plopped down our weary bones for some well-deserved sleep.

25 El Culo Del Diablo

For the next two days we were assigned to help with structure protection, and scouted the small side roads that meandered away from the main highway. We took a left onto a tiny dirt road named Dead Bear Draw and traveled in a ways looking for any kind of structure that could be saved. We soon realized there were no houses to prep, and the road narrowed down to one lane. The sides of the road were choked with oak trees and flanked with a barbed wire fence; it soon became apparent that we were driving into a death trap.

"There is nowhere for us to turn around! If a fire hit we would be screwed!" I said.

"Our only resort is to drive the truck backwards. Guys, we are in deep do-do here," said Diane.

As Phil drove in further, he saw a small fenced pasture with some level ground just ahead of us.

He stopped and suggested, "We could cut away a couple sections of the barbed wire fence and dig out the fence posts to create some kind of turnaround."

"Good idea!" I nodded.

We got out, cut the fence, dug around the metal T-post, and wrapped it with some wire, and then we used the truck jack to pry the fence post up out of the ground.

After identifying the opening with some pink flagging and marking the road on our map, we advised the other units in our task force to avoid the dangerous road altogether, as there was nothing to save down Dead Bear Draw anyway.

On the next road, we joined up with the Type 1 engine from Green Valley. They were assigned to supply water for the hotshot crews, who were helping build some extensive bulldozer firebreaks behind a small subdivision. The crews were burning out a lot of forest and working their way over to Miller Canyon. A water tender from Helmet Peak Volunteer Fire Department was running back and forth to the main highway, fetching loads of water for the engine.

The hotshots had miles of hose and lateral lines set out, starting from the Green Valley engine and ran along the Coronado National Forest boundary. The air was vibrating with the sound of sky cranes and air tankers, and the forest was filled with the buzz of chainsaws, bulldozers, and the sound of hotshot banter. A blue haze covered the area, mostly from the chainsaws, dozer exhaust, and the newly created smoke from the back burns. At the mouth of Miller Canyon were more bulldozers and hand crews cutting a swath of bare earth, five dozer blades wide. The work in Miller Canyon was impressive, and a lot of effort was going into stopping the fire right here.

Phil backed the Triple Nickel next to the Green Valley engine, and we got out to talk with Greg, their engine boss. He was a strong tall fella, with a gap-toothed grin, deep voice, and a great laugh. Their engineer's name was JR, and was about 5 feet 10 inches tall, had a medium build and spoke with one of those classic Texas drawls. He was working the pump panel with goggles pulled down over his eyes and a bandana over his face, protecting him from the smoke. The squad boss was a woman, about 5 feet 3, with olive skin and short black hair flecked with grey. She had a lot of energy and was as quick as a rabbit. Her name was Erin, and she kinda reminded me of Diane.

Their truck was backed in, right up to the National Forest Boundary. The truck engine was in pump mode, and the hood was propped open to help dissipate the motor's heat. They had been supplying water since 08:00 in the morning, and it was now well past 14:00. The motor was red-hot and pumping hard.

"How is the weather up here?" I asked Greg.

He chuckled and said, "Not too bad, the temp is in the nineties today. Who would think ninety would feel cool? The wind has died down some, but I just heard on the weather report that the humidity is reported to be at zero."

"Zero, Like in Z-E-R-O?" I gasped!

"This is our big day," said Greg. "We need to get as much done as possible. Some of the experts are saying the lumber at the Home Depot has more moisture in it than the trees in this forest. The forecast for tomorrow is going to be downright brutal, with high winds, low humidity, and higher temperatures. I can see this fire roaring out of Miller Canyon tomorrow like a lit fart outta the butt hole of the devil."

When I heard that I choked on my Gatorade.

"Diane, come over here," I laughed, and waved Phil and JR over too.

"Greg says the conditions for tomorrow will send fire racing down Miller canyon like what?" still laughing at his remark.

"Like a lit fart outta the butt hole of the devil!"

"*El Culo del Diablo*, the asshole of the devil," laughed Erin.

"There will be an ill wind blowing tomorrow," snickered JR.

We all laughed, picturing the image in our minds.

We finished our Gatorades and moved down the road to the next house. About a quarter mile away was a small wooden house. The front yard was adorned with birdbaths, humming bird feeders and spinning whirligigs. We pulled in the driveway and saw a small barn near the back. As we pulled behind the house, two tiny burros, as cute as can be, came trotting out of the barn like puppies. The property was evacuated, and sadly the burros were left behind.

We walked toward them and to our dismay, there was an older grey mare standing outside of the fence trying to get a drink out of the horse trough just beyond her reach.

Without hesitation, Diane ran inside the pen and cautiously approached the horse.

"Easy girl, let me help you," she whispered, and grabbed her halter.

Diane dipped her hard hat into the trough and held it up. The mare drank like there was no tomorrow.

Phil and I walked around to the other side of the fence, and I rubbed the horse's neck. She nuzzled me and was as gentle as a kitten.

Phil checked her out and said, "She's burned up pretty bad. Her underbelly is blistered and raw, and her legs are peeling."

Phil walked her inside the pen, and she made a beeline to the water.

I radioed Incident Command and was given the phone number to the Sierra Vista Riding Club, and I made the call.

"Sierra Vista Riding Club, this is Roxanne, how can I help you?"

"Hello, my name is Pablo, a firefighter working at the Monument Fire. Our crew has come across three abandoned animals, two burros and a horse. We are in an area that will be overrun with fire either today or tomorrow, and it looks like the horse has already experienced some fire and is in pretty bad shape. Can you help us?"

I gave her some more information and our location.

She was very reassuring and said, "Don't worry, I will have some people heading your way with a couple of horse trailers. They should be there within the hour."

"Are you guys getting many of these calls?" I asked.

"The riding club as well as other organizations have joined forces, and we have taken in about 210 animals so far," Roxanne replied,

"210 animals?" I asked in amazement.

"210 and counting!" she said. "They are being housed at our facility as well as the county fairgrounds and other locations. Local veterinarians are donating their time to tend to the injured animals. And listen to this, the other day a local news station sent a film crew over to the riding club to do a story about the animal rescues. They shot some footage of the chickens, dogs, horses, and goats that we have housed here. After it aired on the evening news, support from the community and the surrounding area has been overwhelming! Feed, hay, dog chow, and money have been pouring in to help defray the costs.

"You guys are amazing," I said.

"You guys are too!" she replied.

As we waited for the animal rescue folks to show up, we sat and fed the animals some of our snacks. The mare really liked the baby carrots and was digging at Phil's pocket to get more.

"I think she really likes you," Diane smiled.

"What's not to like, the older ladies really dig me."

"I think we should give them names," smiled Diane.

"How about naming the burros, Romeo and Juliet," said Phil.

"And we can call the old grey mare, Miss Daisy," I said.

"Perfect, I like that," said Diane, as she rubbed the old horse's neck.

It didn't take long for the animal rescue folks to show up with two horse trailers. Romeo and Juliet tiptoed up the ramp into one trailer. Miss Daisy waltzed right into the other. We patted them on their noses and off they went. Diane had a tear in her eye as they made their way down the dusty road.

"They'll be alright," I told Diane. "I'm just glad we showed up today."

"The guys at the station back home said you were bad juju," smiled Diane. "I think Miss Daisy, Romeo, and Juliet would beg to differ."

We gathered our hand tools and started knocking down weeds and brush. After finishing up with that house, we got the go-ahead to make our way back to base camp. We met up with the Midewin hotshots and the Green Valley guys in the mess tent.

Phil had his plate piled high, like a man on death row. There was a thick slab of meatloaf slathered in ketchup, a pile of roasted potatoes, green beans and three dinner rolls. He set his plate down and headed over to pour a couple of glasses of milk and lemonade.

"That Phil can really pack it away," I said to the table of famished firefighters.

Jerry, from the Midewin bunch replied, "I think every crew has their *Phil*," and nodded his head sideways towards Kate.

Kate sat down between Phil and Jerry with *two* slabs of meatloaf, an even higher pile of potatoes and a slice of chocolate cake!

She looked up at us staring at her and her plate and said defensively, "What?"

We all laughed, and Jerry elbowed her a couple of times.

"She earned it ... you know, I read somewhere that wildland firefighters burn about 5,000 calories per day. Collectively, I bet our task force has burned a million calories so far."

We were laughing and swapping stories when Greg told us he almost ran out of gas coming back to base camp, because they were pumping water all day and didn't realize they were really low on fuel.

"We were running on fumes on the way back." he said, "The needle on the fuel gauge was sticking out the door! It was way past the E! Man, it would have been embarrassing if I had to hold up an empty fuel can to flag down a passing truck."

"I would have stopped, but not before I snapped a photo of you on the side of the road holding up the gas can," I grinned.

Then I told them about Romeo, Juliet, Miss Daisy, and the Sierra Vista Riding Club.

"You know, something like that makes it all worth-while. You guys made my day," smiled Greg.

"Now don't forget," I reminded them, "we have a date with the devil tomorrow."

"Hear, hear!" we all cheered, and raised a glass ... "To tomorrow!"

As we made our way back to our trucks, I noticed the wind was beginning to pick up. Paper cups, litter, and ash, were being swept up into small dust devils around the camp.

"Look at that, dust devils, devils, El Culo del Diablo," I said to the others.

"There seems to be a reoccurring theme here," said Phil.

I shook my head, grabbed my shaving kit, and looked up toward the mountain and saw a menacing glow in the canyon. I stared at it as I made my way to the showers and felt that strange feeling in my gut again.

26 Armageddon

The wind blew hard all night, and I didn't sleep at all, so I decided to get up before sunrise to prepare for the day ahead. I put on two pair of wool socks, a pair of blue jeans and over that, my green Nomex forestry pants. I couldn't shake that ominous feeling as I pulled on a long sleeve cotton T-shirt, and then my yellow long sleeve wildland shirt. It kind of felt like we were going off to war, like this was D-Day, and we were getting ready to storm the beaches of Normandy.

"Damn, where are my leather gloves?" I said out loud in the pre-dawn darkness. Today is the day when all hell was going to break loose and I was feeling anxious. I took a deep breath and tried to calm myself down.

"Remain calm and stay focused, ya gotta stay focused," I mumbled.

It was too early to strap on my chest harness, which contained my radio, a small spiral bound Incident Response Pocket Guide, pad of paper, and a pencil. I laced up my leather boots and wrapped a fresh bandana around my neck. Later I would strap on a waist belt that held two canteens, my Leatherman, and my fire shelter.

Phil was now up and doing a truck check. He removed the air filter and showed it to me. It was choked with dust and ash, and he replaced it with a new one. I saw Diane returning from supply, with a case of water and Gatorade. With determination, she immediately went back for two bags of ice and three sack lunches.

"I'm heading to the morning briefing, "I'll meet you guys later in the mess tent."

"I still have to go to supply and get some fresh batteries for the radios," Diane said.

"OK, hustle up, we're burning daylight," and I marched off.

The camp was beginning to stir as the eastern horizon was starting to brighten. The wind was picking up, and there was not a cloud in the sky.

At the briefing we were presented with grim prospects. All air support was grounded for the day. High winds were predicted, and steady 45 MPH winds would be coming in from the west with 50-60 MPH gusts, definitely horrible conditions to be flying in. Single digit humidity coupled with hotter temperatures, made today's forecast even more dreadful.

Over 10,000 people had been evacuated from their homes over the past two days. The National Guard and various law enforcement agencies were patrolling the streets to keep looters away. The mood at the briefing was solemn. You could have heard a pin drop.

The safety officer spoke next. She told us that she had worked a lot of large Urban/ Wildland interface fires and was brought in to this fire for her expertise.

"I can't tell you how amazed I am with your performance this week. I worked a large fire three weeks ago and couldn't believe what I saw. Some of the crews parked themselves in the subdivisions and waited for the fire to come to them," she informed us. "For them, wishful thinking and luck had become part of their action plan, and they didn't move a muscle until the fire was imminent.

You guys, on the other hand, have been very proactive. As I drove around the Divisions these past few days, I was incredibly pleased to see you out there prepping the land. I have never seen so many firefighters work so hard, for so long, to save so much property. *Wishful thinking should never be a part of anyone's action plan, and I give you all kudos and high praise for a job well done!"*

A cheer went up in the crowd, and the solemn mood was lifted. Engine bosses and crew bosses were given their assignments. Amid eager chatter and back slapping, we dispersed to take on the day.

Entering the mess tent, I found Phil and Diane sitting with the Midewin and Green Valley guys. I grabbed some coffee and a plate of scrambled eggs, hash browns, four sausage links, four strips of bacon, and a cheese Danish.

"Wow, that's a hearty breakfast," Greg said, gawking at my plate.

"No telling when we will get a chance to eat today, we will be so busy, I figure I might as well eat while I can."

"Good idea," Phil and Kate said in unison, as they both got up for seconds. When they came back, their second helping was bigger than their first.

Diane looked at the two chowhounds and laughed. "You guys are like two peas in a pod. You must both have hollow legs."

Kate replied, "We need to keep up our strength, after all, today is the day of reckoning."

"What's the word Boss? Do we have a plan for *the Armageddon?*" asked Phil.

"And just what is your definition of *the Armageddon?*" I inquired.

"Well in a nutshell, during the Armageddon, all the armies of the world gather at the foothills of the *Mountain*. There, they do battle with the *Beast*, the Beast being Satan. Then Christ appears and reigns fire on the land and casts the Beast into the bottomless pit. The *Battle* determines the *End of the Ages*. That's the Cliff Notes version, so don't hold me to it."

"Well that pretty much sums up the morning briefing," I said with a shrug and discussed what was said at the meeting.

We finished our breakfast, bussed our plates, and tossed our trash. The Midewin Crew had been reassigned and was heading up to Carr Canyon Road, the next canyon to the north of Miller Canyon. Carr Canyon Road was the only road that went all the way to the top of the range, and additional manpower was being brought in to help with the back burn. This would be our best and last chance to fire out the area to stop the fire's progress to the north. The IC wanted to stop the fire before it entered Ramsey Canyon, the one with all of the wildlife and endangered species. Green Valley and the Triple Nickel would stay in the foothills and work the last subdivision before Miller Canyon.

I hollered to the Midewin hotshots as they walked away, "Watch out for the rattlesnakes!"

Jerry yelled back, "And killer bees!" They headed toward their transport buggies, and in the silhouette of the dusty morning sunrise, he gave us a reassuring wave.

Traveling on Highway 92, we drove past the destruction once again.

About 30 houses have been lost so far and the count will no doubt go up today," I said with uncertainty. "Fortunately, no lives have been lost."

Driving further north, Phil pointed out that the telephone pole bases were now wrapped in protective foil about 10 feet high.

"I heard at the briefing, over 300 telephone poles have been destroyed so far," I said.

As we entered our assigned subdivision, we were pleased to see that the roads were paved, the houses were rather new, and fire hydrants appeared at regular intervals. The houses were much closer together, were wood frame two story structures with stucco exteriors, and all of them had red tile roofs.

The local news stations have been urging the homeowners to eradicate any brush, cut away any low hanging limbs, and clean out their gutters. This was exactly what we have been doing for the past three days.

"Let's work together and patrol only one street at a time. We can leap frog past each other whenever we are finished with the house we are working on," I suggested.

"Good idea!" said Greg.

"I have an idea that will make it easier for you to deploy your fire hose," I said.

I rummaged around in the Green Valley engineer's compartment and pulled out two, large, 4-inch spanner wrenches. Spanner wrenches are used to break apart hose couplings and resemble big hooks. We secured the spanner wrenches to the grab handles on the outside of their cab using bailing wire and duct tape. We used the spanner wrenches as brackets to hang the lighter, smaller diameter wildland hose to the outside of their truck. I tugged on the hooks a little to see if the bailing wire and duct tape would hold.

"Greg, drape some 1-inch wildland hose over these spanner wrenches. They should hold the hose up pretty good. The 1-inch hose is pretty lightweight and a person can deploy it from these hooks and rerack it a lot faster than the heavy house fire hose. Their house fire attack lines are way too big, too bulky and once they are full of water, are extremely heavy. We will be fighting a lot of fire today and need to be light on our feet and extremely mobile."

Erin brought over several rolls of the smaller wildland hose, and the two of them started to unroll the hose and drape it over the brackets.

"Well looky here!" said JR in his Texas drawl. "We're a lean mean wildland fire fighting machine," and helped us pre-connect the wildland hose to their water pump.

"Here try it out," said Phil.

JR grabbed the entire bunch of hose that was draped over the brackets, lifted it up and plopped the bundle of hose onto the ground. He grabbed the nozzle and ran about 30 feet away from the truck. He was amazed to see how easily the hose played itself out. It looked like a giant snake uncoiling and slithering through the grass.

"We have a similar set up on the back of our brush truck," said Phil.

We walked over to the Nickel and Phil showed off our set up. "We have 200 feet of 1-inch wildland hose laid accordion style in a big wire basket. The hose is pre-connected to the water pump and can be easily deployed and tossed back in the basket when we need to move quickly.

"Ok, we have a full day ahead of us so let's get rolling, we're burning daylight,"I yelled.

We started at the southern end of the subdivision and worked our way to the north. It was business as usual. We cleared weeds and debris from the property. Some of the houses had wooden decks, and their back yards were facing the scenic mountains. Those decks posed a problem because leaves and litter had accumulated under them. If a hot ember flew under there, it could easily catch the deck and then the house on fire.

We sent the smallest people in to crawl under the decks to clear out the debris.

I heard Diane and Erin grunting as they crawled among the litter, "Watch out for spiders, especially the Brown Recluse or the Black Widow," I warned them.

"Spiders! Great! That's just freaking great!" Erin shouted, as she bumped her hard hat on the underside of the deck.

The rest of us carried patio furniture, BBQ grills, and piles of cordwood that were stacked against the houses over to the side sheltered from the wind. We made great progress moving all kinds of stuff over to the leeward side of the houses. After a while, I felt a surge of confidence that everything would to be OK.

Greg went out to the street to check the hydrants. Phil and I walked over as he removed the steamer cap and placed the hydrant wrench on the top valve stem. We wanted to see how much water flowed out of the fire hydrant, and we were curious to see how much pressure was in the system.

"Well here goes nothing," he said optimistically and turned the wrench about a dozen revolutions.

"Nothing! Not a drop! Crap!" he said.

"Nothing, about sums it up, the power must be out at the water plant," I said.

"This sucks!" scowled Greg.

"Big time!" Phil replied. *"It sucks like a skinny straw in a thick chocolate shake."*

"That's a lot of suck," said Greg.

"Uh-huh," nodded Phil as he removed his hard hat and wiped his forehead with his sleeve.

"Well on to plan B," I said, "There is nothing we can do about the hydrants now. We need to keep in direct contact with the guys on the water tenders and make a note of where the port-a-tanks and pumpkins are today."

We were standing in the shade of the next house, sipping water when I commented that the temperature was steadily rising. The wind was strong, and it felt like we were standing in a dry sauna, with a huge fan turned on us. I poured some water on my bandana and tied it around my neck. I poured the rest over my broiling head and placed my hard hat back on.

Phil chirped, "*It's hotter than a two peckered hoot-goat out here.*"

"Hey I'm the hoot-goat around here," I told Phil.

Diane chimed in, "Well Pablo, I always thought you were kinda' hot."

"Ah, get otta' here, you're making me blush," I smiled and turned my head to one side.

Greg walked up to us and said, "Do you notice something strange today?"

"Yeah, I was going to mention it, I can't quite put my finger on it," I replied.

We all stood there and tried to figure out what was so different about today.

Erin looked up in the sky and stated, "It's the noise! There isn't the constant drone of airplanes, air tankers and helicopters. No chain saws or dozers either."

She was right; it was pretty quiet except for the radio traffic and the wind. It was eerie and seemed *too quiet.*

It was 15:45 when we finished prepping the final houses on the northern edge of the subdivision. We grabbed our sack lunches and sat on a low cinder block wall in the back yard of one of the houses. We looked over to the north, and

I couldn't believe my eyes. There in front of us was a huge grassy field almost a half-mile long and a half-mile wide. The field ran all the way up to the mouth of Miller Canyon. We could see the huge dozer line cut across the mouth of the canyon, and the hillside was painted thick with a wide swath of red slurry.

"What the hell is this?" I said pointing at the immense grassland in front of us. "Why hasn't this been burned out?"

The grass was about waist high, picturesque and park-like, filled with wildflowers, butterflies, and humming birds. Up the hill, near the mouth of the canyon, was a thick stand of oak trees. Despite its beauty, this was a huge red flag when it came to wild fires. I called the situation in to the supervisors. They advised me that they knew about the field, and were trying to pull together some manpower to burn out the area. He said it was a low priority on their to-do list, and should be no big deal. They were confident the work done in Miller Canyon would hold.

"*It will hold, my ass!*" I snorted.

The smoke was getting thicker, the wind was blowing hard down the canyon, and the sun looked blood red through the smoky sky.

"Shit damn, this is it!" shouted Greg. "El Culo del Diablo!"

Dense black smoke started rolling out of the canyon with a sinister orange glow behind it. The day was turning into night right before our eyes. There was a heightened sense of intensity, and our portable radios were crackling with chatter.

Greg hollered, "Turn down your radios just for a minute!"

We turned down our noisy radios and I could hear something that made my blood run cold!

I gasped and said, "It sounds like a giant freight train is roaring down the canyon!"

"Look!" shouted Erin and she pointed to the mouth of the canyon.

Through the thick smoke, we could see lots of deer gathering under the oak trees. They were bunching up on each other and getting real skittish. All of a sudden, in a moment of terror, they bolted into the field and started to race toward the highway!

"We gotta go!" I yelled.

Just then giant flames exploded out of the canyon!

We sprinted to our trucks parked in the driveways on the leeward side of the houses, and I could feel the heat on my back as I climbed into the cab.

"Stay in the driveway!" I yelled to Phil. "We have the house to block the heat, and there's nowhere else to go!"

"Good Lord! It feels like a hurricane!" yelled Diane.

The noise was deafening and the truck shook; there was so much wind. We hung tight and watched as flames squeezed between the houses and sweep through the neighborhood.

After the fire front roared by, Greg radioed me. "Let's move out and kick this devil in the teeth!"

We pulled our two units out of the driveways and quickly started to scout the subdivisions.

"Try not to get separated," I radioed to Greg. "In this smoke we could easily crash into each other at the intersections."

"Copy that Pablo!" he replied.

Between the homes, flames were running through the brush filled washes like floodwaters. Wanting to save our tank water for the houses, we had no choice but to let the washes burn. We pulled on our goggles, covered our faces, and jumped out of our trucks to work the neighborhood. We managed to put out several porches and wooden decks but couldn't save any of the landscaping, sheds, or playground sets. Greg cooled off some exposed north facing walls with his tank water. The spray sizzled and steamed as it hit the hot stucco.

We made a quick double check of our area and noticed that the large garbage cans left at the curbs had melted into pools of colored plastic. The yards were black, but the houses were OK. After determining that our sector was secure, we pulled out of the subdivision and headed down the highway.

As I had feared, the fire devoured the big grassy field and easily jumped the highway. It was charging into the adjoining suburbs with a vengeance. Firebrands and hot embers were falling from the sky like artillery fire. We pulled onto one of the side streets and saw a firebrand land in a field right next to our trucks. We stopped and Diane and Erin immediately hopped out and pulled the fire hose from the brackets.

Phil and JR manned the pump panels while Greg and I helped play out the hose. The girls didn't hesitate and jumped right into the center of the spot fire. They were standing in the black, surrounded by fire about the size of a living room and were franticly trying to spray its leading edge. In an instant, it quickly spread to the size of a basketball court and then doubled in size. They ran as fast as they could, dousing the flames as they went, but with the wind raging, they couldn't run fast enough. Running until their hoses were fully extended, they stood there exasperated, watching helplessly as the fire pulled away from them.

The fire consumed everything it touched and was now bearing down on a mobile home park less than a half-mile away. It had its sights set on it like a guided missile.

My adrenaline was pumping and my heart was racing, everything was happening so fast! We gathered up the hose trying not to make a mess of it and placed it on the brackets. Pulling up to the mobile home park, we decided to attempt a dangerous frontal attack. Feeling the fire storming toward us, my goggles and bandana provided little protection against the intense heat, and my face felt like it was frying!

We somehow managed to knock down the fire before it devoured the mobile home park. Columns of black smoke continued to rise throughout the adjoining neighborhoods, and Diane said "Holy Crap we're out of water!"

The Green Valley engine topped off our tank and we were ready for the next round. Their Type 1 engine carries 1,000 gallons of water, which sounds like a lot, but in reality it isn't, and we knew they were low on water too.

I radioed our task force leader, to let him know our location. And after a moment of chaos, our task force regrouped and we tried to form a plan.

We felt helpless as the Type 1 engines poured into the neighborhoods. But without working hydrants we knew the big engines would be empty in no time.

We could hear task force leaders on the radios, desperately trying to locate the water tenders. The wind was howling, fire was everywhere, and it was mayhem!

Suddenly, from out of nowhere, big air tankers flew in low and loud! Hitting the leading edge of the flames hard, they dropped their contents over entire neighborhoods! Houses, cars, and yards were blanketed in the thick red slurry!

"Look at that!" I hollered, peering through my filthy goggles and breathing heavily through my bandana, as another heavy roared in, skimming mere feet above the rooftops.

The wind was screaming like a banshee, and I knew flying in these conditions was crazy and extremely risky, but desperate times called for desperate measures! And at that moment we couldn't have been more desperate!

The assault was intense, and our task force was ordered to keep clear of the slurry drops. We watched in awe as the flame front was being beaten into submission by the heavies! The onslaught was over before we knew it, and an eerie calm settled in, as we stood there fatigued and flabbergasted.

Our division leader came up on the radio and gave us the location of the tenders. After topping off our tanks, he said, "OK you guys, go-ahead and move in and extinguish any remaining fire."

The sun was now setting and the hellacious wind was beginning to die down. I was drenched with sweat and wiped my blackened face with my already blackened bandana. I took a minute to catch my breath as I scanned the scene. The sight was staggering! There was a massive smoldering river of blackened earth, which lead from where we stood, all the way back into bowels of Miller Canyon!

While looking up at the blood red sky, I said, "Thank God for the air tankers!"

I turned around and yelled to my exhausted crew, "OK guys, let's move out and mop this bad boy up!"

Diane stood next to me and with a weak smile said, "It looks like El Diablo just got his butt handed to him."

27 A Trip Back In Time

The morning briefing was scheduled for 08:00 instead of 06:00. Without much objection, all personnel were mercifully allowed to sleep in. After the slurry drops yesterday, our task force was split up to scout for smaller fires. Once we knew the fires were out, we endured unrelenting hours of fatiguing mop up. Everyone worked past 23:30 and eventually pulled into base camp around midnight. In all of my years as a wildland firefighter, that was the most intense and longest day I had ever experienced.

The weather system that was responsible for the ferocious winds had passed, and the fire was estimated to be 70 percent contained. The Midewin hotshots, along with the other assigned crews, created enough black off of Carr Canyon Road to prevent the fire from jumping into Ramsey Canyon. The miles of dozer lines closer to the town were holding the remainder of the fire back. The fire was now surrounded by black and was in the process of having its heart and soul squeezed out of it.

We met up with the Green Valley and Midewin guys at breakfast. Everyone looked haggard, unshaven and exhausted. Despite the bone numbing fatigue, there was a sense of optimism in the air to go along with the smell of sausages and pancakes.

"Man I'm spent!" sighed Diane as she plopped down at the table.

"Me too, I could hardly get my sorry ass out of bed this morning," I said, yawning and stretching my arms above my head.

"God dang! Wasn't that *Hell on Earth* yesterday?" asked Greg.

He attacked his pancakes like he attacked the fire the day before. Those poor flapjacks didn't stand a chance and were gone in an instant. He forked the last piece and started sliding it around in his plate, soaking up every last bit of butter and syrup. Pushing his plate aside, he wiped his wind burned, fire scorched face with a paper napkin. You could see where his goggles had left a distinct contrast of white and red around his eyes.

"From what I hear, nobody was killed yesterday," he said with surprise.

Phil approached the table with a second helping of pancakes and sat next to Kate. "It looks like the devil has been thrown into the bottomless pit."

"How long does the devil stay in the pit?" asked JR in his Texas drawl.

"A millennium," said Phil

"None too soon if you ask me," said JR, taking a sip of some hot black coffee.

After breakfast I went to the briefing. We were going to be released and assigned to the Horseshoe 2 Fire, already in progress in the Chiricahua Mountains. It was about 60 miles to the east, near the New Mexico, Arizona border. Even though there was still a lot of work to be done here, a bunch of units would be joining up with resources already working that fire. There was no rush to get there and Incident Command said we didn't have to check in until later this afternoon.

"The Chiricahua Mountains are rugged and cover about 50 linear miles. The area is about four times larger than the Huachuca Mountains, and the base camp is located just outside of a small town named Portal," I said.

We pulled out our road map and located Portal on the eastern flank of the mountains.

Diane handed me the clipboard, and as always, the time sheets were accurate and complete. Tucked in behind our time sheets was our Demob paperwork. Every evening before going to bed, Diane documented the hours we worked and made sure all of our paperwork was in order. I was glad she kept track of it all. My main priority each night was to have a close encounter with my pillow. After glancing at the time sheets, I did some quick math in my head. We put in 75 hours in our five days here, so that came out to a little over 15 hours worked per day, and not a single one of them were so-called fluff hours either.

I worked my way through the checkout process and returned to the Nickel. We were stocked up, gassed up, and were soon heading east on I-80. After about 30 minutes into our trek, we decided to exit the highway to drive through scenic Bisbee, a quaint mining town nestled at the foot of the Mule Mountains.

"I love these little western towns," Diane sighed. "The old buildings downtown and the little colorful houses clustered up in the hills. It looks like we've traveled back in time!"

The town was rustic and the buildings that lined the downtown streets were authentic two and three story brick buildings, showing off a dramatic Victorian flair. Several fires gutted Bisbee back in the day, but the citizens rolled up their sleeves and rebuilt the town to its former glory. The copper had since played out, but the town has survived because of its eclectic artisan, artsy community. Combine that with seasonal special events and tours of the old Copper Queen Mine, the town of Bisbee had become quite a tourist attraction.

"From what I hear, in the early 1900s, she was the largest city between St. Louis and San Francisco," I recounted. "She was known as *The Queen of the Copper Camps*. They estimated about eight billion pounds of copper was unearthed here along with three million ounces of gold. At that time Bisbee was considered to be one of the richest mineral sites in the world."

"Can you imagine what it was like back then," said Diane.

"Yeah, from what I have read, Bisbee had over 50 saloons on Brewery Gulch!" I grinned.

"Can you imagine 50 saloons packed to the gills with filthy miners reeking of whiskey breath, cheap cigars and knee buckling B.O.!" laughed Diane.

"Don't forget all of the floozies. There must have been some serious carousing going on back then."

"Pablo, you really know quite a bit about the Old West," said Phil.

"Yup, the days of the Old West have always fascinated me. Just up the road from here is a town called Tombstone, *The Town Too Tough to Die*. Wyatt Earp, Doc Holiday, Big Nose Kate, the Shootout at the OK Corral, all of that happened right here, when the West was open and raw, and life was as hard as steel."

After leaving Bisbee, our journey took us southeast along the Mexican border; from our vantage point we could see about 30 miles into Old Mexico. As we approached the town of Douglas, I noticed a lot of Border Patrol trucks scouting the grasslands. I was staring south across the border, mesmerized in thought when Phil elbowed me and snapped me out of my daydream.

"It is hard to believe that Mexico is right there. It doesn't look very secure. It looks like you can waltz right across," Phil remarked.

"From here it looks like that. I bet if we tried to drive across the border right now we wouldn't get very far. They have the border pretty well locked down these days with motorized patrols, motion sensors, aerial surveillance and boots on the ground. See those shiny boxes on stilts off in the distance? Well, those are manned observation towers with heavy lenses fixed on the border. At night they use infrared to spot any activity. And if you take a look up above us, you will probably see the radar balloons keeping tabs on the sky. Yup! It is pretty much locked down."

"There are still a lot of people trying to get in though," said Diane.

"It wasn't like that when Billy and I rode horseback in and around these parts after the war," I said. "We would cross the border on a regular basis and there was nothing here to stop us. It was all open range."

"Who was Billy again?" asked Diane.

"He was my best friend ... we grew up together in Mimbres Springs. We both decided to become Marines after high school to fight in the Vietnam War."

"So you two crossed the border a lot after the war, where did you go?" asked Phil.

"None of your damn business Phil, shut your pie hole and keep your eyes on the road," I snorted.

Diane snapped back, "Whoa their cowboy, did someone piss in your Cheerios this morning? He just asked you a simple question. You don't have to bite his head off! Phil has done you a big favor by cancelling his vacation and signing on with us for this assignment. Remember nobody else wanted to work with your sorry ass, so cut him some slack, and show him some respect you old coot!"

"OK, OK, I'm sorry Phil for being such a crab, maybe I'm just tired or something, can we just drop it?"

"Consider it dropped and I accept your apology," said Phil. He looked right at me and gave me one of his cheesy grins.

I chuckled and whacked him over the head with the road map.

Phil grabbed Mortie off of the dashboard and threw him at me.

"Hey! Keep Mortie out of this!" yelled Diane. "He's just an innocent bystander!"

Phil and I looked at each other ... smiled, and then started whipping empty Gatorade bottles and candy wrappers at Diane sitting in the back seat. For the next few minutes there was a garbage tossing war between the front and back seat. Diane was winning only because she had more ammo, but Phil and I got in a few good licks.

"We better stop," I said, holding up a plastic water bottle. "I can see the Vehicle Damage Report now. *Cause of Motor Vehicle Accident: Empty Gatorade Bottle.* Chief has me on a short leash already, I don't want to do any more explaining about damages to the Triple Nickel."

"OK, let's call a truce," said Diane.

We all raised our right hand and said, "Garbage war truce!"

Diane was laughing as she started to pick up the trash scattered all over the back seat.

I turned to Phil and next thing I knew, Mortie came flying up from the back seat and bonked me in the head.

"Hey! What gives?" I yelled, holding the stuffed sock monkey, shaking him at Diane.

"You should know better White Dog. We are in Indian Territory and you know as well as I, that truces are made to be broken."

I sat Mortie back on the dashboard as we made our way to Portal.

We continued driving north past the Pedragosa Mountains, which merged right into the Chiricahua Mountains. Up ahead we saw the Geronimo Surrender Memorial and decided to stop. It was a simple stone tower off to the right of the highway, was about 20 feet tall with a bronze plaque attached at the base. We got out to read the plaque, which stated that Geronimo and his warriors surrendered in nearby Skeleton Canyon on September 6th 1886, ending the Apache Wars that plagued the West during that time. There was a small ramada next to the tower that shaded two picnic tables. We pulled some cold sodas from our ice chest and sat in the shade.

"Initially the government sent in troops to secure trade routes from the west coast to the east. Once gold was discovered in the 1800s, prospectors came in droves to stake their claims," I informed them. "The Native Americans living here at the time were considered to be savages, and the miners enslaved them to become beasts of burden in the mines. If the natives resisted, the white man felt it was in their best interest to wipe the Apaches off the face of the earth. The Spanish Conquistadors did it in South America, and it was happening again in the Old West."

"So it was the prospectors and settlers who were responsible for the Apache Wars in the 1800s, and it all boiled down to the white man wanting everything they laid their eyes on," said Phil.

"Yup, the mentality back then was, the white man was the superior race. In their minds they felt it was their *God given right* to be masters of their domain. The Indian leaders, Cochise and Geronimo would have none of that, and for the next 25 years they embarked on brutal guerilla warfare to save their people, their heritage, and their land."

"The Apache wreaked havoc on the settlers and the U.S. Army, who were sent in to eradicate them. During that time, the government spent an estimated 40 million dollars to kill about 100 Apaches, however, 1,000 soldiers and settlers lost their lives in the process."

"40 million dollars!" cried Phil. "Can you imagine if that 40 million was spent on some diplomacy, how the outcome could have changed? *That makes about as much sense as tits on a boar hog!*"

"I don't think the concept of diplomacy existed back then. I think the white man wanted all the marbles," I said flatly.

"Greedy bastards," scowled Diane.

We looked across the grasslands and up at the smoke in the Chiricahuas.

"Let's saddle up, we're burning daylight."

Diane jumped in behind the wheel and we headed for Portal. The road was flat and there were distorted mirages up ahead on the hot asphalt. They shimmered on the horizon like lakes in the desert. It was funny how, the closer we got to them the faster they evaporated.

While driving toward Portal, Phil asked me, "Pablo, how did you end up becoming a firefighter?"

"Well kid, after my two-year tour as a Marine was over, I came home to New Mexico and worked some construction, ranching, and other jobs. I realized I was addicted to the adrenalin rushes I experienced in the war. When I came home, the slow pace of my mundane job was boring me to tears. If you must know, I eventually hooked up with Billy again, hung out with the wrong crowd and did things that almost got us thrown in prison or killed."

"Pablo! Were you breaking the law, *like a criminal?*" Phil said with a surprised look on his face.

"Yeah, I was an idiot and finally came to my senses. I realized what the consequences would be to my family so I quit that lifestyle. They said I knew too much about their operations, and that I owed them for a deal gone bad. When those goons threatened my family and me, we got in a scuffle and I beat the shit out of the two of them, almost killing them. I told them never to threaten my family again or they could wake up dead! They knew I was a Marine and a trained killer. They must have taken me seriously because they haven't bothered me since. I still don't trust them, and to this day, I keep a loaded handgun on my nightstand. I go to the shooting range about once a month to keep my skills up, and during the day I keep the gun in the glove box of my pick-up truck."

"What kind is it?" asked Phil.

"It's a Glock 19, 9mm, semi-automatic, with a 15 round magazine. Plus, I have a couple of extra magazines, just in case."

"God Pablo! I would have never guessed," said Diane.

"Don't tell anyone, I have this clean cut image to uphold," I said half seriously.

"Don't worry Pablo, what is said in the Nickel stays in the Nickel," vowed Diane.

"After that, I felt I needed to do something that would make a difference. Something that would offset the killing I did back in Nam and the stupid crap Billy and I did when we came home. I had a young daughter and a wife, so going back to school was not an option. I had bills to pay and mouths to feed."

"So then what happened?" asked Diane.

"The Mimbres Springs Fire Department was holding a fire academy. Classes were held on two weeknights and all day on Saturday. I felt if I could persevere the six months of training, being a firefighter could be my ticket to fulfillment. I could repent for my evil ways and balance the scales. I must admit the whole firefighting thing has been a godsend, a real life-changing experience for me."

"And the rest is history," spouted Phil.

"Well, I didn't get a full-time job right away. I was a part-timer, filling in when guys took vacation, called in sick, or went on wildland assignments like this. I took night classes to become an EMT, worked on the ambulance and after about two years of that, I landed a full-time position as a firefighter."

"Can you tell us about when you were in Vietnam?" asked Phil.

"Vietnam, now that was a real quagmire. We called it a giant *Charlie Foxtrot* (Cluster Fuck). We worked in fire teams of three or four, kinda like what we do now at the fire station and on these wildland assignments. I liked the camaraderie of it all and the occasional adrenaline rushes. As a kid, my older brother and I watched a lot of John Wayne movies. We watched all of his Westerns and war movies. We loved them because they were real good shoot-em-ups. The only one I didn't like was *The Quiet Man.* I thought it was kinda lame, except for the fight scene of course. My dad was a Marine and so was my grandpa. They both saw action and we would sit up late at night listening to their war stories.

"So, being a Marine was in your blood," said Diane

"Yup, after graduating high school, Billy and I signed on to fight in the Vietnam War. We figured we were going to get drafted anyway so we felt enlisting voluntarily was the way to go. We were all fired up to take on those *Commies*. We were going to single handedly rid the world of Communism. At the time we didn't really know what Communism was and didn't have a clue what we were getting ourselves into. We both chose to be Marines. We figured if we were going to see action, we might as well be on the cutting edge and prepare ourselves to be the best damn soldiers we could be."

"*The few, the proud, the Marines!*" huffed Phil.

"Yeah right! It didn't take long to figure out that we were all just a bunch of young kids, put in harm's way by a bunch of fat ass, cigar-smoking congressmen. The decision makers weren't over there feeling the stifling heat of the jungle or experiencing the relentless months of the monsoon."

"It must have been hell! I bet you didn't see that coming," said Diane.

"You got that right Missy! When we got off the plane in Nam, the old-timers let us know we were the *Cherries* (new guys) and were being sent in to replace the ones who didn't make it out. Let me tell you, after seeing my first action, I didn't want to become a decorated war hero anymore. My priorities changed in a hurry. All of that John Wayne crap went right out the window! My new goals were to lie low, follow orders, and stay sharp. I needed to look out for my buddies and get through my tour in one piece."

"Well it looks like you made it back in one piece," said Diane.

"It wasn't easy, we all suffered mentally and physically. We would trudge through miles of mud and walk through leech filled rice patties. The stench was awful as we stepped over the bloated bodies of dead enemy troops, and marched through the ruins of decimated villages. The big wigs closed their eyes to the utter destruction of that country and the senseless waste of young American lives."

"They were probably making those decisions from some cushy air-conditioned office on Capital Hill! Damned politicians!" said Diane.

"Were you scared, Pablo?" asked Phil.

"Scared shitless! We realized we were now trapped in a crazy, deadly game. The generals drew up action plans and we were the pawns, the X's on the map. If a unit got wiped out, they would just send in another one. We were considered disposable ... casualties of war. Do you know what my response to all that was?"

"I bet I know," said Diane raising an eyebrow.

"My response to it all was, *fuck this!* I wanted to get back to the States and see my friends and family again. I sure as hell didn't want to become a statistic in a war that nobody gave a rat's ass about."

"How did you get through it all?" asked Phil.

"I did my time. My M16 and I became best of friends, and I took out quite a few enemy with it. I saw some guys get blown to bits, nearly got killed a few times myself and earned a couple of medals in the process. A lot of the time we just tried to fight off boredom and fatigue. The guys in my unit would sometimes mess with guys from the other companies back at base camp." I started to laugh just thinking about it. "We would play jokes on them just to break up the monotony."

"Like what?" asked Diane, as she gave me a sideways grin.

"Oh, like putting rash cream in their toothpaste tubes. Sometimes we would pour Tabasco on their toilet paper packs or put coffee grounds in their boots, you know stupid shit."

"Is that where your life as a practical joker started?" asked Diane.

"What me, a practical joker*? Never!*"

I laughed out loud, "There was this guy in our unit. His name was Luther ... Luther Tucker was from Gary, Indiana. He was the blackest black man I ever saw and could really hide under the cover of darkness. He was a real killing machine on night patrols and ambushes. He was so stealthy; nobody would know he was there. If he didn't fire his weapon or crack a smile he was pretty much invisible. When we would go to the rear area for a little R&R, he would slip into the other company's tents and catch those guys totally off guard with some awesome pranks. Hey, get this; he would set up trip wires in their tents, attached to multi-colored smoke grenades. When they set them off there was so much smoke pouring out, the poor guys would be stumbling over each other, coughing and cussing as they exited the thick Technicolor haze.

He was the master of disaster. Some companies would set up a sentry when they heard Luther was in the area. Whenever he pranked another unit, word got out that they got *Tucked*. They called him *Luther Tucker, The Mother Fucker!*"

"I suppose he taught you everything you know?" laughed Diane.

"Well not everything, boy that man could cuss! Cuss as if they were his first spoken words. He would drop F-bombs like a Phantom jet. Cussing was second nature to him, part of his every day vocabulary, but we just got use to the casualness of his vulgarity."

"How come you don't cuss like a Marine?" asked Phil.

"I cuss a little, but I reckon I am too much of a country boy and not a tough inner city kid like Luther. My momma would have washed my mouth out with soap and then have me gargle with bleach if she heard me cuss like that. I figure cussing doesn't make a man any tougher. It was just a part of who Luther was."

"Do you guys still stay in touch after the war?" asked Phil.

"Wait a minute Phil, I'm not done with the story ... anyway, most guys would do one tour of duty and get the hell out, but Luther served three tours and was a seasoned veteran and a true warrior. Luther never rose above the rank of corporal, yet he was the most important man in our unit. We were a long-ways from home, and he knew that. He loved the Cherries and would always watch out for us. He was the one the Cherries would go to for advice and support. Luther was our rock, a mentor, and true friend. When we were under a lot of stress, during the most intense barrage of enemy fire, he would crack a joke and make us laugh. *Luther was the glue that kept us loose*, if that makes any sense. *God, we loved that guy.*"

"Anyway, when Luther was finally a *short timer,* meaning he had less than 30 days left of his tour, he placed three playing cards in his helmet band, a 10 of spades, a 10 of hearts and a 10 of diamonds. Every night he would punch a new hole in a card with the tip of a bullet. He would announce something like ... one day down, 17 to go! And hold it up for all to see. He had big plans and was eager to get back to Gary, Indiana!"

Diane chimed in, "You know the war had to be bad if someone was looking forward to going back to *Gary, Indiana!*"

"Yeah, he grew up in the projects, and his Momma and four younger brothers and sisters still lived there. His

Daddy was never around, so his momma worked two jobs to make ends meet, and Luther would always send his pay back to them. He never spent it on a little boom-boom or a bag of weed, he never kept a dime for himself."

"I remember one hot muggy day, our unit was recruited to help fortify an artillery fire support base (FSB) with sandbags. We worked on it all morning. We must have unloaded and carried a thousand sandbags up to the top of a hill to build walls around the howitzers. When we were finished, we sat down to enjoy some homemade cookies Luther's momma sent to him. He passed the box around and showed off a funny crayon drawing his little sister sent him. From out of nowhere, a sniper nailed him! Luther took a bullet right between the eyes!" I shook my head and looked down at the floorboards, "Damn it to hell ... he only had eight days left before going home!" I wiped my eyes with my sleeve and said, "He was sent home all right ... in a pine box!"

"Son of a bitch!" said Diane.

"We were all devastated. Our outfit got pretty tight after we lost Luther. We stayed on our toes and hoped we wouldn't become the next poor schmuck to be taken out. We lost some more guys that year, and it seemed like an eternity before I got my orders to go home. I kept one of his playing cards and tucked it in my helmet band for the remainder of my tour, as a reminder to stay sharp and to remember him by. I still have it and always keep it in my wallet."

"No kidding, can I see it?" asked Phil.

"Sure kid." I replied, and rummaged through my wallet, pulled it from a protective plastic sleeve, and handed him the stained and yellowed playing card.

"Wow!" said Phil as he ran his finger over the card with the holes in it. "Only 8 hearts left ... how sad."

"The Vietnam War was a totally different kind of war. A lot different than the ones my dad and my grandfather fought. That war made no sense, and at times it was stupid as hell!

"What a waste! What a god-damned waste!" Diane said with anger and sorrow.

I wiped my eyes and took a deep sigh, "So to answer your question Phil ... do we still stay in touch? Yeah we do ... I find myself talking to Luther all the time. I get this feeling he's still there, looking out for me."

We drove in silence for the next half hour. Up ahead we could see a sign that read, PORTAL: Population 831. It wasn't hard to find base camp. It was as big as the town itself.

28 A Faraway Ranch

We drove through the town of Portal and arrived at the command post, and the place was being over-run with incoming units. After enduring a miserable three-hour check-in process, we were on the books for the *Horse Shoe 2 Fire.* We were assigned to a task force called the *Chiricahua National Monument Protection Group.* Our orders were to report to the western side of the mountain range and meet up at the school by 18:00. Phil was at the wheel as we headed to our new destination.

I briefly scanned the road map, folded it up and placed it on the seat. "Let's head north, get on Interstate 10 and go around the tip of the mountain range to meet up with the others on the western side."

"Why don't you take another look at the map, just to make sure, you barely looked at it and I don't trust your navigation skills," Phil said with concern in his voice.

"I have great navigational skills!"

"Oh yeah, remember up in Nevada last year, we took a wrong turn and ended up in Idaho!" Phil recalled, raising his voice as he shoved the map back in my lap.

"So we got a little sidetracked. Big deal! We got to fight a lot of fire that day! And didn't I get us to Bryce Canyon with no problems?" I said defending myself.

"Only because I knew the area!" Phil glanced over at me and gave me a challenging look.

"Trust me I know where we're going, so shut your yap and keep your eyes on the road," I snarled and slapped the map back down on the seat.

"It's a free country, I can say whatever I want!" stated Phil defiantly.

"Both of you shut your traps! I'm trying to get some shut-eye back here! You're starting to sound like an old married couple," bellowed Diane.

After about 40 minutes into our drive, a large yellow billboard came into view on I-10 that read, *THE THING? Have you seen it?*"

"Hey look at that!" shouted Phil.

"We can't get away from it!" I laughed.

Diane sat up and gazed out the front windshield. "I can't believe it! The Thing ... it will haunt us for the rest of our lives!"

After passing the big yellow billboard we exited the interstate and drove into a small town called Willcox. It was 100 degrees outside and the powers of the town's Dairy Queen pulled us in for a chocolate dipped cone.

While walking out of the Dairy Queen, Diane commented, "Yup, the Willcox folks sure know how to do a dipped cone right. They dip the soft serve into the chocolate right up to the cone part. There's no ice cream gap between the chocolate and the cone." She looked at it and said, "If there's a gap, the ice cream melts out of the bottom faster than you can eat it."

"You got that right," I said. "Hey, Phil, do you have a hayseed saying for *faster than?*"

He thought for a moment, bit the top off of his cone and said, "Yup, *faster than a buttered bullet.*"

"OK, pretty good, that's pretty fast," I laughed.

After finishing our cones, we hopped in the Nickel and drove south. I glanced up and saw a sign that read, Dos Cabezas 20 miles. An uneasy feeling came over me and I grabbed the IAP to distract myself.

The IAP included a weather forecast, some statistics about the fire's progress, a topography map of the area, and a list of resources assigned to the fire.

"It says here the fire is about 14,000 acres with zero containment. The fire is on the eastern flank, mostly in the upper elevations, and so far, no structures are being threatened. If this fire works its way into the west valley and into this waist-high grass, there will be no stopping it. It could be as bad or maybe even worse than the fire we just fought in Sierra Vista," I said grimly.

I pointed on the map and showed them where the fire was now and where it will be heading. We looked up at the mountains for signs of smoke. Diane grabbed the IAP and looked for other units assigned to our sector.

"It looks like we will be working with some crews from California," laughed Diane. "Remember the last time we worked with those California guys in Nevada, we had to R.A! Run Away! And later that day we got slurried."

"Yeah, my yellow shirt was never the same after that. I couldn't get the red stains out," laughed Phil.

We soon passed a sign that read, Dos Cabezas, 5 miles.

"It will be strange to see the town again," I reminisced.

"How so, have you been here before?" asked Diane.

"Back in junior high and high school, Billy and I would come out here every summer to visit his grandfather. We rode horses, helped Gramps fix his fences, and clean up the property. Billy and I would hike up in the hills looking for old mines and walked the arroyos to flush out quail and jackrabbits. We tried to take them out with our 22s, but had better luck shooting up old pop bottles and rusty tin cans. Yup, we could take out a tin can at 20 paces. The jackrabbits were a lot tougher. Those were fun times, but sometimes we would get in trouble with the locals.

"Ok Pablo, what kind of trouble did you get into?" asked Diane.

I remember one night we were hanging out at the local bar. We were under aged teenagers acting all grown up and started to mess with the wrong people. Of course a fight broke out and all hell broke loose! Billy ended up getting smacked across the teeth with a chair.

"It's all fun and games until someone loses a couple teeth," laughed Diane.

"Boy, that Billy had a bad temper and went ape shit on the guy who hit him and threw him up against the pinball machine. It started to go haywire! All of the bells started clanging and the lights started flashing! It was kind of funny until the guy's drunken buddy picked up Billy and threw him on top of it, shattering all of the glass!"

"Then what happened?" asked Phil.

"Someone called the cops, and the sheriff brought us to Gramps' doorstep around 2 a.m. Gramps was an ornery cuss and grabbed Billy by his shirt collar and pinned him up against the wall. He chewed his ass up one side and down the other and immediately sent us back home to New Mexico. My folks were madder than hornets when we got back. My dad read me the riot act and I ended up getting grounded for a month! There's nothing worse than being grounded during summer vacation. Even though I was grounded, I still snuck out and did other stupid things with Billy."

"Soooo ... What other kind of trouble did you guys get into?" asked Phil with peaked interest.

"None of your damn business Phil, that's classified information between Billy and me. I don't want to talk about it any more, so drop it!"

"Ahhh, a little touchy Pablo?" Diane asked in a motherly tone.

"Whoa, consider it dropped," said Phil as he rolled his eyes over to Diane.

Diane rolled her eyes back at Phil and said, "Don't look at me, Pablo was the one that brought it up."

We drove through the remnants of the town. Dos Cabezas was a classic study of an old mining town that went from boom to bust like so many others in the area.

"You're right, this place is almost a ghost town except for some dilapidated buildings and an ancient cemetery," said Phil, I wonder if ghosts walk the streets at night?"

"I've never seen any, but it doesn't mean there aren't any ghosts out there. I've heard some pretty creepy stories and strange happenings," I replied.

We drove a little further and dropped into the valley south of Dos Cabezas. Off in the distance were wisps of smoke curling over the rim of the Chiricahuas, and the valley below was beginning to fill with a light blue haze, giving the area an ominous look.

"I don't see a lot of smoke," commented Phil. "Where is the massive smoke plume?"

"The fire is a long ways away right now. The National Forest Service informed us that there are a lot of Historical Landmarks in this area. The Chiricahua National Monument and its headquarters are lying in the projected path of the fire. If the winds remain constant it will take about five or six days before it gets there."

I told Phil, "Follow the signs into the Chiricahua National Monument. Drive a short ways up the canyon and pull into a parking lot so we could stretch our legs." We got out and I said, "Hey, come with me, I've got something special to show you."

After walking down a path shaded by oak trees, we arrived at an old ranch house surrounded with corrals, out buildings, and sheds. We came upon a sign at the entrance and Phil read it out loud.

"FARAWAY RANCH"

A Forest Service Ranger greeted us and said enthusiastically, "Welcome to the Faraway Ranch. I'm Henry Witherspoon, but most people call me Hank. Where are you guys from?"

Phil replied, "We're from New Mexico, Mimbres Springs to be exact."

The Ranger was about 65ish, bald, with a rim of white hair that circled the back of his head from ear to ear. He had a little paunch but still looked pretty sharp in his Park Service uniform. He was about 5 foot 10, and walked with a slight hitch in his giddy-up.

Hank told us, "A lot of tourists come here to see how the pioneers lived back in the 1800s. As of today, we are prohibiting visitors from entering the park. The place is getting a little smoky, and a lot of firefighters are moving into the area to work. We have been getting a steady stream of fire trucks passing through here since early this afternoon. A new fire camp is being set up at the school on Turkey Creek Road and the other units left here about 20 minutes ago to meet there."

"How about if you take a few minutes and let me show you around," smiled Hank, proud as a peacock.

Phil and Diane were eager to see the place and we still had some time on our hands before we checked in at the school.

They began to march off when Hank asked me, "Are you coming?"

"You guys go ahead, I've seen the place before when I was younger. I'll just poke around the main ranch house here."

"Suit yourself," Diane said and off they went with Hank leading the way.

I puttered around the main house's living room intrigued by the Sepia toned photographs, western antiques, and homespun knick-knacks. I found a book on the sideboard that looked interesting, *Pioneer Spirit, The Faraway Ranch ... Neil and Emma Erikson.* I just love reading about the Old West, it was like an addiction to me. I couldn't pass up the opportunity to learn more, so I settled down in an ancient rocking chair and cracked the book open.

* * *

... It was an early morning in late May 1892. The sun came up bright and clear, illuminating the small two-room cabin that Neil Erikson and his wife Emma had built with their own two hands. Their 160-acre homestead, called the Faraway Ranch, was snuggled in Bonita Canyon, a side canyon on the western aspect of the Chiricahua Mountains. The Eriksons were both hard workers, had a pioneer spirit, and were proud to call this place home. It was only 8 a.m. and the air was already hot and there was no hint of rain in the forecast. Neil could immediately feel the sun begin to scorch his skin once it cleared the crest of the mountain range. He rolled down his sleeves and knew this was a bad sign. These past two seasons have produced the same scenario, drought and tough times for his crops and cattle.

Neil kissed his wife and climbed onto the buckboard. She handed him a basket filled with bread, dried meat, and fruit. He flicked the reigns and gave a sharp whistle to his two-horse team, Dala and Hans. He was headed for Bisbee to find carpentry work. He hoped he would find something, anything that would bring in some much-needed cash. After purchasing this ranch five years ago and having served in the U.S. Calvary, he felt confident enough about horses, cattle, and ranching to get by, but these past two years have been hard and lean. They had sunk their entire life savings into this place and were now strapped for cash and needed the work, even if it meant leaving his wife and the ranch they loved so much. He was good with a saw and could swing a hammer. After all, he had built everything on the ranch, and the buckboard was loaded with carpenter tools. There were hammers, hatchets, wood chisels, levels, saws, and planers. He thought that by bringing his own tools he had a better chance of finding work, and hoped his carpenter skills would pay off in the booming mine town.

Although the Apache wars were over, he still felt uneasy leaving his wife alone for three months. Emma reassured him that she was no weakling and could take care of herself and the ranch. She was a crackerjack with the rifle and pistol, and he knew the neighboring ranchers, Zackary and Amanda would check in on her from time to time while he was away. Pioneer folks looked out for each other during tough times and Neil wished that these tough times would soon come to an end.

Neil approached the fence line that marked the edge of his property, hopped off the buckboard and opened the gate. Nipping at the wheels were his two faithful dogs, Swed and Hondo. They were good cattle dogs, and he roughhoused with them for a minute. With orders to "Stay and take care of Emma," he laughed and gave them a final scruffy pet. They must have known he was leaving and backed up a few paces, and watched him close the gate. Looking at the hand carved sign that read FARAWAY RANCH, Neil slowly ran his finger over each of the chiseled letters. After a moment of reflection, he climbed up, flicked the reigns, and could hear the dog's despondent barking as he pulled away.

While riding his rig along the rough roads that bordered the Chiricahuas, he watched the waist high grasslands blowing in the wind, and they looked like golden waves in an inland sea. Up in the canyons stood majestic domes and rock formations, and flowing out of the foothills were cottonwood-lined steams that spread out like giant green fingers into the meadows. The streams were now silent and as dry as gunpowder. Neil and Emma had fallen in love with this part of the country, and vowed they would do whatever it took to make it work. Despite the tough times, he was still optimistic about the future. He envisioned the ranch being prosperous with an orchard of fruit trees and fields of hay for the stock. He thought they could raise maybe 30 head of cattle, and convert their cabin into a nice two-story house with white clapboard siding and a green gabled roof. Yes, they had plans for the place all right; they just had to work like the dickens to get there...

* * *

I put the book down and walked out to the front porch. I squinted in the bright sunshine and was surprised to see an orchard of fruit trees near Bonita Creek. There were fields of hay nearby, and off in the distance was a herd of cattle grazing in the hills. I walked off of the porch, looked up and marveled at the main house. It was two stories tall and by-golly it had a green gabled roof. Up in the mountains were majestic granite rock formations and the streams were now as silent as they were back then. Dry as gunpowder.

"Damn, they must have worked like hell to keep this place going. The pioneers back then were as tough as nails! I hope we can keep this place from going up in flames. This isn't just a bunch of old buildings we're trying to save. This represents their hopes and dreams, their passion for life. We owe them that much," I said out loud realizing how important this was. "This is why we do what we do."

Just then, I could hear Hank, Phil and Diane laughing as they rounded the bend.

Hank was in his glory, telling them about the place, and Phil and Diane were captivated, hanging on his every word.

"How was your little tour?" I asked.

"Hank is a wealth of information, he knows as much about the Old West as you do," said Phil.

Diane remarked, "We told Hank about the fire and what needs to be done to protect the ranch. There are a lot of structures on the property and it looks like the fire crews have their work cut out for them."

"I hope to God the fire doesn't take out the ranch," said Hank shaking his head. "Everything here is over 100 years old, and as dry as tinder. I love this place. It would be a damn shame if we lost it."

"The fire is still a ways off, mostly on the eastern side of the mountains. Lucky for us we have time to create some defensible space around this place. We will have to prep the buildings, trim back vegetation, and cut some line. Then back burn some areas, set up portable water tanks, water pumps, and sprinklers. We will just have to prepare for the worst and hope for the best," I said with assurance.

We wandered back to the truck, climbed into the Triple Nickel and pulled away.

Hank gave us a friendly wave and shouted, "Good luck Mimbres Springs, and be safe!"

We made our way down the road to the rendezvous spot on Turkey Creek Road. We had eight days left on our tour and I hoped this week's assignment would be a bit calmer and less grueling than our last assignment in Sierra Vista.

29 Like A Moth To A Flame

After traveling from the fire in Sierra Vista, driving through Bisbee, stopping off at the Geronimo Memorial, and arriving at Portal, we must have covered over 100 miles. It took us the rest of the day to travel to the western flank of the Chiricahuas, which consisted of another 100-mile drive. After our quick visit with Hank at the Faraway Ranch, it was now close to sunset. We rolled in just as the sun dropped below the horizon. This was the first day the school was being used as the western operations headquarters and the place was beginning to fill up with firefighters, equipment, and trucks. We entered the school to check in and were pleased to find the process was much faster than in Portal. We were told we would get our assignment at tomorrow morning's briefing. When the clerk handed us our paperwork she made a point to tell us not to use the restrooms inside the school.

"I don't blame them," said Diane. "I can imagine what the restrooms would look like after hundreds of dirty firefighters trampled through them. You guys dirty up the restrooms at our station in Mimbres Springs pretty good."

"What do you mean you *guys?*" I said.

"Hey, I'm not calling you out or anything, but have you noticed the difference between the condition of the ladies' room and the condition of the men's room at the station?" said Diane defiantly.

"Well uhh," I mumbled.

"I rest my case," said Diane.

As we drove around the building, I noticed this was a nice little set up. The football field was behind the school, and quite a few pup tents were already scattered throughout the dry stubble, with a line of port-a-potties in the north end zone. Phil, showed off some of his newly acquired wildland knowledge, and parked plenty clear of the porta-potties, to avoid the stink and the occasional crapper-flapper.

I was eager to get started, but cautioned them, "Don't set up camp tonight, let's wait until we get our assignment tomorrow. I can't predict if we're going to base our operations from here or get spiked out somewhere else. This mountain range is really big."

We were surprised to find out the evening meal was being flown in from the main base camp on the Portal side of the mountain. I rubbed my hands together as we walked toward the school cafeteria. "Let's see what the choppers brought us for dinner."

When walking in, we could see several large Styrofoam hotboxes of chow. Nestled inside of the big boxes were smaller Styrofoam take-out containers. We each picked up a dinner box; some napkin wrapped plastic ware, and poured a couple glasses of lemonade.

"This has got to be the ultimate take-out," grinned Diane as we sat down.

The cafeteria tables had long light green speckled Formica tops with dark green benches to match. They must have been made for elementary school kids, as it took a little effort to squeeze in there, and my knees bumped the underside of the table.

"Stop!" cried Phil, waving his arms. "Try to guess what is in the boxes before you open them."

Phil held his boxed dinner up to his nose and smelled the length of the container. He did it twice and was prepared to make his guess. We took turns sniffing our dinners and I decided to go first.

"I think it is BBQ chicken."

"I think we are having meat loaf and potatoes," said Diane.

Phil cleared his throat and announced, "I think its Carolina Pulled Pork on a homemade sourdough roll, with a side of creamy coleslaw." He held it up to his nose again and said, "I think there's a kosher dill pickle in there and a bag of potato chips and wait ... I think I smell a hint of peppermint hard candy for dessert."

"That's my Phil, always going way over the top!" We all laughed at his outlandish prediction.

We eagerly opened up the containers and low and behold ... there sat a big pulled pork sandwich, coleslaw, a pickle, and a bag of potato chips! Not to mention, a peppermint candy.

"No way!" said Diane. "Are you psychic or what?"

"He must have X-Ray eyes or the nose of a blood hound! I must admit Phil, you are one freak of nature."

We enjoyed our ultimate take-out, and couldn't get over how Phil could detect our dinner by smell alone.

Weary from the daylong drive, we returned to the camp with full bellies. While lying on the grass, I could hear a chorus of crickets in the nearby field and the soft solitary hoot of an owl in the distance trees. It was pitch black and the moon was starting to rise over the ridge. I was kinda excited about the Horseshoe 2 Fire assignment, anticipating what was in store for us. I settled in, punched down my

pillow and knew I would be asleep in no time, if it weren't
for the constant noise of the crapper flappers.

***

At the morning briefing we learned that our assignment
would be structure protection of the Faraway Ranch, the
Chiricahua National Monument Headquarters, Ranger
Station, and Visitor Center. Our task force consisted of
three, Type 6 engines, two Type 3 engines, two water
tenders, and a hand crew from Arizona.

We hightailed it over to the Faraway Ranch, and along
the way, we passed fire crews already at work, cutting and
clearing vegetation. We soon found our group's staging area.
Our group leader greeted us as we pulled in the parking lot.
We shook hands, and he told me his name was Jesse, the
crew boss from the Arizona hand crew. He was a well-
muscled stocky guy, about five feet eight inches tall, had a
well-trimmed blond beard, and a chaw of tobacco in his lower
lip.

Right off the bat he stated, "The fire is heading directly
toward this area. These structures are listed in the National
Register of Historic Places. The Chiricahua Monument and
the Faraway Ranch have to be *saved at all costs*. The ranch
has been here for over a 100 years and I'll be damned if we
lose it on my watch!"

It was the words *save at all costs* that bother me the most.
I really hate it when those words are ever spoken. Yes, this
place is a showpiece, the pride and joy of the Park Service,
and there is a lot of history in all of this. Sometimes
however, firefighters are blinded by the phrase, *save at all
costs*, and get tunnel vision when trying to do so. They act
like *a moth to a flame*, and are drawn into accomplishing the

task at hand, and become oblivious to the deteriorating and dangerous conditions surrounding them. It's that can-do attitude that gets firefighters into the most trouble. I've known firefighters who have died trying to save something *at all costs*.

I recalled the words our battalion chief said just before we left Mimbres Springs, "You guys be careful, people could get killed and a lot of property could, and most likely, will be lost. So keep on your toes, and don't do anything heroic or stupid." Words to remember.

Jesse told us we would be working with his hand crew from Arizona. We met up with them and started to unload huge rolls of fire protective aluminum sheeting. They consisted of a thin layer of aluminum, glued to fiberglass fabric. It was the same material used in the Sierra Vista Fire to protect the telephone poles, and today we were to wrap all of the historic buildings on our site map.

The buildings on the list were; The Faraway Ranch Main House, The Stafford Cabin, The Bunkhouse, Martha Riggs House, a large tack room and the barn. The secondary structures included some storage sheds, tool sheds, and the original outhouse. If we had time after that, we were instructed to wrap some original fence posts that dotted the property. It looked like this was an all-out effort to save history.

With so many structures on the list, we were given carte blanche, and used our own discretion as to how we would accomplish the task. The task force divvied up the workload among us, and made quick work finishing the main structures. When we stepped back, the place looked like a make-believe fairy tale setting. There were silver, foil-covered houses scattered here and there. We chuckled at the sight and began to work on the secondary list.

As Diane held up a piece of aluminum sheeting against the outhouse, Phil and I stapled the material to the structure.

"Can you believe it," laughed Phil. "we're saving an *outhouse!*"

"Just doing our part to save history. You can bring your grandkids here and point to this very crapper and tell them, 'I saved this!' " I laughed.

"I can't believe I'm saying this but, this is a real *shitty job*," grinned Phil.

"I knew it! I knew sooner or later we would get Phil to cuss!" I howled.

Diane chimed in, "I remember he said *ass* last year, but I guess an ass is an animal. Shit is shit! That's real cussing!"

"Wait 'til I tell your Momma," I said with a wink.

"Go ahead, tell her. She won't believe you," said Phil with confidence.

He turned to walk away and I noticed he was getting a little pink in the cheeks.

As we were wrapping it up, no pun intended, Phil saw a water tender pulling into the parking lot.

"Hey look, it says Green Valley Fire on it," shouted Phil.

We hustled over and helped them dump their load.

"We just got demobed from the Monument Fire in Sierra Vista and were on the same task force as one of your Green Valley trucks!" said Phil.

"No kidding? Who was on the truck?" they asked.

"Greg, JR, and Erin," said Phil.

"Those guys are crazy. They jump at every chance to go to a wildland fire. What truck were they on?" asked one of the Green Valley guys.

"A Type 1 engine, E156. We helped them adapt their engine and set up a system where they didn't have to pull their heavy 1¾-inch attack lines. We jury-rigged some wildland hose to the outside of their truck, and they got to fight a mess of fire with it. We worked together for four days, and our division didn't lose a single house!" Phil said with excitement.

"I'm Mike, and this here is Chris."

"My name is Phil, we are from Mimbres Springs, New Mexico," and they shook hands.

Mike said, "We've been here since almost the beginning. I guess it's been 10 days now. All the days run together. What day is it anyway?"

"I think it's Tuesday, I'm not quite sure," said Phil.

"Mimbres Springs sent a water tender to this fire last week, have you seen them?"

"Haven't seen them," said Mike. "They must be on the east side of the mountain. We've been mostly running loads of water back and forth from Willcox. Before that we were tapping into some of the local water tanks and stock ponds in the area, and almost sucked them dry. The ranchers said they needed the water for their livestock, and were afraid they would lose the fish that were stocked in them, so we had to stop."

"Fish in the stock tanks?" asked Phil.

"Yeah, some of the fish were keepers, nice and big," said Chris. He held up his hands about a foot apart.

"Well guys, this is Diane and I am Pablo," I said.

"Man, if I'm not mistaken you could be a dead ringer for Erin, you could be her twin." Chris said to Diane.

"Sisters in fire," replied Diane with a proud grin.

"Ahh, I know Mimbres Springs," recalled Mike. "Does the Glory Road Hot Springs ring a bell?"

"Yup, that's one fine establishment, if you know what I mean," I winked. We both grinned at each other.

Diane jumped in and asked, "Hey Mike, have you ever been to Joey Patron's Bar and Grill?"

"Been there! Are you kidding? I've shut the place down!" Mike held his head in mock inebriation.

We all laughed.

Chris added, "My whole family goes there for Pioneer Daze! We especially like the flea market. Once my wife bought a bunch of old books from some old guy. The books were kinda ratty looking and smelled like mildew. Anyway, tucked inside one of them were 3, one-dollar bills, Silver Certificates! They were dated 1886. Believe it or not, they had a portrait of *Martha Washington* on them!"

"No kidding?" asked Diane, "*Martha* Washington?"

"Yup, they are authentic one dollar bills, I looked them up," said Chris. "They must have been in those books the whole time and never saw the light of day. I don't know how much they're worth, they look brand spanking new and are in mint condition."

"Probably worth a lot!" said Diane.

Phil said, "Hey, when you see Greg, ask him about the *butthole of the devil.*"

"The butt hole of the devil? I bet there is a story behind that one!" laughed Mike. "Oh, sorry guys, we've got to go! The crew boss is giving us the hairy eyeball."

They jumped in the tender and headed back to Willcox for another load.

We got back to work and started setting up potable water tanks next to the structures, hooked up a series of hoses, pumps, and portable sprinklers. The day's work was halted at 18:00, and we were given the option to either go back to the school or stay here and set up at one of the nearby campsites.

We choose to stay in the campground. The Bonita Canyon Campground was located near the entrance of the park, and there were over 20 campsites, complete with picnic tables, bear boxes, fire rings, and easily accessible pit toilets.

As we drove to a campsite, we were awestruck by Bonita Canyon's beauty. Arizona cypress, Emory oaks, and sycamores, lined the canyon's streambed, and a thread of water meandered through the rocks. As we traveled farther in, there were huge sculptured rock formations, towering 100 feet above the trees. They filled the canyon walls on both sides, giving a surrealistic and magical look to the place.

"This place is beautiful, gorgeous!" marveled Diane.

"I can understand why someone would choose to settle in this canyon and put so much work into their homestead," said Phil.

"This is definitely worth saving. We will do our best!" I said, while looking at the sight. "Oh, by the way, the crew boss told me that base camp will bring in dinner for all of us staying in the campground. He took a head count and said the food should arrive around 19:00, but we will be on our own for breakfast."

Diane got out and helped Phil back the truck into the campsite.

"What's your prediction for supper, *Oh Great Swami?*" Diane asked Phil.

Phil put his fingers to his forehead, closed his eyes and predicted, "Chili and beans with cornbread."

"I'll take that, Oh Great Swami," said Diane.

The meals came right on time. As Diane held up her Styrofoam container for all to see, I did a drum roll on the picnic table to heighten the anticipation.

She opened the box with a, "Ta-da!"

"Wow, look at that! Just like you predicted, it's chili! You nailed it Phil!" she said with surprise.

The meal consisted of thick spicy chili with lots of beans, and even more beef. It also came with a big hunk of cornbread. His psychic ability amazed us again, and we wolfed down our supper like cast-a-ways recently rescued from a deserted island.

After supper we laid down on the picnic tables and looked up into the evening sky. The white wispy clouds slowly turned cotton candy pink and quietly faded. After about an hour, the sky was ink black and showcased an unbelievable amount of stars. Just then, a huge shooting star raced across the sky, leaving behind a long sparkly tail. At the end of its trek, it split in two with a bright flash of green.

"Did you see that?" asked Phil.

"Fantastic!" I said.

"Far out!" gasped Diane.

I got up, rolled out my sleeping bag and said, "Everything is so serene, doesn't it feels like we are on a nice family campout. It's kind of ashamed that these hills are unaware that the other side of the mountain is raging with fire."

As we laid on top of our bedrolls in the cool darkness, Phil cleared his throat and giggled. "I have a confession to make ... while you guys were checking us in yesterday, I peeked inside the food containers in the school cafeteria."

Diane and I both groaned.

"Hah! You Fake Swami! You lose all credibility as a psychic in my book!" I shouted.

"You big fat cheater!" laughed Diane. "I have to admit, it *was* pretty funny. You got us on that one Phil. But what about your prediction of chili and beans tonight?"

"Oh that! Well, that was just dumb luck on my part," laughed Phil.

In the darkness I watched Phil laugh it up with Diane and had to admit Phil has come a long way since last year's fires. He has learned quite a bit about wildfire. He works well with us, keeps a cool head, always works hard and is no longer intimidated with all of this. He has also gotten use to our off-the-wall humor and can prank us pretty good to boot. I think we make an effective team. I really need to thank them both when we get back home. After all, Diane and Phil cancelled their vacation plans to work with me, and I have to give them credit. All the guys back at the station called off of the assignment once they found out I was going to be the engine boss. Yup, Diane and Phil stepped up to the plate on this one, and I realize it's great to have true-blue friends.

I looked up at the stars one last time and rolled over. As I was lying there listening to the soft rustle of a breeze in the trees, I detected the faint odor of smoke in the cool night air.

30 To Hell In A Hand Basket

The raspy sound of hand tools being sharpened with a file woke me from my slumber.

"Good morning Captain Sunshine, how was your sleep?" Phil said with a smile.

"Excellent! All I need now is some of Diane's coffee, and I will be ready to conquer the world. How are you guys doing?"

"I'm feeling finer than frog hair, and twice as fluffy."

"I take it, that's pretty fine," I remarked.

"Can't get finer than frog hair," he said and continued to file a Pulaski.

I stretched my arms and felt as if a ten-pound hammer had pulverized every muscle in my body. I stretched my arms again and realized it didn't help, so I stopped that nonsense.

Phil stopped sharpening his tool, looked around and said, "I have this strange feeling something is going down."

I asked Diane what she thought.

"I don't know, but I think he might be right. The Arizona hand crew lit out of here before first light, and there are a lot of choppers heading south, slinging buckets. Word is being passed around camp that fire conditions have drastically changed."

I looked around and saw everyone hastily eating breakfast and getting their trucks ready for the day.

"We need to find out what is happening," I said and started getting dressed.

Diane turned around, looked at me with narrowed eyes, and in a serious tone said, "Let's stay frosty and keep on our toes. There's no telling what might be coming our way."

"Diane, you know it bothers me when you give me that look and say crap like that," I said.

Phil chimed in, "It's Showtime!"

After a moment of thought, I said to Phil, "OK, you heard the lady, let's get ready!"

Phil put his hands on his hips and jokingly gave me the what-for. "Diane and I have been ready for the last hour. You're the lollygagger here, so hop to it Captain Sunshine."

I looked over at Diane's camp stove and pleaded my case, "Guys, I haven't even had a cup of coffee yet!"

Diane smiled and poured me a cup of the Horny Toad Joe, "Here you go you big whiner!"

"Ahhh! Now that's more like it. That Lupe is the best! This is the best dang coffee ever!"

"Now hold the cup to your heart and say a blessing," said Diane. "Do you know, to the Native Americans, the horny toad is known as the *little grandfather*. He is supposed to provide healing and bring good luck."

Phil said, "Is that why we have a picture of a little horny toad on our fire department's logo?"

Diane replied, "Most fire departments have the same old, over-used images on their Maltese crosses. You know, a fire hydrant, a ground ladder and a pike pole. *Boring!* I love how Mimbres Springs has little pictures of a lizard, a fish, a jackrabbit, and a horny toad on our Maltese cross."

"I think it's cool, it really makes us unique," said Phil.

Diane added, "Some experts have speculated about the style of artwork found on the ancient Mimbres pottery. They can only give us an educated guess about what it means, but from what I've gathered, the symbol of the fish represents a person's soul, the jackrabbit is associated with the phases of the moon and also symbolizes *The Trickster*."

"You mean like Pablo, our resident practical joker!" said Phil.

"Yeah, I guess we can call him our fire department's jackrabbit, however, I can think of another animal whose name starts with the word *jack* that can be associated with Pablo," said Diane.

She smiled and continued, "The lizard is associated with our dreams and our ability to interpret them, and lastly there is the horny toad, a symbol of healing and good luck. I like the fact that those little symbols go everywhere we go."

"Well, we can use all the luck we can muster today. It looks like things are picking up. Something is happening," I told my crew.

Diane and I poured a second cup, and we all gathered for the morning briefing. The supervisor had a stack of IAPs and copies of topography maps on the hood of his truck.

He cleared his throat and said, "We have a new situation that has taken place during the last 12 hours. An early arrival of a weather front, and some resulting spot fires, has created a game change. Due to the lack of immediate resources, some of our units will head to Division AA, just south of here, to assist with back burn operations. It seems the fire, that was mostly running north, is starting to make a strong run to the west, down several of the side canyons. A drastic wind change predicted today will make our job of keeping the fire out of the western valley extremely difficult."

I took a hard swallow, and a shiver went down my spine.

He ended with, "For the units heading south, stay on your toes, it is going to get real dicey down there. Everyone else report to your team leaders for assignments. Crews heading south, report to me after the briefing."

I started to head over to the supervisor's truck to get our assignment when Phil grabbed me by the arm, and with a big grin, handed me the IAP. Diane was standing behind him with even a bigger grin.

They said in unison, "We're heading south!"

I held my coffee cup close to my heart, and looked up to the heavens. "Good Lord, help us all."

Phil handed me the IAP and I began to read our assignment.

After getting the details from the supervisor, we were on the road heading south to meet up with two other Type 6-brush trucks, a water tender, and two, 20-man hand crews. One was from Utah, and the other was from South Dakota. I could hear Diane wrestling with the large topography map in the back seat. She unfolded the map and began to study it.

My thoughts drifted off, recalling the last time I was in this part of the mountain range. It was in the spring of 1976. Billy and I returned to these mountains after the war. What we got ourselves into during that time was insanely horrible, and we only had ourselves to blame for that. Our poor decisions ruined these mountains for me, and I vowed never to return.

Snapping out my daydream, I blurted out, "Are the radios charged and are you two ready?"

Diane replied, "I'm not even going to answer that!"

Phil added sharply, "Are you charged and ready?"

We rendezvoused with our new group leader at Hunt Canyon around 08:30. This left us with plenty of time for a good day's work. The Triple Nickel was going to assist with back burn operations deep in the canyon. The group leader explained that the fire was working its way over the ridge and would come down this canyon later today. There were several ranch homes, structures and corrals in harms-way. We didn't have enough time and resources to save everything.

He spoke to the group, as we huddled in to hear, "Yesterday the sheriff's department made a sweep through the area, and everyone has been evacuated. Strong easterly winds are predicted to start up around noon as the new weather front moves in. That wind will blow over the existing fires and push them toward us. Save what can be saved. Leave the rest."

Diane quickly transcribed the details onto our map, as he spoke and pointed to his map.

He continued, "The plan will be to triage and prep as much as possible. At the same time, cut line between the existing dirt roadways and burn everything on the east side of the scratch lines. That way we can create some black before the main fire works its way down the canyon. Air attack will try to hold the upper canyon. We don't have the heavies we had in Sierra Vista; they are being assigned to a larger fire in the White Mountains. We only have the choppers doing bucket drops. The other half of our group will cut line near the mouth of the canyon." He pointed to his map and added, "The final burnout will start as soon as all the units are out of the upper canyon and are accounted for. We need to complete the operation by late this afternoon."

We drove along a winding, narrow dirt road and could see the flames in the distance, creeping down the mountain. Diane told us she had already picked out several escape routes and safety zones, and marked them on the map.

"Yes sir, this could get a little dangerous, there are a lot of dirt roads scattered all over the place." She put her finger on a road she highlighted with a bright yellow marker. "This is the only road that can take us to the highway, so stay sharp, we can't afford to get lost in here!"

"Super-duper! It looks like there will be some good action today, I can't wait!" said Phil.

"It looks like this is going to be a long day, it's going to be hot, so drink a lot of water, and don't exhaust yourselves," I said

While driving in, we passed another brush truck prepping a small house and barn. We stopped to let them know that we were moving up to the next ranch.

Up the road, we passed the dilapidated remains of an old structure with a rusty pickup truck and an ancient tractor sitting in high weeds. About a mile farther down, we came upon a side road leading to an old ranch. The entrance had a grand steel arch, welded with scrap metal and horseshoes.

Phil read it out loud, before we crossed over the cattle guard, "FALCON RANCH, SINCE 1898."

We meandered through a mesquite grove and eventually saw some structures snuggled back in the trees.

"Let's see what we got!" I said as we pulled up to the house.

While walking to the back of the property, we were surprised to find an elderly gentleman rhythmically raking leaves away from the house. He had a big red dog dozing by his side that quickly jumped to its feet when it heard us approach. With its hair raised up along its back, it let loose a barrage of defensive barking.

"Ruby! Stop!" shouted the old man. The dog sat down, let out a low growl, and kept a watchful eye, as we got closer.

The old man was about 80 years old and was wearing a white; sweat stained cowboy hat, and a light blue long sleeve shirt. His denim pants were faded and threadbare. He looked up at us with a grizzled scowl, looked down and continued with his work.

"Sir, drop the rake and get in your truck. You need to evacuate now!"

The dog gave me a menacing growl.

The rancher let me have the full brunt of his frustration. With the brim of his cowboy hat almost touching my forehead, he said in a loud shaky voice, "Looky here sonny, I have lived here for over 80 years. This is where I grew up, and this is where my folks lived. I ain't about to leave because some smarty pants firemen tell me to."

He rested his head on the end of his rake and took in a few deep breaths and continued. "Did you see the old burnt up tractor and pickup truck up the road a piece? The ones with weeds and bushes growing through them?" he said, pointing a withered finger to the road. "Well that's all that is left of the Jericho Ranch. They turned tail and ran when we had a big fire here 40 years ago, and do you see what's left. We didn't run! Daddy and us fought that fire with everything we had, because this was *all we had!* This ranch is my entire life. I love this place with my whole heart, love it with my whole soul."

Taking a hankie out of his back pocket, he wiped his teary eyes and blew his nose. "I've seen other fires come and go through these parts since then, and goldarn I'm still standing here ain't I?"

I looked at him and didn't know what to say. "But it's for your own good sir."

"Don't tell me what you think is good for me. I have every right to stay," he demanded. "You just try and call the sheriff, it won't do you any good 'cause he was here yesterday, and he knows I'm not budging. If you have any smarts up there under that yellow brain bucket, you can stop wasting your time and leave me be!"

"The fire is just past the crest of the ridge, we don't have much time!" I said urgently.

Spittle started to form at the corners of his mouth. He stepped forward, tilted his hat back and said, "You must be deaf as well as stupid mister. Read my lips, N! O! NO! I ain't-a-goin'! Now get off my land!"

I thought, "Holy crap what did I walk into?"

When I walked back to the truck, Phil and Diane immediately ambushed me.

Diane said, "You really have a knack of winning over the hearts and minds of men!"

"What did you say to piss him off so much?" asked Phil.

"The old guy refuses to evacuate, and wants us off his property. I need to report this to our group leader."

"Let me talk to him," pleaded Phil.

"Don't bother! You'll only be wasting your breath!" I grunted and climbed in the Nickel to radio in.

Before I could say 10 words about our problem, the group leader broke in and replied. "Command is aware of the situation and they have been trying for the past two days to convince him to leave. He's not budging. The division supervisor has written off his property, due to the fuel load. We just don't have the equipment or the time to clear that stuff from around his house. You have permission to do what you can, that is ... if he allows you to stay. If he refuses your help, go ahead and leave. I know we could use your help somewhere else ... Keep us advised."

"Copy that," I responded.

I thought, "There is no way in hell we will get this old coot off the property. He's going to go down with the ship."

Just then, Phil popped into the truck, grabbed his gloves and said, "Come on we're burning daylight, we have a lot of work to do. We have a ranch to save!"

Diane climbed in looking for her gloves, and I asked her, "What did Phil say to him?"

"Beats me, I was looking at the neat old stuff in his barn. When I got back, Phil told me, 'It's Showtime, get your gloves!' "

I scratched my head and said, "What the ... ?"

Diane explained, "It's like they became good friends all of a sudden, they're even on a first name basis. The old guy's name is Theodore, but his friends call him Teddy. And by the way, you may want to take lessons from Phil about diplomacy."

After putting me in my place, Diane grabbed her gloves and jogged over to the house.

Phil was topside, grabbing tools off the truck, when I ask him nicely, "What did you say that changed his mind?"

He hopped down and told me, "I just talked to him politely, like family. Like he was my grandpa. I told him about the fire and how it has gained intensity, and how upset I would be if anything happened to him. After getting him a cold glass of water, I told him that we know how important this place is to him, and we will do everything in our power to save his home."

Phil started walking to the ranch house with the tools on his shoulder. He turned around and shouted, "I found out we are from the same church and know the same people.

And get this! We are related. We're kin!" He jogged back to me and said in my ear, "Like my momma always said, '*You can catch more flies with honey than with vinegar.*'"

As Phil walked away, I stood there dumbfounded, thinking, "That Phil is wise beyond his years."

Phil yelled at me, "Come on we're burning daylight!"

After grabbing my gloves, I went to the barn, pulled open the weathered door and was greeted with the warm familiar smell of alfalfa, dust, and leather. Walking past a couple of western saddles, some tack, and two pair of old riding chaps, I kicked a hay bale and startled two barn cats. They flew past me, careened off the bales of hay and scurried out the door.

Off in the back were some farm implements and an old Ford 8N tractor. I immediately went over to check out the tractor, but was disappointed to see that parts of its engine were missing.

While walking to the house, I could see why command wrote the place off. There was just too much dying vegetation and dead trees around the house and barn.

Within minutes Phil came to me and said, "Pablo, Teddy and I have been looking the place over, and we have come up with a plan."

All right, that's just great; Phil and Teddy have come up with a plan! I hope it's a good one, I pondered.

Phil told Diane, "I want you to be our sawyer and go after those dead trees and shrubs around the house. We will come over later and help you move the slash. Pablo will be cutting line around the house and barn. Teddy will be raking away all burnable items the best he can. Keep an eye out for him, so he doesn't over extend himself. After that, I want Teddy to load up his pick-up truck with his most treasured keepsakes. He knows he can't take them all, and needs to be selective."

Phil looked at his watch, and then scouted the property. "I will use this section of chain Teddy found, and hook it up to some of this scrap cast iron and railroad ties, and wrap them with a piece of chain link fence. I will use the Triple Nickel and drag it around the house and barn. It will work just like a scraper. When we're done it should look pretty clean. But first we need to let the livestock out of the corral. When the fire approaches, they have a better chance in the open. OK, Let's roll!"

Diane exclaimed, "Wow! Phil, nice plan! Especially the part about using the Nickel as a scraper."

"Great idea Phil!" I said and then thought, *how does he come up with this stuff? His idea would never have crossed my mind ... Hmm, adapt and overcome, I guess that's the name of the game.*

Theodore and I started taking away the slash Diane had created with the chainsaw. I carried the heavier brush while Teddy raked the leaves and smaller branches. As we worked I found out a little more about this ranch and Teddy.

"I had an older brother. He was a lot older than me, and his name was Travis." Teddy looked pale and tired, as he pointed to a small knoll just west of the barn. "His grave marker is up there next to Mom and Daddy's. He was a member of the New Mexico 200th/515th Coast Guard Artillery, stationed in the Philippines when World War II broke out. The Japanese, early in the war, overran the Bataan Peninsula. The Japanese captured Travis along with 70,000 Americans and Filipinos. They all became POWs, and were sent on the Bataan Death March. They endured a 65-mile trek in brutal heat, without food or water.

More than 11,000 POW's died on the 10-day march, and an additional 35,000 died during their stay at the prison camp."

"I've heard about that, did he make it?" I asked.

"Well, along the way, Travis was beat up pretty bad, from what the guys who survived told Daddy. But he managed to finish the march, probably because he was a stubborn cuss like me."

"The survivors told Daddy, they all suffered miserably at the hands of the Japs. The camp was infested with lice, mosquitos, cockroaches, and maggots. There was dehydration, starvation, and a lot of senseless beatings. Dysentery, malaria, and dengue fever ran unchecked, and they said the worst part was burying the huge piles of rotting corpses."

"God, how awful, it must have been hell," I said.

Teddy stiffly bent over and picked up a bunch of sticks and tossed them over the scratch line, "Travis felt it was his sworn duty to try and escape, so a bunch of them made a break for it one night, and all of them were shot. They never recovered their bodies. So we remember him with a marker up on the hill."

I noticed he was getting winded. "Let's take a quick break, we've done quite a bit."

We sat down on an old swing-set in the backyard. The poles used to be white, with a pink and blue candy cane stripe running to the top, but were now mostly rusty, and creaked when we sat on them.

"Me and my wife Carol had two boys, the youngest one, Carl, got real sick when he was 7 years old and didn't make it. My older boy Caleb grew up to be a strong young man and lived on the ranch his whole life. My boy married when he was 21. His wife was named Samantha, and she was the sweetest thing this side of a sugarplum. I gave this place to them when they got married, you know, as a wedding gift. Caleb and Samantha were so proud, and promised they would work hard to keep the ranch going. They had a son, and I was tickled pink when they told me they named him Theodore Jr."

Ted wiped his brow and explained, "One night Caleb and the family was coming back from the movies in Willcox, when a drunk driver crossed the centerline and hit 'em head on. The whole family was killed. Carol and I was broke up real bad, and life hasn't been the same after that. Carol passed just three years ago, and I am alone on this place now. Just me and Ruby here," he sighed, and stroked the big red dog on the head. "There's nobody left to carry on."

"Man I'm sorry," I said, and placed my hand on his shoulder. "Life seems so unfair sometimes."

"Oh don't feel sorry for me, nobody said life was supposed to be fair. We had a whole lotta of good times along the way," Teddy smiled, as he struggled to stand up.

"Wouldn't trade it for anything in the world."

He turned and looked at the rusty swing set, and with a glint in his eye, softly gave the empty seat a little push.

We had been working for a little over three hours, and things were shaping up nicely. Diane commented that the air was getting heavier with smoke, and the down canyon wind was starting to pick up.

I got a call from the burnout operations up canyon. It was the handcrew leader from South Dakota. "The situation is changing rapidly for the worse, the wind is throwing fire brands everywhere! We are starting the upper canyon burnout now!"

I looked at my watch and realized they were way ahead of schedule.

Our group leader came on the radio and explained, "Keep your eyes up canyon. I want all units to be ready to bail if the situation goes *to Hell in a Hand Basket!*"

I yelled to my crew, "Holy crap! They've started the burnout up canyon. We don't have much time!"

"Diane, go help Teddy pack his truck!"

"Phil, we need to do something about those old dilapidated wood sheds, they are way too close to the house."

I headed out to do a walk around on Phil's makeshift scraper line and was amazed to see what a clean, down to the mineral earth, line his invention had made. As I made my way around the barn, I witnessed the first of the two sheds next to the house, collapsing into a heap. Phil, using a long section of one-inch wildland hose, had wrapped it around the shed three or four times, and using the Triple Nickel, he dragged the shed away from the house until it fell apart.

"He is a genius, adapt and overcome ... how does he come up with this stuff?" I said out loud to no one. He proceeded to knock down the second shed.

I looked up canyon and saw fire trucks emerging from the thickening smoke. The main fire was not far behind them. Just then our group leader pulled up in his vehicle, and walked up to me.

He paused as he looked around and said, "Nice dozer line! I'm impressed ... All of the resources are pulling out, what about the old rancher?"

"I think he is ready to leave. He just wanted to make sure we did the best we could to secure his place."

"OK, I'm glad you convinced him," he looked again at the dozer line and said, "I'm not sure how you did this but we've got to go now!"

I told him, "It looks like we have maybe 15 minutes still. Once the other trucks pass us, we can start the burnout from our line. We need to create some black between the main fire and the ranch, before the fire front hits us. I think we can save this place!"

He checked on the radio with the other units and gave us an, "OK! You've got 15 minutes. Go for it! We will wait for you down at the next house, keep me posted."

Phil and Diane were standing with flares and drip torches in hand, ready for action. Teddy and Ruby were sitting in their pickup truck; the bed was full of his precious few belongings, and was covered with a canvas tarp.

I yelled to Diane, *"Burn out!"* They started from the back near the barn and preceded around to the front of the house."

I walked over to the rancher and heard his engine trying to turn over. It sputtered and slowly whined to a pitiful halt.

"Crap! The battery is dead!" I marched over to him and shouted, "Sir, you will need to come with us in our truck."

"I won't leave my things, these things mean everything to me, this is all I have left!"

I looked behind the house, and could see the distant hillside in flames. Diane and Phil completed the burnout, and their back burn was slowly heading toward the main fire.

"We don't have time to argue!" I shouted to Theodore.

Against my better judgment, I quickly hooked the tow chain to his pickup truck and yelled to Phil, "Jump in the rancher's truck and steer it. We're going to tow it out!"

I grabbed the rancher by the arm and sternly escorted him over to our truck, and could see the look on his face. He was in shock, as he stared at the fire coming down the canyon.

Diane was spraying down the house and barn, using all of our tank water and the last five-gallon bucket of foam. The buildings were now coated with a layer of soapy bubbles.

While disconnecting the hose, we could feel the heat from the flames. Leaving our hose on the ground, we jumped into the Nickel. Putting the truck in gear, I slowly pulled forward and felt the tow chain thunk, and get taught. The Triple Nickel strained a bit as she began to tow the rancher's truck to the main road. In my dusty rear view mirror, I saw Phil giving me a thumbs-up, with Ruby hanging her head out the window. She was happily barking, and her ears were flapping in the wind.

At least someone was having a great time, I grinned.

As we gained a little speed, I could tell Phil was trying to bump start the truck. Every time he popped the clutch, the truck would jerk but nothing would happen.

As we crossed over the cattle guard and under the Falcon Ranch archway, I could no longer see the ranch house through the smoke.

I radioed the group leader, "We are all out, everyone is safe, and we are heading to your position."

"Copy that Mimbres Springs," he replied.

The group leader saw us towing the rancher's truck behind us and advised, "Go back to the school, we are all heading there to resupply."

"Copy," I replied, and turned to Diane and shouted, "The Nickel pulls us through again, I love this truck!"

"Holy crap, talk about dicey!" Diane said. "I hope everything we did at the ranch will hold!"

A few minutes later, I could see Theodore sitting in the back seat, staring in silence, as we drove past the remains of the old Jericho Ranch.

Arriving at the school, our group leader came up and said, "Strong work guys!"

As Phil was helping unhook the pickup, Ted said with teary eyes, "Thank you for everything. We did the best we could, didn't we?"

"Yes we did. We did the best we could. It's in God's hands now," Phil said, and gave him a little hug.

We refilled our tank water, grabbed a couple buckets of foam, and stocked up on bottled water and Gatorade.

Our task force regrouped, discussed what needed to be done, and went back to work. Two hours later, the burnout operation was complete. From our vantage point, we could see our backfires meeting up with the main fire.

All the crews gathered for the evening briefing, and got a *job well done,* from command. We were dismissed, and were told to either stay at the school, or go to the makeshift spike camp at Bonita Canyon, for a hot trucked-in meal.

"Get some rest," yelled the group leader. "It has been one hell of a day! And there's plenty more where that came from!"

Diane looked at her watch, "Hokey smokes it's 20:30! Boy, time really flies when you're having fun!"

Phil added, "Let's go, I'm starving!"

"Any predictions for the evening supper Oh Fake Swami?" asked Diane.

"Yup, I predict it will be ... lip smackin' good."

I chuckled at Phil and looked back at the mountain. I stared at it for a moment and cursed under my breath, "Damn you hellfire, and to hell with you and your crummy hand basket."

31 Communion With The Past

Golden rays of sunshine were breaking over the ridge when I crawled out of my bedroll. The wind had died down during the night, and a layer of smoke settled in the valley below, covering it like a down comforter.

Diane was still snuggled in her sleeping bag, and the backdoor of the Triple Nickel was open, with Phil's big gunboats sticking out.

Hmm, I'm the first one awake this morning. I said to myself, stretching my arms, trying to work the stiffness from my body. Yesterday my body felt like someone took a hammer to it; today my muscles felt like they have been run through a meat grinder. Every inch of me was screaming, and I felt like a 100-year-old man. Our two-week tour was winding down, and after yesterday's action, I really could use a jolt of Lupe's Horny Toad coffee.

I looked over at them and thought, *those two worked their butts off yesterday, and I don't want to wake them up with me rummaging around, trying to find the coffee pot, camp stove, and coffee. I will wait until they are up before I make some Joe. They deserve every extra minute of sleep.*

Looking around the spike camp, I could see the early risers walking around at a snail's pace. Everyone looked a little fried, and the whole place reminded me of the old zombie movie, *Dawn of the Dead.* Off in the distance, I noticed some guys huddled around several 5-gallon metal thermoses.

"Great day in the morning! There's coffee! Incident Command must have trucked it in!"

Making my way over there, I thought to myself, *nobody is going to deprive this zombie of his morning Joe.*

Approaching the group, I said in a gruff voice, "How are all of you zombies this morning?"

They gave me a collective living-dead grumble.

We crowded around the coffee spigot and growled, "Oooh, coff-ee, aaah, me like coff-ee."

After pouring myself a cup, I noticed next to the coffee station was a small table that the Willcox Women's Auxiliary set up, and on it were several white bakery boxes of powdered jelly donuts. I made my way over to the donuts.

"How nice," I said and wiggled my fingers over them, pondering which donut to take.

I picked a winner, growled as I bit into it, and thick red jelly splooged out of the back end of the donut. I was feeling very cannibalistic as powdered sugar covered my lips. The other guys played along, grunting and growling as they sloppily tore into their jelly donuts.

"Aagggh, dough-nut, me like dough-nut," one of the guys said, as powdered sugar fell to the ground and bright red jelly ran down his chin and dribbled onto his shirt.

After brushing off the sugar and accumulated donut crumbs, we all held up our coffee cups, grunted a collective zombie salute and shuffled our aching bodies and powder sugared lips back to our camps.

I was decked out in my trusty brown Jesus Slippers, an old pair of ratty gym shorts, and the *Custer's Last Shirt,*

Élan gave me. It had been well over a week since I shaved, my hair was a mess, and I was as filthy as junkyard dog. "We must look like death warmed over, but I really don't give a rat's ass," I said raising my cup to an inquisitive Mexican Jay perched in a branch above me. I added while scratching my privates, "This ain't a prissy fashion show honey!" The blue bird looked annoyed, squawked twice and flew away. I took another hit of coffee, sat at the picnic table and tried to ease into the morning.

I put off donning my fire shirt and pants. They were crusted with salt and sweat, dirty as all get out, and could probably stand up on their own. Not to mention they were now beginning to give off that classic, putrid, wildland stink.

Diane was up, and I motioned quietly toward the coffee station down the way and whispered, "Donuts!"

She lowered her head and stifled a muffled laugh.

"What's so funny?"

"Pablo, it's written all over your face!"

I rubbed the back of my hand across my lips and said, "It was a feeding frenzy over there! They were animals!"

Diane headed over to the coffee station, and I looked over to Phil. He was still out cold.

I sat there for a while and savored my coffee. After about 15 minutes, the caffeine started to kick in and I began to feel human again.

Instead of feeling like a zombie or a 100-year-old man, I now felt like a spry 80-year old.

I looked over to Phil and thought, *I can't help myself.* I hesitated for a moment but gave in to my old trickster ways.

I tiptoed up to Phil, grabbed his feet and vigorously shook them!

"The fire has jumped the line! Run Away, Run Away! Our truck is on fire! Man the lifeboats! Women and children first! We're losing altitude, Mayday, Mayday, Mayday! *Oh the Humanity!*"

Phil shot up like a bottle rocket! He flew off the back seat and got tangled up in his sleeping bag, tripped, and ended up rolling around in the dirt.

Meanwhile, Diane was on her way back and saw the whole thing.

Phil was dusting off his T-shirt when Diane came over to me and said in an annoyed voice, "Pablo, you're such a jackass!"

I chuckled and shrugged my shoulders. "The opportunity was there. I couldn't pass it up."

"Pablo why do you always pick on me?" whined Phil, as he gathered up his sleeping bag, shook off the dust, and stuffed it in a side compartment."

"Hey, you're the new guy and I don't mess with Diane anymore, especially first thing in the morning."

"Phil, listen to this," said Diane as she sat on the picnic table and sipped her coffee. "One time about five years ago, we were at a fire in the Four Corners region. We were spiked out in the San Juan Mountains and Pablo thought it would be cute to mess with me one morning."

"No! Don't tell that story! Jeeze Louise!" I pleaded. I placed my hands on top of my head in surrender, turned and walked away. "Not that one!" I pleaded again.

"Hey Pablo, you brought this on yourself, and I feel Phil needs to hear this," grinned Diane.

"Anyway ... Pablo thought it would be cute to mess with me one morning while I was sleeping. He quietly straddled my sleeping bag and started to tickle my nose with a long blade of grass."

"Yeah, then what happened?" asked Phil with a grin.

"You should have seen the look on his face when he was on the receiving end of a swift kick in the nuts!" Diane hooted! "He went down like a sack of potatoes!"

Phil was laughing his ass off, and I walked over to them and said, "Ha, ha, very funny! It pains me today, just thinking about it."

"Your wife was pretty sore at me after that, because it took you a while to recover," said Diane.

"She wasn't the only one that was sore!" I said, hiking up my gym shorts.

Diane walked over to Phil and jerked her knee up. He immediately did a duck and cover.

"OK, stop horsing around Miss Kung Fu," I grumbled. "We need to go to the morning briefing."

The supervisor called for order, and let the group leader fill us in on the details.

The group leader pointed to the map and stated. "We will start deep in this canyon and work our way back to the Rocking K Ranch, near its mouth. This strategy worked yesterday and the winds have died down a lot, so I feel real good about the burnouts today. Take a double sack lunch with you. The area is quite a bit larger than the area we worked yesterday, so I figure we will be busy until dark and might not make it back in time for supper."

All the crew bosses huddled up, and discussed the safety zones and escape routes. Everyone seemed to be on the same page and decided we were good to go. Today would be pretty much the same as yesterday. *Same fire, different canyon.* The next canyon to the north was in the fire's path, but the good thing about today was, we were getting an earlier start.

"Mount up boys and move 'em out!" cried the group leader The supervisor shook the group leader's hand and then waved me over to his truck. I was thinking, "This can't be good. The *supervisor* wants to talk to me. We must have screwed something up yesterday."

"Mimbres Springs Fire" he said, as I walked over to him. "There was an old gentleman at the Portal Incident Command Center early this morning. He said his name was Theodore, and he had a big red dog with him. He was snooping around the IC and wanted to know the status of his ranch. We radioed West Command to find out about the fire in Division AA. They reported the night shift was in there last night and worked some hot spots and cold trailed the black. They reported a lot of structures sustained some damage; some of them were pretty bad.   However, Theodore's Falcon Ranch came through with flying colors. It looks like two of the sheds have been reduced to a pile of hot coals, but the house and barn are 100 percent intact!"

I grinned and shook my head. "Teddy ... How did he get to Portal? We had to tow his pick-up truck to the school."

"Theodore told us the guys at the school put his car battery on a charger. It was dead as a doornail, and the truck was out of gas, but they managed to find him some gasoline and after about two hours they jump-started the truck. He drove over last night and stayed in Portal, only because he had nowhere else to go. He told the guys at IC, that a crackerjack crew from Mimbres Springs worked like the dickens yesterday to clear out the area surrounding his place. He said you guys were on it like *Ants on a Honey Bun.*"

"Wow, that old coot really is a character, they don't make 'em like that anymore. And now that you mention it, I didn't know that phrase was so popular. This is the third time I heard someone say that," I said.

"He told us your leader's name was Phil, and he wanted to thank him in particular, and your crew as well, for a job well done. The guys at IC are always pleased to hear such glowing praise from one of the locals. I am sending a copy of the report to your fire department back in New Mexico. Keep up the good work Mimbres Springs!"

The supervisor gave me a firm and grateful handshake, and I felt fantastic. I couldn't wait to tell my crew.

As we headed out to our assigned area, I told my crew about the praises the supervisor relayed to me.

"Phil, you keep this up, and you will become Engine Boss in no time," I said. "Someone needs to take my place when I retire."

"Naw," replied Phil, "I'm not even halfway done with my Wildland Task Book."

"Hey, you've got what it takes," said Diane. "We are all independent thinkers out here, and I can see that you are not afraid to think outside the box. A lot of people can't or won't do that. Not only that, you have empathy for your crew and show a lot of compassion for others."

"You either have it, or you don't," I said. "I'll tell you right now Phil, you've got what it takes to be a leader. You've got the right stuff."

Phil responded modestly, "We all did our part. It was a team effort."

I could tell Phil was a happy camper, he was grinning like a fox in a hen house. A few words of praise can go a long ways out here. I know it's nice when a crew boss thanks his crew, but it is especially nice when a supervisor notices.

We soon arrived at our destination. The task force leader sent the hand crews up the canyon to cut line and burn out. The brush trucks were assigned to triage and prep the structures. The two ranches at the canyons base were pretty much protected by their plowed fields and well-grazed cattle pastures. The hillsides were steeper and rockier than the last canyon. It was obvious by the look of it, that this canyon had experienced fire a few years ago, which thinned out a lot of the dead trees and heavy ground fuels. There was still enough brush left to cause concern, and, we didn't want the fire to work its way to the valley below.

After about an hour, the few structures we found up canyon were prepped, and the canyon was filling up with smoke. As the backfires progressed, we were given the assignment to cold trail the black and make sure there was no slop over into the green. We needed to work our way 30 feet into the black and stomp out any hot spots. Everything needed to be cold before we moved on.

Eventually we tied in with the hotshot crew from South Dakota and started cold trailing together.

"Hello friend, my name is Pablo," and extended a hand to their crew boss.

"The name's Lionel, but most everybody calls me Dutch," he said.

"Dutch huh?" I asked.

"Yup, my last name is Dutchendorff, and I really am not that fond of Lionel."

"Well Dutch, what part of South Dakota are boys from?" I asked as we worked our way along the black.

"We are the Tatanka Hotshots out of Custer, South Dakota!" he said proudly. "It's a small town located in the southwestern part of the state."

"You guys are a long ways from home!"

"Yeah, this is the furthest south we have ever traveled," said Dutch.

"Travel any further south and you will need a passport!"

The Tatanka Hotshots were all tall young men, wearing red hard hats. It's kinda difficult sometimes to tell who is who, working these fires, as everyone starts to look the same. We all had dirty yellow shirts, dirty green pants, filthy backpacks, boots and gloves. The only distinguishing feature was probably the color of our hard hats. The Tatanka Hotshots were mostly Anglo guys, with full shaggy beards, but there were two women and a Native American mixed in with their group as well.

"I'm finding out Arizona can be pretty harsh," laughed Dutch. "Everything either has a hook, thorn, or spine attached to it. I'm beginning to feel like a pin cushion."

He removed his leather gloves to show me his hands. They were chingered up pretty good with cactus spines and cat claw. Dutch put on his gloves and promptly backed up into a cholla cactus. One of the spiked cactus balls latched on to his forearm.

"Oh God!" he winced, and tried to pull the cactus off.

"Stop! Stop!" cried Phil, and ran over and grabbed Dutch's arm. Phil dug into his cargo pants pocket and pulled out a large plastic comb, and carefully slid it under the cactus ball.

"Hold on, this is gonna hurt a bit."

They both winced as Phil pulled up on the comb. The cactus resisted at first, but with a little more pressure, the gnarly clump cleanly flicked off of his skin. You could see where the cholla barbs were anchored on his forearm, and now tiny drops of blood were pooling to the surface.

"Thanks man," Dutch said with relief. "I need to get me one of those."

"Let me see that comb," I said to Phil.

He handed over the comb and I examined it closer.

"It's one of those Afro picks black guys use to fluff out their hair-do's," smiled Phil. "It has a nice ergonomic design and a non-slip grip!"

Now he was starting to sound like one of them TV ads on The Home Shopping Network.

"Where did you get this?" I asked him.

"Maxine's Mercantile," he said flatly.

"Maxine's, well what do ya know," I smiled and handed back the comb. "It looks like everything you need can be found there. Maybe the comb could be classified as a sundry. I'm still trying to find out what a sundry is."

"The girl at the counter gave me a strange look when I bought it," Phil smiled "I just turned and walked out fluffing up my hair with it."

"Phil, you don't have an Afro, it's practically a crew cut! You're such a dope sometimes," I laughed.

As the Tatanka Hotshots made their way up the main canyon, we split off and began to tackle a smaller ravine to the left. It was narrower than the main canyon and curved around so we couldn't see where it went. It looked burnt out, but we still had to go in there to make sure it was cold.

After a while, Phil called out that he needed to take a pit stop and went behind a big boulder for a little privacy.

"Needs to drop the kids off at school," grinned Diane.

After a few minutes Phil hollered, "Diane! Pablo! You got to come on over here and check this out!"

"Don't make us walk all the way over there to show off your steaming pile of poo!" I yelled.

"No, for reals, this is pretty cool!" he answered.

Diane and I shrugged our shoulders and made our way over there. Phil was kneeling down, looking in a small cave at the base of a rock wall. The opening was about two feet wide and two feet tall, and not too deep. He proceeded to clear away a bunch of burned up Rabbitbrush and Manzanita.

"What's that?" asked Diane.

"I don't know," said Phil as he reached in the little cave. "Heee Doggie, look at that!"

Phil began to gingerly pull out a large earthen pot. It was about the size of a basketball, greyish brown in color and had tiny shiny flecks imbedded throughout the clay. It was a simple pot, as there were no symbols or decorations painted on it. It had a short turned up rim, like you would see on a vase, with a small decorative edge embossed on it.

"God, look at that!" Diane said, reaching out towards the pot. "Can I hold it Phil?"

Phil handed it off, and Diane sat down in the dirt, cross-legged, and cradled it in her arms like a newborn baby.

"This thing is completely intact, no cracks, no chips. It's beautiful," smiled Diane, as she ran her hand over the surface, brushing off the dust. "It looks like it was made yesterday, but somehow it feels so ancient."

"No telling how long that pot has been sitting in that cave," I said. "Can I hold it?"

Diane gave me a daunting look and cautiously handed me the pot.

I held it at arm's length and said, "Hey guys, we could probably make a killing on e-Bay with this thing."

Diane snatched it out of my hands, and handed it back to Phil.

"That pot is not going anywhere bub!" Diane said sternly. "You have this bad juju thing following you around. If we remove this pot, bad things could happen to us! The last thing we need is bad juju."

"Oh, come on, listen to yourself, bad luck, bad juju. It's all a lot of bull-pucky as far as I am concerned! If the spirits were out to get me, I would be dead by now."

Phil and Diane both gave me the stare, and Diane said, "Be careful what you say Pablo, and don't press your luck."

"I'm with Diane," said Phil. "It's not ours. It would be considered stealing! This pot was placed in the cave for a reason; someone cherished it, and wanted to keep it safe. I just happened to see it because the fire burned away the brush, and I was squatting down to do a number two."

He cleaned the pot with his sleeve, held it up and gave it a small kiss, and then placed it back in the little cave.

"OK, OK, calm down guys, it was just an idea. I don't want to be responsible for upsetting the balance of the universe," I grunted.

Phil found a big flat rock and Diane helped him place it over the entrance of the cave. It must have been the original cover because it was a perfect fit. Phil stacked a few large rocks up against it to make sure the covering stayed in place.

Phil got up and wiped his hands on his pants. "I can't believe we found a Leverite Artifact while working a brushfire."

"What do you mean a Leverite Artifact?" I asked.

Phil stated, "A leave 'er right there, artifact!"

"OK, OK, I guess you guys are right. I just got a little excited, that's all. Don't make me out to be the bad guy. I'm not always the bad guy."

"Wow, those people lived and breathed right here, and stood right where we are standing now. That pot was something they made with their own two hands, and we touched it and held it with *our two hands* ... We just made a connection. It's like touching the past!" said Phil.

"Yeah, things like this don't happen every day. Some ancient people placed it there for a reason. I think it's kind of cool that we came across something spiritual sitting in that little cave out here in the middle of nowhere," added Diane.

"And we have enough sense to just *let it be,*" said Phil.

We looked around pondering about what kind of people and events took place at this remote spot, when a small breeze worked its way up the ravine.

"Did you feel that?" whispered Phil, as the wind rustled some of the burned up grass.

"Yeah, I felt it," whispered Diane.

"Me too!" I said.

Just then, a small ashy dust devil skirted past us. The hair on the back of my neck began to stand up, and I felt as if someone was standing behind me. I turned around and the only thing behind me was a blackened wait-a-minute bush.

It was getting late when we regrouped with the hotshots and made our way back to the trucks. To the west, the sun was gracefully balanced on a distant hill, like a golden glass marble ready to roll down the western slope. Without much fanfare, today's burnout went as planned and the main fire never reached the valley below. While stowing away our gear, we could hear the sounds of coyotes calling in the distance, as the evening shadows began to creep towards us.

As we reflected on the profound events of the day, Phil commented, "Man, for all we know, that could be the burial site of a great Indian leader!"

"Maybe so, and nobody will ever find out, as far as I'm concerned," Diane said with a grin.

She got an approving nod from us, as we climbed in the Nickel and headed back to the spike camp. For a day that produced no real fire drama, it still turned out to be pretty darned awesome.

32 Ghosts Of Turkey Creek

Same fire, different canyon. Turkey Creek was one of the few creeks that flowed year round in this area and it had been the home to Native Americans for hundreds of years. I had read multiple stories about the events and people that made Turkey Creek famous, with prospectors and ranchers settling in the area during the boom days of Tombstone and Bisbee. Stagecoach robbers, horse thieves and cattle rustlers, used it as a hideout, back when the West was wild. Billy and I spent many days on horseback exploring those canyons. I was a little hesitant at first, but still kind of curious to see it again.

Our assignment took us deep into the upper canyon. With each passing day the head of the fire was getting smaller. It was as if we were throwing a lasso around it and pulling the rope tighter and tighter. It still had potential to cause mayhem, and could flare up and run amok, so we had to remain diligent.

As the day dragged on, the sun became especially hot and the air was filled with the loud buzzing of cicadas. The din was everywhere as cicadas almost always emerge during the hottest time of year. The sound was welcoming to me, because it signified the approach of the summer rains.

"Man those little buggers sure can make a racket," noted Phil. "It sounds like we are all in a giant sizzling frying pan. The sound kind of makes the desert feel extra hot."

"Talking about frying pans, I was at a friend's house for a party several years back, and his Nana was visiting from Oaxaca, Mexico. She made this incredible *cicada* dish," Diane said.

"No kidding, you guys *ate* them?" blurted Phil.

"Yeah, Nana went out in the morning and gathered a bunch of those critters, just as they were emerging from their shells. This was during one of those 17-year locust blooms, so there were a bazillion of them. She blanched them in boiling water for about 5 minutes, pulled the wings and legs off and put them on a cookie sheet and baked them with a little salt and lime. While that was in the oven, she made a sauce using several cups of chicken broth, cilantro, garlic, tomatillos and some Serrano chilies in a blender. After browning some rice in a big cast iron skillet, she added the liquid from the blender, along with some zucchini, white corn, and sliced carrots. It simmered for 20 minutes, and just before she served it, she tossed the roasted cicadas on top. The cicadas had a nice nutty flavor and everyone loved it!"

"Doesn't sound too bad, in fact it sounds pretty tasty," said Phil.

"Everything except the bug part," I replied.

Diane went on to say, "Some people call them land shrimp, because cicadas are in the same classification as shrimp and lobster. I asked her for the recipe and she wrote it down for me. Maybe I will make it at the fire station some time."

"No thanks, you can count me out! I would have to be pretty desperate to eat a bug," I said hacking, pretending to dry heave.

"I might give it a try. I will try anything once!" announced Phil. "All of this talk is making me hungry, let's eat some lunch."

"This is proof positive, anything will make you hungry," I said.

After a full morning of cutting line and back burning, we looked for a good spot to eat. We could see some large trees by the creek, and as we got closer, noticed they were some of the biggest cottonwoods I've ever seen. Taking refuge in the shade, I removed my hard hat, and looked up into the branches of the largest tree. I ran my hand along the deep furrows of its massive trunk, gave it a couple of sound pats and pondered what stories this old one could tell us if it could talk. After clearing out a spot in the shade, we sat down and started in on our warm baloney sandwiches. After squeezing on a little mustard, I packed about seven or eight potato chips between the bread and meat, crunched it all down, and took a big bite.

Diane was busy eating her sandwich when, after taking a couple of bites, peeked inside and remarked, "Do you guys really know what goes into baloney?"

"I really don't want to know while I'm eating it, but I guess you are going to tell us anyway," I said, while stuffing back in some escaping potato chips.

She went right down the list, "Let's start with muscle scraps, animal skin, tongues, ears, head meat like lips, snouts and jowls, connective tendons, salivary glands, lymph nodes, hearts, livers and copious amounts of animal fat, and other ... how can I put this, other *edible slaughter by-products*. It is churned into a thick liquid slurry and put into intestinal casings and steamed or smoked."

"But they are tasty, edible, slaughter by-products!" grinned Phil, as he raised his sandwich in a baloney salute.

"Hear, hear!" I said in return. "To baloney! Let no one come between a man and his tasty, edible, slaughter by-products!"

"I'm just saying, eating bugs is probably a lot more healthy. They contain as much protein as meat. They are high in fiber, low in fat, contain a lot of vitamins and minerals and are lactose and gluten free," said Diane. "What's not to love?"

"They're bugs! That's what!" I said sarcastically. "OK, OK, when the end of the world comes, then and only then will I eat bugs."

As we sat there enjoying our lunch, Dutch called us on the radio. "One of my guys just saw a rancher on horseback just down the road. He said he called out to warn him about the approaching fire, but the man didn't respond. The guy didn't even look back or slow down, and just kept heading north. The sheriff's office cleared out the residents yesterday, and the area is supposed to be evacuated. So keep an eye open for him."

"Copy that Dutch," I said.

I told my crew, "The South Dakota hotshots are working down the road a bit, so the rancher must not be too far away. He's probably an old cuss like Theodore and can't be told what to do."

After lunch we started to work, clearing some brush along the newly cut fire line. Diane was limbing some trees with the chain saw, when I noticed some movement in the wash. I walked over and signaled her to shut off the saw. We stood there momentarily and then saw him through the smoky haze. He was riding a black horse, trailing a mule on a lead. Wearing a long black riding coat, chaps and a black wide brimmed hat, he emerged from the wash about 100 yards from us. He then crossed the dirt road and dropped back down into the wash. He moved at a slow, steady pace and appeared to be in no particular hurry, and didn't even look our way when he crossed the road.

"He must have heard the chainsaw and noticed all of the smoke," I said.

"Don't you think it's odd that he was wearing a long riding coat in this 100-degree heat?" asked Diane.

"Let's talk to the guy," I said.

"Now don't start something Pablo. Just remain calm and find out what's what. Think diplomatic thoughts," cautioned Diane.

I gave her a sideways look and called to Phil, "We are going to check out something in the wash, we won't be long."

He gave me a thumbs-up and continued to work.

We walked to the spot where the rider dropped down into the wash. The creek was a small side drainage that ran off of the main Turkey Creek. Oak, ash, and cottonwood trees lined the banks. There were big boulders scattered here and there, and there was a trickle of water running through it.

"He came in right here," I said. We both looked down stream and saw nothing.

"Lets' go down a bit further," I said and motioned to Diane to follow me.

We rounded a bend and walked down the shaded wash. We immediately started to look for tracks in the wet sand.

"Nothing! Nada! We both saw him, right?" I asked almost doubting myself.

"Absolutely, he went right through here. " She pointing over to the road and to the ground we were standing on.

"What the hell? There were two animals, he was riding a horse and trailing a mule. There has to be tracks!"

The breeze stopped and a thin smoky haze began to settle into the creek bed. I looked up at Diane and I will never forget the look on her face.

"There is something wrong here," she barely whispered. "Listen, do you hear it?"

"What? I don't hear anything," I whispered back.

"That's just it. The cicadas, *they stopped!*"

I slowly looked around and noticed it was dead quiet. There were no birds, no breeze, *no nothing!*

"I'm getting really creeped out!" said Diane. "Are you?"

"Hell yeah." I hoarsely whispered.

We were breathing kinda heavy and I could feel my heart pounding. At that moment the air suddenly got real cold, like *ice cold!* I looked at Diane and she looked *freaked.* I have never seen her look freaked, *ever!*

"Look! I can see my breath!" I gasped and blew out a big frosty breath!

"Same here! Look at this!" She blew out a long white breath and her eyes grew as large as saucers! "I'm getting the hell out of here!"

"Jeezus H. Christ!" I blurted.

Like a coward, I shoved her behind me and ran like crazy! Diane caught up to me, grabbed my arm and elbowed past me. We couldn't get out of that wash fast enough! We ran up the bank, busting through cat claw and tree branches and didn't stop until we hit the open grass and started to feel the hot Arizona sun!

"God damn!" I gasped, with my heart still pounding! "What was that?"

"I'll tell you what that was," Diane yelled. "That was nuts! *Freaking creepy nuts!*"

Bent over, with our hands on our knees trying to catch our breath, we looked back at the wash and then at each other.

"This is some weird shit!" shouted Diane.

I rolled up my sleeves and said, "Look! My arms, they're all goose bumpy!"

She looked at hers and said, "Me too!" and started rubbing her arms, trying to warm them up.

Taking in some more deep breaths, we gathered our wits and briskly walked back to the truck.

When Phil saw us he asked, "Are you guys OK? You look like you've just seen a ghost."

"A ghost? Don't be silly," said Diane, slightly winded.

I glanced at Diane and we nodded in agreement, "No nothing's wrong, don't be crazy, we're fine."

I didn't want to admit to Phil that, *Yeah, as a matter of fact, we just saw a freaking honest-to-God ghost!* Some people already think I am little wacked, but I didn't want everyone to think I was a raving lunatic!

We gathered up our tools and decided not to tell Phil about our ghostly encounter. We drove up the road and met up with the Tatanka Hotshots.

Dutch asked us if we ever met up with the rancher.

"Must of headed south," I said, and looked back at Diane.

She looked at me and did an involuntary shiver.

We all caravanned down the road and soon found ourselves working the property around the Sander's Ranch.

This ranch has always been a working cattle ranch and dates back to the early 1800s. It was rumored that the ranch was the headquarters for some of the most notorious desperados of their time, and they used Turkey Creek as their hideout.

Down the road, about 50 yards from the ranch, Dutch saw a sign that read, *RINGO'S GRAVE,* with an arrow pointing to the creek. I remembered reading stories about the grave, but never took the time to check it out.

"Let's take a look!" said Dutch.

It was about 16:00 in the afternoon. The group was planning on taking a break, but we soon found ourselves hiking down the trail to Ringo's Grave. Diane and I were reluctant to go at first, but we figured there was safety in numbers, so we went with them.

Just past an open field, we found an odd pile of river rocks about two feet high and eight feet long that were stacked on the riverbank next to Turkey Creek. To the left was a low pile of whitewashed stones, with the largest one perched on top that read, JOHN RINGO JULY 13 1892. A short-ways away was a historical marker with a bronze plaque mounted on it.

"What does it say?" asked Phil.

Dutch read it out loud for all to hear. *JOHN RINGO. THE REMAINS OF THIS NOTED GUNMAN AND OUTLAW LIE HERE. A TEAMSTER TRAVELING FROM WEST TURKEY CREEK FOUND THE BODY SITTING IN THE FORK OF THE NEARBY OAK TREE WITH A BULLET HOLE IN THE RIGHT TEMPLE. A CORONER'S JURY REPORTED THE DEATH TO BE SUICIDE AND RINGO WAS BURIED ON THE SPOT. THERE WERE OTHERS WHO VIEWED THE BODY AND MAINTAINED THAT THE JULY 13, 1882, DEATH OF RINGO WAS MURDER ... Cochise County Historical Society.*

"Do you think that it could have been him?" I whispered to Diane.

"No telling who it was," said Diane with a shrug.

"Who?" asked Phil.

"I'll tell you all about it at camp tonight," I said.

We all gathered around the gravesite and had the group leader take a group photo. One of the Tatanka hotshots was lying on the rock pile, acting like the dead Johnny Ringo.

Another was pointing a Pulaski at him as if it were a rifle. Three others were standing stoically with their shovels at their side, at attention ready for burial. Diane was standing in profile, with her hard hat over her heart. Phil had his head bowed, kneeling in prayer, and Dutch had his hand tucked in his shirt like Napoleon. Everyone else was posing, *old timey, Wild West style,* with their arms either crossed over their chests, or on their lapels. We were all hamming it up, posing all-important like, and I must admit, it was kinda corny, but funny as all get out.

As we dispersed, I told the group leader, "I would really like a copy of that photo."

We all got in our trucks and headed to the main highway. The group leader gathered the task forces together on the side of the highway and told us today's burnout operation was a success. If everything goes according to plan, we will take on Rustler's Park Canyon tomorrow, and possibly, the Faraway Ranch. He told us this would be the last day we would be allowed to spike out at the Faraway Ranch. After tonight, we would all have to camp at the school.   A collective "awwww" went up in the group and everyone started to throw empty plastic water bottles at him.

"Sorry boys! The fire is getting too close for it to be safe," he cried, ducking and taking cover behind his truck.

With that said, we headed to the spike camp one last time, for a nice hot meal.

This hot weather was making my face itch. After we got back, I decided to shave. Normally, us full-time structure fire fighters need to be clean-shaven when we show up for work at the fire station, just in case we get called to a house fire. While fighting those fires, we need to wear an SCBA (Self-Contained Breathing Apparatus). The SCBA consists of a metal backpack holding an air bottle. The bottle is connected to a facemask, similar to what a scuba diver wears. But unlike a scuba diver, instead of going under water, we go into fire. The SCBA facemask needs to have an airtight seal on our face, so we don't breathe in anything toxic, and having a beard would compromise that airtight seal. Out here on these wild fires, we can't afford the luxury of an SCBA. The SCBA weighs about 35 pounds. They are too heavy, too hot, and impractical. Out here, we wear a bandana to cover our faces when the air gets thick with smoke, and at the end of the day we just deal with the pounding headaches. We hawk up a lot of black goobers and blow some gross black boogers to boot.

A lot of times, the professional hotshots or wildland guys sport a full beard, kinda like a badge of honor. It seems the longer the season, the longer the beard. I myself can't stand having a hot itchy face and neck, so I broke out my shaving kit and lathered up.

While shaving, Phil came over and asked, "You being the resident Wild West know-it-all, who was that Johnny Ringo character anyway?"

I started to tell Phil, "Back in the day, Johnny Ringo and Curly Bill Brocius were said to be best of friends, and were members of the *Clanton Gang*, also known as *The Cowboy's*. From the stories I heard, Curly Bill was an excellent shot with a pistol, and could snuff the flame off a candle and could shoot a silver dollar from between the fingers of anyone brave enough to hold one up.

"That's impressive, I'm a pretty good shot with my rifle, but not that good with a hand gun," said Phil.

"I heard Johnny Ringo shot a man in a saloon because he wouldn't accept a drink of whiskey from him. The man stated he preferred beer. Johnny was insulted and shot him on the spot."

"Sounds like the guy was a real loose cannon!" said Phil.

"Yeah, the whole Clanton Gang was a lawless bunch, and wreaked havoc in these parts. They cheated at cards, drank with a vengeance, and robbed the stagecoaches that ran between Bisbee and Tombstone. They stole horses, rustled cattle, and even killed the marshal in Tombstone. The worst thing the Clanton Gang did was ambush some Mexicans just south of here, in Skeleton Canyon."

"That's the same canyon where Geronimo surrendered," recalled Phil.

"Phil, you've got a good memory," I nodded.

"Those Mexicans were bandits themselves, known as the *Estrada Gang*. They had 30 mules laden with about $75,000 worth of stolen coins, jewelry and religious artifacts, and were trying to sneak their way into Arizona, to fence their ill-gotten loot. *The Cowboys* got word of the caravan and set up an ambush and opened fire on them while they were taking their siesta. When the mules started to scatter, they couldn't control them and ended up shooting them all. After the smoke cleared, 19 Mexicans and 30 mules lay dead. With all the mules shot dead, they couldn't carry it all and had to stash a lot of it in the canyon. Some say a bunch of it is still hidden up there."

"Wow! We need to check out Skeleton Canyon one of these days," said Phil with amazement.

"You won't be the only one. For years people have tried to find the hidden treasure, but with no luck," I answered.

"Anyway, the Clanton Gang was pretty much a bunch of evil men. If something illegal took place, you could probably bet Curly Bill or Johnny Ringo had something to do with it. Unfortunately, Curly Bill thought he was above the law and Wyatt Earp, who was Tombstone's deputy town marshal at the time, got tired of his lawlessness. His sheriff's posse caught up with their gang in a wash just west of Tombstone. Wyatt Earp let Curly have it with both barrels of his shotgun. They say the blasts nearly cut Curly Bill clean in two. Yup, that Wyatt Earp was a pretty mean bastard himself."

"Good Lord!" said Phil. "What eventually happened to Johnny Ringo?"

"Hold on pardner, this is the tricky part," as I carefully started to shave around my upper lip and chin.

"You missed a spot," said Phil, pointing to just under my chin.

"Ahhhh, that's better!" I rinsed off my face and continued, "The story of him killing himself could be true. Johnny Ringo was drunk and despondent most of his adult life and was a real pain in the ass to be around. Other than Curly Bill, he had no family or real close friends. In fact, most people were happy to hear he was dead. Some speculate that either Wyatt Earp or Doc Holiday hunted him down here in Turkey Creek and Johnny got what was coming to him. Nothing could be proven, one way or another and the rest is history. Someone once asked Doc Holiday what he thought about the demise of Johnny Ringo. Holiday remarked that he thought Johnny must have died of an acute case of *Lead Poisoning*. So there you have it," I said, patting my clean-shaven face. "If I'm not mistaken, I think I smell supper."

Chow had arrived and we all got in line. There were some grilled steaks a local rancher donated, a garden salad, corn on the cob, mashed potatoes and a big lemon sheet cake with cream cheese frosting.

"I could never be a vegetarian," I said as I cut into my steak and let that charbroiled, juicy, grass-fed beef melt in my mouth.

"Me neither," said Dutch. "I would miss bacon too much."

After dinner we chatted it up with the Tatanka Hotshots, and I asked Dutch if any of their guys had a copy of the photo they could email me.

"Sure thing man, what's your email address? I'll send it to you right now," he said.

Out of curiosity, I asked Dutch to identify each member of his crew.

"OK starting from left to right, there's Junior and Samuel. That's Rusty, Tony, and Lucas, holding the shovels. Then there's Aaron, he's the dead guy on the pile of rocks. Kyle is shooting him with the Pulaski. Standing behind the rock pile with their arms folded across their chests are Andrew, Donna, Cameron, John and Milo. That's me with my hand tucked in my shirt, Napoleon style. Off to the side, holding their lapels are Seth, Owen, and another Andrew."

"You have two Andrews?" Diane asked.

"We have three actually! First there's Andrew number one, then Andrew number two goes by Drew and the third Andrew goes by Skip, just to keep things simple. Then there's Chankoowashtay. He's a Sioux Indian, but we just call him Chank, and then there's Mitch and Lily."

I spotted Diane in the picture with her hard hat over her heart. Phil was on one knee praying, and I was standing next to the whitewashed grave marker with my foot propped on it.

"All in all, a fine bunch of unprincipled scoundrels!" said Dutch.

"Indeed!" I laughed, looked at the photo again and did a double take. My eyes widened and a cold shiver went down my spine!

While walking back to the truck Phil remarked, "Hey Pablo, you're looking a little pale, you have the same look you had earlier, like you just saw a ghost!"

With an uneasy tone I said, "Look at this picture again and tell me how many guys *don't* have beards?"

"Is this a trick question?" asked Diane.

Diane looked at it and noted, "Everyone has a beard except Phil, you know, Mr. Baby Face. Then there's Chank, because he is a Native American, Donna, Lily and then me, obviously because we're girls, oh and then this guy standing right behind you. Who is that?"

I looked at Diane then back at the photo.

"I've never seen him before, who is it Pablo?" she asked again, with concern in her voice.

Barely able to speak, I told her in the calmest voice I could muster, "You're not going to believe it. I don't know if I can believe it!"

"What?"

"Don't freak out but ... It's my buddy Billy! Christ that's Billy! He's standing right behind me looking over my shoulder!"

33 Black Jack, Jughead And Tank

"Good God!" gasped Diane. "Are you sure?"

"I'm positive!" and stared at the image in disbelief.

I quickly turned off the phone and shoved it in my pocket. After a few minutes, I cleared my throat and explained. "I think it's time I come clean. I've never told anyone about this, not even my wife!"

It was about 22:00 and we sat down at the picnic table. In the dark I began to tell them my most guarded secret.

"When Billy got back from the war, he inherited his grandfather's ranch. Very few people were living in Dos Cabezas anymore and Billy didn't have anything lined up after the war, so he moved in, cleaned up the place and decided to live there. Billy wasn't much of a rancher, but he found alternate ways to make money, none of which was legal. He kept several horses and about four mules, and had no other livestock on the ranch. He eventually got in with some thugs and started to run drugs up from Mexico. He ferried bales of dope across the border and hid out in the Pedregosas or the Chiricahuas. Somehow I got involved with the whole thing. It seemed exciting to me at the time and I couldn't say no to the money. It was a *lot* of cash!

"Billy always rode his prized quarter horse. It was a tall black stallion with a big chrome of white on his forehead, and his name was *Black Jack*. Billy called him *Jackie* for short. He was smart as a whip, could sense a rattlesnake on the trail, and find water in the desert. I, on the other hand, rode a much shorter and stockier horse. It was dusty grey, kinda stupid but gentle. His name was Jughead. I thought it was a good name for a Marine like me to ride. You know, a Jughead for a jarhead.

"Billy traveled with two handguns around his waist and a rifle in a scabbard on his mount. He let me borrow a colt revolver, since I didn't own a handgun at the time. Traveling with us was his dog *Tank*. Tank was a cross between a coyote and a pit-bull and he looked very primal. He had eyesight like an eagle, was an excellent sentry, and could hear the smallest twig snap. When hearing something at camp, he would perk up and give us a soft gruff whisper, and point his nose toward the sound. Nobody was going to get the drop on us with Tank on guard.

"The plan was, we would trailer two horses and two mules, drive down and park in a designated side canyon, unload the horses and mules, and head down Mexico Way to meet up with the *Dopers* on the other side of the border. That is what we called them, the Dopers. We didn't trust them at all, and cautiously did business with them. We started each trip at sundown and later met up at the designated site. The encounters were always tense as we transferred the load onto the mules, keeping a watchful eye for trouble. After returning to the trailers in the hideout canyon, we would anxiously wait for the buyers to show, I really hated those transactions. The tension was thick and my stomach was always in knots because I didn't know whom we were dealing with. Billy however, loved those encounters. He lived for the adrenaline rush, and could hardly wait to make the exchanges and get paid. We counted the cash before we left, to make sure we weren't short-changed, and then hightailed it outta there before sun up.

"After about two and a half years, we were making runs more frequently and I felt the odds were stacking up against us. It was only a matter of time before something went wrong, like getting busted or maybe even killed. I was beginning to feel uneasy about the whole thing, and let Billy know how I felt. But Billy liked that lifestyle; it was covert, dangerous and exciting. He insisted I stay on, and said we were a team, and I was the only person he could trust. There was a lot of money to be made and he didn't want to give that up. I could see that Billy had become exceedingly greedy and I couldn't trust him anymore. He was now a different person than the one I knew growing up.

"My life had changed in those two and a half years. I had a wife and a kid and didn't want to take a chance of losing it all. I figured it was time for me to grow up and accept my responsibilities as a husband and father.

"One night I flat out told Billy, *I'm out! No Mas!'*

"Billy blew a gasket! I remember he gave me the most hateful, evil stare and snarled, 'You ungrateful son-of-a-bitch! You're gonna cut loose and leave me hanging?'

"I tried to reason with him but he would have none of that. He started to kick chairs and flipped over the kitchen table. Grabbing a knife off of the kitchen counter, he yelled, 'You can take your pantywaist attitude and stuff it up your ass! I don't need you anyway! I'm the brains of this outfit and you are more trouble than you are worth, you jackass coward. I don't ever want to see you again, now get the hell otta here!'

"He threw the knife at me but missed by a mile. I slowly backed out the kitchen door, climbed into my truck, and tore out of there. Those were the last words he ever spoke to me.

"Billy had a run planned for the following week, and to help him with the trip, he recruited a local from Dos Cabezas named Cooter. They made the exchange in Mexico, but something went wrong in the Chiricahuas. Some ranchers heard gunshots just before dawn and went to investigate. They heard the frantic barking from Tank and found Billy and Cooter, unconscious, lying in some tall grass. The ranchers said if Tank wasn't there, they would have never found them in time.

"Cooter was beat up pretty bad and couldn't remember anything about that night. It took him three weeks just to remember his own name. He was never the same after that. Billy, on the other hand, was shot three times. One bullet went through his right shoulder, the other two ended up in his gut. His insides were all tore up, and one of the bullets severed his spinal cord. He was in the hospital for months. All in all, he had seven surgeries, could no longer eat like a normal person, and had to wear a colostomy bag to poop.

"One year later, I went to visit him at his ranch and was shocked to see him. Billy was messed up pretty bad, and I didn't recognize him. He was real pale and gaunt like a skeleton, could hardly eat and was unable to walk. He had a caregiver living with him 24/7 and Tank never left his side. I tried to make conversation with him, but he didn't say a word to me the entire time I was there. While leaving, I gave Tank a scruffy pet and I felt like hell. That was the only time I visited him.

"Billy died before the year was over, on New Year's Eve. I didn't go to the funeral. He was buried in the Dos Cabezas Cemetery.

"Ever since then, I have been beating myself up thinking that somehow, if I had been there that night, the whole thing wouldn't have happened."

"So that is why you have been so testy with us on this trip," said Diane. "Pablo, let me tell you right now, as a friend. You did the right thing. You made your decision and Billy made his. You don't know for sure what was going to go down that night. It sounds like someone was setting you up. For all we know, you could be dead! Your wife would have ended up being a widow and your little girl would have grown up without ever knowing her Dad. Do you ever think about that?"

I turned away, wiped my eyes with my hands and stood there for a moment to let it all sink in. I walked to the Igloo to get a drink and splash a little water on my face.

Phil came over to me and put his hand on my shoulder, "Pablo let it go man! Billy chose that lifestyle and paid a severe price. You on the other hand could see the handwriting on the wall. You were right; it was only a matter of time before something bad happened. I know it's hard and you will never forget it ... but starting right now, you need to let it all go. What's done is done!"

Phil took a sip of water and asked me, "Pablo, think about it. What kind of person would you be today if you stayed on with Billy? Now step back and look at the man you've become. You're a husband, you have a great family and your wife and daughter adore you. You're a firefighter, and you are my friend. You really make a difference in a lot of people's lives."

I looked him in the eye and felt a sudden wave of relief wash over me, like a huge burden had been lifted off of my shoulders.

"You're right Phil, you're absolutely right!"

Phil slapped me on the back and said with conviction, "Without a doubt I'm right, without a doubt."

I raised my cup and said, "Amen to that."

34 Baby Cakes

It was a new morning and I woke up refreshed. I couldn't remember when I had slept so soundly and knew it was because I cleared my conscience.

We muddled through our morning routine. As expected, we were assigned to Rustler Park Canyon. *Same fire, different canyon.* It was starting to sound like a broken record. Not that I was complaining though, work is work and every day can't be an Armageddon. We grabbed some coffee, but unfortunately, there were no zombie donuts.

The cicadas were buzzing in full force as we headed out for the day's work. It was 06:30 and already hot. We were going to work with a crew from California and were instructed to burn everything starting from the edge of the road east toward the approaching fire. We used road flares and a drip torch and walked on the shoulder setting the grass on fire. About two miles separated the California crew and us, and it looked like today was going to be pretty easy but involved a lot of walking.

As we burned the roadside grass, the dry field incinerated with ease and became a moonscape of black rocks and burnt stubble. The burnt rocks kinda resembled black Easter eggs, thousands of black Easter eggs. Near the edge of the road mixed in with the charred grass, were hundreds of old beer bottles, liquor bottles, and rusty beer cans. No matter where we go, whether it's Nevada or Colorado, New Mexico or Texas, it boggles my mind to see that much trash in the weeds. During the burnout, I found a couple of horseshoes, a rusty license plate dated 1948 and a leather cowboy boot, nestled in the burnt stubble.

I held up the boot and stared at it, "How can you lose just one boot? I think you would know if you were walking around in one boot." I looked down at all of the empty liquor bottles, shook my head, and re-evaluated my quandary.

As the day progressed, the back burn moved quickly along the grasslands. The fire was gaining in intensity as the fields turned into a mix of heavier brush and mesquite trees. The wind was picking up, and this was a little disconcerting to me, but I figured, if we patrolled the black and made sure the fire didn't cross the road, we should be OK. I radioed the hand crew working down the road to let them know my concerns about the changing weather.

"Thanks Mimbres Springs, keep us posted on how you Truck Princesses are holding up," he laughed.

"You got it, ya bunch of Knuckle Draggers," I replied.

We continued burning out when Phil yelled, "Hey, there's a spot fire on the other side of the road!"

"Cripes!" shouted Diane, "Where did that come from?"

"Phil, get on it!" I yelled.

"I'm on it like dip on a chip!"

He put the truck in reverse and drove backwards to the fire. We hustled out and pulled hose. It took some effort and every bit of our 200 gallons of tank water, but we managed to knock it down. We scraped along the edges to make sure there were no hot spots and I was confident that the spot fire was completely out.

"That should do it," I said, and radioed to the California hand crew to see if they knew where we could top off our water tank.

They said the nearest pumpkin was up the road about a mile.

"Let's fill her up," I said.

While driving down the dirt road, we could see where a small side road entered the main road and the barbed wire fence formed a corner. In the corner were about 20 heifers and cows huddled up along the fence in the high grass. Mixed in with them were about a dozen or so calves. We parked the truck and hurried over to the fence and looked for a gate. There was no gate, and the smoke from the fire was working its way toward us. The cows were getting a little panicked.

Phil grabbed the bolt cutters from the truck and made a plan. "We need to cut a hole in the barbed wire on the other side of the road first. That way when we cut this side, the cattle can cross the road to the other pasture," Phil explained. "That should make things a lot easier."

"Good idea," I said and we ran across the road and started to cut fence.

Phil told Diane, "Park the Triple Nickel sideways across the road next to the opening. That way the cattle can use the truck as a guide into the new pasture."

Diane pulled the truck around, and we all began to herd the cattle to the new pasture. After a few minutes passed, the fire was gaining speed and was less than a quarter mile away. I glanced over and saw Diane running down the fence line about 100 yards away from us. A cow had knocked over a section of fence, and she and her calf were tangled up in it. Phil and I finished with the cows and I ran up to Diane. We started to franticly cut away at the wire. We managed to free momma and Phil herded her toward the others. I looked up to see the fire was moving in on us fast. The baby was still tangled up and had wrapped herself around a metal fence post so badly we couldn't get the bolt cutters in between her and the post. She was lying down on the ground and was stuck to that pole like Brer Rabbit was stuck to the Tar Baby.

"We need to get ourselves outta here," I yelled to Diane.

"We can't just leave her here!"

"Oh yes we can!"

Diane ran to the truck and grabbed 2 shovels.

"Help me!" she hollered and tossed me a shovel.

I grabbed a shovel and we started to create a scratch line around the calf. After creating a large circle, I reached into my backpack and pulled out a couple of fusees. Phil and I started to fire off the grass next to the scratch line with the road flares. We proceeded to work our way away from the calf and enlarged the black until it was about 10 feet deep.

When I looked up, the fire was bearing down on us.

"We gotta go NOW!" I yelled. "We don't have any water in the tank and there is nothing more we can do!"

We all ran to the truck and I made the comment,

"She just might make it, but then again, she could become a casualty of war, you know, collateral damage. If she doesn't make it, at least we will have some nice tasty veal steaks for supper."

Diane glared at me and yelled, "You asshole!"

She turned and started to run back to the calf. I grabbed her by the arm and yanked her around.

"You aren't going anywhere lady!" I yelled.

The next thing I knew I was seeing stars and ended up flat on my back! *Diane cold cocked me!* I got up with watery eyes, shook my head and realized I had a bloody nose and a split lip. I could see Diane running toward the calf. She got there just as the fire was almost on top of them. She whipped off her backpack and deployed her fire shelter, shook it open and flopped spread eagle on the calf. Within seconds she was under the silver shelter, tucking the corners under her and the calf. There was a lot of wiggling and struggle and I heard Diane come up on the radio.

She was out of breath and the calf was bawling in the background. "Pablo, radio me when the fire front has passed." Diane must have had the transmit button depressed when I heard her say, "It's OK Baby Cakes we will be alright, everything will be just fine, now hold tight!"

There was a lot of bawling and Diane must have shifted and released the transmit button. The radio went quiet just as the fire hit them.

It was all happening so quickly, and yet, seemed like an eternity. As the flames poured over them, I prayed the fire would skirt around them because of the black we created. The words our BC said to us just before we left rang in my ears. *Stay on your toes and don't do anything heroic or stupid.* In my mind I knew this qualified as both *heroic and stupid.*

The fire front worked its way past them and was now heading toward Phil and me. We hid behind the truck and could feel the intense heat, as the flames hissed past us, like a living-breathing thing.

As the fire traveled down the road, I radioed to Diane that it was all clear and I could see her peek out from under the shelter. Phil ran up to her and helped her up.

I ran up to her, grabbed her by the collar and yelled, "That was a God-damned, jackass stunt you just pulled! If you were a guy I would flat out punch you right now!"

I winced a little and pulled out my hankie and held it to my bloody nose.

She looked me in the eye and then, unexpectedly, broke down and started crying. I have seen Diane tear up a little from time to time, but in all the years I have worked with her, I have never seen Diane flat out cry, *ever!*

"I am so sorry, really sorry Pablo!" she sobbed. "I don't know what got into me. I just lost it when you made the comment about collateral damage."

Deploying a shelter is serious business on a fire scene, but when I saw Diane crying, my anger subsided and I felt my heart melting.

"I am just a sucker for a woman in tears," I said, and pulled her close, crooked my arm around her neck, and rapped on her hard hat a couple of times with my knuckles.

"What's done is done Missy. Now help me with Baby Cakes over here, we need to get her freed up and back to the herd."

We walked over to the calf and tried to calm her down, and get her out of her predicament. There was a piece of barbed wire wrapped around the calf's neck; it was twisted so deep it was cutting into her flesh. I figured if the fire didn't kill her she would have hung herself in the struggle. We dug in under the wire a lot harder and snipped it off. Her hind legs were also tangled and cut up. Phil ran to the truck and retrieved the first aid kit and a short section of pencil line. Diane sniffed back some tears, wiped her nose on her sleeve, and began to work on freeing the calf's rear legs.

I looked at the gash in her neck and remarked, "This probably will need quite a few stitches. She's lucky the barbed wire didn't sever an artery."

After rummaging through the first aid kit, I pulled out some antibiotic cream, squirted some into the wound and spread it around. Then I pulled out a tube of Crazy Glue and poured a bead along the edge of the gash. I squeezed the two sides together and held them for a couple of seconds.

"This is a trick I picked up in Nam, I always put a tube or two of Crazy Glue in the first aid kit just in case. In fact, Crazy Glue was invented for this very reason. It was made to close wounds in the battlefield. It was meant to be a temporary fix until we could get the wounded over to medical. Don't worry Baby Cakes, it looks like you will be just fine," I said, trying to calm her down while waiting for the Crazy Glue to set up.

Phil fashioned a lasso with the wildland hose and we stood her up, slipped it around her waist and walked her over to the hole in the fence. After loosening the hose, Phil smacked her on the rump, and she ran hobbling and bawling to mamma and the rest of the herd.

We cut a few long pieces of barbed wire and did some field repairs to the fence on the other side of the road, marking them with bright pink flagging, so the ranchers could do a proper fix later. We marveled at our handiwork and walked back to the truck.

I radioed ahead and informed the hand crew that the fire was quickly heading their way.

Deploying a fire shelter in the field is indeed serious business. It is mandatory that with any deployment of a fire shelter, that the act needs to be documented and an official report be generated.

"I am now making an official decision as the engine boss. *None of this will ever be reported to the IC!* We have extra fire shelters on the truck, and I don't want them kicking us off of this fire. Yes, what Diane did was pretty heroic, but hair-brained stupid. I think what goes on between us, stays with us. We need to make a pact never say a word about this incident to anyone. We need to act as if none of this ever happened."

"I'm all for that," agreed Phil. "My lips are sealed." He made a locking motion across the front of his mouth with his fingers.

"Incident? What Incident?" asked Diane.

Diane miraculously found the packaging materials the fire shelter came in, laying on the ground under the fire shelter. She folded the fire shelter very carefully and stuffed it back in the protective wrapper and slid it into its protective hard plastic case. We squeezed the whole thing back into its blue nylon cover. We took the shelter and placed it on the dirt road. Phil started up the truck and drove the Triple Nickel over the shelter, back and forth about six or seven times. When we were done, it was squished flatter than a pancake, and was barely recognizable. So now the Triple Nickel was involved with the cover up as well.

"It looks like we're all in this together," I grinned.

"Even Mortie the monkey?" asked Diane.

"Yup, even Mortie. He saw the whole thing, didn't ya fella?"

I walked over and peeled the shelter up off of the dirt road.

"I don't know how this happened," I said sarcastically, holding the smashed blue fire shelter up in the air for all to see. "The truck's compartment must have popped open on these bumpy dirt roads and the dang thing fell out. The entire task force must have rolled over it before we realized it was missing."

"That's unfortunate," said Diane with a wink. "I will fill out a damaged property report when we get back to base camp. I'm sure supply will issue us a new one."

We climbed in the Triple Nickel and headed north. "Hey Mortie," I asked. "What's the word, ya little fur ball?"

The sock monkey sat there motionless on the dashboard with those little beady black eyes staring back at me.

"That's what I like, a man of few words. You know what they say, *loose lips sink ships."*

We drove about a mile up the road, topped off our tank from the pumpkin and eventually met up with the California hand crew. They managed to get ahead of the fire and back burned a section of grassland, thereby stopping the fire from jumping a narrow dirt road further down the way.

"Sounds like you guys had your hands full back there!" said their crew boss.

"Why's that?" I asked.

"Well we heard you guys come up on the radio and heard some heavy breathing and a whole lot of mooing!"

"Oh the mooing!" I stammered. "We had to herd a bunch of cattle out of harm's way. They were trapped along the fence line and were getting panicky. They were about to get over run by fire!"

"Sounds kind of exciting. It looks like you got a split lip and a bloody nose in the process," said the crew boss.

I held my hankie up to my nose and dabbed at it a bit. Staring directly at Diane I said sarcastically, "Heck, cattle are pretty stupid and they don't follow orders very well," and gave her my most daunting evil eye. "One of them reared her head and clipped me good. It's nothing really, no big deal,"

Without their crew boss seeing her, she looked back at me, clasped her hands together and looked up to the heavens. I could see her silently mouth, "Thank you God."

The crew boss from California then asked, "Who the heck is Baby Cakes?"

"Oh that," laughed Diane awkwardly. "That's just a pet name I have for Pablo. I know I shouldn't be saying those things over the airwaves," and she gave me a quick swat on the rump. "Isn't that right Baby Cakes?"

She flashed me a cheesy smile, and we turned and walked back to the truck. I laughed, pushed her hard hat down over her eyes and gave her a sideways shove.

"Move along little doggie, we're burning daylight."

The group leader arrived, gathered us up, and went over the day's events. He told us the burnout went well, and he was going to release us a little early today. I was glad, because I about had it for the day. These past few days have been pretty damn hot and it was nice that we were getting off a little early today.

I climbed behind the wheel of the Nickel, cranked up the AC, and told Phil I was going to drive us back to the school.

35 The Queen Of The Night

Since we had a little extra down time I wanted to make a quick detour before heading back to the school. We turned north on the main highway that headed toward Willcox. More precisely, it was the main highway that went through Dos Cabezas. We passed the ramshackle remains of the town and turned left onto a narrow dirt road.

"What gives?" asked Diane as I pulled off the highway.

"I have a little unfinished business to take care of if you guys don't mind. It won't take long."

"No problem-o," said Diane.

We drove through Dos Cabezas and pulled up next to an old cemetery that was about half an acre in size. The sign above the gate read *Pioneer Cemetery*. It was a far cry from the Mimbres Springs cemetery, lacking the bright flowers and shiny trinkets. This one looked forgotten and sadly neglected. A rusty wire fence circled the grounds to keep the cattle out. It was a good thing because we had to chase a bunch of them away to get inside the gate. We spread out and worked our way through the waist-high weeds, looking at the old grave markers.

"What are we looking for?" asked Phil.

"Billy's grave," I replied. "I didn't attend his funeral so I don't know where he is. I know he didn't want to be buried in Mimbres Springs and insisted on being buried next to his grandpa, you know, to keep him company I guess. I never did meet Billy's grandmother. Gramps was a cantankerous cuss and lived a solitary life, but I could tell he really liked it when we came to visit him during those summers. Even though we were just kids, Billy always managed to bring a fifth of Wild Turkey to help ease his arthritis."

"Medicinal right?" questioned Phil.

"Yup, it worked wonders, no better medicine," I grinned.

"Did you kids pass the bottle with the old man?" asked Diane.

"Of course we did. No man should drink alone!" I said with conviction.

We scoured the cemetery marveling at the various grave markers. Some were old weathered wooden boards shaped in a cross and were held together with barbed wire. Some were just flat cement slabs with a name scribed on the surface with a stick or finger while the cement was still wet. Others were large and elaborate carved marble headstones clustered together in family plots. The larger plots were circled with fancy ancient wrought iron fencing. Others were just large piles of rocks with weeds growing up through them. No names or other identifying markers were on them, and I was hoping Billy's grave wasn't simply a nameless pile of rocks.

I pulled out my cell phone and called my brother back in Mimbres Springs. I needed to know in what general direction was Billy's grave. When I got a hold of him, he said he remembered Billy's family saying he was buried right next to the Pacheco family plot. Outside of that, he couldn't tell me anything else.

"Look for the Pachecos," I hollered.

After about 15 minutes, Phil called out, "The Pachecos, they're over here!"

There were about a dozen Pachecos. Their markers were large elaborate granite headstones, with crisp incised words and dates.

"Wow, the Pachecos have been here for quite some time," reflected Diane.

We noted that some of the Pachecos were born as early as 1845 and died as early as 1896. We pushed around the grass looking for Billy when I stumbled over a low stone and fell on my face. I looked up and there he was!

WILLIAM "BILLY" WHITE, BORN 1949, DIED 1976.

He was only 27 when he died. Next to him was another low marker. It was a plain white stone that read,

EDWIN WHITE, BORN 1886   DIED 1972.

Surprisingly, next to Gramps, were two markers that read,

ELIZABETH WHITE, BORN 1888   DIED 1916.

EDWIN "EDDIE" WHITE II, BORN 1916 DIED 1917

We stood there in silence with only the sound of the wind rustling through the grass.

"You notice Eddie Jr. was born the same year Elizabeth died? She was only 28," said Diane.

"Maybe from complications giving birth?" I pondered. "Gramps was a real private man. He never told us anything about his wife and family. I didn't know his wife's name was Elizabeth. Heck, I didn't even know his name was Edwin 'til just now."

We rummaged around a little more and I found a dark brown rock about the size of a football to the left of Billy's grave. I cleared the grass away and on the top, chiseled in the stone, was the word *TANK*.

"Ahhh Tank. Man's best friend! You are not forgotten boy." I patted the rock and stood up.

"What now?" asked Diane.

"I think they deserve better than this," I replied. "Do you guys mind if we clear out some of these weeds?"

"No problem, *I'm on it like a wiener on a stick,*" said Phil.

We went to the truck and grabbed some hand tools. I grabbed the shovel, Diane grabbed the Pulaski, and of course Phil grabbed the McCloud. We raked and pulled all the weeds from the site, and created a flat sandy smooth surface. We ventured out to the cow pasture and brought in armfuls of rocks and made a perimeter. I went out and gathered a couple cow pies and brought them back, plopped them on the ground and asked them if they could work the manure into the sandy soil.

"What are those for?" asked Diane.

"You'll see," and walked to the truck to retrieve an old paper lunch bag.

"What you got in there?" asked Diane. "Some Wild Turkey?"

"I wish! But this is better! Ever since we have been in Arizona I have been on the lookout for these." I opened the bag and poured the contents on the ground.

I separated the pile of five slate grey looking sticks. They were about ½ inch in diameter and about 6 inches long. They appeared to be slender ribbed cactus stems minus the spines.

"What are they?" asked Phil.

"They are Night Blooming Cereus Cactus, also known as *The Queen of the Night.* To the untrained eye they mostly look like dead sticks. It took the entire two weeks for me to collect them. I must admit they're kinda hard to find."

"They are a hearty plant and once they become established, they put down deep roots and don't need much water." I placed the cut side down and shouldered the stems with some soil. "They bloom only once a year, usually in late June or early July. The flowers open only at night, and begin to fade with the rising sun. The blossoms are creamy white, and are as big as an open hand. They have a real strong fragrance. They smell as sweet as cotton candy," I smiled.

"Seriously? You're not pulling my leg are you?" asked Phil. "To me they really look like a bunch of dead sticks."

"Phil, I'm serious, and when I die you can place some of these on my grave. I'd like that very much."

I nestled them in with a couple of bigger rocks, to shelter them so the summer rains wouldn't knock them over and wash them away. I poured the contents of my canteen on them and stood up, envisioning what they would look like in about six years.

"Pablo, most of the time you're an ass, but sometimes you're a thoughtful and considerate guy," said Diane with a wide grin.

"Don't let the word out, it would ruin my whole reputation."

"Ha! Don't worry about that," snorted Phil. "You are on A-shift now! Your reputation is already in shambles."

I laughed and gave him a dusty kick in the pants. We gathered up our tools and headed back to the truck.

As we pulled away, I looked back at the cemetery. Cattle were now surrounding it and I couldn't see their graves, due to the high weeds.

I said to Diane and Phil, "Ya' know, when we were yanking out those weeds, I couldn't help but feel as if I was cleansing my own soul."

"Was it like pulling all of your bad memories out by the roots?" asked Diane.

"Yeah, you could say that."

As we drove down the road, I looked off to the south. Thunderheads were beginning to form way down in Mexico. I knew they wouldn't make their way up for another week or so, but still, it was nice to see that rain was on its way.

"Thanks for helping, I don't know why it took me so long to deal with this. I should have done it a long time ago," I said.

"Glad we could help," said Phil. "So how do you feel after letting it all go Pablo?"

"You know Phil, even though I am hot, filthy, sore, and exhausted ... surprisingly, despite all of that, I feel like a brand new man!"

36 Making A Difference

We pulled into the school and found a spot on the football field to park. We then filed into the cafeteria for supper one last time. The cafeteria walls were lined with crayon drawings from the local children. Written on colored paper were the words, *Thank-you firemen.* They had images of fire trucks, firemen, mountains, and lots of flames. It looked like the kids enjoyed drawing fire as much as we liked fighting it. One drawing made by a kid named Carlos, really caught my eye. He drew the forest with deer, an owl, some rabbits, and a lot of fire. He must have used up his entire yellow crayon on that one. I grinned, took it down, folded it in half, and put it in my cargo pants pocket. It reminded me of something my daughter drew when she was little.

We grabbed some chow and took our meals outside. A large white tent was erected next to the cafeteria, shading dozens of adult sized tables with chairs. There were coolers full of ice-cold sodas and next to them was an entire table dedicated to cookies, cakes, and pies, made by the locals. There was a tray of chocolate cupcakes with an American flag on each one. I put two on my plate and read the sign next to them, *Brownie Troop 3042.* I smiled and hoped all of those Brownies got a merit badge for their efforts.

Our two-week tour was over and I knew we were going to be demobed the next morning. I got word from Jesse and the

Arizona hand crew, that the fire had entered the Chiricahua National Monument today, but with all of the prep work done at the Faraway Ranch earlier this week, the fire skirted the complex and the whole area was saved!

As the afternoon dragged on, more units began pulling into the school grounds, and the place soon became packed. There were firefighters from all over the West, Utah, South Dakota, Nevada, Colorado, California, Nevada, Arizona, and New Mexico.

Two-weeks prior, these firefighters arrived as complete strangers, and after all of this is over, some of them may even leave as friends. Regardless of who they were or where they came from, they were all here for the common good of this community.

"I don't even know how things turned out in Sierra Vista, we left in such a hurry. It seems so long ago," I said to Phil.

"Yeah, I can't believe it has been two weeks since we left Mimbres Springs."

"You know Phil, this campaign has truly been unique. Most of the time, the wildland fires I've been assigned to have been in remote areas or in wilderness. We rarely get a chance to interact with the townsfolk. Sometimes we work our two weeks and leave without making contact with any of the locals. They never know who we were or what we did. At times I feel so insignificant and small out there.

Phil said to me, "Never think of yourself as insignificant or small. If I'm not mistaken the Dali Lama once said, '*If you think you are too small to make a difference, try sleeping in the same room with a mosquito!*' "

"Ha! Phil you always seem to amaze me. Where do you get those from?"

He shrugged his shoulders and gave me a palms-up gesture.

"Well Phil, I can't argue with the Dali Lama. You got me on that one."

We finished our supper and made our way to the football field where we parked the truck. I leaned in the cab, picked Mortie off of the dashboard, and signaled to Diane to *go deep!* She took off and did a crossing pattern, while I heaved Mortie in a big arching spiral down field. She grabbed him with one hand and raised her arms in mock victory. She chucked him back my way and Phil intercepted him just as I was about to make the catch.

We played a little round of catch with the sock monkey and when we finished, Phil dusted him off and put him back on the dashboard.

"That little monkey brought us luck on this tour, despite your bad juju," he smiled.

"Phil, we still have to get home, remember what happened to us last year! Hey! I've got one for you, I remember a famous *Yogi* once said, *'It ain't over till it's over.'* "

I sat down, took my boots off, and aired out my tired achy feet.

"Ahhh, that's more like it, I have a mess of laundry to do when I get back. I'm down to my last pair of chonies," I said to Diane, as I wiggled my toes.

I placed my hands behind my head, let out a long sigh, and for the next half hour listened to the hum of the generators and the distant sound of laughter in the camps.

Phil came running up to me and said, "I was just in the cafeteria and they have popsicles!"

He smiled and handed Diane and me a Bomb Pop.

I thought to myself, *Phil, I really love that guy.*

While we sat there, enjoying one of life's simple pleasures, I said to Phil and Diane. "I never told you guys how much I appreciated what you did for me. You cancelled your vacations two weeks ago to work your tails off on these fires. I am really sorry I was such a crab. I don't know what I would have done without you."

"No problem Boss," Phil said. "Remember what I told you last year at the TP fire, I was born to do this. I can go hiking any old time."

"Same here, the planet has plenty of rocks to be climbed," said Diane.

"To us!" I said.

"To the ghosts!" said Diane.

"To Bomb Pops!" said Phil.

I unrolled my sleeping bag in preparation to sleep under the stars and felt especially tired and worn out. As I drifted off I thought to myself, *This might be it for me, my last go round ... my last rodeo. I don't know if these old bones can take this wildland firefighting any more.*

***

The next morning, we packed up our stuff and handed in our paperwork. Despite the fact that a lot of crews were checking out this morning, the process didn't take long, and we were on our way in no time. As we climbed into the Triple Nickel, I asked Diane and Phil if it would be all right if I caught some shuteye in the back seat. For some reason I didn't sleep very well last night, and thought maybe it was because a pesky mosquito was trying to make a point. I was making myself comfortable in the back seat when Diane tossed Mortie to me and said, "Sweet dreams cowboy."

As we pulled out of the school grounds, we were greeted by hundreds of people lining the road! It was as if they came out of nowhere! They were all cheering, holding up signs, and waving American flags. As our convoy slowly made its way down the road, I started to recognize familiar faces. Élan came running up to me and I rolled down the back window.

"Are you guys working on this fire? I didn't see your name on any of the IAPs," I asked shaking his hand.

He said, "No man, we aren't on this fire at all! We are working the Wallow Fire in the White Mountains right now! You are having one of your dreams!"

"No shit! Are you kidding me? I'm dreaming?"

"I'm not kidding! Go ahead and pinch your forearm as hard as you can."

I rolled up my sleeve and pinched my arm as hard as I could. I felt no pain whatsoever! I did it again ... nothing!

He said, "There you go, now enjoy the rest of your dream!"

I looked over to Diane and she laughed out loud and hollered, "Far out! This is awesome!"

"Punch me in the shoulder as hard as you can," I told her.

"Are you sure? You know I can really pack a wallop."

She landed a good one on my right shoulder.

No pain, I felt nothing!

Diane hung out the window and began to high five all of the women on the Apache hand crew. Over on the driver's side, Phil saw the Midewin Hotshots in their white hard hats. Kate ran up to Phil and handed him a big bag of snacks!

"Something for the road," she said and gave him a peck on the cheek.

Phil gushed, "A woman after my own heart." He looked in the bag and said, "Wow, Twinkies, Fritos, Corn Nuts, and *Jujubes! My favorite!*" He leaned out of the window and yelled, "Marry me Kate!"

Phil almost drove us off the road.

Diane grabbed the wheel and said, "Keep your eyes on the road lover boy," and yanked us back in line.

"As dreams go, this is turning out to be a real doozy!" I shouted.

The line cooks from the TP fire were next. Dressed in their sweat stained baseball caps and plastic aprons, they were standing at attention with one arm raised, holding metal serving spoons and ladles. Off in the distance, standing in front of their white transport buggies were the women of the Wild Bunch, wearing their orange Nomex fire gear.

"Hey Phil," I yelled. "They are all waving temple garments and blowing you kisses."

"Aww! Now they are just messing with me," he said with a blush.

The Green Valley engine was driving on the road just in front of us and we heard the sound of a bugle further back in line.

"The Butter Bean Gang!" we all said in unison! I hung out of the window and looked back. There, directly behind us was Chopper, Dylan and Chico, with Butter Bean the dog sitting on Chopper's lap.

Up ahead, standing on the side of the road was the nice elderly lady from the Safari Motel. Standing next to her was the aging hippie Bee Boo, along with Julie, the waitress from the Middle Sister Café.

Julie ran over to Diane and handed her a bag of fresh-made peach empanadas and said, "Thanks for the tip!"

"What tip?" asked Phil.

Diane said shyly, "I gave her a $30 tip after our breakfast in Utah."

Off to the right were the Bryce Canyon rangers, Johnny, Vince, and Jen, pointing to 17 cases of toilet paper and sixteen cases of mousetraps. Jen was holding up a cardboard sign that said, *Thanks Pablo, I got a big fat raise!*

A little further down the way was Benjamin. He was leaning on his shiny red, 1938 Alpha Romero sports car, wearing his white 10-gallon cowboy hat and those expensive ostrich skin cowboy boots. Louise Manning was standing next to him. She was the lady who let us have the cold bottles of Coca- Cola from her fridge. She was smiling and waving the letter Diane found tacked to her front door.

"This is all too unreal, but who am I to say what is too unreal. *This is my freaking dream for crying out loud!*"

My attention was drawn to two horse trailers in the pasture. Standing in front of them were Roxanne and two other co-workers from the Sierra Vista Riding Club. Grazing in the pasture were the two little burros, Romeo and Juliet. And looking right at us, chomping on a mouthful of grass, was a healthy Miss Daisy.

"I'm getting all goose bumpy," I said.

To the left was the rancher Theodore and his big red dog Ruby. As only dreams can do, time became compressed. Teddy was a much younger man. Standing next to him was his wife Carol and Ted's older brother Travis, wearing his World War II uniform.

"I'll be damned!" I marveled.

Next to Theodore was his son Caleb, his wife Samantha, along with their son Teddy Jr. Holding Teddy Jr.'s hand was little Carl, the brother who died when he was 7 years old. The little ones ran over and started to swing on the pink and blue swing set. I recognized them as if I knew them all my life.

On the other side of the road were the Tatanka Hotshots, all standing in the same corny poses as in the Johnny Ringo's Grave photograph. Nobody batted an eye as we rolled by. It looked like they were all frozen in time. Only Dutch broke ranks and gave me a hairy grin, and a sly thumbs-up.

There were so many people running up to the side of the road, it was hard to keep track of them all. I saw Hank Witherspoon, the Park Ranger we met the first day at the Faraway Ranch. Next to him were Emma and Neil Erikson, the pioneers from the 1800s. They looked the same as the picture in the book. And they smiled at me, and somehow they knew who I was. Behind them was a large group of about 30 Native Americans, all dressed in ceremonial clothing. The oldest one in the group watched as we drove by and she was holding the ancient pot.

"Look over there!" pointed Diane. Off in the distance was a herd of heifers and cows, with a little calf prancing out in front, kicking up her heels and showing off.

"Baby Cakes!" we all said at once!

Diane remarked. "You know when I was under that fire shelter, face to face with her, and she was bawling like a baby, it reminded me of something."

"Reminded you of what?" asked Phil.

"Puppy breath!" said Diane. "She smelled like puppy breath!"

Just when I thought things couldn't get any wilder, we turned north to enter the highway that lead to Dos Cabezas and I saw something in the field that made my heart stop!

"*It's Billy!*" I gasped.

I hollered to Phil, "Slow down! Slow down!"

Billy was riding his favorite stallion Black Jack and Tank was up in the saddle with him. He looked as sharp as he did on graduation day at boot camp, proudly wearing his Dress Blues.

We slowed to a crawl and our eyes met. Billy gave me a smile and I could see a tear running down his cheek. He gave me a salute and while returning his salute, my eyes immediately filled to the brim with tears. Billy gave me a reassuring nod, and in an instant, everything was quiet, and everyone had vanished!

Waking with a start, Diane looked towards the back seat and said, "Did you have one of your dreams cowboy?"

"Boy did I!" I said, wiping tears from my eyes in the bright sunshine, "It was fantastic!"

"Was it better than the island girl dream?" asked Diane.

"It was a million times better than that, let me tell you everything I can remember! It was the best dream I ever had!

Glossary

Air Attack: The deployment of fixed-wing or rotary aircraft, to drop retardant or extinguishing agents, shuttle and deploy crews and supplies, or perform aerial reconnaissance of the overall fire situation.

Air Biscuit: A fart.

Air Tankers (Heavies): Fixed-wing aircraft certified by FAA as being capable of transport and delivery of fire retardant solutions.

Anchor Point: A barrier against fire spread, from which a hand crew starts constructing a fire line. The anchor point is used to minimize the chance of firefighters being flanked by the fire while the line is being constructed.

Back Burn, Back Firing: A tactic associated with indirect attack. To intentionally set fire to fuels inside the control line, to slow, knock down, or contain a rapidly spreading fire.

Barking Spiders: Farts

Be Safe: A parting reminder, invocation, or wish to those heading out to fight fire.

Black Line (The Black): In fire suppression, the black denotes the area where the vegetation has been burned away. There is no unburned vegetation between the fire front and the man-made fire line.

Blowup: Sudden increase in fire intensity or rate of spread of a fire. Often accompanied by violent air convection and may have other characteristics that resemble a firestorm.

Box: An Ambulance.

Brain Bucket: Hard hat

Brush Boots: Wildland boots must meet the following requirements:

- Eight-inch minimum height
- All leather construction
- Secured with leather laces (no zippers allowed)
- A defined heel
- Oil resistant soles

- No steel toe or steel shank
- Heat resistant sole, either sewn on, nailed or screwed in place, or all three. (No glued on soles allowed)

Brush Pants: Long trousers worn by wildland firefighters. Theses pants are made of fire resistant material (Nomex), has two pockets at the waist, two cargo pockets on the thigh and two rear pockets. It has ties at the ankle, which prevents ash, dirt or debris from entering up from the bottom.

Brush Shirt: A lightweight, yellow, long sleeve, button-up shirt worn by wildland firefighters. It is made of fire resistant material (Nomex) that has a turn down collar, buttons at the cuffs and two breast pockets. (Inmate crews wear orange shirts)

Buggy: A hand-crew transport bus, normally designed to carry 10 men and their gear. Sometimes referred to as a Crummy, Green Machine, the Short Bus, or a Stink Box.

Cold Trail: A mop up term. To *cold trail a fire* means, firefighters systematically work the entire edge of the fire, scraping embers off remaining fuel, piling up unburned materials, digging out every live spot, and trenching any live edge to create cleared areas of mineral soil, and finally, feeling for heat with the hands.

Contained: The status of a wildfire suppression action signifying that a control line has been completed around the fire. i.e. *The fire is reported to be 75% contained.*

Crapper Slapper: Any unthinking person who lets the porta-pottie door slam loudly in fire camp, usually at the wee hours in the morning, when everyone else is trying to get some sleep. *Don't be a Crapper-Slapper* signs are sometimes posted to deter the abusers.

Demobilization (Demob): The release of resources from an incident in strict accordance with a detailed plan approved by the incident commander.

Divisions: Divisions are used to divide an incident into geographical areas of operation.

"Don't Bogart That Joint": Rather than passing a marijuana joint around the circle, a person hangs onto it and tokes more than his fair share, or has it dangling from his lips like a Humphrey Bogart cigarette in the old movies. First attested in the 1969 movie "Easy Rider".

Dozer Company: A resource that includes a dozer, its transportation unit (low boy) and a standard complement of personnel for its operation to create a dozer line. (Fire line constructed by the front blade of a bulldozer)

Drip Torch: Hand-held metal container for igniting fires by dripping flaming liquid fuel on the materials to be burned; consists of a fuel spout, burner arm, and igniter. Fuel used is generally a mixture of diesel and gasoline.

Dry Bulb: A name given to an ordinary thermometer used to determine the temperature of the air. And combined with a wet bulb thermometer, helps to determine the relative humidity. The temperature of the air is measured in the shade, 4-8 feet above the ground.

Eyes in the Green: Watching the green side of the containment line (unburned vegetated side) as to be on the look-out to catch a potential spot fire.

Fingers of a Fire: The long narrow extensions of a fire projecting from the main body.

Firebrand: Flaming or glowing fuel particles of hot embers that can be carried naturally by wind, convection currents, or by gravity into unburned fuels.

Fire Front: The part of a fire within which continuous flaming combustion is taking place. Unless otherwise specified, the fire front is assumed to be the leading edge of the fire perimeter.

Fire Ground: The operational area on which firefighters combat a fire.

Fire-out: **(burn-out)** The act of setting fire to unburned fuels located between the control line and main fire in burn out operations, as in *to fire-out* an area.

Fire Retardant: Any substance except plain water that by chemical or physical action reduces flammability of fuels or slows their rate of combustion.

Fire Shelter: An aluminized pup tent offering protection by means of reflecting radiant heat and providing a volume of breathable air in a fire entrapment situation. Fire shelters should only be used in life threatening situations, as a last resort. Sometimes referred to as a *shake and bake*.

Fire Shovel: Type of shovel specifically designed for use by firefighters in constructing a fire line. It has a tapered triangle shaped blade with both edges sharpened for scraping, digging, grubbing, cutting, and throwing.

Flanking: Suppression tactics used to attack a fire by working along the sides, (flanks) either simultaneously or successively from a less active or anchor point and eventually connecting the two lines at the head.

Foam (Class A Foam) Foam intended for use on Class A or ordinary, woody fuels. Class A foam is made from a hydrocarbon-based surfactant, possessing excellent wetting and penetrating properties, which is far more superior to using water alone.

Fusee: A red colored flare designed as a railway-warning device or a highway road flare, this hot burning stick is widely used by fire personnel to ignite ground fuels during backfires and other prescribed fires.

GPM: Gallons per minute.

Green: The unburned vegetated side of a fire line. (As opposed to the black, burned side)

Hotshot Crew: A highly trained 20-man fire crew primarily used to create hand line construction, using only hand tools, chainsaws, and firing out devices, such as drip torches and fusees.

IAP, Incident Action Plan: Incident Action Plans provide a coherent means of communicating the overall incident objectives for both operational and support activities.

 They include measurable strategic objectives to be achieved in a time frame, which may be any interval of time but is commonly 12 hours. They may be verbal or written, and are prepared by the Planning Section.

The consolidated IAP is a very important component of the Incident Command System that reduces freelancing and ensures a coordinated response.

All *Incident Action Plans* must have these five elements:

- What do we want to do?
- Who is responsible for doing it?
- How do we communicate with each other?
- What is the procedure if someone is injured?

IC, ICP, Incident Command Post: are set up to host, house and maintain firefighters and support the equipment and services that have been assigned to a wildfire. Offices are set up to direct official business of the wildfire incident, from direction of firefighters on the ground and aerial support, to meals, to supply orders, finance, and health clinics.

ICS, Incident Command System:

(ICS Flow Chart Sections)

- Incident Commander
- Safety Officer

- Liaison Officer

- Operations Section

- Planning Section

- Logistics Section

- Finance/Administration Section

Initial Attack: The first firefighting units to arrive at the fire scene.

Inmate Crew: Any fire crew composed of prison inmates or wards.

Jonesing: A craving, an addiction. The saying originated from Jones Alley in Manhattan, where a lot of homeless drug addicts hung out back in the 60s.

Jump Spot: Selected landing area for smokejumpers.

Knock Down: To reduce or eliminate flame or heat on the more vigorously burning parts of a fire edge.

LCES: *L*ookouts, *C*ommunications, *E*scape Routes, and *S*afety Zones. Elements of a safety system used by fire fighters to routinely assess their current situation with respect to wildland firefighting hazards.

Limbing: Fire crewmembers in the progressive method of line construction, who cut and clear away brush, small saplings, vines, low branches of trees and other obstructions in the path of the fire line; usually equipped with an ax, brush hook, Pulaski or chainsaw.

Lookie-Loo: An inquisitive person who holds up traffic by slowing down to look at a car accident, fire or some other calamity. One who gathers around when a police car, fire engine or ambulance arrives on scene. Also known as a Rubber-Necker.

May Day: International distress signal/call. When repeated three times it indicates imminent and grave danger and that immediate assistance is required.

McCloud: (McLeod) A long handled combination tool used by a member of a hand crew, that has a hoe on one edge and a rake on the other. Used for grubbing and raking vegetation or embers and char.

Military Time: The 24-hour clock system where one minute after midnight is designated as 00:01, one o'clock in the morning is 01:00, noon being 12:00, one o'clock in the afternoon is 13:00, and midnight is 24:00.

Mimbres: Which means "willows" in Spanish, is the name given to a cottonwood and willow-lined rivers in southwestern New Mexico. The spectacular pottery designs found in and around the Mimbres Valley also came to be called Mimbres Style, and the name was soon applied to the ancient people who made the pottery.

Mineral Soil: Soil layers below the predominantly organic layers. It is the bare soil with little or no combustible material.

Monkey Butt: Chaffing and irritation of the posterior region of the human anatomy, the area otherwise known as the buttocks. This rash or irritation is usually located in the general area of ones butt crack. Sometimes known as hotshot butt.

Mop Up: Extinguishing or removing burning material near control lines, felling snags, and trenching logs to prevent rolling after an area has burned, to make a fire safe, or to reduce residual smoke.

Morning Briefing: Crew bosses and team leaders gather each morning to discuss fire conditions. Several presenters take turns, bringing firefighters up to speed on the previous day's/night's activities and inform them about the firefighting objectives for the day.

Napalm: An incendiary mixture with a jelling agent used in flamethrowers and bombs.

Natural Barrier: Any area where lack of flammable material obstructs the spread of wildfires. i.e. a large rock outcropping, lake, reservoir, roadway, etc.

Nomex: Trade name for a fire resistant synthetic material used in the manufacturing of flight suits and clothing used by firefighters. Aramid is the generic name.

Overhead Tones: A radio-based loudspeaker paging system that alerts firefighters in a fire station, that an incoming call is immanent. After a series of *loud tones*, to get a person's attention, a dispatcher then verbally gives information over the loudspeaker.

Pack Test: A physical test used to determine the aerobic capacity of fire suppression support personnel and to assign a physical fitness score. The test consists of walking three miles, with a weighted 45-pound backpack, and is to be completed in 45 minutes or less. (With altitude corrections) This determines whether a wildland firefighter is qualified to perform arduous work.

Pencil Line: The smallest diameter fire hose, usually 3/4 inch and very light weight.

Plume: A large convection column (pyrocumulus cloud) generated by the combustion of wildland fuel.

Port-a-tank: A large portable container, either rigid frame or self-supporting, which sits on the ground and can be filled with water or fire chemical mixture from which fire suppression resources can draw from. It can also be a source for charging hose lays from portable pumps or stationary engines.

Pulaski: A combination chopping and trenching tool widely used in fire line construction, which combines a single-bitted ax blade with a narrow adze-like trenching blade fitted to a straight wooden handle.

Pumpkin: A soft-sided portable water container with a floating collar (4,000 to 6,000 gallons), which sits on the ground, resembling an above ground swimming pool. Pumpkins hold large volumes of water or retardant and are filled by a helicopter. These water tanks are usually orange in color.

Rappelling: Technique of landing specifically trained personnel from hovering helicopters or stationary anchor points; this maneuver involves sliding down ropes with the aid of friction-producing devices.

Red Card: An agency-issued document that certifies that an individual has the training, experience and physical fitness to perform the tasks of a specified position on a wildland or prescribed fire.

Red Flag Warning: Term used by fire weather forecasters to alert firefighters to an ongoing or imminent critical fire weather pattern. These conditions usually consist of a relative humidity of 20 percent or less, with a wind speed of 20 MPH with gusts of 35 MPH or greater, accompanied with extremely dry fuel conditions.

Repeater: A radio signal station that automatically relays a radio transmission, sometimes over a different frequency, thereby increasing the range of a transmission.

Retardant: A substance or chemical agent, which reduces the flammability of combustibles.

Safety Zones: A preplanned area cleared of flammable materials used by firefighters for escape and safety, in the event the fire line is outflanked.

Sawyer: A person who fells trees using a chainsaw. Also known as a Feller or Cutter.

Scratch Line: A preliminary control line hastily established or constructed by the lead member of a hand crew, and expanded by the following members of the hand crew. A line scratched down to mineral soil that eliminates all vegetation and helps stop the forward spread of ground fire.

Self-Contained Breathing Apparatus (SCBA): Portable air (not oxygen) tanks with regulators and a facemask, which allow firefighters to breathe air while in toxic, smoke conditions. Usually rated for 30 minutes of service. Used primarily on fires involving houses, structures or hazardous materials.

Single Resource Boss (SRB): Is a general qualification label that encompasses different position types. SRB leads crew members and resources associated with the different type designations, e.g. the Engine Boss directs operations of a wildland fire engine and crew; a Firing Boss directs a firing operations on a wildland fire, a Dozer Boss directs activities associated with a bulldozer crew.

- Crew Boss (CRWB)
- Engine Boss (ENGB)
- Firing Boss (FIRB)
- Tractor/Plow Boss (TRPB)
- Dozer Boss (DOZB)
- Felling Boss (FELB)

Size Up: The evaluation of the fire to determine a course of action for suppression. Some factors to consider are, firefighter safety, LCES, fuels, terrain, weather, fire behavior, access routes, water sources, land ownership, and public safety concerns.

Slash: Products produced by sawyers or hand crews, as a result of pruning, thinning, or brush cutting. It includes logs, chunks, bark, branches, stumps, and the broken understory of trees.

Slimed: Fire ground personnel hit and covered with a load of fire retardant by an air tanker.

Slop Over: A fire that crosses a control line or natural barrier intended to contain the fire.

Smoke Happy: Someone who sees smoke emanating from every nook and cranny and wants to put it out during mop up.

Smoke Jumper: A specifically trained and certified firefighter who travels to wildland fires by aircraft and parachutes to the fire.

Smokey Bear: The symbol of the Cooperative Forest Fire Prevention

Program since 1945. Smokey's image is protected by US Federal Law and is administered by the USDA Forest Service, the National Association of State Foresters and the Ad Council.

Spanner Wrench: A large metal wrench used to tighten and free hose connections.

Spike camps: (Sometimes known as coyote camps) A progressive line construction team, which builds fire line until the end of the operational period. They remain at or near that point while off duty and set up a temporary camp. They begin building fire line the next operational period where they left off.

Spot Fire: Fire ignited outside the perimeter of the main fire by an airborne hot ember known as a firebrand.

Spotter Plane: A small fixed wing plane used to lead an air tanker (Heavy). It flies over the area and advises where the tanker needs to drop its load. A spotter plane is sometimes called a *bird dog.*

Strike Team: Specified combinations of the *same kind* and type of resources, with common communications, and a leader.   *Same kind* resources meaning a group of four similar water tenders, or a group of five similar Type 6 engines, or a similar group of four hotshot crews.

Strike Team Leader: (STL) The ICS position responsible for supervising a strike team. The STL reports to a Division/Group Supervisor or Operations Section Chief. This position may supervise a strike team of engines (STEN), crews (STCR), dozers (STDZ), or tractor/plows (STPL).

Structure Fire Protection: The protection of homes or other structures from fire.

Supervisor: The ICS title for individuals responsible for command of a division or group.

Task Force: Any combination of *unlike* single resources assembled for a particular tactical need, with common communications and a leader. A task force may be pre-established and sent to an incident, or formed at an incident. The term *unlike* single resources meaning, a group consisting of i.e., One water tender, plus three Type 6 engines, plus two 20-man hand crews.

Task Force Leader: (TFL) The ICS position responsible for supervising a task force. The TFL reports to a Division/Group Supervisor or Operations Section Chief.

Two-Week Bag: A firefighter's large duffle bag, consisting of personal and firefighting clothing, toiletries and other personal gear to sustain them through their two-week tour of duty.

Virga: Precipitation falling from a cloud, but due to low humidity and high ambient temperatures, the rainwater evaporates before reaching the ground.

Wait-A-Minute Bush: *Mimosa aculeaticarpa* is a shrub in the Fabaceae family. It is commonly known as the cat claw mimosa or the wait-a-minute bush and is endemic to upland regions of Mexico, Arizona, New Mexico and Texas.[2]

Water Tenders: Are specialized vehicles capable of bringing water, foam, or dry chemicals to fire trucks in the field that are engaged on the fire line. These vehicles are specifically designed for firefighting often with four-wheel drive, large capacity water tanks, rugged suspension and high wheel clearance for mountainous dirt road conditions.

- Type 1 Tender- 300 gpm pump capacity, 5000-gallon tank.
- Type 2 Tender- 200 gpm pump capacity, 2500-gallon tank.
- Type 3 Tender- 200 gpm pump capacity, 1000-gallon tank.
- Type 4 Tender- no pump, 1000-gallon tank.

Weather Kit: A small, belt-mounted case with pockets fitted for, compass, two thermometers, (one wet bulb, one dry bulb) slide rule, water bottle, pencils, and a book of weather report forms. Used to take weather observations to provide on-site conditions to the fire weather forecaster or fire behavior analyst. Observations include time of day, air temperature, wind speed, wind direction, and relative humidity.

Wet Bulb: A name given to an ordinary thermometer with a small cloth cover over the bulb end, which is wetted with room-air temperature water and used to help determine relative humidity. The temperature of the air is measured in the shade, 4-8 feet above the ground.

Wet Line: A line of water, or water and chemical retardant, sprayed along the ground, and which serves as a temporary control line from which to ignite or slow down or stop a low-intensity fire.

Wildland: An area in which human development is essentially non-existent, except for roads, railroads, power lines, and similar transportation facilities. Structures, if any, are widely scattered.

Wildland Boogers: Black nasty things that grow inside your nose while fighting fire, back burn operations or during mopping up.

Wildland–Urban Interface: Refers to the zone of transition between unoccupied land and human development. These lands and communities are adjacent to and are surrounded by wildlands. These human made structures are at risk during wildfires.

Wildland Fire Engine Classifications:

Type 1- 1000 gpm pump capacity, a 400-1,000 gallon tank, 1,200 feet or more of 2.5 inch hose, 400 feet or more of 1.75 inch hose (attack line), 200 feet or more of one inch hose, one ladder 20 feet or longer, 500 gpm master stream, and 4 crewmembers. Mostly used for structure protection.

Type 3- 120 gpm pump capacity, a 500-gallon tank, 1000 feet or more of 1.5-inch hose, 800 feet or more of 1-inch hose, assorted smaller diameter hose known as pencil line. 3-4 crewmembers.

Type 6- 50 gpm pump capacity, a 200-gallon tank, 1,000 feet or more of 1.5-inch hose, 800 feet or more of 1-inch hose, assorted smaller diameter hose known as pencil line. 2-3 crewmembers.

Wildland Standard Firefighting Orders

- Keep informed on fire weather conditions and forecasts.
- Know what your fire is doing at all times.
- Base all actions on current and expected behavior of the fire.
- Identify escape routes and safety zones and make them known.
- Post lookouts when there is possible danger.
- Be alert. Keep calm. Think clearly. Act decisively.
- Maintain prompt communications with your forces, your supervisor and adjoining forces.
- Give clear instructions and insure they are understood.
- Maintain control of your forces at all times.
- Fight fire aggressively, having provided for safety first.

18 Watch Out Situations

- Fire not scouted and sized up.
- In country not seen in daylight.
- Safety zones and escapes routes not identified.
- Unfamiliar with weather and local factors influencing fire behavior.
- Uninformed on strategy, tactics, and hazards.
- Instructions and assignments not clear.
- No communication link with crewmembers/supervisors.
- Constructing line without safe anchor point.
- Building fire line downhill with fire below.
- Attempting frontal assault on fire.
- Unburned fuel between you and the fire.
- Cannot see main fire, not in contact with anyone who can.
- On a hillside where rolling material can ignite fuel below.
- Weather is getting hotter and drier.
- Wind increases and/or changes direction.
- Getting frequent spot fires across the fire line.
- Terrain and fuels make escape to safety zones difficult.
- Taking a nap near the fire lin
-
-
-
-
-
-
-
- e.

About the Authors

DIANE VETTER

Diane is a recently retired firefighter, having served with the Green Valley Fire Department in southern Arizona, for 18 years. Aside from being a firefighter, she worked as an EMT and a Technical Rescue Technician; she was also a member of their Wildland Division for 16 of those years.

Prior to becoming a firefighter, Diane was a four-time All-American runner in track and field while attending Iowa State University and two of her cross-country teams were crowned National Champions. Vetter was inducted into the Iowa State University, Athletic Hall of Fame, Class of 2012.

Diane loves being in the out-of-doors and her avocations eventually led her to the glorious mountains. Aside from all of her running, she was an avid rock climber and mountaineer for 30 years.

Diane was the president of the Southern Arizona Climber's Coalition (SACC) for 10 years. In collaboration with the US Forest Service, the SACC assisted with peregrine falcon monitoring in the stunning Cochise Stronghold. Along with their dedication to help preserve an endangered species, the SACC also encouraged local rock climbers to develop a better awareness and stewardship for wild places. As a result, the Access Fund bestowed the Sharp End Award, to her and her organization. She still can be seen hiking down a trail or camping, regardless of weather conditions or season.

In response to the prompting of her cohorts, Vetter felt obliged to write about her experiences as a wildland firefighter. It wasn't the high adventures or the harrowing firefights that prompted this book. She instead, wanted to shed light on the laughable escapades and the down-to-earth friendships that arose while working on those fires.

Diane lives in Tucson, Arizona, and shares her home with her two dogs, Bingo and Mr. Jingles. Her writings have appeared in no notable publications and this is her first attempt as a novelist. There is a first time for everything!

She can be reached at:
diane@mimbresspringsfire.com
www.vetterbelt.com
www.facebook.com/dvetterMSFD

PAUL MILLER

Paul has been a full time firefighter for the past 22 years. In addition, he is an engineer, hazardous materials technician, emergency medical technician (EMT), and wildland firefighter.

After leaving the Marine Corps in 1970, Paul spent the next 20 years in the marketing, advertising and graphic design profession.

While still being physically fit and adventurous, his quest for new experiences motivated him to close his business in 1990, to fulfill his childhood dream of becoming a firefighter.

His desire to write grew from his advertising and technical writing background. Paul has a passion for writing and wanted to capture in words, his encounters with the many uncommon people and rare events that can only be found in the fire service. Paul's joy in telling stories and his love for wildland firefighting inspired him to share these unbelievable stories. He joined forces with a close friend and fellow firefighter, Diane Vetter, to help give these tales their unique human perspective and humorous twist.

Paul and his wife Sarah have called Tucson, Arizona home for the past 50 years. He is currently a member of Green Valley Fire Department. After two decades with the department, he will soon be retiring and plans to continue writing about the action packed, humorous and mildly strange events of firefighting.

Paul is also a talented Western oil painter and commercial graphic designer. He has shown his work for the past 16 years, selling the majority of his paintings to private collectors.

He can be reached at:

paul@mimbresspringsfire.com

www.facebook.com/pmillerMSFD

Made in the USA
San Bernardino, CA
27 June 2017